I could not put Junius Podrug's *Dark Passage* down. From the opening pages I was hooked. I can count the really good tales that I've truly enjoyed on my fingers (with a few digits left over), and *Dark Passage* is now one of them. If this book does not grab besteller lists all over the place I'll be shocked. The characters are there, the scenes are vivid and real, there's slam bang action on every page, and best of all *Dark Passage* tells a whiz bang story . . . I truly envy readers who're going to pick up *Dark Passage* and read it for the first time . . . YOU'RE IN FOR A RARE TREAT!"   —David Hagberg, the *USA Today* bestselling author of *Joshua's Hammer*

"*Dark Passage* is a breathtaking two-millennium ride from France, the modern and ancient Holy Land, and the United States, towards Armageddon, with jihad terrorists as traveling companions. Few writers today have Junius Podrug's gifts to pull off such a skyrocket of a story as this one."
                    —Dale L. Walker, the Spur Award winning author of *Pacific Destiny*

"A self-centered actor, an engineer, and a woman of doubtful past are swept into an inexplicable time-warp. They have to go back to the time of Christ to save the world. Well-researched and well-imagined, this book is exciting."
    —Barbara D'Amato, Mary Higgins Clarke Award Winning author of *Authorized Personnel Only*

"Podrug is a talented writer with a knack for startling images and a real gift for capturing the steamy downside of cities."
                                        —*Kirkus Reviews*

"If this thriller doesn't entertain you, you're dead."
                        —David Morrell on *Frost of Heaven*

"*Frost of Heaven* is fast and entertaining . . . an accomplished first novel."   —*Rocky Mountain News*

FORGE BOOKS BY JUNIUS PODRUG

DARK PASSAGE

JUNIUS PODRUG

TOR®

A TOM DOHERTY ASSOCIATES BOOK
NEW YORK

This is a work of fiction. All the characters and events portrayed in this book are either products of the author's imagination or are used fictitiously.

DARK PASSAGE

Copyright © 2002 by Junius Podrug

A Tor Book
Published by Tom Doherty Associates, LLC
175 Fifth Avenue
New York, NY 10010

www.tor.com

Tor® is a registered trademark of Tom Doherty Associates, LLC.

ISBN 0-812-57850-3
EAN 978-0812-57850-8

First edition: October 2002
First mass market edition: April 2004

Printed in the United States of America

0 9 8 7 6 5 4 3 2 1

for

Stuart Lewis, Esq.,

*who has courage, integrity,
and generosity under fire*

Acknowledgments

Many people see to it that a book gets published besides the author. I want to thank the following Tom Doherty Associates staff who brought the book into being: Linda Quinton of Sales, Kathleen Fogarty of Marketing, Irene Gallo and Peter Lutjen, who prepared the cover art; Jennifer Marcus in publicity, Robert Gleason and Brian Callaghan, who came down on my head so often as editors, along with the guy down the block who provides Brian with doughnuts. I also want to thank Fiorella deLima and Deborah Miller who caught my many errors, including the fact that it is doughnuts and not donuts.

In addition, I want to thank my agent, Carol McCleary of the Wilshire Literary Agency, and the following people who helped streamline the manuscript: Michael Zweibel, Amanda Jones Hopper, John Bevard, Ginger Bevard, and Corliss Krische. And special thanks to Hildegarde for once more climbing out the window.

BEHOLD THERE APPEARED A CHARIOT OF FIRE, AND
HORSES OF FIRE, AND PARTED THEM BOTH ASUNDER;
AND ELIJAH WENT UP BY A WHIRLWIND INTO HEAVEN.
— II KINGS 2, 11

THE MAGDALENE

CHAPTER ONE

MARSEILLES, FRANCE
The red-light district

Marie stared at the offending hand cupped around her breast more with stunned curiosity than shock. She had started down the stairs and had turned to exchange taunts with an angry pimp who followed her out of an apartment when someone coming up the steps put a hand on her breast.

She turned to face her assailant—a sailor, drunk, glassy-eyed, so sloshed his sea legs were rubber and he rocked back and forth on the steps like a boat in swells. She had come to the tenement in the red-light district after getting a call from a streetwalker that a pimp was going to kill a girl for spending his share of a trick on a moment of Ecstasy. But the pimp had simply beaten the girl so she could still work and the girl had refused Marie's offer of help when the pimp offered her drugs.

The sailor leered at her, sloppily, barely in control of his facial muscles.

"Do your teats get hard?" he slurred.

One of his friends was coming up behind him, navigating the stairs with difficulty, another vessel pounded by waves.

Her hand went around the reassuring wooden butt of the gun in her coat pocket, the same gun that had kept her from a beating by the angry pimp.

He squeezed her breast. She wasn't wearing a bra and the contact was almost hand to flesh through her skintight silk blouse. Still cupping her breast, he pressed on her nipple with his thumb as if he was pressing a button.

"How much for a fuck?"

She slowly pulled the gun from her coat pocket. With intense deliberation, slow enough for him to follow with his dulled senses, she brought the gun up until the business end of the barrel was point-blank to his eyeball.

The sailor followed the unhurried movement of the gun, watched her grip tensing as her finger tightened on the trigger, the finger slowly pulling back the trigger. He leaned back from the danger, letting go of her breast.

With her free hand, Marie gave him a push.

He stared at her, his drunken leer unfolding into a gape, his body teetering on the brink for a moment before he fell backward. He crashed against the other sailor stumbling up the stairs and the two fell together, becoming a pile of broken heaps at the bottom of the steps.

Marie went down as far as the pile of men and slipped over the banister, jumping to the floor below.

"Kill her!" the pimp shouted from the top of the stairs.

She was out of the building while the sailors were still wresting with their own arms and legs.

On the street, she began to walk quickly, then slowed her pace. Something was wrong. Soldiers and sailors, thieves and beggars, businessmen from Lyon, Eurotrash, Arabs and Africans, brassy whores quoting prices to eager men, drunks hugging a bottle, it all gave the street an international air of indecency and a babel of languages. A half an hour ago she had brushed by whores and johns and gawking tourists to get to the tenement.

Now the street was deserted.

The eerie silence was creepy. She could have handled an aggressive john but the cold deserted street played on preternatural human fear within her; goose bumps crawled up the small of her back and fanned the hair on the back of her neck. She had been on the street hundreds of times and it was never deserted except when the sun was shining. Now the only action was the neon cowgirl prancing on the sign above Le Moulin Rouge de Texas. The gaudy lights of the honky-tonk joint danced on pavement that was still wet from an earlier drizzle, exposing the street's cheap soul in surrealistic images.

She slipped her hand into her coat pocket but the gun gave her no reassurance from a threat she couldn't see. Someone—*something*—had turned a hot street cold and bloodless in a matter of minutes and she had stepped into it. She almost turned to go back into the tenement but the threat from the pimp and the sailors was too strong.

Keep moving, she told herself. An all-night café was around the corner and a couple'blocks down and she headed for that. To her right a cat meowed. Marie turned to the sound, her hand tightening on the gun. A longhaired white cat rubbed against the pant leg of a man hidden in the shadows of a doorway. Panic hit her and she started to run. Almost immediately she was confronted by a man in a brown trench coat who stepped from around the corner.

"You're the one they call St. Marie," he said.

Steps beat the sidewalk behind her—the man she had spotted in the doorway. Behind her the two sailors burst out the door of the tenement with drunken shouts. The man in front of her turned to the loud commotion. She darted around him, dashing into the street, but he caught her by the arm. She spun around, whipping out the gun and shot him in the face, a rank liquid bursting out of the nose of the gun. Jerking back in surprise, his heel caught on the curb and he stumbled, falling backward.

She ran in the gutter with the footsteps of the other man pounding behind her. A black limousine to the rear gunned down the street and came up beside her, forcing her back onto the sidewalk as it swept by her. The limo suddenly turned to block her way, jumping the curb, skidding broad-side, its bumper sideswiping a storefront, showering her with shattered glass and exploding wood.

Throwing up her hands to protect her face, she stumbled headlong into the car and bounced off, going down, hitting the sidewalk hard. Making it to her knees, she brought the gun up. The man chasing her kicked it out of her hand and jerked her onto her feet, throwing her bruised body against the car with her hands behind her. He shook her down, his hands feeling everything inside her tight silk blouse and un-der her short skirt.

The man in the trench coat caught up, breathing hard. He picked up the gun she had shot him in the face with and stared at it in disbelief.

"It's a water pistol!"

He opened the back door of the limo and the man who searched her forced her inside, one hand on her neck, ready to snap it if she resisted, the other hand twisting her right arm behind her back in a painful hammerlock. Inside the limou-sine he slammed her against the backseat. The other man got in, closing the door behind him.

The metal of the undercarriage scraped painfully as the car slid off the curb. The driver slammed it into forward while still backing up and floorboarded it, the limo's tail fanning and tires screeching as the big car accelerated down the street. Police motorcycles with sirens wailing shot out of an alley and roared in front of the vehicle.

Breathless and bruised, her heart beating in her throat, she kept her face blank and straightened her clothes, pulling down on her skirt. She had the wide backseat all to herself—the two men sat on jump seats across from her.

Catching her breath, she asked, "Who are you? Where are you taking me?"

"You'll know when you get there, bitch," the man in the brown trench coat said. He spoke in English with an Ameri-can accent. Built like a college football scholar, he was husky and blunt-faced with cheeks that had been polished to smooth acne scars. His suit under the trench coat was dark blue; shirt, white button-down; tie, Harvard.

He sniffed the barrel of the black plastic water pistol she squirted him with. "This thing smells like piss."

The other man choked, smothering a laugh. "The street girls use their own piss to kiss off men who want amour without paying." His English was laced with a heavy French accent.

The American threw the gun at her. She ducked and it hit the back window.

"You slut!"

"Calm down," the Frenchman told him.

"She sprayed me with piss!"

The Frenchman shrugged. "*C'est la vie*. What do you expect from a whore?"

The American's accent was Midwest, she thought, not Chicago, but more heartland . . . city, not corn . . . maybe Kansas City or St. Louis. "How are things in old St. Louie, sport?" she asked, mimicking his American accent.

The American reacted with more anger. "How the fuck do you know where I'm from?"

The Frenchman chuckled. "*Très bien, ma petite perruche.*" Very good, my little parrot.

She turned her gaze to the Frenchman. Western France, she thought, probably wine country Bordeaux, but his regional accent had been polished by years in Paris. He had slick black hair combed straight back, a nightclub pallor, and thin, purple lips. While the American was blunt and physical, he was suave and manipulative. He wore a caped coat over an expensive brown gabardine suit, a yellow tie, and narrow Italian shoes. She guessed his age at about thirty-five, a few years older than the American.

Stories of pale-complexioned girls being kidnapped off the streets and sold to dark-skinned Arabs across the Mediterranean raced in her mind, but she couldn't imagine a police escort for the activity.

The limo slowed and the American jerked around to the driver. "Don't slow down!"

"People are crossing the boulevard, Monsieur."

"Run them over!"

The driver glanced back. "*Merde!* Insanity."

The American pulled a gun from his shoulder holster and put the cold steel barrel behind the driver's right ear. "*Don't slow down.*"

What was happening? Panic made her breathless again. Men with guns, a black car streaking through the city, police sirens. Marie instinctively knew why she was being taken, but her mind balked at the realization. It was the summons she had been warned from childhood to expect. It had finally happened. They had come for her. And it terrified her.

She dove for the door handle, hitting the door with her shoulder. The door flew open and she fell face-first at the seventy-miles-per-hour pavement flying by. The Frenchman caught her by the hair and blouse and jerked her back, throwing her against the seat.

Turning from the driver, the young American shoved the gun in her face. "Don't try that again."

Marie looked away from the gun and stared at the lights passing in the night, getting her breathing under control by taking deep breaths and exhaling slowly. Panic crowded her thoughts, but she kept her face stone. Not showing fear was something learned early on the streets. But now a dread worse than panic gripped her. She had spent her whole life running from unmentionable demons, the hounds of hell snarling behind her, their hot breath and sharp teeth at the back of her legs, ripping little pieces of flesh, waiting for her to fall so they could tear out her liver. She still wanted to believe that it was a case of mistaken identity, but she knew that the demons had finally caught up with her. A village priest had told her years before that she would get the summons and she had spent a lifetime dreading the day.

The windows of the limo were blurred from the mist outside and the hot breath inside. She turned from the two men, sitting upright, her body tense and sore, and stared at the blur and haze of lights streaking past the window. She recognized the route and that was another surprise.

"Why are you taking me to the airport?"

The Frenchman nodded back toward the street where they found her. "Does it matter? Anything has to be better than being a whore." He eyed her short shirt, tight top, and heavy makeup. "I was told you might not be a whore, but—"

"She's a slut," the American said. He wiped his face with his hands and smelled his fingers, his features souring. "Who the hell knows what goddamn diseases the bitch has."

"France is a civilized country, we make our prostitutes pass health tests and license them." The Frenchman grinned at the other man's fears. "Of course, you can never tell when a dose of AIDS might get past the—"

"Fuck you and the horse you rode in on."

The limo detoured from the traffic lanes leading to the passenger terminals and sped through an open gate directly toward a big jet waiting at the foot of a runway. French army vehicles formed a barricade around the plane with military policemen in combat helmets standing by with automatic weapons at the ready.

What was happening? Confused and frightened, she struggled to keep her composure. What if it was a mistake? What if they had the wrong person? She grabbed at the straw. "You've taken the wrong person! Don't you see? I'm not who you think I am!"

The Frenchman raised his eyebrows. "Marie Gauthier. Born in Marleaux, France. Daughter of Henri and Heloise Gauthier."

She stared at him in shock despite the fact that the information should not have come as a surprise to her. It was hope, not reality, that was crushed. The tension-charged atmosphere in the car closed in on her and her chest muscles contracted. She could hardly breathe again. What else did they know about her? Even as she thought the words she told herself to stop fooling herself. *They knew everything.*

The blockade of military vehicles parted to let the limousine through and it swept past them, coming to a halt near the plane's boarding steps. The American pulled Marie out of the limo and rushed her to the bottom of the steps where a distinguished-looking man with gray hair and a camel-colored cashmere overcoat was waiting. He took Marie firmly by the arm and led her up the steps.

She didn't resist. It was futile, she thought. There was no escape from her fate. Then she saw the eagle emblem on the tail of the airplane and her knees went weak. She grabbed the railing. "That emblem, I've seen it on television."

"This is Air Force One," he said, "the personal plane of the president of the United States."

THE ROMAN

CHAPTER TWO

John Conway hummed and quietly sang a little as he watched the action onstage through a crack in a curtain. Dressed as Julius Caesar for the role in Shakespeare's play of the same name, he had complained earlier about the draft caused by wearing a Roman tunic, basically a woman's dress, instead of pants. However, the dress had proved an asset as a young red-headed actress knelt and gave him a blow job before he was to return to the stage to be betrayed and killed by Brutus and other Roman senators.

He was a very fit fortyish male, good-looking, dynamic, a veteran movie star whose stage presence had been likened to Hollywood golden age actors Errol Flynn and Laurence Olivier, but he knew the young woman was more interested in what he could do for her career than her libido. She was known as Plastic Woman—collagen lips, silicone breasts, liposuction thighs, and pubic hair trimmed in the shape of a heart. She was the type of woman the casting couch was invented for.

He was not really enjoying her tender ministrations. He had enjoyed sex from every possible angle—and orifice—of his and a woman's body. The young actress had offered it. He accepted both out of habit and perhaps a deep-down worry that if he refused, she would think he was gay. Start a rumor like that and he would make the front pages of the tabloids and see his action-hero box-office attraction sink.

The lure of fame and fortune brought out the worst in all of us, he thought, then went on humming and mumbling a little of Bruce Springsteen's "Redheaded Woman."

Songs with words, musical poetry, that's what he liked about Springsteen's music. And hated about music composed of screeching sounds made by someone hopping up and down on a stage while fornicating with a guitar.

Even though the actress was doing a fine job of faking her passions, Conway was more introspective than aroused. There had been a time when a young woman would have given him oral sex because she enjoyed it. And he would have returned the deed with more gusto than he could muster today. He felt that unwittingly he had turned a corner in life sometime in the recent past—*that he was getting old*. It wasn't passing forty; anything under sixty was still a kid in an age where baby boomers spent a fortune to ward off old age. It was something more subtle, more personal. He had been trying to grasp what it was and the phrase, "I'd rather be ashes than dust!" kept popping into his thoughts.

He hummed a few more bars of the song. He couldn't remember the words, something about a man hadn't lived until he had had his tires rotated by a redheaded woman . . . but the song didn't get him into the rhythm of the fellatio. "I'd rather be ashes than dust," kept invading his thoughts.

He even felt sorry for the young woman on her knees before him. She was someone's daughter who probably was taught the wrong things about life, love, and the pursuit of happiness. He didn't need to get her into bed to know that she would fake her orgasms. Old-fashioned romance had died under the hot light of movies and TV and he reduced the current state of lovemaking to three *F* words: Fast-Food Fucking.

MacFucking was getting it in, getting off, and getting out, with all the generic passion of buying a hamburger at the drive-thru window.

The plastic perfection of the young actress blowing him reminded him of a beautiful woman he had seen walking down Rodeo Drive in Beverly Hills when he first arrived on the West Coast. She was with a major male star whom the tourists on the street goggled at, but Conway's eyes had been drawn to the woman. She was absolutely perfect; not charismatic like a movie star, but the perfection supermodels have. He didn't know how much of the perfection came from a plastic surgeon's knife, but it did not matter. The effect was as shiny and stunning as a new luxury car on a showroom floor.

Because she had been so beautifully manufactured, he thought of her as a storebought woman. Pretty to look at. Exciting to drive. But under the hood, there was a metallic soul.

He wondered if he should compose some lyrics for a song about a "storebought woman" and send them to Springsteen. He tried thinking about the words, but "I would rather be ashes than dust" kept jumping in and pushing everything else in his mind away.

Finally, he gave up the ghost and quoted the entire verse aloud:

"I would rather be ashes than dust!
I would rather that my spark should burn out
in a brilliant blaze than it should be stifled by dry rot.
I would rather be a superb meteor, every atom
of me in magnificent glow, than a sleepy and permanent
    planet.
The function of man is to live, not to exist.
I shall not waste my days trying to prolong them.
I shall use my time."

He suddenly realized that the pretty young thing had stopped manipulating his virile part and was staring up at him, puzzled and openmouthed.

"Jack London," he said. "The creed of a man who knew how to live."

———

Onstage, little beads of sweat from the hot lights rolled down his face and he resisted the temptation to wipe his cheek. He had been getting less than enthusiastic reviews and an amateurish move would get him fried by the critics. An American movie actor playing Shakespeare on a London stage didn't sit well with the critics, anyway. The fact that he was half-British didn't help. It was his accent. He could fake a British accent for an American audience but not for a London one.

He pointed to the Roman villa painted on the canvas set and said to a group of Roman senators, "Good friends, go in and taste some wine with me."

Brutus stepped away from the group of senators and looked to the audience, pausing for dramatic effect. Caesar's jaws tightened. He felt like kicking Brutus in the ass every time the man pandered to the audience. Brutus was a *stage* actor and he seemed to be saying to the audience, "Don't pay too much attention to this *movie* actor."

Conway knew he had one great advantage over Brutus and the other actors on the stage—he looked like a noble Roman. Like Olivier and Heston, he could pass for the real thing—the cast-in-bronze features, patriarchal and arrogant, the naturally commanding presence of one who knew others lived to serve him, the haughty mannerisms of noblesse oblige.

He had always believed that in a past life he had been a Roman general, a legion commander and conqueror. Unfortunately, it was a thought he had once shared with a *Playboy* interviewer. After the article came out, *National Inquirer* ran a series on his past lives in which an "informed source" said that he claimed he had been Napoleon and General Patton. What he hadn't told the interviewer was that his secret hero was Alexander the Great, the golden-haired boy king who conquered much of the civilized world while still in his twenties. As a youth, Conway had built models of the battles at Gaugamela and Hydaspes and led charges from the back of an imaginary Bucephalus, the great war horse that Alexander built a city to honor.

———

Brutus raised his eyebrows and cocked his head back a little. "'That every taste is not the same, O Caesar. The heart of Brutus yearns to think upon.'"

Smothering a groan, Conway exited right. Brutus would soon put a dagger in his chest and Conway was almost looking forward to it. The play was to close in a few weeks and he was looking forward to that, too. He needed to get away for a while and figure out what he was going to do when he grew up.

Jack London had been a ghost in his mind of late for weeks. He had been sent a script for a movie entitled *Call of the Wild*, not a remake of the earlier film but the story of Jack London's life. London, raised poor in the San Francisco Bay Area, had quit school at fourteen to seek adventure. He sailed the Pacific as a sailor, rode the rails as a hobo, and chased the pot of gold at the end of the rainbow in the Alaska gold fields. Failing at gaining fame and fortune at everything else, he sat down and wrote stories. Like the medieval alchemists who tried to turn lead into gold, London's pencil scribbles would bring him the pot of gold.

As a teen, Conway had read London's autobiographical novel, *Martin Eden*, and it set the pace for his own life of seeking adventure. Like the eclectic and adventurous Jack London, he had filled his life with movement. He had been raised in a lower-income neighborhood of Philadelphia. His father, a British navy enlisted man, had married a Philly girl of Italian stock and settled down to work in the shipyards.

His mother's brother was a priest and classical scholar and had used his influence to get him admitted free into Catholic schools, in the hopes that he would someday become a servant of God. It was a futile hope. If nothing else, Conway loved women too much to ever consider celibacy.

His priest-uncle was blind and Conway became his right hand and altar boy, learning more about a church than he ever wanted to know.

Being taken out of the mainstream of education and directed by his scholarly uncle had affected Conway's attitudes and lifestyle. Under his uncle's tutelage, he became fluent in

Latin, could read ancient Greek, and was a master of the classics. He found a natural outlet for his education and spirit in acting. The only acting available was college plays and he soon found college and the plays too stifling.

Leaving education behind, he joined the navy and became a frogman. It was exciting, dangerous work, but he hated the structure of the military. Wearing the same uniform each day. Reporting to work on a regular basis. The military pace of "hurry up and wait." Saluting drove him nuts. Everyone had to salute. Generals saluted bigger generals. The biggest general saluted the president. The president saluted back.

He left the navy and got a berth on a fifty-foot sailing yacht that a man with too much money and too little sense was taking on a cruise around the world. Sailing around the world sounded fine to Conway, but he bailed out in Panama. The owner was a rich, stupid man, and Conway was going to jump ship anyway. Knowing that the man intended to cheat him out of his pay, he took it out in trade before he jumped ship, humping the owner's wife in a standing-room-only head.

A chance encounter in Panama with Colombian rebels running guns led him into an unofficial CIA assignment and he ended up on the payroll, working for the Company for two years, impersonating a priest to be able to travel jungle back roads without creating much attention. Stomping around jungles and riding one-horse trains into back country had been exciting. When the gig was over, he found himself transferred back to CIA headquarters at Langley to be trained and groomed into a *real* CIA agent rather than the rough-and-tumble independent operator he had been in the jungle.

He found the CIA to have the same sin as the navy. Everyone wore the same uniform and saluted, even though the clothing and attitude were more subtle than the military. CIA headquarters was a great concrete bureaucracy. When he found he was to be assigned undercover as a cultural attaché at a U.S. embassy in Poland, he jumped ship from the intelligence agency, this time to the lure of Hollywood, where a frogman buddy was now doing stunts.

Conway was more interested in acting than taking punches

for other people, but his features were too "classical" for most modern roles and he discovered the only jobs he could find were as a stunt man. He had to learn sword fighting for a Mel Gibson costume drama and did so well Gibson gave him a minor role; that led to a small part as a Roman officer in *Gladiator*.

Over the years, as audiences grew more bored with car crashes and Hollywood rediscovered the Roman Empire and medieval knights, his classical looks became an asset. His big break came with a remake of *Demetrius and the Gladiators* in which he reprised the Victor Mature role as a Christian pacifist forced into the arena to fight, only to become a champion.

He had taken the challenge of a Broadway play only because, like Edmund Hillary and the mountain, it was there, another notch on his life's adventures.

The Jack London script had heated up his brain juices, making him wonder what he was doing, what his purpose was on earth—a question everyone asks at some point in their life but for Conway it was a recurring theme in his mind. London had lived life to the fullest, dying at forty. He had avoided the three maladies Conway feared most—boredom, chronic illness, old age.

He knew he had to move on, to keep putting his feet down one in front of the other, but only in a different direction than he had been moving. But where would the next adventure take him?

When he entered his dressing room, Jeff Hines, a CIA agent he had worked with in the past, was waiting for him. Hines was a strictly-business agent with the mentality of a government-issued gray metal desk.

"What are you doing here?"

"The president has a role for you, Your Roman Majesty. There's a car waiting outside and a jet standing by at the airport. You're reporting to New Mexico."

"New Mexico! What the hell is in New Mexico?"

"Tumbleweeds and turquoise Indians, for all I know. The orders to bring you in came from the White House and Downing Street. We have a fire raging in the great Southwest and for some reason you're the person they think can put it out. Los Alamos and all that secret atomic stuff is out there, but your guess is as good as mine."

"I have to finish the play. After my scenes—"

Hines nodded at the open door behind Conway. Two military policemen with automatic weapons at the ready were standing just outside the door.

"My orders are very specific. You're coming. Now."

Conway looked at the guns.

" 'Et tu, Brute?' "

THE WANDERING JEW

CHAPTER THREE

ISRAEL, THE JORDAN RIVER VALLEY

David Ben-Dor. The name was stenciled across the top of the thick military file. Colonel Yaffe, Israeli army engineer, sat at a foldable metal command table above the bank of the Jordan River and read the file, occasionally looking down at the man named Ben-Dor knee-deep in the river. The colonel's unit was testing a portable bridge that could be used in rapid water or laid across a dry gully. The design was clever, the colonel thought, light enough for easy handling, strong enough to support an armored vehicle, and able to bleed off and divert the power of fast-flowing water.

But at the moment the colonel was more interested in the man who had designed the bridge than the bridge itself. Command wanted the design updated to use new alloys and they had sent the colonel to test it, along with Ben-Dor, who designed the bridge a dozen years before. Ben-Dor had been lent to them from, of all places, a prison.

Colonel Yaffe glanced up from the file and out at the river again. Ben-Dor and several soldiers were working a segment of the bridge into place. Ben-Dor's natural light complexion was deeply bronzed by the sun. His powerful arms and shoulders glistened from the sweat of exertion. Yaffe wondered whether the muscles were natural or built up with weightlifting. The man was assigned to a prison labor camp and probably spent most daylight hours swinging a sledgehammer or jockeying a jackhammer.

Ben-Dor was thirty-eight, the colonel noted, his own age, but their lives had certainly taken different paths. Besides the usual statistical data about his military service, the first significant entry about Ben-Dor's service was a reprimand for dereliction of duty: As a young soldier on guard duty in Jerusalem, he had not fired his weapon at the approach of an Arab with a suicide bomb strapped around his waist. The teenage Arab boy was running toward a group of Israeli worshippers coming out of a synagogue. Other soldiers opened fire, killing the boy, with a number of people injured in the resulting bomb explosion. Because of his youth and inexperience, Ben-Dor had not been court-martialed. The file noted that Ben-Dor had apparently "frozen" at the sight of the boy and suggested that something from his own past had kept him from reacting to the threat.

The second significant entry in the file was a commendation a few years later for having designed the bridge. By this time Ben-Dor was a young architect and engineer and the only military attachment was mandatory reserve duty with the rank of captain.

The final entry was a memo from the police. Ben-Dor had designed an architectural project in the Negev, Israel's arid southern region. And he had blown up the project as it neared completion. No one had been killed in the destruction.

Why would an architect blow up his own creation? the colonel wondered. That would be like a mother killing her baby. Or a writer burning his book.

Ben-Dor had disappeared into the desert after the explosion and it had taken three years for the authorities to capture and bring him to justice. When they found him, he had been living as a Bedouin.

A Bedouin? The colonel shook his head. An enigma wrapped in mystery. How does a soft-ass architect become a wandering nomad, living off a land that even lizards and snakes have a hard time surviving in?

The entry noted that Ben-Dor's wife had been killed in an Arab attack before he blew up the project. Surely a connection, the colonel thought. But still a puzzle wrapped in an enigma. Why would he destroy an *Israeli* project for the consequences of an *Arab* attack?

CHAPTER FOUR

David looked up to where the colonel sat in the shade, reading the folder. Prison life should have cured him of the feeling, but he still felt an invasion of privacy. He recalled reading a story in his college days about a jungle tribe somewhere—or was it the Greeks?—who believed a person's entire life was set down in a book and if one could get ahold of the book they could change the outcome.

Sloshing in the water, he fantasized for a moment that *that* book was the one in the colonel's hands and that if he rushed out of the water and grabbed it, he would be able to make changes. A few strokes of a pen here, a deletion there, and his life would have taken an entirely different path.

Five men were in the water with him, an army sergeant and four enlisted men, all Israeli soldiers. Between them they were shouldering and positioning part of the portable bridge that he had designed a couple of lifetimes ago—or so it seemed. Three more soldiers were positioned as lookouts on a mound a hundred meters down river. In ancient times the entire Jordan River valley had been part of Israel, but during most of David's lifetime, much of the river valley had been held captive in a struggle with a couple million Arabs on the West Bank and a billion other Muslims scattered from Morocco to Bangladesh.

"Ease it back . . . steady . . . steady," David said.

The girder interlocked with the section already installed and David stepped back, pulling his feet out of the suction of mud. He rinsed sweat from his face with cold river water, shivering as the water ran down his chest and back. The early spring temperature in the Jordan River valley was already over a hundred and by summer would soar to a hundred twenty. The valley was a narrow place filled with thickets, green rushes, and the shocking magenta and violet of bougainvillea.

David scanned both sides of the riverbank and the sergeant next to him did the same. An Israeli battle tank, which would test the strength of the bridge, was overdue. They were keeping an eye out for the tank. And snipers.

"Bring out another girder," David told the four enlisted men.

The bridge girders were on the trucks that had brought them to the spot. In the water, handling the bridge parts, he was obeyed as if he still wore the bars of an army captain on his shoulders. One foot out of the water and he reverted to prisoner.

Another girder in place and the bridge would span halfway across the river. That was as far as they would go. They didn't want to make Arabs on the other side trigger-happy. David was sure they were being watched, either by a Palestinian or Jordanian unit. Perhaps even Islamic fundamentalists, Jihad terrorists, who rejected all Israeli-Arab accords.

"Where the hell is that tank?" asked David.

"Tank jockeys are always late," the sergeant said. "They're like guitar players, always tuning something." He spat downstream and scanned the riverbanks again. "Ever been in the river valley before, Captain?"

It wasn't necessary for the sergeant to use David's former rank, in fact it was completely unnecessary, but respect had grown between the men as they shared a common labor.

"Not this far upstream. Just down to the Dead Sea from Jericho."

They had been working together for two days and the sergeant had become friendlier as the work progressed, impressed not only with David's ability as an engineer but that he went into the water with the rest of the men.

David nodded at the cliffs on the west side of the river. "I used to live up there, south of here, when I was a kid."

"The Judean Hills?"

"My parents were West Bank settlers," David said. "We moved there when I was a teenager."

"I heard your family were pioneers in one of the harsh areas of the Negev."

So he had been told about me, David thought. The colonel probably read aloud his file after the evening mess.

The sergeant shook his head, slightly awed. "Pioneers in the Negev and the West Bank."

David knew his estimation in the sergeant's eyes had gone up several notches despite any more recent history. The southern Negev, alien desert that had to be reclaimed from rock, sand, and blistering winds, and the West Bank, the danger zone where over a million hostile Arabs lived, were places only the toughest of the tough had tried to settle, something like homesteading in the middle of Apache territory.

The sergeant set the last pin and with a critical eye surveyed the portion of the bridge that had been put together like an erector toy. "Damn clever. Lightweight, strong. Bridges your specialty, Captain?"

"I borrowed a few ideas from Archimedes."

Bridges had been his father's specialty, not David's. His own "specialty" was not something he wanted to talk about. His dream had been building a utopia in the desert, an ecologically friendly creation that *Dune* writer Frank Herbert would have been proud of. In the end the project had cost him his wife and his freedom. And almost his sanity.

"Who the hell is Archi—whoever."

"Archimedes, an ancient Greek, the father of engineering. He was doing stuff like this over two thousand years ago."

"He move anything as heavy as a tank over his bridges?"

"I doubt it, but a Persian king named Xerxes built a bridge

across the Hellespont by tying seven hundred ships together and putting a road on top of the ships. He marched a million men across to invade Greece, only to be defeated by a few thousand Greeks."

David put his back to the end girder and leveraged himself into a sitting position with his feet still in the water. Rubbing the top of his numb legs, he looked up at the cliffs.

"Missing the old days?" asked the sergeant.

David chuckled. "Not those old days. I only spent about a year in the West Bank. It was . . . interesting." It was the most neutral word he could think of. Dangerous and combative would have been more accurate. Soul-searing, better yet.

"Ben-Dor," the sergeant said. "I've heard that name before." He took in David's light brown hair, hazel eyes, and sunned complexion. "Have we ever served in the same unit? One of the Lebanon excursions? I went up Fatahland with an armored unit. Think I might have seen one of these contraptions there."

The Bekaa Valley of Lebanon was nicknamed Fatahland after Yasir Arafat's wing of the PLO when fifteen thousand of his followers set up shop there for attacks on Galilee. There had been major and minor battles in Lebanon during most of David's life, often against the Hezbollah, but he knew which one the sergeant was referring to. "My bridge got a workout in Lebanon, but I rode a desk at headquarters." He had never been assigned to a combat unit after the incident in Jerusalem.

The sergeant spat downstream again. "Ben-Dor, I'm sure I know that name. When did your parents immigrate?"

"Back in the '40s, after the war."

"Europe?"

"My father was European. My mother American."

"Maybe your father served with mine back in '48, a Haganah unit that pushed out of Haifa."

"My father was Lehi. He was at Deir Yassin." David didn't know why he said it. He instantly regretted it, as much for the sergeant's sake as his own. The name of the Arab village signaled a controversy whenever it was mentioned.

"Your father was a hero." He spoke a little gruffly, defensively, as if he expected an argument.

"Some people have called him a fanatic."

"Not in front of me, they wouldn't. The Lehi were the toughest soldiers we had back in '48."

They weren't just soldiers, David thought. The Stern Gang is what Western newspapers called them, after Abraham Stern, who headed the group until he was gunned down. And Deir Yassin was not a name associated with heroism. During the War of Independence, members of the Stern Gang and Irgun had massacred all 254 inhabitants of the Arab village called Deir Yassin. In '48 it was a name of infamy as notorious as My Lai became twenty years later when American GIs murdered 500 Vietnamese civilians.

"People who weren't around in '48 don't understand how desperate things were," the sergeant said. "We were not only outnumbered ten to one by Arab armies but there were more Arabs than Jews in the Jewish sector. Your father ever tell you about Gush Etzion? An Arab army took the farm and murdered and raped the defenders—men and women. But first they tortured them.

"The Lehi commandos at Deir Yassin, they knew about Gush Etzion," the sergeant said, "knew they were fighting for the life of every Jew in Palestine when they hit the village. The village occupied a hilltop position on Jerusalem Road and was pouring fire down on our convoys."

David didn't reply. Deir Yassin was not a controversial subject with him but a personal one. His mother told him that his father's unit had arrived at the village with emotions running high. One killing led to another and soon the commandos were racing from house to house, shooting until the village was splattered with blood.

The echoes of Deir Yassin were heard around the world. The leaders of the massacre were arrested, but the charges were later dropped. Simon Ben-Dor had been one of the men arrested.

David understood the path that had taken his father from

being a talented engineer to a bloody militant. His father had lost everything in the Holocaust—family, fortune, perhaps even part of his sanity. It was one thing for people who did not personally experience the Holocaust to give lip-service sympathy to those who survived the horror—it was another thing to be held prisoner by Nazis beasts who murdered everyone you held dear.

The outrage was aggravated as homeless Jews were barred from establishing a safe haven in the Holy Land. Because the immigration of Jews to Palestine was cut off after the Second World War, David's father and other survivors of the Holocaust had to run a naval blockade to get to the Promised Land. His father had waded ashore near the ruins of Caesarea, the Roman capital of ancient Israel, after the leaky fishing boat he and twenty-four other Jews used to sneak past the blockade ran aground. Aided by members of the fishing kibbutz of Sedot Yam, he was hustled off to Haifa under the noses of British patrols.

Angry, bitter, his father was quickly solicited for membership in the Lehi—the Stern Gang—the most violent and radical Jewish underground group fighting the Arabs and British for control of Palestine. His father's family had been the favorite builders for three Austrian emperors and were famed for their Danube bridges. With forged papers, he got a job with the British Mandate's Royal Engineers, designing bridges for Palestine. At night he rode with the Lehi, setting explosives in exactly the right places to bring down bridges.

One night he blew up a bridge he had designed himself.

He never designed anything again.

David tried to stand in his father's shoes and imagine what he went through, the horror of being hunted like an animal by Nazis, of losing family and friends to insane genocide, the need for a homeland, and rage when it was denied. But it was unimaginable.

It had taken the Holocaust and the birth of a nation to make his father violent. What shocked David was that it had taken so much less to drive himself to an act of violence.

"People forget what Deir Yassin did for Israel," the sergeant said. "When the Arabs heard about it they ran from the Israeli sector by the thousands and suddenly we Jews were a majority in our own country."

They were setting the girder into place when the tank rumbled down a hill on the west side of the river. Two black dots were in the sky beyond the hills. Helicopters.

"They're ours," the sergeant said, gazing at the helicopters. "Armored gunships. Rockets strapped to their sides and commandos in their belly." He jerked his thumb at the tank barreling down the hill. "We may need the choppers for ambulance duty if those damn fools roll that tank."

The tank survived the hill and its speed slowed as it approached the river. The men on the rise started down to meet it at the riverbank. One of the soldiers hailed the gunner manning the machine gun mounted on the tank turret. "Point that thing the other way, soldier."

The machine gun exploded into action, twenty rounds a second ripping into the hillside and the three men walking down. The men in the water froze in shock and stared in disbelief. They dropped the bridge section and struggled to shore for their weapons as the tank veered toward them and machine-gun fire chopped the water. David hit the shore with bullets kicking up sand at his bare feet—someone behind him cried out and went down. A truck to his left exploded as the tank cannon thundered.

Overhead a gunship came in low, its point gun blazing at the tank. The tank's cannon and machine gun swiveled to return the fire as rockets roared from the lead chopper and pounded the hill above the tank. The tank swerved wildly and rode sideways up an embankment, flipping over onto its side.

David and the men who came out of the water with him stared numbly at the carnage. A truck was burning to their left. The three men who had been posted as lookouts were down, dead or seriously wounded. He heard someone cussing beside him and glanced to his right—the sergeant was on his feet, but blood gushed from his left shoulder.

The lead helicopter roared by overhead as the other chopper bellied down in a clearing beyond the overturned tank, commandos leaping from the chopper before it even touched ground.

Machine-gun fire again chopped at David's feet. Three men in the tank had gotten out through the escape hatch and were charging directly to where David stood. The colonel stepped away from his table and stood with his feet spread apart and fired a 9mm held in both hands. He caught a round in the chest and was blown backward off his feet.

Commandos from the chopper opened fire on the three tank men, putting two of them down, but the third man was too close to David for the commandos to risk firing.

David dove for the ground as the remaining attacker from the tank, a skinny, olive-skinned Arab in an Israel army uniform with an ammo belt bulging with hand grenades charged. His mouth open, eyes wide with terror, mustache and brow wet with sweat, he fired a machine gun wildly, aiming more from desperation than skill. Bullets spattered dirt into David's face.

The sergeant suddenly dashed into the line of fire, firing an Uzi from his hip. The charging gunman exploded and grenade shrapnel shot out as a swarm of lead death. The sergeant took the brunt of the grenade shrapnel in the face, chest, and legs.

His ears ringing, mind swirling, David knelt beside the downed sergeant. The man was bleeding from a dozen wounds. He grinned weakly up at David and said something David didn't catch.

Boots crunched beside them and David looked up at a commando lieutenant, a woman in her early twenties. "Where's Ben-Dor?"

"I'm Ben-Dor. Get a medic."

"Medic! Over here! Follow me, Captain Ben-Dor. You're being evacuated separately from the rest of the men."

"Like hell I am. I'm staying with him. He saved my life." David stepped back from the sergeant as two medics with a stretcher knelt by the noncom.

Another commando officer, a full colonel, hurried over. "Come with me. Now! Or you'll be cuffed and dragged."

David cursed aloud and followed the colonel to a helicopter, boarding behind the senior officer. The chopper lifted off as soon as David had stepped aboard. He slammed into a seat across from the colonel, cold and clammy from shock.

The colonel indicated a man sitting next to him. "This is General Scott of the U.S. Military Intelligence Agency."

David ignored the introduction. "I'd like to know why I'm being singled out."

"That was a suicide squad," the colonel said. "You're lucky you're alive. That last man was going to detonate himself and take you with him."

"Palestinians?"

The officer shrugged. "Who knows? For sure, one of the Jihad groups. They hijacked the tank at a rest stop, killed the crew, and headed for you."

"They were after you," General Scott said.

Scott stared at David impolitely, even a bit arrogantly, like a man examining a fly who was about to pull its wings off. The American officer was about sixty, with whiskey-veined jowls that were starting to sag. He had the dead stub of a cigar screwed into the right corner of his mouth and packed a U.S. Army automatic on a gun belt slung around his dress uniform jacket. There were more combat ribbons over the man's left breast pocket than in a Tel Aviv pawn shop.

David wasn't in any mood to be under a microscope. He would have said something to Scott, despite the general's stars, when the Israeli commando officer distracted him.

"They were after you *personally*, Captain Ben-Dor."

David was too numb for the statement to register.

The commando colonel eyed David with a mixture of awe and curiosity. "I don't know who you are, Captain, or what you've done, but General Scott arrived in Tel Aviv this morning after a telephone call saying that you're needed by the Americans. You're on your way to Los Alamos, New Mexico."

"What?"

General Scott took the cigar butt out of his mouth, exposing nicotine-stained teeth. "The call was made to the prime minister of Israel. It came from the president of the United States."

THE MIRACLE

CHAPTER FIVE

Marie sat across a table from the man who had escorted her onto Air Force One as the plane lifted off from the Marseilles airport and pointed west. The man was about sixty years old with thick, silken white hair and strong, dignified features. His midnight blue suit was faintly pinstriped, traditional rather than trendy, with medium lapels that were never quite in or out of fashion, his tie quiet red silk with black stripes, shoes black and plain-toed.

"My name is Martin Bornstein." He spoke to her in English. "I'm national security advisor to the president of the United States. It's going to be a long flight."

"Where are you taking me?"

"New Mexico. It's one of the desert states in the American Southwest."

"Why are you doing this? There are laws."

Bornstein studied her, intrigued by the depth of feeling and emotion that he detected. So many secrets, so many hurts were masked by hard eyes and cold lips. "Don't worry," he said, "you have not been kidnapped to be used as a guinea pig in an experiment."

Even as he spoke he realized that he was lying, that that was *exactly what was happening.*

The Marseilles police file on her had been brief: arrested once in a roundup of prostitutes, she had been released because there was no real evidence she was a prostitute. A note scribbled by a police officer on the bottom of the arrest report said she was known as St. Marie on the street because she was an ex-nun who helped battered and drugged-out girls.

About five feet nine and almost too thin, she was saved by the sleek profile of a high-priced model. Hair cropped above her shoulders fell in straight lines with bangs across her forehead. Starved cheeks made her prominent cheekbones sharper and gave her round hazel eyes the intriguing sensuality of a fashion model staring back from a magazine cover.

Her clothes and makeup added to the mystery: ruby rouged cheeks that would make a clown blush and flashy clothes that were expected from a woman of the night. He realized that she deliberately dressed and made herself up to hide her dynamic looks, but character traits shined through that belied her prostitute's disguise. He read idealism, courage, and integrity in her features, along with a depth of innocence and softness no woman who has had to spread her legs for money could possess.

Bornstein was an experienced diplomat who had manipulated presidents and kings in the citadels of world power and it struck him as absurd that the very fate of mankind was in the hands of this skinny French girl who could be a whore or a saint.

"You must be insane," she said. "You—you grab me off the street, force me onto this plane, this is criminal. You are making a terrible mistake. I'm not a spy. Whoever—whatever you think I am, you are wrong."

"Your English is excellent. You have no trace of an accent. I understand you have exceptional abilities with languages. Latin, Hebrew . . ."

"Yes," she snapped. "I speak several languages." The strain was getting to her. The palms of her hands burned and she buried them in her lap.

"It's more than that, isn't it, Marie? You're a human parrot"—he smiled—"if you'll pardon the analogy. You have an amazing talent to mimic any language or dialect you hear while most of us are stumbling over the first syllables."

"I . . . I'm good with languages."

She sensed mid-Atlantic America in his speech, perhaps Maryland, but his English had been internationalized by travel and life as a world citizen.

His name struck her as Jewish and she identified American Jews with New York City, but his countenance was more of what she imagined to be Bostonian, neither of which was an unlikely conclusion to be reached by a French girl whose knowledge of the United States was based upon movies and tourists.

"You lived in Israel for a year," he said, "and became an expert on the daily life of Christ, actually following his paths through the Holy Land. After that you lived in a small village in Lebanon where an almost dead language was spoken, one of the few places on earth where people still spoke Aramaic, the language of the Middle East during the time of Christ."

Her composure cracked and memories flashed through her mind like signposts on a dangerous curb. The village. The disaster that left her wandering half-mad, half-dead, in the mountains. What did they want from her? "Why have you kidnapped me?"

"We had to take you, uh, abruptly, because there was no time for explanations. And no room for a refusal. You are needed desperately by my government, by the whole world. I can only imagine how strange that sounds to you, but from our perspective you are almost unique. You are one of the few people in the world who are completely fluent in Aramaic and English. In addition, you are an expert on the life of Christ and daily life in the Holy Land during His time."

"These are scholarly things, everyone knows about the life

of Christ. You can get history and language from books. You're lying to me."

"No, I'm not lying." Just not telling the whole truth, he thought.

"Whatever you're doing, I don't want to be a part of it. I want to go back."

"Back to the streets?"

"They're my streets, I chose them. You've chosen this"— she gestured at the airplane's luxurious interior—"another form of prostitution. Tell me the truth. What is it you want from me?"

Turning away, he stared at the dark window. After a moment, he met her eyes. "A few days ago in the desert of New Mexico a miracle occurred."

Blood drained from her face and she tottered on the brink of fainting. Her hands stayed hidden in her lap.

"Miracle? What do you mean, a miracle?"

Diplomatic neutrality coated his words and his features, but his eyes took X rays of her. "An expert on A.D. 30," he murmured aloud, but to himself. "Most people are familiar with the era from movies and books but you actually learned the language of that period and its customs. Why? What motivated you?"

"Jesus was crucified during Passover that year. Everybody knows that. And you answer all my questions with questions."

Her hands ached, a stabbing pain she had not felt for years but had once dreaded more than life itself.

More signposts flashed in her mind—a church in the village where she was born, Easter services when she was twelve, the terrible pain, her brother screaming beside her as she opened her hands.

The memories made her nauseated and she struggled to focus on the present, on the man across from her. *What did these people want from her? Did they know everything about her?*

"You look ill. Would you like a glass of water?"

She shook her head; her hands remained hidden in her lap. The ache was becoming unbearable.

There was genuine sympathy in his voice when he spoke. "It's all right, *Sister Marie*. We know about the bleeding."

The bleeding. She was twelve when her hands first bled. Twelve years old and innocent.

CHAPTER SIX

> The luck of little shepherd boys.
> One found the Dead Sea Scrolls and made history.
> Another stumbled onto an even greater secret. . . .

THE HILLS EAST OF THE
SEA OF GALILEE, A.D. 30

"Isaiah!"

"Yes, Father?"

"A lamb is missing. Go back and find it."

"But, Father, the sun is almost gone."

"Hurry. Take the dog."

Isaiah shivered and pulled his tattered sheepskin cloak tighter as he hurried in the direction he had grazed the sheep. The lamb had chosen a fine time to stray! An evil night was falling as a strange cloud blackened the sky like a locust swarm from Egypt. He had returned from a hard day of herding the sheep and had only a moment warming his hands at the fire before he left to obey his father's command.

"Come, dog!"

The dog, whining and barking, ran beside him, giving Isaiah a surge of protective pride. They were friends, he and the dog. One would not abandon the other, even when their stomachs rumbled from hunger and their flesh stung from the cold of night.

A lean, knuckleboned youth with the bold eyes of a lion's cub and an unruly shock of thick brown hair, Isaiah Ben Ebed was twelve years old at a time when a man called Jesus performed miracles along the shores of the Sea of Galilee. Isaiah carried a knobby oak staff in one hand, a leather rock sling in the other, and forged into the night with the untamed spirit of a young David out to slay a giant, but wishing he was back at the one-room earthen-walled hut he shared with his family. He was hungry and his mother would soon serve dinner to his father, two sisters, and baby bother: barley bread leavened from dough left from yesterday's baking and a soup of cabbage and leeks.

Icy wind clawed at him, and fear shivered down his spine. The air was thick with ominous spirits that swirled angrily around him. He could feel the evil in the night and he silently cursed the lamb.

"Don't be afraid, dog," the scared boy said. "We'll return to the hut soon."

The gleeful cry of jackals came from the hills to his right and he prayed that the worthless creatures were not feasting on the lamb—the lamb was his to protect against a pack of jackals, a den of lions, or the devil himself! The flock of sheep and goats provided milk for nourishment and wool for clothes, necessities so vital to the family that lamb found its way to the dinner table only on holy days. To lose one to a pack of jackals was an offense to God!

He cursed the foul night again. "You shouldn't have let the lamb stray, dog."

His criticism was unfair and he patted the dog's head to apologize. Letting the lamb stray had been more his fault than the dog's. "Tonight you'll share my dinner," he told the dog.

Earlier the bitter cloud shadowing the meadow frightened him and he lost track of the lamb as he herded the flock back to the hut. As he retraced his steps, the ugly mass of air grew darker, reaching from the sky to the very earth. His fear tried to drive him back to the safety of the family hut, but he kept his feet moving in the direction he believed the lamb had strayed. "We have to find that lamb, dog. We cannot return without it."

He knew little about the world beyond the hills where his father had built the family hut. To the west was a city called Bethsaida and the great lake called the Sea of Galilee. Further south the hills ran along a deep trench carved by the river Jordan as it flowed to the mysterious Dead Sea, the watery coffin of the once mighty cities of Sodom and Gomorrah.

Somewhere beyond the haunted waters was the holy city of Jerusalem, the Promised Land of the Israelites where the sacred Temple of the One God pierced the very heavens with its crown of gold. He had heard that in Jerusalem people did not grow their own food, nor weave the cloth for their clothes, but bought the necessities of life with coins of the realm, and he wondered what it would be like to live such a life. He had never possessed money—the only money he had ever seen was a few copper coins his father buried in a sack in a corner of the hut's dirt floor.

He had not been to the great city and knew of it only from tales whispered by his grandfather over the crackle of the evening fire—stories of gold and lust, the mighty and the wicked, and of people called Romans who ruled Israel with a cruel whip covered with the blood of Jews.

A gush of wind slapped him and he staggered. The dog whimpered beside him.

"Quiet, dog!" His voice trembled. Late summer brought occasional storms and misty fog, but nothing like this wind and gloom had come before. Bits of dirt and rock and twigs stung his hands and face. He wiped tears from his eyes with his knuckles and trudged on, fearful of his father's wrath if he returned without the lamb.

His father's name, Ebed, meant "slave" and his father had once been a slave on the estate of a rich landowner, winning his freedom by defending the landowner from thieves. He expected no less courage from his son.

He heard something and broke his stride to listen. A faint murmur rode the wind as if the breeze were whispering its secrets.

Shivering, he gripped his leather sling tighter and moved on. He could whirl the sling until the strings sang and hurl a stone that would bring down a rabbit at fifty paces, the same way a shepherd boy named David had once slain a giant. But rabbits and giants were flesh and blood—the cold swirling murk gathering about him was a belch from hell that wrapped around him like the stinking rags of a mummy.

He lost sight of the dog. He heard a bark, but couldn't see the animal. He ran blindly toward the bark and stumbled, pitching headlong down a ravine in a tangle of arms and legs, landing in a clump of thorny bushes at the bottom.

CHAPTER SEVEN

BETHSAIDA, NEAR THE SEA OF GALILEE

Salome was superstitious. The queen of a small Jewish province on the heel of the Roman Empire, she was the product of a family in which murder and debaucheries were matters of state. The Herods had murdered so many, it was said that a lake the size of the Sea of Galilee could be filled with the blood.

Strange, that a dark cloud roiling above the distant hills would bother her.

But it did.

A portent of evil, a dark eye in the sky staring at her, was the sensation she got from the phenomenon as she was carried through the streets of Bethsaida.

Her grandfather, Herod the Great, had likewise been alert to omens. When told of a prophecy that a child born in Bethlehem would take his throne, in the Herod tradition of excess, he ordered the infamous "slaughter of innocents," having every newborn in the town put to death. He even carried his bloody fancies to the grave: Fearing no one would mourn his passing, Herod left instructions that when he died, the head of every household in Israel was to be slain so the whole nation would weep at his passing. Fortunately, the Roman governor had forbidden the insane order.

Many said she had also inherited Herod the Great's most distinguishable trait.

Mad, murderous ambition that knew no bounds.

Crowds, mobbing the way to the gladiator games, parted as the royal pavilion came down the road. The queen sat atop a golden throne carried by twenty tall Nubian slaves and surrounded by a phalanx of Royal Guards, their shields overlapping, spears pointed straight out. Empress of all she surveyed, a chained lion accompanied her on each side of the throne. Behind the throne a naked boy and girl, each twelve years old, fanned the queen with palms. The children had been painted gold—living statues.

Cleopatra of the Nile had not gloried over her subjects with as much pomp as this queen of Jews. The Roman emperor, Tiberius, permitted the docile sons of Herod the Great, now deceased, to assume thrones as long as they remained subservient to Rome and under the thumbs of Pontius Pilate, the prefect in Judea, and Vitellius, the legate in Syria. Salome was the wife of Philip, one of the sons. She was also the daughter of a Herod son, which meant her husband was also her uncle. Prior to her marriage to Philip, her stepfather, another son of Herod, had bedded her as well as her mother, an incestuous coupling motivated, on her part, by ambition, not desire.

As the procession moved through the streets, people shouted, *"Salome, Queen of the Jews!"*

An old man, a maker of sandals, drunk on the cheap, thick wine the queen had distributed on the day of the games, spat as the golden procession came by, and muttered too loud, "Bitch of the Jews."

One of her spies on the street pulled a barbed whip from under his cloak and lashed the old man across the face.

"What is the disturbance?" she asked the commander of her guard.

"An old man spoke words of insult against you."

"Cut out his tongue. Nail it to the city gate."

The crowd at the coliseum was restless as they waited for the arrival of the queen so the games could commence. The ordinary fare for the coliseum was gory matches in which professionals and amateur gladiators—criminals, prisoners of war, political prisoners—fought to the death on foot and chariot. Today, however, the queen had diverted water in the city's aqueducts to the coliseum, creating a lake in the arena. War ships, propelled by galley slaves, awaited battle, the upper decks and towers teeming with gladiators. Hungry crocodiles swarmed the artificial lake, waiting to rip to pieces gladiators who fell from the ships during the fighting. But being speared like a frog or ripped to pieces by a crocodile was a quicker and less agonizing death than being burned alive. Fire arrows and flaming spears were part of a ship's arsenal, and the slave rowers were chained to their posts. When the wood ships caught on fire, they would be burned alive.

The crocs were a gift to the queen from the Roman governor of Egypt. He had sent more off to Rome, for the games there, along with lions and giant snakes. As the crowds grew tired of seeing the same bloody matches, new ways to thrill them were sought.

Bets were placed while the crowd eagerly awaited the spectacle. Seasoned gladiators manned two galleys, amateurs the other two, and the odds were a hundred to one in favor of the professionals.

Trumpets blared, drums rolled, and the coliseum gates opened. The noise died as royal guardsmen marched five abreast on the lower walkway that encircled the arena. The Royal Guard, golden-haired mercenaries from Macedonia, men whose ancestors once sacked most of the known world for the boy-king Alexander, matched the march-step of the drums. Burnished bronze helmets spouting red plumes, breastplates blazing, crimson capes draping their shoulders, spears lethally erect, the legionnaires served the most ruthless queen in the Roman world.

As the queen came into view, trumpets sounded again and the people in the coliseum rose as one, their voices a single roar that shook the foundations of the amphitheater.

Salome wore a long white linen tunic, adorned with pearl-clustered gold braiding as well as a flowing silk body veil of royal purple glistening with silver thread. Her golden reddish hair was parted in the middle and rolled back at the sides, a gold band trimmed with rubies forming a crown around her head. Her only other jewelry was gold drop earrings and a golden snake-bracelet with a single giant sapphire for an eye.

As the crowd roared, *"Salome Queen! Salome Queen! Salome Queen!"* her servants flung coins into the areas of loudest adoration. The lions on the platform roared back at the crowd.

Behind the platform carrying the queen another fifty legionnaires stepped to the beat of the drum. The throne platform and honor guard were a moving monument, a temple of gold and power dedicated to a queen whose lusts for men, wealth, and power knew no bounds.

As acclaim thundered through the coliseum, Salome did nothing to conceal her contempt. She knew they shouted her praise because they were swine and she provided the swill. The coliseum at Bethsaida was not one of the wonders of the world; it would have fit into the center arena of the great Coliseum in Rome, but it served the same purpose—to divert from their miseries the vulgar rabble upon whose shoulders weigh heavily the extravagances and ambitions of their master. That the Herods toadied to the all-conquering Romans, who treated Israel as a slave colony, was a barb in the heart of all good Jews.

The people hated and feared her; she showered them with scorn. Yet her husband, Philip, was beloved by the people. He had wisely administered the prosperous tetarchy, the quarter kingdom he inherited upon the death of his father. Now Philip no longer appeared in public. It was whispered that he never left his bed, that he was dying in the palace from poisons administered by his ambitious wife. But such scandal was never spoken above a whisper because Salome held the reins of power and freely jerked them to strangle anyone who opposed her.

Like the rumors of regicide, market talk proclaimed that a different man shared her bed each night and that the men who failed to satisfy her sexual appetite found themselves in the hands of her notorious torturer the next morning.

Other than satisfying her in bed, she had no need for any man. She had contempt for the priests who were weak and for the Jewish revolutionaries who thought they could defeat Roman legions with faith. She was a realist, not a dreamer. She knew her power was in her cunning, not in force of arms. She dreamed of empire, but never fooled herself. That dream would only come true when the time and events were right. The penalty for failure against Roman legions was humiliation and a death so painful one begged to pass beyond the agony.

She went up the steps to another throne at the top of the coliseum, walking on a carpet of flower petals thrown by women who were rewarded with coins from the queen's agents in the crowd.

Salome was a leaf on a family tree that blossomed murder, lust, kingly ambition, betrayal and madness. The progenitor of the family was the Antipater, her great-grandfather. In a war between Pompey and Julius Caesar, Antipater, who was king of an Arab land called Idumaea, had sided with Caesar. His reward for choosing wisely was the right to govern most of the Palestine.

His son, Herod, called Great, became King of the Jews but was hated by them because they considered him a false Jew, a converted Arab, embracing the religion for political reasons. Like his father, Herod became embroiled in a struggle for mastery of the Roman Empire. When Mark Antony and Augustus fought for control of the Empire, Herod chose unwisely, siding with Antony. Herod's fortunes dimmed when Antony lost the struggle and, along with Cleopatra, committed suicide. But Herod was clever. He confessed his sins to the new Roman emperor, and Augustus, realizing that Herod was the perfect tyrant to rule the troublesome Jewish province, enthroned him over Palestine.

Herod's forty-one-year reign was marked with great prosperity, but he was also possessed by a malignant madness, crazed paranoia fed by the intrigues and deceptions of his own family. He murdered seven of the sons given to him by his eleven wives. The only woman he really loved was the young and beautiful Mariamne, but jealous intriguers around him, including Salome, his sister and namesake of Salome of Bethsaida, directed his insane rage against her. Herod murdered Mariamne, had their two sons strangled, her brother drowned, her grandfather and mother put to death. No tears were shed for Mariamne's mother, a woman of the vilest stamp who whispered lies to Herod about her own daughter to gain his favor.

The emperor in Rome, hearing of Herod's slaughter of his sons, and knowing that Herod would not eat pork, remarked that it was safer to be Herod's pig than his son.

After Mariamne's murder, Herod kept her body near him, preserved in honey and herbs. Servants and palace hangers-on were ordered to act toward the body as if she were still alive, but nothing mitigated the madness. He ran through his palace hounded by her ghost cries that he had murdered her and her sons.

With so much of Herod's murder and madness flowing in her veins, it was not surprising that Salome would recognize that the dark cloud was something other than a common storm cloud.

Seated on her throne at the top rung of the stadium, Salome gave the signal for the games to begin. Four galleys set forth on a lake of death, two manned by professional gladiators and two with prisoner gladiators. Each ship had twenty slaves chained to oars. The crowd immediately began yelling to its favorites, calling seasoned gladiators by name. The professional killers were more poised for battle, though all knew that they could die. The crocodiles were impartial killers.

Salome viewed the mortal combat with equanimity. She tried to keep her mind off the strange storm gathering in the distance and on another form of mortal combat: the intrigues that advanced her ambitions.

The Roman Empire encompassed Europe, North Africa, and the Middle East, encircling the entire Mediterranean. The Jewish provinces of the Palestine were a small part of the vast empire, but more trouble was bred in Jerusalem and Galilee than by the savage barbarians on the empire's frontiers. While patriotic Zealots planned revolution and gathered an army in the wilderness, and fanatical Sicarii assassins plotted the deaths of Romans and their Jewish supporters, the people themselves prayed for the Messiah that was to deliver them from under the iron heel of Roman legions.

In this boiling cauldron of murder and revolution, of paid spies and fanatical assassins, burning religious fervor and patriotic zeal waiting to boil over and explode as it would inevitably do, the strong levitated to the top like cream rising in a milk jug.

Only Salome inherited Herod's treachery and cunning. She alone possessed his ambitions, a strong woman surrounded by weak men. Herod's sons who inherited his kingdom had survived his homicidal rages because they were weak-kneed. They bent to the omnipotent Romans, just as they had cowered before their preternaturally bloodthirsty father.

As the galleys came together in mortal battle, Salome's vizier approached her. A tall, gaunt twig who kept his hands chest high, palm to palm, like a praying mantis, the vizier was the queen's chief advisor. A maggot-souled Merlin with a white beard and crocodile eyes, his alchemy was murder and politics. She purchased his loyalty with filthy lucre and the certain knowledge that if he ever betrayed her, she would have him flayed whole and packed in salt.

"A messenger is here," he whispered, stroking his beard, "sent by your uncle, Herod Antipas."

Salome looked beyond him, to the eastern hills where the dark cloud spiraled as if it were eating a hole in the sky.

"Strange, a storm cloud on so bright a day," he said.

It *was* strange. The cloud rose as if the bowels of hell were erupting. Her superstitious mind swirled like the cloud with doubts and fears. She often consulted soothsayers and was tempted to send for one now.

Her vizier squinted at the phenomenon. "A bad omen."

"No! There are no ill omens in my future. Anyone who speaks of one will have his tongue ripped out."

"Of course, my queen, of course. Did you wish to speak to your uncle's messenger?"

"Bring him forth."

"Ah, a galley is aflame."

On the lake, a rain of fiery spears had come down on a galley of amateurs. The wood caught fire instantly. Her vizier chuckled. "I ordered the wood for the galley soaked in oil so it would burn faster."

"Not the ships of my gladiators, I would hope."

He bowed. "Of course not, Highness, only the ships of the worthless criminals who are meant to die today. Only a quick death at the hands of the opposing gladiators will spare the fighters leaping from the burning ship from being taken under and drowned by crocs before being eaten. For the chained galley slaves, there will be no reprieve. The crowd is enjoying the action, wouldn't you say, Highness?"

Salome barely glanced at the drama in the arena while she waited for the messenger. Instead, her attention was again drawn to the dark storm atop the eastern hills. An evil portent, perhaps, but she refused to surrender to fear. If the cloud was an evil omen, it was a bad sign for her enemies.

Not for herself.

CHAPTER EIGHT

THE HILLS TO THE EAST OF BETHSAIDA

Isaiah crawled out of the bushes and pulled biting thorns off his clothes. He called for the dog again, but there was no answer, but he was not worried for its safety—the dog was no fool. It would return home after it became separated from him. Fighting back panic, he began making his way up the hill, using his hands for eyes, shivering from the cold and fear, wondering if something in the fog was stalking him.

His staff had flown away and he held his sling in hand, loaded with a rock. What came for him would be given a fight. He could see things in the swirling murk, dark things that took shape and then faded, appearing again and fading. And sounds, words that had no meaning except to frighten him, words that seemed to be uttered by the maelstrom itself. He was a brave boy, but was certain that demons were loose in the night. Terrified, for a moment he froze, unable to move as fear overwhelmed him.

The lamb baaed!

Isaiah stopped and listened, his heart pounding. He slid down a foot and braced himself. The lamb cried again! He couldn't see anything through the ugly gloom. He shouted and the lamb baaed in answer. Crawling to the right, he found the little creature shivering from cold and fright, its leg trapped between boulders. He worked the leg free and gathered the lamb in his arms.

As he stood up, words twisted around him, ghost voices using a strange tongue, riding the haunted breeze. He spun around, trying to find the makers of the words and fell onto his rear with the lamb in his lap. Still clutching the lamb, he got up to run, but his feet dragged as the murky gloom gripped him, turning him about until he spun like an ant caught in a whirlpool.

He cried out, but his words were lost in the babel of strange voices and the roar of the whirlwind. He felt the very essence torn from his soul and tossed to the wind.

CHAPTER NINE

THE COLISEUM AT BETHSAIDA

On the lake, the galley slaves aboard the burning vessel screamed as they burned, still chained to their oar mounts. The smell of their burning flesh reached Salome in the upper tiers of the stadium and she put a perfumed nosegay to her face. The battle had become such a bloody slaughter, her attention was drawn from the growing black maelstrom in the eastern sky. The second prisoner ship was afire and amateur gladiators flung themselves into the water to face the crocs rather than burn alive. The screams of the burning men were worse than that of victims in previous performances who had been thrown to wild animals. Men and women throughout the coliseum surged to their feet, intoxicated by the chorus of horror, wild-eyed, shouting, waving their fists, drugged mindless with the exciting lust of blood. An old man clutched his heart as it burst in his chest and a pregnant woman fell to the floor and began to give birth.

The vizier laughed gleefully as the amateur gladiators threw down their weapons and jumped from the burning ships, one after another grabbed by crocodiles and drawn under before body parts floated to the surface. Those not already grabbed by crocs were kept from clutching on to the other galleys by gladiators with long spears, who forced them back until they were pulled under by crocs. One superior swimmer made it to the wall of the arena and began to scale it. A citizen who had bet there would be no survivors of the prisoners' galley used his knife to chop at the man's hands to stop him from coming over the top. The swimmer frantically yelled and waved at the queen.

Her vizier stroked his beard. "The man is Galen, captain of your guard . . . until you, uh, demoted him."

A gladiator on the galley looked to Salome and she nodded. Spears flew, striking the climbing man in the back, pinning him to the wall. . . .

The messenger stumbled up the stairs toward Salome, looking back in mute awe and horror at the sea battle. The lake was turning red. When he didn't move fast enough, Salome's current captain of the guard, a tall bronze-blond Macedonian who was the queen's present lover, gave him a shove.

He stumbled forward and knelt before the queen, uttering the long greeting given royalty. Salome was not listening, her attention had again been drawn to the dark mass in the distance. It had spread aggressively in the sky, now covering the whole horizon to the east and spreading toward Bethsaida. She shivered and struggled to keep from showing fear.

The spectators in the coliseum had not noticed the phenomenon. The savage entertainment on the sea of blood was too captivating.

Keeping her nerves together, Salome stared contemptuously down at the messenger. Few communications from her uncle, who was also her stepfather, pleased her. Herod Antipas was hare-hearted. Dominated by fears—fear of the Romans who made him a king and who could unmake him, fear of the people he ruled and who hated him—Herod Antipas had none of his father's greatness. He was Tetrarch of Galilee and ruled from Tiberias, a city he built on the western shore of the Sea of Galilee and named after the emperor Tiberius. In line with the insensitivity he had for the religion of his people, he built the city on a sacred burial ground.

When the emperor divided Palestine between Herod's surviving sons, Philip had gotten the poorest of the kingdoms, an area north and east of the Sea of Galilee. Anger that she married the least of the Palestinian kings poisoned Salome's mind as effectively as the poisons said to be slowly killing her husband. Raised around impotent men, and women who failed to use their feminine powers except to seduce, she had looked for strong women for inspiration and found them in two queens who asserted themselves to claim an empire—Cleopatra and Semiramis.

Cleopatra, Queen of Egypt, who had seduced both Julius Caesar and Mark Antony and had the entire Roman Empire as her personal fiefdom, died before Salome was born. But the legend of Cleopatra continued. She had become queen by marrying her brother upon the death of her father. Later, after a falling out with her brother, she became the lover of Julius Caesar and convinced him to defeat her brother. After the defeat, she married another of her brothers and reassumed the throne, traveling to Rome where she displayed her hostile sister, Arsinoë, in a cage during a victory parade. She was known also by a derisive Greek name, Meriochane, "she who spreads her legs for a thousand men." Salome had heard Romans boast that Cleopatra had fellated a hundred Roman senators during an orgy in Rome, but she attributed all the slander about her to weaker fools who envied the Egyptian queen.

When Julius Caesar fell to assassins blades, Cleopatra returned to Egypt. Mark Antony, whom she had met when he was a young staff officer in Alexandria, rose to power and sent for her. She had been fourteen when she met him and she was now twenty-eight and considered the most sensuous woman in the world. She came to Antony in a barge filled with treasure and seduced him body and soul. When Antony's star fell, she joined him in suicide.

Salome considered Cleopatra's blind loyalty to Antony—even in defeat—and her eventual suicide, the Queen of the Nile's only failings.

The other woman she admired was Semiramis, the Queen

of Babylon. What a cruel, scheming, cunning bitch! Her ambitions knew no bounds, her willingness to do anything to
achieve them had been without limit. Like Salome, she was
consort to a king, but lost her royal position on the death of
her husband. Unwilling to be shoved into oblivion on the
death of the king, she imprisoned her own son, the heir to the
throne. Dressed as a man, she took the throne and imperson-
ated him. Anyone who questioned the guise had their eyes
gouged and tongue ripped out before being impaled alive at
the palace gates.

Her uncle-stepfather's messenger started to praise Salome
for her wisdom and beauty but she snapped impatiently,
"Speak my uncle's words."

"Great Queen, some in Palestine would drive our Roman
friends from the land."

Salome's attitude toward the Romans was different than
Herod Antipas's. He was content being a Roman stooge. She
admired the Romans for success and envied them their empire. If she could unite Palestine, recreating the old Kingdom
of Israel, and rule with the power that Cleopatra had had over
Egypt, she could challenge even Rome.

"Continue," she commanded.

"There is talk among the common people of rebellion. The
traitorous Zealots have a cache of arms and food in the
wilderness. In their crazed zeal, they seek to drive the Romans from the land."

The concern of her uncle was no less than her own. The
Zealots opposed not just the Romans but the Herods, too. After they drove the Romans from Palestine, they would kill the
puppet kings that had hidden behind Roman legions to op-
press them.

"This talk of rebellion is not new," Salome said. "The
Zealots plot in secret while the Sicarii assassinate Romans
and those who support them. We know well of these matters."

"Yes, great Queen, but our spies have brought urgent news
to the ears of Herod Antipas. People whisper in the market-

places and baths that a Messiah is rising who will lead the people of Israel in battle."

Salome scoffed. "The people have more Messiahs than the Herods have had kings. These stories flare up, then are forgotten."

"True, O Queen, but this Messiah performs miracles. He is a healer who has cured the sick and raised the dead."

Salome laughed. "Bring this miracle worker to me. I will have him turn stone into gold."

"Would that it were so simple," the messenger said. "Your uncle believes it is John the Baptist, risen from the dead."

The mention of that name made Salome flinch. When her uncle Herod Antipas divorced his wife and married Herodias, Salome's mother, he was reproached by the Baptist because Herodias had been the wife of his half brother and the mating violated Mosaic law.

Both Herodias and Salome had feared the allegations of the Baptist. Herodias, because of the threat that Herod Antipas might be coerced into divorcing her, and Salome because she had planned an incestuous marriage with her uncle Philip.

Herodias goaded her husband to imprison and murder the Baptist, but like all the Herods, Antipas was superstitious. He feared killing a man deemed to be holy.

Herod the Great's sons were all ruled by their gonads. Herodias, knowing that her husband lusted after her daughter, convinced Salome to dance for him on his birthday. Disrobing, she then satisfied him as her mother instructed her, taking his member into her mouth.

In exchange, he beheaded the Baptist.

The day John the Baptist had been separated from his head, she went to the dungeon to watch the beheading. Out of a sense of curiosity. As a princess, she had not experienced the darker sides of life. She knew her uncles had the power of life and death over their subjects, but she was curious about how the power was exercised. What happened when one of the Herod kings pointed his finger and commanded that someone die?

She stood in the shadowy dungeon and watched as the man was brought from his cell. His long hair fell below his shoulders, his beard fell below his neck. His eyes were red and wild, almost feral in their intensity.

Four strong men forced him over a large wooden block, the stump of a tree, and chained him down. Secured so he could not move, the dungeon master stood beside him with a large-bladed ax. With one swift move he lifted the ax and brought it down across the man's neck.

What happened next she had seen before with chickens: when the head flew off, blood sprayed and gushed from the gaping hole between the shoulder blades.

When the head separated, it flew from the wood block and rolled across the floor to her feet. As she looked down at it, the eyes in the head stared up at her. The lips moved and she ran screaming from the dungeon.

She never revealed to anyone what the head had said, but she relived the memory every day.

It had whispered, *"Salome!"*

Salome ignored the chorus of horror coming from the arena and the messenger before her. Her rational mind fought the notion that this new Messiah was the Baptist risen, but her fear of the holy man rankled. But unlike her stepfather, fears did not deter her. She would have this miracle worker hunted down before his disruptions brought Roman legions upon all of them.

Gasps rose from the people in the coliseum. The malignant black cloud roiling in the horizon, raced toward the coliseum, thundering like hell itself.

All action except the screams of the fire victims stopped in the coliseum.

The black mass was an angry violent tempest, not just a storm but a violent maelstrom reeking of power and evil as it spread across the sky. A wind, wild and harsh, came ahead of the tempest, howling as if all the demons of the Underworld had been turned loose in the sky, causing the earth itself to

shudder. Mortified for the second time in her life, Salome
heard the wails of all the thousands the Herods had tortured
and murdered.

No one had ever seen such intensity in a storm.

Such power could not be wielded except by the hand of
God.

Petrified by stark terror, immobilized by the wind that
pushed her back against her throne when she tried to rise, Salome sat helpless as the black mass reached the coliseum. The
huge structure trembled and shook as the storm hit it. Terrified people who tried to run were knocked down, others were
blown off their feet and into the crocodile-infested waters.

The roaring wind was gone in a flash. In its wake came
darkness, the sky midnight in the middle of the day.

The screaming spectators, linked in terror with the dying
men in the arena lake, knelt en masse, praying for deliver-
ance. Salome remained seated, her mind swirling, her arms
and legs petrified.

All at once it began to rain—sprinkles and then huge drops
that made a plop! sound as they struck.

She was hit in the face with something, a hailstone, she
thought. More hit her, plummeting down from the sky. She
looked down at the creatures crawling in her lap and
screamed.

Frogs.

It was raining frogs.

To every thing there is a season . . .
A time to be born, and a time to die.
A time to kill, and a time to heal . . .
A time to love, and a time to hate;
A time of war, and a time of peace.

—Ecclesiastes, Old Testament

THE INCIDENT

CHAPTER TEN

NEW MEXICO

"That damn dust devil is creating havoc with the sensors."

Dr. Carla Jennings stood at the control-room window and stared down into the "doughnut hole" area in the center of the synchrotron. It was early morning, just after seven o'clock on a bright, blue-sky, New Mexico day.

The facility was near a corner of the enormous Los Alamos scientific complex, a sprawling empire of science covering nearly a hundred square miles of desert where the first atomic bomb was developed. It was still the heart of nuclear and solar research.

The control room of the synchrotron was in a circular building that surrounded the dirt area where the dust devil, a miniature tornado common in desert areas, was spinning. The synchrotron itself was in two parts: an underground particle accelerator that stretched for a hundred miles, but not in a single circle. Rather, the accelerator was coil shaped, not unlike the heat coils of electric stove burners. The building above was also circular shaped, a facility built in the round with a first and second floor. The administrative facilities were on the first floor, while the second floor was all solar panel. From the air the facility looked like a gigantic tire lying on the desert floor.

The underground portion of the facility drew energy from the magnetic force field of the earth, the power source at the heart of the planet that operated like a gigantic world-sized electric generator. The roof panels drew power from the sun, not to generate heat but to draw in the energy of solar winds that burst across the solar system and collided with the earth's magnetic force field, creating cosmic electromagnetic storms that disrupted broadcasting and telephones.

The anticipated result was a duplication of a magnetic storm within the synchrotron, similar to the storm created by the cosmic collision of solar winds and the magnetosphere.

But a disturbance on the surface was not anticipated.

"We built this radically new technomonster to explore the very origins of the universe," she muttered, referring to the synchrotron, " 'exploration of that mysterious force called magnetism that may be the glue that keeps the earth, the sun and the stars, the very universe, together . . . ,' " she said, mimicking the national press release on the project, "and we can't build a sensor housing that will keep out a little dust."

It didn't take much wind to raise dust in the New Mexico desert—grass had not been planted yet and the doughnut hole in the center of the facility was in its virgin state of sand and sagebrush.

Carla didn't get a response to her remark, not even a grunt from Dr. Hakim, her associate. She looked to where he sat behind the control panel. The synchrotron had become operational the previous afternoon, barely twelve hours ago. She and Dr. Hakim were the only physicists on duty, baby-sitting the facility until the morning shift came on.

The dust devil had been their first "crisis." The swirling little creatures related to tornadoes were common enough in the desert, although this one was darker and thicker than others she had seen.

"I should go out there and put the cover over the sensor post," she told the taciturn Dr. Hakim.

"Strange." Dr. Hakim peered intently at the computer screen tracking the speed of the particles in an agitated state in the synchrotron. "The speed of the particles seems to be increasing on their own. These speeds are superluminal."

"Maybe the interference from the dust devil is back-feeding your data." She thought about her suggestion, imagining the electronic circuitry, calculating the probabilities that dust in sensors was affecting the whole system.

She had turned thirty-four three weeks ago and it did nothing to change her lifestyle—her marriage was to her career, her children conceived in the laboratory and published in scientific journals. She kept her hair cut short so she could towel it dry coming out of the shower and maintained a regiment of simple, dark colored pants and white blouses so she wouldn't have to clutter her mind about what clothes to wear, reserving all mental energy for her one and only love: science.

She had engaged in coitus (her name for it) just once, when she was seventeen and in her second year of college, making sex, not love, in a classroom closet with a sixty-two-year-old professor who wheezed and coughed while he humped her doggy style and nearly had a coronary as he prematurely ejaculated. She had assumed some sort of relationship between the professor's big brain and his penis, and had been disappointed to discover that despite his enormous intellect, he was just a little prick.

After analyzing the data generated by that experience, she decided she would get better results by masturbation, a process that was more satisfying and less time-consuming.

She had never sought God except in a test tube and the Miracle that occurred that day at the synchrotron would make her reevaluate a great deal about her life and the nature of the universe.

It was Wednesday morning, approximately the time of day Carla would normally be getting out of bed and going into the bathroom to wash up. Wednesday differed in her routine only because it was the day she masturbated, having logically chosen the middle of the week to spread the benefit of the experience evenly over the week.

She had been on duty all night and her body, accustomed

to the Wednesday morning routine, tingled a little, causing her to look at Dr. Hakim and wonder what it would be like to have coitus with him. It was not that she was particularly infatuated by Dr. Hakim, he just happened to be the only male in the room. She decided sex with Dr. Hakim would not stimulate her. Even though she found him physically attractive, he was Arab and she had preconceived notions about Arab men and the way they treated women. Also, she heard he had problems with his daughter and assumed the problems were rooted in Hakim's old fashioned, male-dominated attitudes.

Across the room Dr. Hakim concentrated on the computer screen, unaware he was the object of Carla's thoughts. A forty-eight-year-old Jordanian, he had an unusual background for a scientist at an installation in the American Southwest. Born in the Old City, the Arab sector of Jerusalem, he was raised in Jordan after his Muslim family fled the Israeli occupation of the West Bank. Sent to Cambridge to study economics at Harvard, Hakim displayed a brilliance for science that led him away from money and into physics, changing classrooms to those at MIT.

Since his own country lacked significant scientific facilities, he participated in U.S. and British projects. His appointment to the elite cadre of scientists assembled at the synchrotron was in recognition of his abilities and as a "bone" thrown to the Arab world, although there were allegations that the motive was to keep him from helping Arab nations develop atomic power. A world-class atomic physicist with an Arab nationality did not sit well with certain quarters in the United States and Israel. However, Dr. Hakim was a devoted scientist and maintained an indifference toward politics similar to Carla Jennings's attitude toward clothes.

Unfortunately, his twenty-year-old daughter did not inherit his apathy toward politics.

An awkwardly arranged young woman, Fatima had a prominent nose, uneven teeth, and an old-fashioned mother who had sent her to school in formless dresses and layers of underclothes, earning poor Fatima the nickname of "tent lady" from her classmates.

She got her first taste of male attention and male anatomy when she returned to Jordan for college and was recruited by an element swearing alliance to the most radical wing of Islamic fundamentalists. Visiting refugee camps, drinking muddy coffee side by side with jihad activists, making explosives in a hut in sight of the captive West Bank, mouthing slogans and getting laid, fulfilled Fatima's need to belong.

She had not come to New Mexico for a family visit but to convince her father to join the holy war against Israel, to become one of the mujahideen, a warrior for Islam. Implicit in the request was that he use his knowledge of atomic energy to build a bomb. Ironically it would be in the New Mexico desert, not the Middle East, that Fatima would strike a blow for Islam, firing a crisis that placed the very existence of civilization at stake.

Dr. Hakim studied the data appearing on his computer screen. "I'm beginning to believe your theory that dust is affecting the sensors. It's impossible, the speed of the particles is beyond anything imaginable even by the superluminal people."

"Do you think we should wake Dr. Delasak and the others?"

Delasak was the project director, a Nobel laureate for his work with magnetic particle theory. The director and the three other scientists had worked half the night before retiring to the sleeping quarters provided to the staff.

Hakim and Jennings had the same thought. If it was a simple malfunction due to dust, the director would not be happy being awakened. If it was something else, some sort of startling scientific breakthrough and they were the ones on duty at the time . . .

Her eyes shot to the window. The sensor post was hardly visible through the whirling dust. "I'm going down and put on the cover. If I get carried away by that dust devil, call the air force."

"Good luck, Dorothy." Dr. Hakim giggled at his joke without looking up from the controls. "Don't forget to take Toto. . . ."

Wind ripped the door from her hands as Carla stepped outside.

"Oh, Christ!"

The dust devil had turned into a real blow. A trash can had gone over and some of yesterday's lunch bags were airborne along with sand and sagebrush. She was halfway to the sensor post when the wind became a fury.

My God, it's a tornado.

She tried to turn back, but the dust blinded her and she became confused. She squatted down, burying her face in her arms and legs, her bare head and the back of her neck stinging from the storm of sand. Crying out in panic as the wind pushed her, feeling weightless, she threw herself flat onto the ground to keep from being taken airborne.

Her ears were ringing when she saw the light of day again, the storm spending itself in seconds, leaving sand and sagebrush piled a foot thick against the walls of the building.

Getting to her feet, she was coughing and spitting out dirt when she saw the little boy holding the lamb. He stood perfectly still, covered by a thick coat of dust, his mouth gaped open, his eyes wide, hugging the lamb like a child hugging a teddy bear as he awoke from a bad dream.

A shepherd boy, probably from the Navajo Indian tribe, that much registered instantly with her. The boy, about twelve or thirteen, wore a tattered cloak of sheepskin over a coarse garment that looked like a peasant woman's homespun dress. His face and bare legs were coated with as much dirt as that clinging to his garments. How did he get into the doughnut hole? she wondered.

Dr. Hakim came up beside her, his eyes glued to the strange young shepherd boy.

"How did an Indian boy . . ." Her voice tapered off.

Something was wrong with her Indian-boy theory, not just with the boy's features but his clothes. Hell, Indian kids worn blue jeans and wise-cracking T-shirts.

Dr. Hakim stared at the boy with a mixture of awe and shock, as if he were confronting the first alien on earth. "He's not Indian, he's Middle Eastern."

His explanation did not compute with Dr. Jennings. Israelis and Arabs are Middle Eastern. Dr. Hakim was Middle Eastern. What was a shepherd boy from the Middle East doing in New Mexico?

She heard the alarm going off inside the building. Dr. Hakim must have hit the panic button before leaving his post to help her.

Dr. Hakim spoke to the boy in Arabic, but got no response. He switched to Hebrew. *"Shalom. May-ei-fo ba-ta?"* Peace. Where did you come from?

The boy's eyes lit up. He stammered something in a language that sounded familiar to Dr. Hakim's ear, but which he could not identify. Hakim stepped closer to the boy as the doors behind them burst open and staff members rushed into the doughnut hole.

The boy dropped the lamb and made a run for it.

"Stop him!" Dr. Hakim yelled.

The project director, Dr. Delasak, ran in front of the boy and flailed his arms as if he were flagging in an airplane. The boy hit him with his shoulder and sent the Nobel Laureate sprawling in the dust.

Neil Smithers, Oxford don and International Science Award winner for his work in molecular fission theory, caught the boy by the arm. The boy spun around, swinging his rock-loaded leather sling, coldcocking the man's 182-IQ brain. Two other genius-level physicists turned tail and ran as the boy's sling whirled. A secretary from Albuquerque, a Navajo with six kids and an IQ of 98, dove at the boy in a flying tackle, slamming him to the ground. The secretary sat on the boy's chest while two skinny geniuses held down his legs.

The boy yelled at them in his strange language.

"Where did he come from?" Dr. Delasak asked.

"He suddenly materialized, right here, during the dust storm," Dr. Hakim said. "It's incredible, I think he's—he's Semitic, from the Middle East—"

"Nonsense," Dr. Delasak snapped. "The boy must be Indian."

Martha Johnson, a physicist from Georgia, stepped closer to the boy, listening intently to the strange words he was shouting at them. Dr. Johnson was a black Baptist whose hobby was biblical scholarship.

"That sounds like Aramaic," she said.

"You mean Arabic," Dr. Delasak said.

"No, Aramaic. It's been a dead language for over a thousand years."

"Then how do you know—" Dr. Delasak started.

"I spent last summer in Jerusalem taking a Bible study course. The New Testament was originally written in Aramaic and the minister read passages aloud in that language so we could experience the original Bible."

"That doesn't make any sense," Carla Jennings said. "If Aramaic has been a dead language for over a thousand years that would mean . . . that he was . . . oh, my God!"

They stared at the boy, a half dozen of the finest minds in America and a tough Navajo secretary. Each of them realized what had happened.

The dusty little shepherd boy with the tattered clothes of homespun thread was a Pressed Rose from another Time.

CHAPTER ELEVEN

Dr. Hakim called his daughter two hours later, waking her up. He made the surreptitious call while the others were crowded into the project director's office, analyzing what changes might have taken place in the magnetic field to have opened a door to Time.

The project director had called the national director in Washington and after a flurry of excited calls back and forth the project director was ordered to keep the synchrotron shut down and permit no one to leave—a crisis team from the National Security Council was being rushed to the facility.

Hakim's wife was living in Jordan with their other children, an arrangement decided upon to give the children an opportunity to experience their homeland. Only Fatima was in New Mexico, arriving a few days earlier, making demands on her father, quoting old PLO catchphrases and the newer, more violent, vocabulary of a reactionary Muslim religious movement. Words like "lackey" and "coward" spouted from her mouth, "fanatic" and "terrorist" from his.

Dr. Hakim probably couldn't have explained why he had made the call if he had been asked. Perhaps it was because he was a Palestinian and what occurred had an incredible link to his homeland. More likely it was because of pride. His daughter had belittled him as a bootlicker for the Americans, and he wanted to share with her the fact that he was involved in the most astonishing scientific event in history.

The call would cost him his life.

"It's a miracle," he whispered over the phone. "We broke a hole in Time itself. Imagine, Fatima, we may be able to go back in Time, perhaps even change history, erase all the evil."

The call from her father was brief and when it was over Fatima Hakim sat on the edge of the bed and thought about the incredible news.

A hole in Time itself. Going back to change history. Erasing the evil.

Fatima had a different view of history from her father's, a different criterion for judging evils: The West, the Great Satanic Conspiracy—the Americans, British, French, Italians and other Europeans—dominated by Jewish money, was a vampire that enslaved the Arab world and sucked the essence from it, keeping tens of millions of Arabs poor, diseased, and downtrodden in order to maintain an industrial complex that cocooned Westerners in an oasis of comfortable homes, powerful cars, the world's best medical care and a gluttony of consumer products.

All created by cheap Arab oil—the very life blood of a region that lacked enough water for a good spit but which floated on a sea of liquid black gold.

And when Arabs dreamed of their own economic oasis and tried to break the chain of oil serfdom, as Baghdad did, a nightmare of lethal missiles and bombs rained from the West.

She dialed a number in Los Angeles that was forwarded electronically to a number in New York and by the same method to the Little Algiers district of Paris. The call was answered at a barber shop and once she had convinced the barber of the urgency of the communication, the barber took her number and told her to hang up and expect a call within the hour.

The precautions were for security purposes. Fatima's lover, Amir Zayyad, and his brother, Jair, were Palestinian terrorists whose methods were considered extreme even by much of the Islamic movement. Wanted by the police in six countries, they were at the top of the kill-on-sight list of Israel's counterterrorist agency. No peaceful coexistence agreements between Israel and Arab nations mattered to them. Their purpose in life was a war of extermination with the Jewish state. Until Israel ceased to exist, they would continue the fight.

Amir Zayyad's romantic involvement with Fatima was no accident but a scheme by his brother, Jair, the older of the two, to enlist her father into jihad activities.

Jair Zayyad, a tall, lean, cold bastard with the premeditated manners of a coiled snake, had decided it was time to strike the greatest blow possible against Israel: an atomic one. Newspaper accounts that Dr. Hakim's children were returning to Jordan and a picture of chunky, dour-faced Fatima convinced him that Allah was smiling on the endeavor. His brother, Amir, was a little shorter than he, and like Fatima, ran to the chunky side, but Amir had a pleasantly handsome face and a line of shallow charm that some women fell for. Looking at Fatima's picture, Jair, who had survived a dozen attempts on his life by on his serpentine survival instincts, decided Fatima would easily fall under his brother's brand of charm.

It was Jair, anxious for news about Dr. Hakim, who returned Fatima's phone call. When he finished speaking to her, his mind was analyzing data as quickly and efficiently as any of the beyond-genius scientists at the synchrotron.

When the door to his bedroom crashed open, Amir was fucking a girl on the bed. The girl was young enough to get him a jail sentence in most countries. He rolled off her, reaching for his pistol on the nightstand until he realized the intruder was Jair.

Jair stared at the naked girl, a French-Algerian, dark skinned, with black curly hair that was almost kinky. Her legs were spread and she didn't bother closing them. She wasn't any older than twelve or thirteen, but her breasts were well developed, even a little bloated—a slight bulging in her abdomen hinted she was pregnant. Jair didn't have his brother's success with women. The only women he had been with were ones he screwed after his brother had finished with them, beating them if they objected too strongly about the sudden switch in partners.

His cold eyes went to his brother. "Get dressed. We're going to make a hit."

"What are we hitting?"

"The whole damn world."

"What are you talking about?"

"Get dressed. Now."

The girl started to get up, and Jair said, "No, you stay put. It's my turn."

"I don't want you."

A switchblade knife flipped open in Jair's hand. "When I'm through you're going to tell me how much you liked it," he whispered.

Seven days later Carla Jennings and Dr. Hakim were in the operations room just before dawn when an explosion rocked the building. They ran into the corridor to find it filled with smoke and dust from a blast that created a gaping hole where the front door had been.

A shadowy figure came at them from out of the smoke, taking shape as a terrorist in olive drab combat fatigues and wearing a heavy black scarf wrapped from head to neck, covering everything but the eyes. The eyes were popped wide from drugs, making the AK47 assault rifle in the terrorist's trembling hands all the more threatening.

Carla Jennings froze in pure fright.

Dr. Hakim stared in shock as he recognized the terrorist. He stepped forward. "Fatima, what are you—"

Fatima Hakim stepped back and the automatic weapon went off in her hands. The burst caught Dr. Hakim in the face and chest.

Carla Jennings had turned to run and was struck in the back by a bullet that had gone through Dr. Hakim. She started to fall forward and was hit twice more. She lived ten seconds longer than Dr. Hakim.

"Silicone melts in the sun."

THE MISSION

CHAPTER TWELVE

NEW MEXICO

David had the cold feeling of being a prisoner from the moment he was hustled aboard a U.S. Air Force jet bristling with an airborne assault team. Fighter jets rode shotgun as the plane winged halfway around the world to the American Southwest. Explanations came slow from the cigar-chomping general and only after David demanded them. David felt a grave opening under his feet as the general talked.

"You're the only one alive who can identify the Zayyad brothers. Right now you're number one on the hit list of every fanatic with a gun from Tripoli to Beirut."

The Zayyad brothers.

Ghosts from his past back to haunt him.

Blood for blood.

David listened with growing dread. Two terrorists with bloody footprints that led from assassinations, bombings, and hijackings had struck an American scientific installation. They had damaged the facility and killed a number of people, that much David got out of Scott, but the general was holding back from telling him everything. It was obvious the terrorists had gotten away with something, something very important to the Americans.

"Jesus H. Christ. A terrorist attack in New Mexico." Scott glared at David and sucked bitter juice from his cigar. "The fallout from the shit you Jews have stirred up in the Middle East gives the whole world a headache."

David deliberately stared at the general's Vietnam and Gulf War ribbons. "Piss off anybody in the world lately, General?"

An instant mutual dislike had arisen between the two. The general was the type who expected everyone around him to snap to attention and salute the minute he walked into a room. David had spent the last few years in a prison uniform, not a military one. Everything about General Scott, from his stinking cigars to his Let's-get-'em-cowboy attitude, annoyed him.

Tight jawed, Scott left his seat.

The general was being evasive about why David was being brought to the New Mexico installation, but David was sure the Americans wanted to debrief him about the elusive brothers. He was the only person known to the Israeli police able to identify them.

The Zayyad brothers. Not just names in the newspapers—his own father had helped them on the road to becoming terrorists. They were psychopaths who would have found a way to vent their murderous rage on the world regardless of whether their paths crossed his father's. But his father had given them direction, a target for the insane hate that fueled them.

He stared out the plane window, thinking about the path that led him into a blood feud with two of the world's most notorious terrorists.

After the War of Independence, Israel still had enemies on three sides, the sea to their back and several hundred thousand displaced Arabs who stared across barbed-wire fences at Jews plowing the fields they had once sowed. The cease-fire hadn't brought peace to his father, either. Despite the fact that he was still a young man, his father couldn't return to his profession as an engineer—the Holocaust and war in the Palestine had killed something in him and he couldn't push a pencil across a blueprint, couldn't design bridges to replace the ones destroyed in battle.

Few Americans had heeded Israel's cry of homeland as the new country threw open its doors to the Jews of the world. David's mother had been one who answered the call.

She had an upbringing that was unusual for even the Israeli melting pot. Her own mother was the product of an orthodox Jewish family, but she married a Yankee Presbyterian and sent her daughter, Rebecca Ben-Dor née Wallace, to the synagogue on Saturday and church on Sunday. Artistic, intellectual, impulsive, and romantic, Rebecca "discovered" her Jewishness when the Jews had their back to the sea and Arab armies pushing from every direction. As it turned out, she was more in love with the spirit of giving birth to a nation than the harsh reality, more attracted to the heroic concept of being a pioneer in the Wilderness than she was of kosher chicken and the Burning Bush. Full of revolutionary ardor, she came to Israel to help give birth to a nation, met and loved and married Simon Ben-Dor, a man as practical as she was whimsical, as disciplined and angry as she was highspirited. Opposites attracted, but in the end they nearly destroyed each other.

In many ways, David's family history reflected the extremes of Israel's own history: the courage, the toil, and even the violence and tragedy. His mother had romantic ideas of what it would be like working side by side with other members of a kibbutz and they went north to a farm near the Sea of Galilee where David's cry at birth was chorused by the boom of Syrian artillery in the Golan Heights. A very pregnant Rebecca had been returning from the fields when the artillery barrage started and she took cover in a barn where she gave birth to David.

His name was born in battle, too, as Israeli commandos opened fire with a battery of Davidkas, the mighty "Little David" mortars that had earlier pounded the hell out of Arab League armies. "Davidka," Simon told Rebecca as he stood in the barn and held eight pounds of red, wrinkled, and wiggling new life against his breast. "He'll be strong like the metal of Israeli guns and fight for his homeland."

Years later his father stopped calling him Davidka when David disgraced his uniform by not firing on a terrorist in Jerusalem.

Life on the kibbutz was a frantic time of learning and hard work as his city-bred parents became farmers, but problems soon arose as his mother's romantic notions of life on a collective farm met the reality of living in a utopian-socialist environment with assigned sleeping quarters, toilets down the hall, and a communal dining room.

Kibbutz children were raised by specially trained members in Children's House. Each evening after the adults returned from the fields, the children were sent over for a two-hour visit with their parents before dinnertime. Rebecca wanted David raised by her and conflicts arose.

His father became head of security for the farm, but his aggressive philosophy was shared by only a small percentage of the other members—kibbutz policy was a defensive one, leaving retaliation to the Israeli army. After Simon led an unauthorized raiding party into the Golan Heights to silence Syrian guns that had found the range of a section of the kibbutz fields, angry members stripped him of his position.

They left the kibbutz when David was six. Rebecca wanted to return to city life, to violin lessons and life as the wife of an engineer, but Simon took them south to become pioneers in a raw and savage frontier—the southern Negev, the dark side of the moon, the bitter part of Israel's frontier province, part steppe of semiarid grasslands, part desert inferno with tortured ridges sculptured from the burning earth.

Two savage enemies awaited them: the desert itself, a land of rocks and snakes where blistering sun could bake a person's brains while shearing winds stripped flesh from bone, and the Bedouins who claimed the land as their own, nomadic tribes as fierce and savage as the desert, wandering vast, brooding plains in an endless search for water to keep their herds of sheep and goats alive.

A battered, bullet-nicked Land Rover that had been armor-plated in a blacksmith's shop, took them to a moshav in the desert, another type of collective farm, but one that emphasized personal freedom—each family owning their own farm, but banding together for protection and common use of equipment.

David still remembered vividly the Land Rover stopping on a rise to give them their first sight of their new home: farmhouses set out in a protective circle like a wagon train in Indian country. Farmlands fanned out from the houses like spokes of a wheel, with barns and stalls inside the circle. The south end of the farm extended to the edge of a wide wadi, a riverbed that was dry most of the year, becoming a raging torrent during the brief rainy season. Large irrigation hoses disappeared into the dry riverbed.

"Where are they getting the water for irrigation?" his mother asked.

"From archaeologists," their driver said. "They discovered how the ancient Nabataeans turned the Negev into a garden."

Nabataea was a kingdom that had flourished in the Negev before the Romans conquered Palestine. In Roman times the Negev, like Egypt, was a bread basket for the empire, producing vast amounts of grain.

"The Nabataeans put rock dams across wadis and dug cisterns underground for the water to drain into during the rainy season. They drew out water for crops the rest of the year. We're doing the same thing and the Bedouins aren't too happy about it."

"Why would they care?" Simon asked.

"The underground cisterns in the wadi feed a spring they use for their herds. When we pull out water for irrigation, the water table drops and the spring goes dry."

"Can't they get more water?" It was an innocent question from David, but one that haunted him in later years after he had learned the way of the Bedouins. To a Bedouin, water was everything, life itself, and water rights were legal holdings of ancient origin. To ride up to a waterhole in the desert to relieve your thirst without getting permission was as insulting to a Bedouin as someone barging uninvited into a stranger's house for a drink of water.

The struggle for water brought the Israeli farmers into conflict with the Bedouins. "And we have to worry about roaming marauders and Egyptian irregulars. Shelled us with mortar a couple weeks ago. Blew the roof off a barn." He gave David's father a long look. "We're glad you're joining us. We can use a Lehi."

Rebecca's arm was around David's shoulder and at the mention of Lehi her hand unconsciously moved up to cover David's ear.

David was immediately infatuated with the desert, attracted by its very uniqueness. His mother hated it, hated the rocks and snakes and spiders and especially the khamsin, the dry, hot wind that was the curse of the Pharaohs on the Jews that defied them. She hated the sound of gunfire as Arab marauders attacked the little settlement, the long nights when Simon and other settlers went out to retaliate, leaving her home, lying awake with little David sleeping on one side of her, a rifle on the other side.

David grew up in a household of conflict, caught between a mother who never lost her love for music or romantic notions of people and events, and a father who never came out from behind walls he had erected around himself that were as thick as the concrete walls protecting the settlement. The desert became a childhood refuge.

"You're truly a sabra," his mother told him. *Sabra*, the fruit of the cactus, tough on the outside, sweet and tender inside, like the children of the First Generation who worked beside their parents to build a nation.

By the time David was in his teens the sabras were taking their place in a dynamic Israel, taller and stronger and healthier than their parents. Because they had not experienced Jewish ghettos, the Holocaust, or even anti-Semitism, their attitudes were different from those of their parents. David, like the other sabras, was not so much Jewish as he was Israeli.

To Simon Ben-Dor they were the Espresso Generation,

lazy young people who knew more about music and movies and soccer than an Uzi and stopping a Syrian tank with a Molotov cocktail. They never beached a leaky boat and waded ashore under the nose of British guns, hadn't defended kibbutz Safed against the Arabs with ammunition running so low soldiers were fined for missing shots, weren't in the street fighting at Jaffa when one of the first Israeli air force planes, a two-seater Piper Cub donated by a Nebraska farmer, dived at Arab bunkers while a girl in the passenger seat leaned out the window and dropped homemade bombs.

The Six Day War had opened up a new "frontier" for Israeli pioneers: the West Bank—Old Jerusalem, Jericho, the Judean Hills, the Jordan River valley and the Dead Sea—the very heart of ancient Israel.

To Jewish visionaries and Jewish fanatics, it meant a fulfillment of prophecy, a return to the Kingdom of David. To Simon Ben-Dor it meant a raw new challenge, but this time there weren't some ragged Bedouins to push away from water. The West Bank was already extensively settled by Arab farmers.

Rebecca resisted the move for years. Israel's destiny meant another hardship and more danger for her child. The West Bank had a million Arabs and they weren't going anywhere—not without another Deir Yassin.

CHAPTER THIRTEEN

General Scott brought back two bottles of beer when he returned. He sat down in the airplane seat beside David and handed him a bottle. "German dark, only damn beer fit to drink. Everyone's drinking that Mexican piss nowadays, but I like the Old World brew." The general took a swig from his own bottle.

He's patronizing me because he needs me, David thought. He wondered how Scott would treat him once he got the information he wanted. He was surprised the man bothered taking the cigar out of his mouth prior to taking a drink. Probably slept with the cigar in place. And made love the same way.

David set the beer on the fold-down table and looked out the window. The high New Mexico desert was sinister yet fascinating, a moonscape of sculptured plateaus that rose from the pale sands like prehistoric tombs. More scenic than the Negev, New Mexico was a land of stark contrasts with flat deserts, mighty plateaus, and the magic Sangre de Cristo, the 'Blood of Christ' mountains, stained red by the sunset as the plane neared Los Alamos.

"Strange country," Scott said. "There are Indians down there still living in caves—the ones that aren't dead from TB and booze."

"It looks like a lost world," David said. "I can imagine wandering behind a plateau and finding a dinosaur burial ground."

General Scott responded with a grunt. "You'd find rattlesnakes and tarantulas. The tarantulas are as big as your fist. They used to be smaller, but they thrive on the radioactive soil. This is atomic country, son. You've heard of the Manhattan Project, haven't you?"

The Manhattan Project. Los Alamos. The first atomic bomb. Hiroshima. David had not put the names together. The landscape suddenly took on frightening dimensions.

From the air the synchrotron resembled a tire that had fallen onto its side, a circular building with a hundred meters of bare sand and sagebrush in the center.

"It's designed like an atom," the general said. "The nucleus is a natural deposit of magnetite ore beneath the surface. They say that it's able to tap into the magnetic core of the earth itself. And that stuff on top creates a solar storm. Disrupted communications around the world when everything went to hell. TV, radio, telephone, the Internet, for a few minutes the whole world of communications shut down."

The landing field outside Los Alamos looked like a war zone as they stepped off the plane and boarded a staff car. Jeeps with 50mm machine guns escorted the car past tanks rumbling alongside the road while jet fighters and attack copters patrolled overhead. It reminded David of home.

"The president ordered in a special tactical unit," the general said. "Security is a hundred-fold what it was before the attack." General Scott leaned closer to David. He smelled of stale cigar smoke. "We're into something so hairy it even scares the crap out of me."

He's baiting me—wants me to ask what the game's all about so he can make a power play and refuse to tell.

David was curious as hell, but he wasn't going to let the bastard make points at his expense. He had already decided the Zayyad brothers had grabbed an atomic bomb. It fit with Los Alamos.

The faces of the young warriors in battle helmets and fatigues looked little different from the ones in the Israeli army. Or even the youths of the Arab armies. Uniforms were different, skin tones varied, but the rugged innocence, late-blooming pimples and white walls around the ears were universal. As they drove by an all-male platoon jogging in fatigue pants and T-shirts, David heard a fragment of the men's running song:

"If I should die on the Iraqi front,
bury me with an Iraqi cunt. . . ."

The jogging platoon and strong male voices keeping pace with the cadence stirred memories in David of his own military training. Military service in Israel was as expected as going to college was in America. *Hemmed in by enemies, every woman and man has a duty to defend the country.* Words spoken by his father. They came back to haunt him now, along with bitter memories of a day in Jerusalem when his past exploded in his face.

"Those marines," General Scott said, "are from the same unit that took it in Lebanon when I had captain's bars. Nearly three hundred of our boys blown to hell in their sleep by fuckin' terrorists in a truck loaded with explosives. We should have sent a division into Lebanon and kicked ass after that. Wouldn't be fuckin' with the Zayyads if we had." His demeanor told David that he held him personally responsible for the lack of action.

David didn't agree with Scott about what a division in Lebanon would have accomplished, but he didn't say anything. The Israelis had stayed in Lebanon nearly two decades and while it provided Israel with a buffer against repeated Arab attacks, it did nothing to promote long-term peace. Of even more significance was the fact that the Zayyads were a product of the West Bank—and his father—not Lebanon.

An infantry unit had dug in around the synchrotron. The

concrete-and-glass facility was still wounded from the terrorist attack—bullet-chipped walls, broken windows, and a gaping hole that had once been the front entrance.

"They ran a suicide truck loaded with explosives past the guard post at the gate and up to the front entrance," General Scott said. "Crazy bastards. Same trick they used in Lebanon and a dozen other places, only this time they just wanted the front knocked out. Probably all on drugs." He chomped on his cold cigar. The right side of his mouth was darkened by nicotine stain. "You were involved in a suicide attack, weren't you?"

David turned back to the window. Scott already knew the answer. Everybody had a file on him.

"Quite a bloodbath, wasn't it?"

Bloodbath. The roots of it had been in the West Bank, too.

He had been fourteen years old when his father uprooted him and his mother from a prosperous Negev farm and moved them to a Judean hilltop where a dozen Jewish families had squatted in the heart of the West Bank.

The Six Day War in 1967 erupted when Arab troops massed in the Sinai and Jordan, giving every sign of an imminent pan-Arab attack against Israel. Israeli decided on a preemptive attack rather than wait to be slaughtered. Its air force destroyed the Egyptian air force, which was caught flat-footed on the ground. In six days of fighting, the Israeli army overran the Sinai, the West Bank of the Jordan, including the Old City of Jerusalem, and the strategic Golan Heights on the Syrian front.

The West Bank had suddenly become a hostile territory that the little state of Israel had to control. On a map, the West Bank fitted nicely with Israel, restoring the ancient Kingdom of the Jews. The problem was that there were about a million Arabs living there.

"The Arabs took the land with the sword and we'll reclaim it with the sword," his father told David and his mother. "Every conqueror, every conquest, in history resulted in the losing side giving up their freedom and land. It's the way of war. Why should it be any different this time? *What would these Arab bastards have done to us if we had been defeated instead of them?"*

His father slammed his fist on the table. "We own the West Bank because we conquered it. You don't see the Americans giving the country back to the native Americans, the Arabs giving North Africa back to the native Africans. It's the spoils of war. This was Jewish land. Arabs took it from us in the past and we are taking it back. But there's another good reason. These people are wild animals who will never be satisfied until every Jew in Israel is dead. And behind them are another billion Muslims, their minds twisted by killer phrases from their holy book, all hungry for our blood, all waiting for us to show a weakness or falter so they can rip our hearts out. They came before to murder us in our beds, that's why we are occupying the West Bank. Now we need the territory as a buffer against the next time they come."

An Arab village occupied a hilltop several miles to the north of the new Israeli settlement. West Bank Arabs were not nomads but fellahin, peasants who worked their own small plots of land or the lands of a large owner. Fields cultivated by the Arabs reached almost to the hill that the Israelis choose for their settlement. To the south was a broad belt of land the Arabs lacked the agricultural technology to farm, and this was the land the Israelis would farm with water piped from deep wells.

It meant starting all over again for his mother, back to her hands bleeding in preparing the fields, breaking her back over a scrub board, fighting flies away from dinner cooked on a kerosene camp stove in the front yard before permanent housing went up.

Her arguments with Simon made things worse. "The Negev is part of Israel," she told him, "but the West Bank is Arab. I don't want to live in the middle of a million Arabs. I don't want to have to worry about snipers when we step out of the house, to set a night watch every time we go to bed, to have our son carry a rifle to school. I want to go to a concert, see a movie, know my son is safe."

"There is no place safe in Israel," his father said. "If we don't take the fight to them, they will bring it to us. These Arabs on the West Bank *attacked* us. That's why we are here. Only after they came after us with guns, allied with Arab nations, attacking us not with the intent of conquering us but with the intent to *annihilate* us. There will never be another Holocaust because this time we will fight to the death."

After they settled in, Simon led the men to the village, armed and unannounced. David went with them, clutching a rifle he would have preferred using to hunt rabbits.

Arabs gathered in front of their houses along the dusty street leading into the little village—men, women, children, and elders—some standing against the walls in front of the houses that lined the street, others squatting in the dirt. They uttered no word of welcome, no sign of threat, but blind hate—and fear—showed in their eyes. Every man in the village owned a weapon. They could have wiped out the intruders, but they were not fools—massacre Jews and Israeli jets would be strafing the village before nightfall.

His father led the way boldly, not stopping until he reached the flagpole in the center of the village square. Flapping in the wind at the top of the pole was the emblem of the PLO. "Go ahead," Simon told one of the men. The man stepped up to the flagpole and grabbed the rope to lower the Arab organization flag while another man took an Israeli flag out of a sack.

A sudden buzz went up from the villagers as another procession entered the square: Abdul Zayyad and his two sons, Jair and Amir. Zayyad was the mukhtar, the mayor of the village, and the biggest landowner in the area. He was a large man, not tall but built like a tree stump. His long brown robes parted as he walked, exposing white linen and a red belt.

No emotions were revealed in his stony countenance, not even the hatred the villagers revealed with their eyes—this was no poor fellahin shuffling toward them but a sheik, proud and defiant, with noble lineage traceable further back than most European nobility.

The younger Zayyad boy, Amir, was about David's age, a heavy-set youth built broad like his father, but fleshier, while the older, Jair, was taller and leaner. It was the penned-up emotion of Jair that drew David's attention—a stark, wild frenzy in his eyes that David had once seen in the eyes of a mad rabbi in Jerusalem.

Abdul Zayyad paused a couple feet from David's father and locked eyes with him, two predators with their claws in the same territory. The older Zayyad was no fool. And on his shoulders rested the safety of the village. An overt attack on the settlers and the village would be hit with rockets by Israeli gunships in hours. Zayyad did something that stunned the onlookers, Jew and Arab alike. He stuck out his hand, offering it to Simon Ben-Dor.

"*Shalom,*" he said. Peace.

David trembled and gripped his rifle tighter, the thought flashing through his mind that Zayyad might put a dagger in his father's belly with his other hand if his father took the offered hand.

Simon turned from the handshake. "Take down that stinkin' rag."

The man holding the flagpole rope let it fly and the PLO flag dropped.

"The flag," Abdul Zayyad said, holding out his hand. He spoke Arabic, but everyone there knew what he was talking about.

The Israeli holding the flag started to hand it to Zayyad but stopped when he caught Simon's eye. The man jerked the flag back, spat on it and threw it on the ground at Zayyad's feet.

A wounded animal cry went up from the crowd. There was often no love lost between West Bank villagers and the PLO but the insult was to them personally. The oldest boy, Jair, tried to spring at the man, but was stopped by his father's powerful hand. The Israelis went back to back with each other, their weapons at the ready, facing the hostile crowd surrounding them.

David stood rooted, his knees wobbling, the rifle shaking in his hand, mesmerized by the emotional contortions of Abdul Zayyad's face as the Arab leader struggled to maintain his composure. Still holding his son Jair with his right hand, he slowly raised his left hand. David's heart pounded, sure that it was a signal to start a massacre, but instead of gunfire, the cry of the onlookers died.

Zayyad's signal had been to stay calm, not to do something foolish and give the Israelis an excuse to send fighter planes and commandos. Before he turned to leave the square, he stopped and stared coldly at the man who had defiled the flag. The man jutted his jaw out defiantly at the Arab leader, nervously clicking his weapon's safety on and off.

At Simon's command, the Israel flag was raised. When it hit the top of the pole, a shout of victory went out and the men fired a round into the air. They left the village quickly, carefully covering all sides as they hurried back to the truck. All the men except the driver piled into the back of the truck, their weapons pointed at the village. It was only when they were out of rifle range that they relaxed, grinning and joking—all except Simon.

"Come here, Davidka."

David stepped up to his father, keeping his balance in the moving truck. "Yes, Father."

"You were the only one who didn't take a defensive stance. Why?"

"I . . . I forgot."

Simon hit him with his open palm, sending him crashing into the side rail of the truck. "Don't forget a command—ever."

"Simon, he's just a boy," said one of the men.

"And he'll never live to be a *man* if he lets an Arab get the drop on him."

That night at dinner his mother quietly brought up the subject of the raid. "The minute you left the village the Arabs burned the flag you left behind. We watched them with binoculars."

"Yes, I know," said his father.

"You knew they would burn it, yet you left it behind. Why?"

His father shrugged and said nothing. David stared down at his plate, listening. He didn't have an appetite.

"I know what you're up to," she said, "You're picking a fight, insulting them so they'll fight back."

"Since when do we have to pick fights with Arabs? How long do you think we can stay here before they attack us, murder us?"

"This time we're in their territory, Simon. This isn't Israel."

"Don't you ever say that, not in front of me, not in front of the boy. This is Israel and those bastard Arabs are trespassing! This is the ancient land of Israel. The Arabs took it from us with the sword. Now we're taking it back. We have to fight for it, just as we had to fight for every inch we've gained elsewhere."

"Don't shout at me. I fought for Israel, too. I'm tried of fighting. I want peace. To enjoy life while I still can. I want David to experience something besides guns and enemies. You took a child into an armed camp today and then humiliated him in front of the men when he was brave enough to have gone in the first place."

"Davidka is a Jewish warrior. He will fight for Israel. If necessary, he will die for Israel."

"Is that all there is, Simon, fighting and dying? What about art and love, music and learning?"

"Davidka was born in battle. Do you remember—the pounding of Syrian guns nearly drowning out his cries?"

"I remember, Simon, by chance I was present at my own son's birth. I remember the guns, but war didn't create our son. Love did." She spoke the word bitterly, as someone hurt by love.

"We're here for Israel. I can't help it if the sacrifices a pioneer must make don't satisfy your romantic inclinations."

"I've made sacrifices, made them in Galilee, made them in the Negev when we turned sand and rock into farmland, I even came to the West Bank with you—"

"Reluctantly."

"But making the sacrifice. Now I regret it because I know you're up to something. You deliberately left that flag to be burned."

"Why don't you just say it? Get it out of your mind and onto the table."

"You went to that village to bait the Arabs. Your old Lehi friends in Tel Aviv, the ones providing the money and weapons for this settlement, will leak the flag-burning incident to the press without mentioning the fact that an Arab flag was defiled."

Simon shrugged. "It's not a major incident."

"What's frightening me is the fact that you're deliberately picking a fight."

"We have to let the Arabs know who is boss right away or they will be picking us off one by one."

Rebecca shook her head. "But how can you imagine you can barge into the middle of a million Arabs and throw around your weight? This isn't the Negev, there aren't a few nomads roaming hundreds of square miles of wasteland. These people have homes and farms and businesses—"

"So did the Arabs in the Jewish sector in '48, and most of them left. Perhaps the West Bank Arabs won't care to live under Israeli rule and will move out, too."

Rebecca started to say something and stopped, taking a sharp breath.

"Simon," she whispered, "no, no . . ."

His father stared at her impassively, his stony features revealing nothing.

"So that's it, that's why you left the flag."

David looked up from his plate, fork and knife in hand. He watched the conversation, puzzled, but realizing his mother had just gained some insight about his father's motives that had eluded her earlier. It was not the first time he had heard the argument between the two—his mother, burned out and frightened by life on the fringe, wanted to live peacefully in a city, his father, driven by the ghosts of his past, wanted to make a dangerous world safe for his family and country.

"You're not trying to settle in and live peacefully with the

Arabs. You're trying to start a fight that will give you an excuse to drive them out—you want another Deir Yassin!"

David had a flash of what he heard at school about the incident, a battle in an Arab village that terrified the entire Arab population of Israel, causing hundreds of thousands to flee Israel, leaving behind homes and farms. It wasn't until he was an adult that his mother told him the attack had been a massacre by a small number of extremists, his father included. It had been intended to terrify Arabs in the new Israeli state—and had succeeded.

"You remember what we did," his father yelled, "but you forget all the massacres the Arabs did. A dozen for our one! This time we won't suffer a dozen before getting in our one. You forget that most Arabs left the Israeli sector because their leaders told them we Jews would be purged and when they returned they would have our lands too. And you forget that just as many Jews were forced to flee from the Arab sectors because of massacres and pogroms. Why weren't these Arabs taken in by their own kind? Tens of millions of people were refugees after the World War and they were absorbed by their own. We absorbed over half a million of our refugee people from Arab lands."

"I don't care about your damn history or—"

Simon yelled at David. "Listen to me, son, don't listen to this defeatism. This is our land, we've been here continuously for over three thousand years. King David built Jerusalem, it's not a Moslem city, it's a Jewish one. Before we ruled the land, the British governed it, and before that the Turks. In over a thousand years since Muhammad, Arabs have hardly ruled the land. Listen to me," he shouted, "we have our back to the sea and they want to kill us, they don't know any other way, they think like animals. We have to kill them before they kill us."

"You're crazy!" she screamed. "You're nothing but a damned fanatic!"

"Shut up!" Simon jumped up, sending the chair he was sitting on flying over backwards.

"Fanatic!" she screamed.

"Shut up, damnit!" Simon went around the table at her and David flew out of his chair and leaped in front of him, half a head shorter than his father.

"Leave my mother alone!"

Simon looked at him, his face flushed with anger. David waited, sure the man was going to bat him across the room, but the anger slowly faded and his father smiled, not at David but at the knife David was holding.

Simon nodded at the knife. "Good. Only next time, use it."

CHAPTER FOURTEEN

General Scott escorted David past a sandbag barrier hastily thrown up where glass doors had once marked the entrance to the synchrotron building. Inside, Scott hurried him down a corridor crowded with military and civilian personnel.

A door opened on David's right and a military police-woman came out escorting a woman. The woman didn't have the appearance of someone connected with the personnel in the hallway. Her clothes had a disheveled, borrowed look and her expression was harried. Their eyes met briefly and the look told him that she was in the same position he was—an involuntary guest of the Americans. She was no happier about the situation than he was. Could she identify the Zayyad brothers, too? he wondered.

They escorted her to a room off the hallway and secured the door with a metal bar.

She was a prisoner.

General Scott led him toward a room that was next to where the woman was placed. It had a duplicate lock on the door.

He was a prisoner! These bastards flew him halfway around the world because they needed him but were going to keep him prisoner. No matter what had happened in Israel, he was not their prisoner. And they were not going to get anything from him as long as they treated him like one. He turned and confronted the general. Anger from the arbitrary way Scott had treated him exploded. "I'm not your goddamn prisoner!"

"The lock is for your own protection."

"I can protect myself."

"What's your problem, Ben-Dor? We just jerked you out of a prison."

"Then take me back, because I'm not letting you lock me up."

Scott took his arm. "Calm down, Captain. I told you it's for your own protection."

David jerked his arm away. "Touch me again and I'll knock you on your ass. I've had it with you and your fucking superiority."

The general gave a signal and military police closed in on David. Someone grabbed his arm and he jerked loose. "Keep your damn hands off of me!"

A military policeman grabbed his arm to twist it into a hammerlock but David spun out of his grip and kicked the man's feet out from under, sending him crashing to the floor. An MP with an automatic pistol jumped in front of David in a gunfighter's stance.

"Freeze!"

Other MP's with drawn weapons surrounded him.

"Take him to his room." General Scott said. "You'll be briefed later, Ben-Dor."

Inside the room, he stood in a daze for a moment. What the hell was happening? He looked around the room—a twin bed, Formica nightstand with lamp and clock radio, a cheap TV, portable closet—the ambiance of a budget motel room.

The only window in the room had iron bars on it. Sawdust created from their installation was still on the floor. He opened the door to the bathroom and stepped in. The window had been sealed.

The toilet was gone. A big sandbox had been put in its place.

Cats use sandboxes, not people.

What were they trying to tell him?

CHAPTER FIFTEEN

John Conway watched Marie being escorted to her room and the action between David and the military police. He found Marie to be an interesting woman, attractive ... sensuous, not sexy in the way hot bods are portrayed in magazines, the plastic *Baywatch* look, but the kind that radiates from a woman's inner glow.

His own escort was led by a marine policewoman, a lieutenant, about twenty-five years old, with green eyes and red hair. He almost groaned aloud when he first saw her. She was definitely *Baywatch* material, but red hair was his downfall. No doubt the devil was a woman with red hair.

He hadn't been told any more about the mission than David or Marie. He had tried pumping Jeff Hines, the CIA operative who took him into custody in London, and soon gave up. Hines only knew Conway was needed at the Los Alamos installation. And that terrorists had struck it. Nothing else. Conway deduced that the terrorists had gotten away with something, maybe a bomb. Not an unlikely scenario in an age of psychopaths who mixed religious fanaticism with an underground war to cripple Israel and the world's superpower that had supported the Israelis for over fifty years.

As he approached his room door, he quickly understood that despite his intelligence agency background, and his movie star status, he was in the same position as the other two people being escorted down the corridor: There was an outside metal bar on the door he was being led to.

He admired the way David had dropped the MP who had jumped him from behind and told the female marine escorting him so. "Take away the guns, and he probably could have handled several of your people."

"Yes-sir," she said.

"Who's the woman?"

"You'll-be-briefed, sir."

He gave her a smile that melted women.

"Am I being locked in, too?"

"Yes-sir."

The same crisp responses had been about the extent of their conversations since she escorted him from the plane. The answers had the machine precision of a computerized voice.

It annoyed him. Not only because he was used to young women fawning over him but he disliked the air of military superiority that surrounded her. It wasn't just yes-sirring him; there was an unspoken sense of superiority being conveyed: she was an officer and carried a gun, there was something special about her.

She was probably hated by her underlings and feared by her superiors. But she was built like the proverbial brick shithouse and had red hair—aspects that excused a lot of sin in his eyes. Thinking about how lonely the night was going to be, he decided to test the waters.

"Those green eyes of yours could steal a man's soul," he said. Corn, but lots of women ate it up, especially when it came from a movie hero.

"Yes-sir."

Not a smile, not a blink.

"I understand the hot desert gets cold at night," he said. "I could use a little company to keep me warm. Can you do something about that?"

"Yes-sir. I'll-get-you-a-hot-water-bottle."

No change of expression. Not the hint of a smile to make the staccato remark funny. But her eyes glinted with superiority. And her pert little nose went up just a bit.

It was time for a cheap shot.

Conway considered himself a gentleman, but he could not stand a snob of either sex. He generally rolled with the punches in life. When he made an ass out of himself, he usually laughed it off. And he did not pick on dogs or small children. But he did tend to take a snob down a few pegs.

He nodded sympathetically at a bit of sunburn on the tip of her nose. "Been doing a little sunbathing under the desert sun?"

"Yes-sir."

She opened the door of his room. He started to step in and then turned around, looking into her eyes for just a moment and then stared rudely at her perfectly round breasts, breasts too perfect to be natural.

"Better be careful. Silicone melts in the sun."

He checked out the room, noticing the cleverly placed monitoring devices. He lacked the resentment that David felt at being a prisoner. Actually, he kind of enjoyed it. Something superimportant was going down and he was happy to be away from the London play and be part of fresh excitement.

He went into the bathroom and stared at the sandbox where the toilet should have been. And smiled.

Whatever the mission was, it was beginning to look interesting.

CHAPTER SIXTEEN

Two men were in the conference room when General Scott burst in.

Martin Bornstein, the presidential advisor, stood at the window that overlooked the center of the facility.

Allen Holt, director of the Central Intelligence Agency, sat at the conference table. Holt was a short, swarthy man with a heavy brow, thick, tousled black hair, and intense eyes that drilled holes into anything that came within his line of sight. He had two open packs of cigarettes next to an ashtray that looked like a junkyard of cigarette butts. With one cigarette burning between his fingers and another dying in the ashtray, Holt smoked compulsively as they talked.

"Ben-Dor is trouble," General Scott said.

"We've been watching the monitors," Holt said. "Mr. Bornstein thinks he has some insight to Ben-Dor's attitude."

"Through the Israelis, we've gathered everything known about Ben-Dor since birth," Bornstein said. "His father was an Israeli activist, a Stern Gang member during the War of Independence, a West Bank settler—or intruder, depending on whether you want to hear the Israeli or Arab side. Ben-Dor appears to have been traumatized by his father's lifestyle. The reason he can identify the Zayyad brothers is a good one—Ben-Dor's father executed their father."

Scott grunted. "All you are telling me is that the man is trouble."

"I'm telling you he didn't have a typical upbringing and can't be expected to react in a typical manner. The bottomline issue is his ability to assist in the mission. In terms of his physical ability, you saw him handle that MP. His prison records state that when he was first imprisoned he was involved in a couple fights as other prisoners tested his mettle. He handled himself well. In terms of his brains, he was considered a brilliant architect and engineer."

"Before he went nuts and blew up his own project."

"He—"

"Gentlemen, with due respect, who the fuck cares who or what Ben-Dor is, was, or will be," Holt said. "There are no pictures of the Zayyad brothers. He's the only one who can ID them. End of discussion. He's what we have. We need to make the best use of him possible. If he's a loose cannon, we need a contingency plan for that, too."

"I don't like it," General Scott said. "I told the president I didn't like it the minute I heard the plan. A Jew and a prostitute on a mission like this?" Scott glanced at Bornstein. "Not that I have anything personal against Jews. It's just the nature of the mission."

"Of course not, General," Bornstein murmured, thinking to himself that the old bastard should have been retired years ago, a fact Bornstein had suggested to the president more than once. The president kept Scott around because the general was the darling of the guns-and-guts crowd in Congress. The man only became dangerous when he got into a situation that could not be solved by increasing military appropriations. "Ben-Dor is a bright man and can take care of himself in a fight." He held up his hand to ward off Scott's verbal attack. "I know. He froze once when confronted by a Palestinian terrorist. That's something we have to deal with. As for the woman, admittedly, Marie Gauthier is a very complex young woman. She has experienced incidents of stigmata during which the palms of her hands bleed like the crucifixion wounds of Christ."

"You hear those stories every Easter," Scott snorted. "There's always some religious nut running around with bleeding hands."

"Exactly," Bornstein said. "Most incidences of stigmata have been exposed as fraud or frenzy and that is what makes Marie Gauthier so unique. Her wounds appeared while she was in public and in no obvious religious passion." He stared through the window at the "doughnut hole" where the shepherd boy had miraculously appeared. "A freak or a saint," he mused. "Those two words have dominated Marie Gauthier's life. The stigmata set her apart from others. It was either a sign of God's favor . . . or the mark of Cain."

"Considering her chosen profession a good guess would be the latter," General Scott said.

"There's no real proof she's a prostitute," Bornstein said. "She might be working to help prostitutes in Marseilles, perhaps dressing like one to be accepted."

"Where there's smoke, there's fire," said General Scott.

Bornstein ignored him and spoke directly to Holt. "Like Ben-Dor, she brings critical skills to the table. She speaks Aramaic and is familiar with social customs in the first century. But I have two main concerns about her. One is her willingness to cooperate. She has incredible fears about the situation. I think she is more aware of what we are going to ask of them than the other two. Second, she dreads it."

"You told her about the mission?" Holt asked.

"Not a word. All she knows is what we agreed to tell them—the Zayyad brothers attacked the facility. But Marie has . . . I don't know what to call it. Intuition? I suspect she has somehow guessed the nature of the mission we're sending them on—and it's unleashed deep-rooted fears within her."

"You think she'll balk when we tell them about the mission?"

"I'm certain of it. Part of it's the stigmata, of course. But there's another piece missing. Something happened to Marie in Lebanon. But we don't know exactly what happened."

"I don't like it at all," General Scott said. "We're dealing with a couple amateurs with a history of unreliability. The woman is God-knows-what and Ben-Dor is a criminal, a foreigner with a history of terrorism, blowing up a building he designed himself. Thank God we have Conway. He's a pro and can be relied upon."

"Which Conway are you speaking of, General?" Holt asked. "Are you talking about his screen persona or his personal one? From what I've heard, he's known as a womanizer and sometimes boozer, a man who moves from one profession to another. His CIA record reflects a man who followed orders and did a terrific job when he wanted to . . . and discarded the rules whenever he felt like it. He's no loose cannon, but he's certainly a maverick. I don't think we should fool ourselves into thinking that he's the same man off the set as he is before the cameras."

"Compared to the other two, he's Jesus H. Christ in my estimation. He's served honorably in the U.S. military and has even been with the Company."

"Back to basics, General, we're stuck with the hand we were dealt," Holt said.

"Not necessarily," Scott said. "I think that the woman is expendable and Ben-Dor may be more trouble than he's worth. At the very minimum, Conway has to be given the authority to terminate them if they get out of line."

"Why don't we just terminate them now!" Bornstein snapped. "That way we can be sure the mission fails before it even gets off the ground."

"Gentlemen, that's enough," Holt said. "Obviously Ben-Dor and the woman would not be on this mission if we had a choice, but we're stuck with them." Holt lit a cigarette before meeting Bornstein's eye. "I do have to admit that General Scott's concern keeps coming back to me. At this moment Gauthier and Ben-Dor are the two most important people in the world. The fate of mankind, the world as we know it, is in their hands." He took a deep drag and leaned back in his chair, slowly exhaling smoke toward the ceiling. "Considering the nature of this mission, it's rather ironic, wouldn't you say? A Jew and a prostitute?"

A military police lieutenant suddenly burst into the room. "Sorry, sir, but we have a problem. Ben-Dor just kicked open his door."

CHAPTER SEVENTEEN

General Scott brought Conway, David, and Marie into the conference room.

"No introductions have been made," General Scott said.

"Then let's do it." Holt quickly introduced himself, Bornstein, and then each of the three prisoners.

Conway shook hands with David and mentally noted the firm but not overpowering grip. He then shook hands with Marie, who seemed a little surprised that he offered to shake hands with her.

"Mr. Conway is an actor," he said to David and Marie. "From the lack of recognition on your faces, I assume neither of you have ever seen his movies."

Both indicated in the affirmative and Conway laughed. "That's all right, they were pretty bad movies."

"Damn good movies if you ask me," General Scott said. "And you've been a good soldier and intelligence agent for our country."

Conway shot Holt a questioning glance. He had signed an agreement when entering the agency that he would not voluntarily disclose his employment with the CIA, even after he left it.

"Everybody take a seat," said Holt, after a grimaced look to Scott. The CIA director was behind a sea of cigarette butts at the head of the table, Bornstein to his right. General Scott stood back from the table, leaning against the wall, his arms folded across his chest.

Displaying a blank face, David took measure of the three men, deciding that Holt was direct and blunt, Bornstein quietly manipulative, and that Scott was a pit bull with a brain, albeit an older dog with a shaggy coat and cigar-stained mouth, but still with some bite. Scott was the most dangerous of the bunch. He sensed the other two might be dangerous only if it was warranted. Scott could do so erratically.

Holt blew a cloud of smoke in the direction of David. "We had anticipated giving all of you a briefing tomorrow after you had a good night's rest, but Captain Ben-Dor caused us to advance the meeting by kicking open his door."

David lifted his eyebrows. "A good night's sleep? I don't know about these other people, but I was kidnapped and flown here from halfway around the world. And the only answers I know so far are this gentleman's"—he gestured at Scott—"preference for German beer and stinking cigars." He didn't bother neutralizing his tone. He didn't like Scott.

"Captain—"

"Excuse me, Mr. Holt, but my name is David Ben-Dor. If you're not comfortable calling me David, you can use Mr. Ben-Dor. My military rank was long ago preempted by penal rank in a prison work camp."

"You seem to speak perfect English, but maybe you don't understand—" Scott started.

"How does 'fuck you' translate, General? I understand my situation perfectly. You want something from me and that something is identifying the Zayyad brothers. What I don't understand is *your* situation. What have they taken and exactly how do you intend to get it back? And what are you offering me to help?"

"I'll handle this, General." Holt took another drag and blew it out, leaning back, sizing up David over the stream of smoke. "You're a hundred percent right, David. John," he indicated Conway, "has been in the Agency and at least understood he was being pulled in, activated, for a mission, but you and Marie are civilians, foreigners. You deserve an explanation. The first one I can give you is that at no time in history has there been a greater threat to world survival than what we are facing today. We all know that atomic weapons changed the face of war and that there's been a couple of times—the Cuban missile crisis, the Lebanon crisis a couple decades ago—when there was a serious threat of atomic annihilation.

"Let's start first with who the Zayyad brothers are. They are the worst kind of terrorist because they have no particular group that they are glued to. Being part of a pact means you have communications and meetings with other terrorists that inevitably bring you into the purview of the various police agencies that keep track of terrorist organizations and occasionally arrest them. The Zayyad brothers are lone wolves who make contact with other groups only when they need help in an action, the Hezbollah one day, Iranian extremists the next. We call them Islamic fundamentalists, but that is more because of their alliance to various Islamic fundamentalist groups than the nature of any extremist religious view that we can substantiate they personally possess. We know they studied in Dammaj, Yemen, where Sheik Muhammad bin Shajea spent years ranting that America was the Great Satan, but we do not believe they have any particular alliance, past or present, to people like Shajea and bin Laden. We know surprisingly little about them and don't have any photos.

"Bottom line, they are part of that horde of unconventional, fanatical, September eleventh–type enemy that stealth bombers, antimissile defense systems, and thermonuclear bombs cannot defend against. Just as the U.S.S. *Cole,* an American navy supership, equipped with almost everything money and the best military science could provide, a ship able to single-handedly take on a small nation or an alien invasion of Martians, was crippled by a couple fanatics with a homemade bomb aboard a dingy, these two blew their way into a scientific facility and put the whole world at risk."

"The terrorists, these Zayyad brothers," Conway said, "got away with a nuke?"

Holt shook his head. "I wish it was that simple. The fact is, the terrorists took *nothing* from the facility. In terms of armaments, our best analysis is that at this moment they are armed with nothing more than a single semiautomatic pistol with only about four rounds in it."

Holt trained his drill-bit eyes on David, Marie, and Conway in turn. No one spoke, no one moved. Holt had dark circles under his eyes. Gray cigarette ash surrounded the ashtray in front of him. He lit a Camel, leaving a Sherman smoldering in the ashtray, and smoked with short, jerky movements, bringing the cigarette up to his mouth between his thumb and forefinger and pulling a drag. He coughed the smoke out. "Disgusting habit," he told the others. "We used to call cigarettes coffin nails. That was in the days before we put warnings on the packs."

David wondered how long the man had been riding the crisis. Holt looked exhausted.

The CIA director pushed back his chair and stood up. "The story I'm going to tell you really comes in two parts. The first part was pure serendipity: a freak scientific event knocked a hole in Time."

"In time? You mean—?" Conway asked.

"Time with a capital *T*. A door to the past."

Conway and David exchanged looks. *A hole in Time, a door to the past*. Excitement surged in Conway. Marie didn't appear to be surprised and showed no emotion. David looked at her and realized she probably already knew, either she'd been told—or had guessed it.

"How did it happen?" David asked. "How could a door to the past open?"

"You'll be briefed by a scientist, one of those guys who can't tie his shoelaces but has an IQ somewhere in the stratosphere. But I can tell you this: The facility was conducting an experiment in universal energy, the power source that keeps everything from planets to galaxies in motion. The result, a hole in Time, wasn't anticipated.

"It's a two-way door," Bornstein said, "and the possibilities it raises are incredible. So incredible that it is nothing we can handle, nothing the world is ready for at this time."

"That's a matter of opinion," General Scott said.

"That's a matter of policy," Bornstein said. "What occurred here is not completely understood. To ensure that it doesn't get out of hand, that fanatics or terrorists don't take advantage of it, the facility is going to be destroyed when we're finished with our mission. We are already evaluating people for miles in every direction. That decision was made by the president in consultation not only with America's leaders but the leaders of the world. The whole damn world is paranoid and so is our own leadership. No one can afford to run the risk of us rearranging history to their detriment—or even some future American administration doing it. A time machine would be the ultimate weapon, militarily and economically. The Japanese prime minister is already making noises about rumors that we'll try to sabotage their economy to better our own."

"But before we can destroy it, we have to undo the damage it's already done." Holt paused as if to prepare himself for the magnitude of what he was about to say.

"They went back in time," David said, as much to himself as to the others, "the Zayyad brothers made it back in time." The magnitude of the problem hit him. The Zayyad brothers in the *past*. The reason for the crisis management was now clear to David. The Zayyad brothers had not gotten away with a bomb—*they* were the bomb!

Holt nodded. "They went to the first century, the time of the Roman Empire, when Palestine was a Jewish homeland and Jesus was walking along the shores of the Sea of Galilee performing miracles and gathering followers." He coughed and took another puff before he went on. "Two men who would be institutionalized as psychopaths in any civilized community have slipped through a door to the past and are loose in the ancient world with a ruthlessly insane scheme." He described how the experiment went astray, the shepherd boy being drawn forward in time. And the Zayyads storming the facility.

"Only the two brothers made it back in time, but these two maniacs have a gun! *A gun, damnit, in a world where the height of military technology is a double-edged sword.* And they have something even deadlier. Knowledge! A hundred men with ball and cap muskets could conquer the ancient world and these terrorists have the knowledge to make machine guns.

"Introduce modern weapons into the first century and you'll have atomic bombs by the next century without the cultural advances that keep them from being dropped. Can you imagine Emperor Nero pressing the Button rather than burning Rome? Pagan armies dropping atomic bombs on cities rather than pounding at the gates with battering rams? If the terrorists run amok in the ancient world with modern knowledge, their actions will affect everyone on earth." He spoke very slowly and his eyes bored into each of them. "And that includes each person in this room."

"How do we know for sure the present can be altered by changes in the past?" David asked.

"The shepherd boy is our proof," Bornstein said. "His appearance here in New Mexico created a related incident on the other side of the world. We had the story played up as mass hysteria like a UFO sighting and finally killed it entirely."

"The incident on the West Bank near the Jordan River!" Conway said.

David knew what Conway meant. He had heard the soldiers at the bridge project discussing it. Panic had broken out in an area where people had disappeared. "Are you saying that the people who disappeared are descendants of the shepherd boy who were never born because he altered history by coming forward in time?" he asked Bornstein.

"Yes. The people who disappeared all had roots back to the region where the boy came from. And there have been other incidents we've managed to keep entirely out of the news. We believe the Zayyads have already killed someone, perhaps even more than one person, in the past and the deaths caused more ripples in time. Unless they're stopped, the ripples will become tidal waves."

"But why Israel two thousand years ago?" David asked.

"Why not New Mexico last week or a thousand years ago? Why did they choose the first century?"

"They didn't. The mechanism did. The hole it broke in time was set for a particular time and place, and First Century Palestine was it." Bornstein threw up his hands. "It could as well have been the Ice Age. Then we could just sit back and hope that the two terrorists would be eaten by some dinosaur down to its last meal."

Holt swept the table again with his probing eyes. "Each of you has a clue as to why you're here. We have a young woman who speaks an ancient language and is an expert on daily life at the time of Christ, a man who can identify the two terrorists, and an experienced covert operative who speaks Latin and has passed for a Roman—at least onstage."

David knew what was coming and electric anticipation surged through him with the spine-chilling ecstasy of a religious vision. He spoke quietly, but his heart was pounding. "You want us to go back in time to the ancient world."

Conway was breathless. "Back to the first century?"

"We're sending you back," said Holt, "on a rescue mission, the most daring adventure in the history of mankind. Back to the Holy Land just before Passover in the year A.D. 30. Your job will be to stop the Zayyad brothers before they can spread modern knowledge and to bring back their gun."

Conway stared around the table, a grin spreading across his face. "My God, that's the most exciting period in history, the height of power of the Roman Empire. The glory of Greece is still alive everywhere Alexander marched."

"You haven't told us everything," Marie said, speaking for the first time. Her voice was tight and grim. "Christ was crucified at Passover time in A.D. 30."

David had seen the tension building in her as Holt spoke. He had had immediate empathy for her from the first moment he saw her. She had the look of a trapped animal, which is how he felt since he had fallen into the hands of the Americans.

"You're right, Ms. Gauthier, I haven't told you everything. Haven't told you what these crazy bastards plan to do."

He lit another cigarette and made a complete walk around the table before facing them again. He bent forward, leaning on the table with both hands and spoke in a strained whisper.

"They plan to kill Jesus Christ before He is martyred on the cross."

Marie sat rigid, her hands hidden in her lap. She tried to keep her face devoid of expression but David could see waves of emotion gripping her.

What were the devils she was fighting? he wondered. He suddenly realized that he had his own to combat. A time machine that could change history. He did not care about the future of the world. But a device that could send him back to the ancient world could send him back a few years, to a moment of time when he lost everything he ever loved.

"It's madness," Bornstein said. "Never in the history of man, not even in the darkest days of maniacs like Genghis Khan and Adolf Hitler, has there been a threat to civilization itself. It doesn't matter if you believe Jesus is the Son of God or just a carpenter from Galilee. Our image of him is the core of Western civilization. These terrorists are fanatics waging a holy war against the West. They don't understand that the consequences of their actions would be catastrophic for the entire world."

"If they kill Jesus before he's martyred on the Cross," Bornstein continued, "there'll be no Battle of Tours stopping the sons of Islam from taking Western Europe, no Christian army saving Eastern Europe by stopping the armies of Islam at the walls of Vienna. Even more probable, if Jesus had not been martyred on the Cross, Christianity would never have risen above the status of a small sect and the Muslims would have wrestled pagan armies for control of the Western world." His voice wavered. "Science, art, literature, all the achievements that make the world what it is today, would be lost. You must stop them or this world, as we know it, will be hell and our lives and the lives of our children may never be."

"The dangers of the mission should be obvious," Holt said. "We can't permit more modern weapons to be taken back. The dangers are too great. You'll be armed only with swords and daggers and pitted against two vicious killers with an automatic weapon. Obviously, it's not the sort of task you will be forced to participate in. I can see from the expressions of these two gentlemen that they're just waiting for the word to go, but what about you, Ms. Gauthier?"

Marie stood up and met Holt's eyes without flinching. "I'm not going."

She turned and left the room, leaving an uneasy quietness behind her. An MP followed behind her.

David's chair scraped noisily as he scooted back from the table and got up to follow her.

"Are you bowing out, too?" Holt asked.

"I don't know. I need to think about it."

"Before you go, young man, I want you to give thought to the peculiar situation you'll find yourself in." General Scott sucked nicotine juice from his cigar. "I'm speaking in terms of your religion."

David frowned in confusion. "My religion?"

Holt and Bornstein exchanged looks.

General Scott took the cigar out of his mouth and stared at the soggy, mashed end. "Has it occurred to you that if the terrorists kill Jesus before he is martyred on the cross, Christianity will never come about?" Scott raised his eyebrows. "If you don't have Christianity, you don't have the Holocaust and two thousand years of persecution of the Jews."

Bornstein jumped up so fast his chair fell over backward. "If the Zayyad brothers win, by our own time mankind will have gone back to swinging from trees. If trees still grow."

David left the room. When the door was closed behind him, Holt turned his ire on General Scott. "What the hell are you trying to do? Drive Ben-Dor away!"

Holt turned to Conway, whose mind was flying, and gave him a sour grin. "Well, John Conway, you managed to antagonize just about everyone at Langley with your contempt for your former employment in the Agency. What do you think now?"

"Who gets the movie rights?"

Bornstein laughed. "You can have them. If you live."

"I'm in, if that's what you're asking. I don't know about the woman. Her language skills would certainly help, but Ben-Dor seems to be indispensable. There's not a single picture of these terrorists?"

"None that can help identify them. Not unless they're wearing ski masks in ancient Israel," Holt said.

"I need to talk to Ben-Dor. See if we can work together."

Scott snorted. "The man's more of a problem than he's worth. He needs the kind of handling that comes from the business end of a gun."

CHAPTER EIGHTEEN

NEAR THE SEA OF GALILEE, A.D. 30

Amir Zayyad, leading a cart pulled by a donkey, and his brother, Jair, walked down a dirt road on the east side of the lake. Something in the cart was covered by blankets. They looked like typical farmers, returning from market in Bethsaida. As children and adolescents on the West Bank, they had led a donkey cart to the village and their father's fields many times.

It was late afternoon, the time when travelers looked for fire and shelter. The punishment for robbery was a slow painful death, but there were always men foolish enough—or stupid enough—to attempt it. But it was not fear of thieves that made Amir nervous. They had been in the ancient Holy Land for five days and were about to make their first major contact. A dangerous one.

He wondered if time was passing the same way nearly two thousand years in the future. Had the same five days passed at the scientific facility they had attacked? He had asked Jair what he thought people were thinking about them back in their own time. The answer had been one of his short, sharp phrases.

"They're shitting."

His brother said he thought too much. And worried too

much. Amir's nickname, Mouse, fit him because his quick, bulging eyes and short, pudgy build reminded Jair of a bottom-heavy, nervous little mouse.

The five days had been busy, as they assimilated into an ancient culture. They had not found the transition particularly difficult. They had been raised in an agrarian Middle Eastern culture that still maintained many of its ancient vestiges. Men herding sheep and goats, women spinning cloth, camel-hair blankets and hand-sewn sandals was a familiar way of life to them. They were Semitic and the ancient Palestine was a land of Semitic people.

Their clothes were acceptable. Jair, who planned everything, while Amir used his legs and mouth in carrying out the plans, had made sure that they wore the homespun garb of Bedouins when they attacked the science facility.

To look at them, one would see nothing inherently alien about them in comparison to the people of ancient Palestine. Only their language drew them apart. They both spoke Arabic and rough Hebrew. But even language was not a great bar because Palestine was on the crossroads of much of the trade that occurred in the civilized world. In the marketplace at Bethsaida, one could hear a dozen different languages being spoken—and Bethsaida was not one of the largest cities of the Palestine. There was always somebody who could understand a little of their modern Hebrew, and Amir, who was better at languages than Jair, was already adding many words of Aramaic and ancient Hebrew to his vocabulary.

The one regret Jair had expressed to Amir was that they would not be taken for Jews. Jewish men wore their hair long, curled hair down their temples, and had full beards. But since Palestine was a beehive of traders and travelers, it was not mandatory that they appear Jewish. Their greatest asset was their stealth. They had spent two decades of their lives penetrating Israeli cities. They were used to blending into the social milieu of wherever they were standing at the moment. They did it by acting naturally and flowing with people around them.

Their first imperative had been to get information that

would lead them to Jesus. At this stage of his life he was known to be a member of the underground army called the Zealots. According to the Christian Bible, he had performed miracles in Bethsaida and on the shore of Galilee and helped feed the Zealot army hiding in the wilderness.

Jair had rejected the notion that the Zealots would be of any help to them. The Zealots were too idealistic. Instead, he had set his sights on making contacts with the Sicarii. The choice had been a simple one: Judas, the betrayer of Jesus, was a Sicarii. The Sicarii assassins practiced a form of fanaticism Jair understood completely. Only in the way they murdered Romans and other political enemies did their methods differ from Jair and Amir—knives instead of guns and bombs.

"The Zealots would think too much if we went to them with a proposition," Jair had told Amir. "Like you, they ask too many questions. The Sicarii have simpler goals. They kill Romans and their Jewish sympathizers. If we show them we can kill Romans, they'll help us with what we want."

Amir asked questions but he never argued with his brother. Jair was always right. His brother had an instinct for gathering information from strangers, always able to pick out a person in a crowd who could tell them what they needed to know. In this case they needed to contact the Sicarii. The cover story Jair created was that they were emissaries of an unnamed Arab potentate who wanted allies in a war against Rome. In an age when war was epidemic, it was not an unlikely tale.

They had brought gold coins with them, coins minted in France and whose imprints would be unreadable, but gold was valued by weight. A single coin had purchased the information in the marketplace from a man whom Jair noticed displayed a particular look of hatred toward a Roman soldier walking by. The man had first tried to trick them. But he did not fool Jair. Amir had often boasted that his brother knew what men were thinking just by looking into their eyes. Jair had seen a lie in the informant's eyes and raised the ante by putting his dagger to one of the man's eyes and telling him he would pop out the eye if the man continued to lie.

The informant's information had set them upon the road, leading the donkey cart, on their way to what they hoped would be a nest of Sicarii daggermen. Everything about the plan worried Amir and he exposed his anxieties to Jair with constant what-if questions until Jair told him to shut up or he'd cut off his ears. Their destination was a tavern and they approached it as dusk was settling upon the land.

They tied the donkey to a post outside and Amir led the way inside. He always entered before Jair. If there was an ambush, it gave Jair an extra second to react.

The place smelled of sour sweat and moldy wine. Six men, besides the tavernkeeper, were in the place, all gathered around a table where dice were being thrown. Every man turned to look at them as they entered. Amir kept his face blank as they sat down at a table. As the owner approached, he spoke to them in Aramaic. Amir replied in Hebrew, but since the man shook his head, indicating he did not understand the language of priests, Amir reverted to Aramaic, having already learned how to order wine in a tavern.

"He understands Hebrew," Jair said.

"How do you know?"

"He's a bartender and Hebrew is one of the two major languages in the area. This fool is pretending to be ignorant because we're strangers."

When the man came back with two small jars of wine, Jair addressed him in Hebrew. "We seek the Sicarii."

The man tried to pretend that he did not understand the words, but the way he flinched said otherwise. Jair's words had been spoken loud enough for the men at the adjoining table to hear. A whisper went around the table.

"We are no friends of Romans," Jair said. "We come to forge an alliance with the Sicarii."

"You are mad!" the tavern owner blurted out in Hebrew.

Amir leaned over and whispered in Arabic to Jair. "How do you know they're Sicarii?"

"I know," Jair said, smiling. When he smiled, his mouth and teeth had the snarling grin of a skull.

Amir was so nervous, he fidgeted on the chair.

The men stared back, with no pretense. They were hard, murderous fanatics beneath the skin.

"Last week," Jair said, "a Roman officer raped the wife of a Jewish merchant in Bethsaida and almost killed her husband."

Amir knew the statement was not true. The officer had been caught by the husband making love to his wife and had cut the husband with his sword when he escaped. But the story grew and became distorted in the marketplace. Jair had simply embellished it a bit more.

"I have something outside to show you," Jair said to the men.

He rose and Amir jumped up with him. They walked to the door, Amir nervously looking behind him in case a dagger came flying across the room. Outside, he and Jair stood by the cart until the men slowly filed out of the tavern. Each man had his hand inside his clothing, clutching a dagger. Amir's throat was dry, but he tried to keep his face stoic. He had supreme confidence in Jair to handle situations. Even if it came to violence. But this time there were seven men, including the tavern owner, against the two of them. And each was a professional killer.

After the last man silently filed out, Jair reached into the cart and jerked off a large blanket. A Roman cavalry officer, bearing the rank of decurio, commander of a horse unit of about forty men, lay in the cart. He was tied and gagged. A bloody wound to his head indicated that he had required some persuasion to get into the cart and be tied.

Jair cut the ropes holding his legs. "Help me get him to his feet," he told Amir.

They pulled the man off the cart and stood him up. As soon as the man was on his feet, Amir backed away and Jair walked slowly toward the men assembled in front of the tavern.

"I have power," Jair said, "power that can destroy Roman legions, power that will drive the Romans from the land of Israel for all time."

He turned and faced the Roman officer, drawing his gun from under his robe without the men behind him seeing it. He fired a single shot. It hit the legionnaire in the forehead, throwing the man backward.

The shot was a blast of thunder to the Sicarii, thunder that came from Jair wielding magic. None of them had ever heard of or seen a man strike another dead without touching him except in the tales told of ancient gods who walked the earth as men.

Jair had killed the man from a dozen feet away.

As he turned to the Sicarii, the gun secreted back in his robes, the sound of the shot was echoing off the hills. The brave Sicarii, assassins who frequently gave their own lives to kill a Roman, had run back inside the tavern.

CHAPTER NINETEEN

Marie ignored the army cot along the wall of her room and sat on the floor in a corner. She leaned back against the wall, resting her head, and closed her eyes. Her mind was tired; it needed the peace and release of sleep, but she was too wound up to fall asleep. She had been told no more about why she had been brought to the New Mexico desert than the little Bornstein revealed on the plane. She soon realized that he wanted to probe her about her life. They knew a lot about her, but not *everything*.

The sun had fallen behind mountains, draping a shadow across the desert. She was being enveloped by the growing gloom of night falling and her tired eyes drooped. She wanted to get out of her head and into the limbo of sleep but thoughts kept flying through her mind, images from the past that swirled in her head like ghosts in an attic.

They knew about the bleeding.

She had led a normal life until that day in church when she was twelve years old. Raised in a small village on the French side of the Alps, she had gone to school, picked flowers, learned to bake bread, flirted with boys, and had thoughts about what she wanted to be when she grew up. One of her teachers so captivated her, an older woman with a polio limp, who turned her lessons in history into living dramas, that she decided she wanted to be a teacher. She had a special ability for languages that no one recognized because her village life gave her little contact with foreigners.

She was too young to realize that the future a child sees at twelve usually has little connection to what is lived a dozen years later.

In her case, the future was preordained. Destined. That was how she thought of it. Most lives are capricious—people are born, bred, educated, and turned out onto the world where education, genetics, maladies, and luck lead them this way and that way until they finally get on a track that sometimes gets derailed a few times before they die. But her life had always had a purpose. Even though the purpose had never been revealed to her, the fact that a purpose had been set out for her had always been in her mind from the age of twelve, hovering around her as an invisible force, too ethereal to grasp, but inescapable.

Although her path was determined in a church at the age of twelve, so much pain had been engendered from that moment that she thought of herself as a prisoner of the devil. It began with her experiencing the stigmata.

The Crucifixion wounds of Christ.

She was in church on Easter Sunday sitting next to her ten-year-old brother, her mother and father on the other side of him, when she began to feel pain in the palm of her hands. The pain, hot and searing, increased until she had gasped and cried out. When she unfolded her hands, her palms were bleeding and her brother was screaming.

From that moment on her life was indelibly altered.

The news story had been reported worldwide—mostly covered by TV shows and paper magazines that reported stories about alien rape and two-headed babies. Reports of stigmata were not unusual—they occasionally popped up, usually in a devout Christian around Eastertime. But what had been unusual was that the incidents rarely could be duplicated by the bleeders and were always accompanied by reports of visions and feverish religious ecstasy.

Marie's village priest reported to his bishop, who in turn reported to Rome, that Marie did not experience visions nor had ever expressed fervor toward her faith other than what would be expected of a proper young French girl.

Incidents of the stigmata were not taken lightly by the Church. Over sixty sufferers of the wounds of Christ, including such notables as St. Francis of Assisi and St. Catherine of Siena, had been declared saints or blessed by the Church.

Nor was the incident taken lightly by believers of the faith. People flocked to the village, sick and lame, seeking a miracle cure from the young girl that God seemed to have chosen to bear the wounds of the Son. Her parents had become caught up in the frenzy and failed to protect her from the inevitable chaos. Soon miracle cures were attributed to her and she couldn't leave her home without people trying to touch her or beg her to save them from some malady. The attention was frightening. She no longer had friends—to them she was a freak.

At the age of fourteen she suffered a nervous breakdown and had to be hospitalized.

No longer able to attend school, she received private tutoring from priests and nuns. Delegations were sent from other areas to examine her and question her about the incident of palm bleeding. Many of the examiners were foreigners and it was soon discovered that she was a linguistic savant who could parrot back languages.

By the age of fifteen, the Church owned her: She left her parents and went to live in a convent where she could be protected—and studied. It was natural that she would become a "wife of Christ" by taking vows of a nun. She knew that one of the reasons she had taken the vows was the terrible fear of facing the world. A convent was a place to hide. But the knowledge didn't lessen her fears or her needs for shelter.

Why she had been chosen, as priests and other nuns commonly called it, wasn't clear to her. But she did know that it wasn't just a fluke of nature, that God had marked her for a reason.

And it terrified her.

All she had ever wanted out of life was to be normal. To love and be loved, have a career, a home, a family. She had none of those things. And her fate had hung over her for over two decades. She thought that if she studied the history of the age when Christ had walked the earth and suffered his death on the cross there would be a clue as to why she had been marked. But that knowledge gave her neither clues nor relief.

When the opportunity arose for her to be sent to a small village in southern Lebanon near the war-turbulent Golan Heights, she eagerly took the opportunity. The village was one of the few places left on earth where Aramaic, the language of biblical Palestine, was still spoken. The Church wanted to keep alive the language spoken by Jesus and the Disciples and Marie had the linguistic talents to carry out the mission.

The road from that small village in Lebanon to the sleazy back streets of Marseilles had been filled with as much pain and terror as the stigmata.

They knew about her work with the prostitutes of Marseilles. But how much did they know about what happened to her in Lebanon? she wondered. She had not even told the doctors who treated her after she was found wandering in the desert.

It was her secret.

CHAPTER TWENTY

David turned on the light in his bedroom and began making a detailed examination of the room for sound and camera bugging. He found a sound device in a vase of plastic flowers and a video camera, similar to an instrument doctors use for a colon examination, draped atop a picture frame. He continued his hunt because the two devices were such obvious dummies intended to be found.

To reduce the potential search areas where monitoring devices could be hidden, he did some architectural analysis. He eliminated the ceiling. Although it was a two-story building, he knew from the design that there was no room for a crawl space between the two floors, so it was unlikely they would put a camera there. Three walls—one facing the outside, one facing the interior hallway of the building, and the common wall with the bathroom—were eliminated because the butt end of the camera would be visible outside the room.

Only the wall to the left as he entered was a candidate. Even at that he would never have found out where the camera lens was exposed if he hadn't figured out where on the wall a camera would best be mounted to capture the room as a whole. The camera, with a lens little more than the size of a dull pencil mark, poked in plain sight through a wall. And was almost impossible to see.

He found sound bugs on a lamp that was centrally located

in the room and in the light fixture in the bathroom. He left all the devices in place, knowing that if he destroyed them, they'd just be replaced. The discovery had been more of a game than anything else. They would have observed him in his search and know he spotted the devices.

He lay on the bed and stared up at the ceiling. The interior was the typical inexpensive American building techniques used in temperate zones: Sheetrock walls supported by two by six's in the walls, and probably lightweight insulation; the exterior was plywood covered with a layer of stucco. He could kick a hole in the wall and keep kicking until he reached the outside. But he would have six MPs sitting on his head by the third kick.

As darkness filled the room he did not bother getting up and turning on the light. He enjoyed the privacy from the spying camera that the darkness provided, though he realized the camera was probably a night-vision unit.

He responded to a knock on the door and opened it to find a soldier with a food cart. He thanked the soldier and took the cart in, eating in the dark to maintain his sense of privacy.

When it was completely dark he got quietly up from the bed and went into the bathroom. He closed the bathroom door and turned on the water in the tub. While the water was running, he lay down on the floor facing the wall that adjoined Marie's room. Using the dull dinner knife from the tray, he hacked a small hole in the Sheetrock between studs and slowly enlarged it, breaking away pieces with his hands. When he had a big enough hole, he used the knife to chop a hole in her wall. As soon as he had a hole large enough to speak through, he whispered her name.

"Who is it?"

"David Ben-Dor. Turn on your bathwater."

A few moments later he was able to put both his fists through the hole. "I'm not fooling anyone, they'll know I'm talking to you," he said, "but we can have at least a few minutes of private conversation before they figure out a way to filter out the running water with their sound equipment."

"I didn't realize walls are so hollow."

"They are in warm climates like the American Southwest and the Middle East."

They were silent for a moment. Then David said, "It's all pretty weird, isn't it."

"Pretty weird," she repeated. There was a trace of accent to his ear. She was speaking English with the same slight Israeli accent he had. He wondered if she adapted to her listener's tone deliberately or if it happened unconsciously.

"Where are you from?" he asked.

"Marseilles. And you?"

"Israel. Been there?"

There was a thick silence before she answered. "There and . . . other places."

"It must be wonderful to have such an ability with languages. God forced people to speak different tongues as punishment. It's caused a lot of hell."

"My ability with languages has caused me 'a lot of hell.' I would rather have been born mute."

He sensed a No Trespassing sign in her voice and he respected her privacy as much as he needed his own. Yet there was something compelling about her, something that drew him to speak to her. Part of it was the fact that she was a fellow prisoner. But there was something else, a quality about her that he could not put his finger on, yet drew his interest.

"And you. How is it you can identify the terrorists?"

"Their family were our neighbors. A long time ago."

"They said you're an architect and engineer. What do you build?"

"Nothing, I build nothing. The last thing I built I destroyed. I'll never build anything again."

There was silence between them again and then he said, "I know it's none of my business, but I have to ask. You said you don't want to go on the mission. I'm trying to understand my own feelings. I would like to know why you don't want to go."

It was a long moment before she answered.

"I'm afraid."

He heard her get up and turn off the water, then footsteps

leaving the room. He stuck a hand towel in the hole and went back to his bed.

It had been a long time since he'd had a personal conversation with a woman. He had not sought out a woman's company since his wife died. He tried not to think of his wife. He had experienced the pain over and over until it had become a part of every atom of his being. Now as he lay on the bed and stared up at the dark ceiling, the memories flowed back to him.

He first saw Leila when he was camping in October in the southern part of the Negev, the area that was itself the southernmost region of Israel.

His mother had died earlier in the year. She had left his father and their West Bank farm and moved to Tel Aviv where she worked in a library and enjoyed the culture she had missed. David had lived with her until he finished college. He went on to get advanced degrees in both engineering and architecture.

His father had remained behind on the West Bank for a year, before loneliness and the government forced him to give up his squatter's rights. With his health slowly getting worse, he went to Galilee and lived on a kibbutz. David had kept in contact with him, but their relationship was never warm. After the incident in Jerusalem where he was reprimanded for failing to shoot a suicide terrorist, the few conversations with his father were tightlipped on both sides. His father disowned him when David married. He died a year after the wedding.

The day he met Leila he had ridden into the desert on horseback with surveying equipment to take measurements for the desert project he designed. He wore the clothes of a Bedouin, not because he was trying to ape them but because they were the most efficient clothing to wear in the desert where the sun was hot, the nights cold, and the winds knifing.

He had camped in a wadi, a dry riverbed. Wadis were frequently used as roads in the dry season. She came down it in a Land Rover that reminded him of the vehicle used to transport his family to the Negev when he was small. Her Land Rover was old enough and battered enough to have been the very vehicle.

She drove by him without stopping. As she went by, he waved and yelled a greeting in Hebrew, thinking she was Jewish.

The Land Rover came back a few minutes later.

"I took a wrong turn an hour ago," she said, "and got lost. It's getting dark and I'm going to have to camp."

She was tall, almost as tall as he was, and much more outgoing than any Arab woman he had ever met. Her dark hair with tints of red was worn short in a fashionable cut, the sort of look you see on international models staring at you from a magazine cover. Her eyes were liquid brown, large and moist; they stole his heart and soul from him immediately. She was efficient, professional, inquisitive, and knowledgeable. And there was a bit of cynicism to her. She was a worldly doctor in an other-worldly Arab culture in which women were expected to stay in the home and be virgins before marriage— even if they were flying off to Switzerland to get their hymens sewn before marriage so they could be a virgin on their wedding night. And she shared that culture with a Jewish one in which Arabs were not just the enemy but were commonly despised.

She had passed him by because of his Bedouin robes, thinking at first that he was a hashish smuggler. Coming back she saw his surveyor's level, a telescope fitted with a spirit level and mounted on a tripod.

"I realized it was safe to return and share a camp because you were probably a government surveyor," she later told him. She had left Hezeva earlier, intending to make it to a Bedouin camp at an oasis.

As they talked, he discovered that she was Arab. And a doctor. Her father, also a doctor, had sent her to London to study. She worked for a United Nations health organization as a health officer for Bedouins.

"It's as much research as treatment," she told him, "and it has its drawbacks. Few Arab males would let me touch them, so most of my treatment is with women and children."

They both shared a love for the desert. That night as they sat across from a campfire he told her of the project he designed.

"It's not just a building, a structure, but a living organism," he said. "It takes in air and water and thrives on sunshine."

"Does it say Mama and pee when you pull its string?" She laughed.

"If I draw it into the plans." He told her about the Nabataean, how they grew grain in the desert by their clever storage and retrieval of rainwater in underground cisterns.

"The building is going above one of the ancient cisterns," he told her. "There will be no generators, no power lines, no gas lines, no conventional air conditioning or heat." It would draw cold air from the cistern in the summer, warm air heated by solar panels and water plates in the cold periods, and create light from panels that were almost self-illuminating. Building materials, light metals, and glass that conserved energy, were more similar to what was used to build space stations than a building.

"It will be entirely self-sufficient, drawing energy only from its natural environment. At my office, they call it the Mars Probe, but I think of it as an oasis. I'm even going to put date palms in the atriums area."

He called it the Oasis Project. Built to house classrooms and dorms for a university extension campus of biologists and geologists, in an era in which humans were stamping out the natural environment everywhere they stepped, it was David's dream to build a complex in the desert that was one with the environment.

She laughed a great deal as he described the project to her, not because she thought the project was funny but because he was so enthused as he was waving his hands and pacing around.

Thinking back now, he realized he had needed something to fill voids in his life and had filled it with architecture. Leila had been the rest of the life he wanted.

Love developed between them almost from the first moment they had seen each other. She had believed one doesn't choose whom one loves, that love was God-given. She left in the morning but came back the next day and camped with him, and they made love under the desert sky, a night sky glittering with more stars than there were anywhere else.

Their life in the desert had been idyllic. But it was hell everywhere else.

His father refused to speak another word to him when he told him he was marrying an Arab. His co-workers took the news impassively to his face—and spoke angry words behind his back. Her family and friends were as horrified as his. A mixed Jewish-Arab marriage had a similar stigma to mixed marriages in the American Deep South before the civil rights movement.

They married during a storm and had little time to honeymoon because both had projects in progress with critical time frames. The Oasis Project was rising from the sand above ancient cisterns and the World Health Organization's Bedouin study was nearly complete.

She became pregnant, unplanned but not unwelcomed, and they set up home in a temporary trailer in the desert to live in while he supervised construction and it served as a base for daily excursions among the nomads. As he watched his space-age oasis take shape, as life grew in her belly, he had everything he needed to make him happy. But there is a snake in every paradise.

Trouble rose with the project, the worst kind of trouble for David. A controversy that brought home everything he had tried to forget and leave behind from his youth. Unwittingly, he became a victim of the fatal flaw that God put in mankind to keep men and women from being perfect. History repeats itself.

The diversion of water to the underground cistern caused a Bedouin waterhole a mile away to go dry. To the nomadic Bedouins, roaming empty valleys and plains, wherever they herded their goats and camels belonged to them. Water was their most important possession. Life itself, survival at its most basic level, depended on the availability of water.

The project could not compensate them for the loss of the waterhole. The single water source permitted them to graze their animals over dozens of square miles of desert. Without the water, their entire lifestyle, their life cycle, would be destroyed.

Millions of dollars had poured into the project. It was not going to be abandoned.

Despite his efforts to rectify the problem, tempers flared between the Bedouins and the security people guarding the construction materials and equipment. Accusations were made that equipment was sabotaged and materials stolen by the Arabs. The Arabs in return accused them of killing their animals.

He began to see his dream project not as something that flowed with the desert but as an ugly sore upon it. He was an intruder in the desert not one with it.

David was in his trailer when he heard shots and ran outside. Security guards on one side of the wadi were exchanging shots with Bedouins on the other side. The shooting stopped as men on both sides scrambled for cover.

He saw Leila's Land Rover coming down the wadi—she was in danger of being caught in a cross fire. He went wild, running for the dry riverbed, shouting for both sides to hold their fire.

His cries were drowned out as the shooting began again. Holes ripped the front windshield of the vehicle as automatic rifle fire hit it. The Land Rover swerved and went into a ditch, rolling over in a cloud of dust. When he reached the vehicle, she was still inside. One side of her head was covered with blood.

He took her in his arms and screamed her name.

CHAPTER TWENTY-ONE

David had fallen into sleep when a knock on the door awoke him. He was surprised to find Conway at the door. "Can I talk to you?"

David turned on the light and gestured for him to come in. "I'd offer you a drink but the only thing I have is water from the bathroom sink."

"I'll get straight to the point. The woman is important for this mission. I don't want to lose her, but she can't be forced. You're different. The mission can't be done without you. Things are going to have to move fast around here, we need to cram a lifetime of knowledge into a few days. Training starts early tomorrow. I'd like to know if you're in or out."

"I haven't made up my mind."

"That's what you told the guys in charge. No matter what impression you got, I'm a fellow grunt on this mission. There's a lock on my door, too. I don't understand your hesitation. You're not scared. You're not leaving anything but a prison cell behind. And it's the only chance to save the world."

David shrugged. "Are you sure? History's written by the victors. We don't know for certain that Islam would dominate. It's another five or six hundred years from the death of Jesus before the Muslims rise. Maybe if barbarians had atomic weapons a couple thousand years ago, we'd be soar-ing around the galaxy today."

"If the Zayyads run loose in the ancient world with their fanaticism and their knowledge of modern technology, these nutcases will create a world more gruesome than Dante's In-ferno. We're talking about psychopaths."

"Maybe the Zayyads will die in a plague before they intro-duce Islam. Be poisoned by rivals. Get their heads cut off by the Romans. Or a thousand other possibilities."

"I don't get you." Conway shook his head. "You seem to have a hard-on for the whole world."

"Maybe I'm not satisfied with the status quo. I'm not a big, tough matinee hero. Just a sometime criminal. And hell, who knows, maybe this whole thing is God's plan. He once spat on the slate and wiped the earth clean with the Flood. Maybe he's using electronics this time. This is a culture that brought us the Inquisition, the Holocaust, atomic warfare, genocide in the Balkans and Africa, slavery, and the death of tens of millions of Native Americans to satisfy the avarice of Europeans."

"Fuck you," Conway said. He stopped at the door. "I'll go it alone. You stay back in your comfortable little prison cell and feel sorry for yourself."

David looked to the surveillance camera. "I'll go, but there has to be something in it for *me*. If we take out the Zayyads, my reward will be that I will be sent back in time exactly three years, five months, twelve days"—he looked at his watch—"nine hours, and forty-three minutes."

Holt exchanged looks with Bornstein and Scott. The three men had been watching the interaction between Conway and David on a monitor.

"Three years, five months . . ." Scott mulled.

"It's really quite simple," Bornstein said. He picked up a file with David's name on it and opened it. "It's back to the date and time his wife died."

He tossed the file back on the table. "He wants to go back in time to save her."

Holt put his hands on his head. "Jesus. What a twist. It can't be done, you know that."

"We can't tell him that," Bornstein said.

Holt turned off the monitor displaying David's room. He took a deep drag and sighed, letting the smoke out. "Well, gentlemen, we have one Israeli with a tragic romantic past, and one nun-whore, or whatever she is, with a tragic past. Ironic, isn't it? Both haunted by ghosts of the past, with probable signs of an early attraction between them. All the right ingredients for a Gothic tale, but it plays hell for the mission. We can't send Conway alone." Holt shook his head. "The Operations Evaluation computer gives a lone operator with no knowledge of the language a five percent success factor."

"Fuck the computer," Scott said. "It's only as good as the people who programmed it. And most of them are shit-faced nerds."

"I think it's time Marie meets the shepherd boy," Bornstein said. "She blames herself for the death of another little boy, one of life's twists that took her to the brink of madness in Lebanon. This little boy's plight might stir her heart."

General Scott grinned. "The golden heart of a prostitute." He left the conference room in a fury. He had been a combat platoon leader when Holt was ROTC and Bornstein had a draft deferment. As usual, the civilians were going to screw things up and force him to step in and save their asses.

CHAPTER TWENTY-TWO

BETHSAIDA

Salome was in conference with an aide to the governor of Syria, the Roman administrator who oversaw the Middle East for the emperor. In her mind, the meetings were becoming too frequent because each dealt with a problem that would be reported to the emperor. Tiberius ran the empire from the Isle of Capri. Sometimes his madness traveled all over the Roman world, toppling kings and administrators, often irrationally. She preferred not bringing news of her husband's domain too often before him. She even began avoiding opportunities to improve her image with the emperor. One never knew when a mad dog would bite.

"You know the problem," she told the procurator's aide, "these Jews are repulsed by graven images, even the likeness of our godly emperor on coins. They rioted in my uncle's territory when he introduced the coins and in Jerusalem when Pontius Pilate distributed them. Now we have trouble here."

"The Jews are inherent troublemakers," the aide said. "They need a strong hand."

"Exactly," Salome said. "But every time there is an offense against order, it gets reported to the emperor. At some point he may believe that his servants in the region cannot manage his affairs."

The threat was to the governor, who knew as well as anyone that Tiberius could be capricious.

"It would be best," she went on, "if we avoided the problem by not distributing the coins publicly. We can use them among others than Jews and for payment of taxes to Rome."

"What is bothering the governor most," the aide said, "is that the emperor's features on the coin are being defaced by Jews. He has sent a messenger to the emperor for guidance in the matter. There is also the matter of the continual threat of insurrection from these Jews."

He is a fool, Salome thought. But she said, "We are in the process of breaking the back of the resistance. Soon we will have good news for the governor to report."

It was a lie, but when the time came to report, she would make up something appropriate, perhaps have some Jews arrested and tortured until they confessed to being Zealots.

Alone with her vizier, she was informed about a foul remark about her painted on the side of a house. The remark was stimulated by her incestuous marriage to her uncle and rumors that she behaved licentiously.

"Have the offending building burnt," she instructed her vizier.

"But it is no fault of the building owner. Someone else painted the offensive language."

"Burn it anyway. And arrest the owner. That will frighten other building owners to keep closer watch and report any possible infraction."

The praying mantis bowed. "As you wish, Your Highness."

She threw on the floor a gift, a thin gold necklace, that the governor's aide had brought from Syria. "I would not permit my servants to wear this cheap rubbish."

She paced, angry. "I can well imagine what message the governor has sent to the emperor. No doubt he reported that his servants in Palestine lack the ability to keep this Jewish rabble in order as my grandfather Herod did. There is trouble brewing and that will mean trouble with the emperor. These damn Zealots plot to drive the Romans from the land while their brother Sicarii put daggers in the backs of our friends. And Galilee is the center of it. Pontius Pilate has a fraction of the problems in Judea that we have in Galilee. When problems arise, it's usually at Passover from Galileans visiting Jerusalem. But my uncle in Tiberias and I both know that the rebels are brewing trouble under our feet. When it happens, we will be swept away before Rome can restore order."

The vizier went to get her next visitor while she mulled over the dynamics of Roman rule in Palestine.

The Romans kept control more by intimidation than by actual physical force. The mere thought of a Roman legion marching on a city was enough to make most rebels throw down their swords and plea for peace. But the Jews did not give up as easily as other people. She thought it was an error to assume that they would stay in line as other nationalities did.

There were amazingly few Roman troops in the region. Pontius Pilate, the governor of Judea, had a cohort, a few hundred men, garrisoned at the Antonia fortress in Jerusalem and more in Caesarea where he lived. There were only a couple hundred legionnaires spread between Bethsaida and her uncle Herod Antipas in Tiberias. Order was maintained by the local rulers, with armies made up of mercenaries from Greece, Gaul, and Spain, but they were not large enough to put down a major rebellion. That required Roman legions and the legions would not come unless order broke down. And they would not leave until they brutally ensured that the problem would not arise again and that the local rulers, Salome among them, were punished for letting the situation get out of hand.

Galilee was the hot cauldron where the problems ignited. From there, the trouble would spread. Her uncle Herod Antipas lacked the talent to deal with the Jewish rabble. He alternately alienated them with restrictions and tried to appease them with promises he failed to keep. Pilate, who administered the heart of the Palestine, was strong willed and authoritarian. He came to the Palestine intent upon making the Jews kneel to Rome and had run into one problem after another by his actions, causing riots by ordering the emperor's image to appear on coins, and when he had legionnaires march through the streets of Jerusalem carrying ensigns with the emperor's image on it. When hundreds of citizens protested, he had them surrounded by his soldiers and gave them the choice of dying or going home. To massacre them would have launched a general uprising and he had to back down from his command when the men bared their chests—they would sooner die than allow their religion to be offended by the worship of graven images of the god-emperor. More trouble arose when he ruled that the Temple in Jerusalem would have to bear the expense of a new aqueduct bringing water to the city from twenty-five miles away.

Despite his own feelings that the Jews needed the whip more than coddling, he had to keep order with a minimum of violence or face charges in Rome. Like Salome, Pilate was smart enough to avoid involving the emperor.

Now the marketplace was buzzing with talk of a man who could perform miracles, who people believed could drive the Romans from their land. Salome knew that the pot would boil over in Jerusalem during Passover. The question was how she would ride out the storm. Or turn the wind to her advantage.

Her thoughts were interrupted by the appearance of her vizier with a dark cloaked man.

"He has been searched," the vizier said. "No weapons." He whispered to her, "This is the Sicarii of whom I spoke. I have heard his tale. It is imperative that you hear it from his own lips."

Sicarii. Daggerman. Assassin. She should have him ripped slowly to pieces with a torturer's hot pinchers in her dungeon. But her expedient nature left her door open to all who could serve her ambitions. Two of the chained rowers burned to death on her arena lake were captured Sicarii assassins. If she was not pleased with the man who had requested her audience, he would fare worse than being burned to death.

"Speak your business and do not waste my time," she said.

"I come with urgent news, my Queen. Two men have come

to Palestine from an unknown land. These strangers claim to have a power mightier than Roman legions. They killed a Roman sympathizer to demonstrate their power."

"What nonsense is this? Rome has more legions than the miserable rabble around me have lice."

"Great Queen, I would not risk my life to beg audience with you if I did not believe it was important. One of the men burned in the sea battle at the arena recently was my brother. I come here because we know these men have some sort of wizardry, a power that can strike a man dead merely with the wave of a hand."

"What is this power you speak of?"

"The man killed was struck by a bolt of lightning that made the sound of thunder. He fell instantly. Part of his head was blown away as if he had been struck in the head by an invisible ax."

"An ax that no one sees?" the vizier asked.

"No one saw the weapon that struck the man. It hit him and knocked him backwards. He was as dead when he hit the ground as he would be if his head had been chopped off."

Salome exchanged looks with her vizier. The story was incredible, but it could not be ignored. She had always believed that her destiny was to rule an empire. Perhaps her Julius Caesar had arrived in Palestine.

"Why do you come to me? Use these men to drive out the Romans . . . if they have the power."

"They have the power, great Queen. It is the leader of the two men who has sent us to you. He says we need resources, money and men that you command."

"Bring these two men to me and you will be rewarded for your deed."

After he left, Salome asked, "I trust you are having him followed?"

"Of course. But it never does any good. His comrades will kill whoever we send to follow him."

"I want this power. At any cost." Her dark eyes were afire with the possibilities of an empire. "Get it for me. If I don't get it, I will have your eyes gouged and your tongue cut out. *I want it.*"

The Sicarii's claim about thundering power possessed by strangers to the land brought back the memory of the terrifying black cloud that recently passed over Bethsaida, blowing down houses and raining frogs.

Power to destroy Roman legions.

Her intuition told her that the strangers from the unknown land had something to do with the terrifying black storm.

CHAPTER TWENTY-THREE

NEW MEXICO

"When you two were a glint in your mother's eyes, I helped choreograph the fight scenes in *Ben-Hur* and *Spartacus*," the combat instructor told David and Conway. "And I did the same for *Gladiator*, showing those young choreographers how to stage arena battles. I'm going to teach you how to defend yourself with the Roman short sword, shield, and dagger. And how to kill with them." In his breastplate, Roman helmet, and white beard, the choreographer looked like a grizzled gladiator who fed on the smell of blood.

The clash of swords and shields echoed off the cement walls of the surrounding building as Conway and the fight choreographer battled.

The lesson took place on a field at the rear of the compound. The weapons were real, forged around the time of Christ, antique pieces hastily borrowed from museums and collectors. The CIA director told them at breakfast that the best swords, the ones they would actually take back with them, had been taken by gunpoint from an Italian duke at a villa outside Rome and flown to New Mexico in an ultra high-speed air force jet. The duke had been awakened in the middle of the night by a frantic call from an Italian cabinet minister who told him the men breaking down his front door were police who had come to rob him of his collection of weapons of antiquity.

David and Conway both wore wool tunics and leather sandals. The clothes were flown to the site from a village in Syria where the cloth was woven in the same manner it had been during the time of Christ. Women who worked the cloth were brought to make alterations. A Hollywood costume designer and a curator from the Metropolitan Museum worked frantically with the equipment, money, and clothing pouring in, the curator authenticating and the costume designer improvising.

As he watched the action, David decided Conway was a better swordsman than the choreographer. The movie expert knew the technical moves, but Conway had speed, strength, and was impulsively high-spirited. Even David had been better than the choreographer, but he had no particular pride about it; he and Conway were half the man's age. They would get a tougher fight from a younger choreographer.

In some ways he envied Conway. The man had enjoyed stardom and all of the perks that came with it. Movie stars were America's royalty and although Conway was not a top box office star, he was certainly a prince among a few kings. He wondered what it would be like to enjoy the glittering world of diamond-studded women and tuxedo-clad men in places like Monte Carlo and St. Moritz. And to be a secret agent, which Conway had once been. Putting his fingers around the walnut grip of a pistol must be as exciting as masturbating to him.

Danger wasn't sexual to David. He had been raised in a war zone and believed that the only honorable battles were the ones that could not be avoided.

Working with Conway was going to be interesting. More than working with him—tackling the most daring mission in all history. The thought of going back in time to the ancient world gave him a shot of adrenaline that made him almost quiver with excitement. He had made a deal with Holt and the others: If he returned successfully from the mission, he would be sent back in time to ten minutes before his wife was shot, enough time to save her. What he did not tell them was that he would not have traded a trip to the ancient world for man's first step on the moon.

Now that he had a personal goal in the unimaginable journey, he had adopted it wholeheartedly.

The drapes were tightly drawn at the window to Marie's room. He had not seen her since the conference, nearly thirty-six frantic hours ago, a day and a half of almost nonstop preparation. Her name had not been mentioned after his brief meeting with the project managers. Whatever devils she was fighting, he wished her well.

After gulping down a cup of coffee, David reported to the training field, joining Conway already in arms. As his turn came to practice with Conway, the difference between him and Conway was evident from the beginning. Conway had taken fencing lessons and learned to use a lightsaber and lightweight fake movie sword with precision. Like everything Conway did, he did it well.

David had spent several years at hard labor. His muscles were bulging, his swing powerful. With the Roman short sword, his strength made up for any tactical advantage the quick-footed, well-trained Conway had. David had broken the instructor's sword in half with a single swing of his own blade.

Up against Conway, the two ended in a draw. Conway refused to meet his stronger arm head-on—and David carefully sidestepped deceptive maneuvers that Conway employed.

He had to admit one thing: Conway was truly a Roman. Garbed in Roman helmet, breastplate, and tunic, Conway looked as if he had stepped from the set of a Cecil B. DeMille costume extravaganza. He was every bit the Roman, even in his mannerisms. Within minutes, he was giving commands to David and the instructor as if he were Julius Caesar himself.

Bornstein and Holt watched the fight lesson from the window in the conference room.

Holt stubbed out a cigarette and wiped gray ash from the tips of his fingers with his handkerchief. "This past week has aged me ten years. It's too damn bad about the Gauthier woman. She's needed on this mission."

"Don't give up on her yet," Bornstein said. "I'm hoping that she will sacrifice herself for the boy." He shook his head at Holt. "We're in a hell of a business, you know that. This stuff about sacrificing people for the fate of nations. I hope to hell I don't have to answer for this—in this life or the next."

"At least we're lucky that we have Conway leading the mission." Holt lit another cigarette. "Hell, look at him, doesn't he look the part? The guy's a regular method actor."

Bornstein's eyes followed Conway racing a chariot around the doughnut hole. He was enjoying himself and made it look effortless, as if he had handled the reins all his life. And was trying out for a starring role in a remake of *Ben-Hur*.

"I wonder whether a man who plays Julius Caesar on the stage may have the most dangerous personality trait of all."

"What's that?"

"A big ego."

CHAPTER TWENTY-FOUR

"We call him Isie," Bornstein told Marie as he escorted her down the corridor. It was late and the only other people in the corridor were military police.

"His name is Isaiah. We've had a problem communicating with him. People today understand there is something called the future and that the future will probably be different from the past, but Isie came from a culture that was unchanged for thousands of years before his birth. He has no concept of a future any different than the life he's been living. We haven't been able to explain to him that he's come forward in time. He believes we're some sort of demons who have captured him and taken him to a strange land."

"I don't see how I can help."

"We brought in a professor from Damascus who speaks Aramaic but he hasn't gained the boy's confidence. His Aramaic isn't good enough and his approach is too stiff. We need to get closer to the boy, to make him understand he can trust us."

Marie shot a glance at him.

He paused in front of the door to the boy's room. "I know how you feel. We grabbed you off a street and brought you halfway around the world. But keep in mind that there's good and bad in this world, and regardless of how we manage things, or bungle them, our motives are for the good."

Isie sat on the edge of the bed and watched as Marie and the presidential advisor entered. His eyes were alive with curiosity and caution. The Damascus professor rose stiffly from a chair next to the bed.

Bornstein introduced Marie to the professor, using Marie to translate the introduction into Arabic. After a moment of polite conversation with the professor in Arabic, Marie switched to Aramaic and then spoke to Bornstein in English.

"His Aramaic is terrible. So is his attitude. He's a fundamentalist Muslim and the boy's Jewish. I want to speak to the boy alone, without the guards. No wonder the boy is frightened. Look at those helmets and guns and bully clubs."

"The MPs have to stay. Those are orders from the president and I don't have authority to change them."

"The guards go," she said, "or you can speak to the boy in Aramaic yourself."

He locked eyes with her for a moment, but he knew he had no leverage in the negotiation. "The president could have used you at the last summit. I'll take one of the guards."

"Both."

"One," he said, and smiled. "That's a diplomatic concession."

"Both. That's an offer you can't refuse. And take the professor with you."

He left, taking the professor and one of the guards with him. The professor didn't bother saying good-bye to the boy. The old man had only cooperated because his government told him to, but no one said he had to be friendly.

Marie sat on the edge of the bed.

"My name is Mariam," she said, using the version of her name that she hoped the boy would recognize.

He tried to keep his face rigid, but a shy smile slipped out. "My sister's name is Mariam."

As Bornstein predicted, Isie kindled in Marie the memory of another little boy, one whose image was never far from her and whose death she had relived in a thousand nightmares. She put her arm around his shoulders and pulled him close, feeling him trembling against her.

"I need your help," she said. "The people in this place are good. They are friends. But soon we will be returning to your land. And I will need your protection."

Little boys had not changed in thousands of years. Isie, like the boys today where he was born, were raised to protect women. She would protect him with her life, but he had to think that he was protecting her.

"Will you help me?" she asked.

The boy hesitated for a moment, looking at her, wondering if she was tricking him.

"If you don't want to help me, it's all right."

The boy's eyes darted to the door where the military policeman was standing. "I don't trust these foreigners with their strange tongue and ways. I think they're demons!"

She held the boy, calming his fears as well as her own. She was the one who was tricked. Bornstein knew about Lebanon. At least what she had revealed when she was brought out and hospitalized. He knew she wouldn't be able to resist the boy's plight, that she would not let the boy be put in danger without her at his side. She had seen one boy like him die. She would not let it happen again.

She was going to be sent back to the past. Not her own past but to a time and place found only in books and that had dominated her entire life.

The past. A place before the here and now. She wondered what it would be like to go back in time, back to a world in which she had no past.

The palms of her hands burned.

CHAPTER TWENTY-FIVE

Lunch and history were served in the conference room.

One instructor was a woman, a professor of antiquity from the Sorbonne, the other, a rabbi, held a similar position with Hebrew University in Jerusalem. They were two of the three most distinguished experts in the world on first-century Israel. The other distinguished expert, a Jesuit priest, was dying of old age at the Vatican hospital in Rome.

Like the other experts rushed to the facility, they had been told what they had to do, but had not been given the slightest clue about the mission.

"You know the history of Israel at the time of Christ from movies, books, and religious schooling," the rabbi told them in a thick Israeli accent, "and those media have trained you to think in terms of the spiritual qualities of the era.

"For the Jew it was the last days of the great Temple before the Romans crushed Jewish autonomy and the nation of Israel lay dormant for two thousand years. For the Christian, it was the agony of the Crucifixion and the birth of Christianity.

"In terms of the daily life of the average man in first-century Israel, spiritualism had as much effect as it does in the present Middle East. It was important, but fanatics were in the minority. For most people, the dominating influences were survival in terms of food and shelter, and a political climate not a far cry different than the war and terrorism that has gripped the Middle East for the past fifty years or so."

The French professor cleared her throat. She was short with disproportionately shorter legs and a faint black mustache. She reminded David of a female Toulouse-Lautrec. "The two historical eras that are the most analogous to first-century Israel are the present turbulent conditions in the Middle East and the time of Nazi Germany."

"The Nazis?" Conway said.

"Think," the rabbi said, tapping his temple area, "the storm troopers of the ancient world were Roman legions that swiftly conquered nations and brutalized enough of the population to ensure the rest would cower. The Romans then established puppet regimes under local rulers who were kept in office by the presence of Roman legions and a network of secret police and spies. Hitler copied Roman methods. And before him, the British with their empire.

"Herod the Great was an important ruler enthroned by the Romans. But Herod was more of an Arab than an Israeli, born in the desert region around what is now Jordan and the Negev. He was considered a foreigner by the Jews. His people had been forcefully converted to Judaism and his practice of it was merely ceremonial, giving lip service to the local religion when, if anything, for political reasons he gave allegiance to the pantheon of Roman gods.

"He served his Roman masters well and was generally hated and feared by the Jews. At Herod's death the clever Romans divided Israel into three territories and placed a son of Herod on each throne. When one of the sons, the one ruling Judea, the heart of Israel, proved unfit, he was replaced by a Roman governor named Pontius Pilate.

"The other two territories bordered the Sea of Galilee, one ruled by Herod Antipas and the other by his brother, Philip. They ruled as petty Oriental potentates, burdening the population with outrageous taxes to pay for Roman protection."

The French professor took the floor. "At the time Christ began his ministry along the Sea of Galilee, Philip was dying and his wife, Salome, controlled the kingdom. Salome was Philip's wife-niece and the grandniece of Herod the Great. She alone inherited the cleverness and ambitions of Herod the Great. She entered into the incestuous marriage with Philip, her elderly uncle, and schemed to carve out an empire. She was the Cleopatra of the Jews, a beautiful, ambitious, and ruthless woman."

"Tell them about the Zealots and the Sicarii," Holt said, impatiently.

Both professors cast him a dour look, but the Israeli picked up the subject.

"The main resistance against Roman rule was a secret Jewish militant group called the Zealots. The Zealots wanted to drive the Romans and despots like Salome out of Israel. They fought in guerrilla fashion, gathering their forces in the wilderness and launching surprise attacks on Roman convoys. An extremist element—Jewish terrorists called the Sicarii, whose method was to lie in wait for Romans and Jews who were Roman sympathizers—broke off from the Zealots.

"The Romans and the Herodian tyrants crucified thousands of Jewish patriots, Zealots, Sicarii, and anyone else who made their objections to their tyranny too loud. I must mention that crucifixion was not frequently used for common crimes. It was introduced into Israel by the Romans and was usually reserved for the rebels battling Roman rule or that of its Jewish puppets."

It occurred to David that the situation in Palestine during Roman times was not unlike that of Palestine under the British Mandate when the Lehi broke off from the rank and file of the Jewish underground to wage a terrorist campaign against the British and Arabs.

"Salome was too immoral and corrupt for the Zealots," the French woman said, "but not for the murderous Sicarii, the assassins of that era. Her capital city, Bethsaida, was a scandalous town, the Sodom and Gomorra of the times. Bethsaida had such an immoral reputation that after Jesus restored the sight of a blind man from Bethsaida, he warned the man not to go back into the city because of the evils the man would see.

"Salome allowed the Sicarii to use Bethsaida as their headquarters. They fed her gold in return and occasionally slipped a knife between the ribs of a righteous Jew who complained too loudly about her incestuous marriage to her uncle and her debauchery. She had one executed occasionally to keep them in line and keep up appearances.

"Judas Iscariot was a Sicarii, Iscariot not being a proper Jewish name but a corruption of the Greek word Sicarii, meaning daggerman. Judas may in fact have been planted among Jesus' followers by the Sicarii because Jesus was attracting a great deal of public attention. It's probable that all the other eleven Disciples were Zealots. Three have definitely been identified as Zealots and considering that Jesus was feeding a secret Zealot army in the wilderness, it's most likely that Jesus was also a Zealot. Why else would he be feeding a rebel army that planned to attack the Romans?"

Holt walked to the podium. "If you don't mind," he said to the scholars, "you can finish your history lecture and get into the daily customs a little later. Right now I need to speak to these gentlemen alone."

CHAPTER TWENTY-SIX

After the scholars left, Holt sat across from David and Conway and flicked ashes from a cigarette onto the floor. General Scott stood nearby with his arms folded, while Bornstein took a chair off to the side of the conference table.

"Those two professors will be back to tell you which hand you eat with and how to take a crap without a toilet, if you haven't already learned that one from the sandboxes. And there'll be language instructors to point out differences between ancient Hebrew and Latin and how the languages are spoken in modern times. But while the history lesson's fresh, I want to drive home a few points.

"Palestine was important to the Romans as a crossroads of east-west trade, just as Middle East oil is to Europeans today. Cut off the trade pipeline and the Romans would have had to tighten their belts. There were secret police and storm troopers, revolutionaries, terrorists, and a scheming bitch named Salome. Now, where would a couple of terrorists like the Zayyad brothers head?"

"The Sicarii," Conway said.

"The Sicarii, Salome, Bethsaida, the whole nine yards. That's the information we got from a terrorist who talked under truth serum before he died. We only took one alive and got limited information before he kicked. He said the objective was Bethsaida. The city's wide open, Salome's hungry for power and gold, and the Sicarii are ready-made allies for the Zayyad brothers, not to mention that Jesus is out on the lake walking on water. His first miracle was at Bethsaida and three of his disciples hail from the town."

Conway rubbed his chin. "Why can't we put a squad of men back in time moments before the Zayyad brothers landed? They can retire the two terrorists when they appear and be back in time for lunch."

"I wish it was that easy. We don't know exactly how the time warp works, except that it's affected by where you're standing and the speed of the atoms. We know *almost* exactly where the Zayyad brothers were standing and *almost* exactly the speed of the atoms when they disappeared.

"The almosts are very important. We can get you close to the same time and place as the Zayyad brothers, but "close" may mean days either way and miles' difference. We did a test with a video camera before the ban on experimenting with time came from the Oval Office. We altered the speed and position slightly and ended up in an incredibly different time and place."

"Where?" Conway asked.

"We're not sure. We got a quick shot of swampy terrain before something with jaws big enough to swallow a car ate the camera."

"Jesus. We could end up in the Stone Age."

Holt left a filtered cigarette burning in the ashtray and lit a brown Sherman. "If this mission isn't a success, you might be better off living in a prehistoric cave than a modern city. Think about it, gentlemen. The Zayyad brothers, the Sicarii, and Salome, represent the whole spectrum of evil: murder, lust, greed, and insane ambitions. You will be entering a culture radically different than anything you have experienced. We'll feed you as much training and information as we can in the short time we have, but it will be up you to improvise as problems arise. If you can't fake it, you're finished."

Holt blew smoke at Conway. "You are Marcus Claudius Verro, a wealthy Roman trader. You're a long way from your home on the Iberian Peninsula. Your trusty servant is David

Ben-Dor, a Jew raised in your family's household since he was a baby. There's no need to change your name, David. It was as good a Jewish name in the first century as it is today. But be prepared to explain your hair. First-century Jews wore temple locks and beards. Your excuse is that you were raised by Romans, a race of clean shavers at this time."

"The loss of the Gauthier woman will be damaging. The Romans spoke Latin—you can cover that." Holt nodded at Conway. "Hebrew was spoken by Jewish priests and the upper classes—your language, of course, David—but unfortunately, most of the people used Aramaic. It was the language of the common man, the language spoken by Jesus and the Disciples. Not knowing how to speak it is going to increase the odds against success.

"You will each be issued a sword and dagger. Keep your sword hidden," Holt told David. "Jews were prohibited from bearing arms because too many Jewish blades ended up in Roman backs. Galilee was the hotbed of dissent against Roman rule. Watch yourself. The friendly soul you meet on the roadside may be a Sicarii assassin or a Roman spy.

"Your equipment will be authentic, but sparse. We can't send you back fully equipped because you'd need pack animals to carry the stuff. Rich Romans like Marcus Claudius traveled in style. Your cover story is that you fought off robbers who got away with the pack animals and drove off the other servants.

"You'll have plenty of gold to make purchases. I regret we can't provide you with equalizers to compensate for Jair Zayyad's gun, but we can't afford to let you carry back a modern weapon that could fall into the hands of the ancients. We're just lucky they only have one gun. Amir Zayyad had actually thrown down his weapon and surrendered before that devil Jair turned the tide."

"What type of gun? How many bullets?" Conway asked.

General Scott chomped on his cigar with pleasure. "Spoken like a professional."

"A Korth nine millimeter, double action, semiautomatic," Holt said. "An efficient German weapon. We know from the videotapes of the attack that Jair Zayyad used all but five of the rounds in the clip. He had two hundred more rounds in a backpack discarded during the fighting. The attackers, by the way, all wore masks and our only clue to their identity was from the one we took alive."

"Remember," Bornstein said, "at no time can you fall back on modern technology. I want to emphasize that point especially with you, Mr. Ben-Dor. You're a trained engineer, a skilled and knowledgeable technician by modern standards. But in the ancient world you will be the greatest scientist on the face of the earth, a genius magician who could build weapons and machines capable of enslaving the ancient world."

Bornstein paused and locked eyes with David to drive the point home. "No one, not the Zayyad brothers, not even Mr. Conway here, can compete with your technical knowledge. Don't let it go to your head."

"Are you afraid I'm going to succumb to temptation?" David asked.

Holt took a deep drag off the smoldering brown cigarillo, fired the tobacco a quarter of an inch back. "In a word, yes." He stubbed out the cigarette. "Your return after completing the mission will be accomplished by getting back to the same spot you arrived. The mechanism will be left on so you can return immediately after getting back to the entry point."

Bornstein stood up. The presidential advisor had been studying each of them as Holt spoke. Now he addressed David and Conway.

"There are a couple other matters of grave importance, more promises we must exact from you. We've impressed upon you how dangerous it would be to introduce modern knowledge into the ancient world, but knowledge is a two-edged sword. Each of you might be exposed to the greatest secret of the ages, a secret with such incredible consequences, its revelation could destroy the world we live in, pit nations and people against each other.

"You are going to be a witness to the times of Jesus Christ. It may be within your power to discover whether Jesus

Christ was a man of flesh or the Son of God. Christ's holiness is a two-thousand-year-old secret. Incredible consequences would follow in the wake of revelations about it. The religious bloodshed that has ripped apart the Middle East, Northern Ireland, India, and Pakistan would be trivial in comparison to the violence that would erupt if the religious beliefs of billions were refuted.

"Come back with knowledge that would cause one religion to triumph over another, and you will set the world aflame, rip it asunder."

"Very little is actually known about Christ," Holt said. "There are no pictures of him. Although he is believed to have lived into his thirties, we know little about his actual life other than a few episodes concerning his ministry and his death. In this regard, there is one last covenant we must exact from each of you.

"You must promise not to look at the face of Jesus."

David and Conway exchanged looks. The responsibility they were being handed was greater than anyone had ever been asked to bear.

David cleared his throat. "Everything centers around getting to Jesus before the Zayyad brothers. I suppose no one knows exactly how to find him."

"There's very little factual information about the daily life of Jesus," Holt said. "However, he was a public figure and shouldn't be that hard to find."

"That's not true," Marie spoke from the doorway. "Jesus was known by name and deed, not by sight. He preached in desolate places to avoid the prying eye of the Romans who feared a Messiah would become a heroic figure for the Jews to rally around. The Temple priests had to bribe Judas with thirty pieces of silver to get him to point out Jesus for them because they didn't know what he looked like."

There was no fear in her as her eyes swept the room. "The Romans and the Herod tyrants considered Jesus a rabble-rouser. He was a heretic in politics and religion. In an era where heretics were killed when discovered, it was inevitable he would die violently. It's only among the little people, the small merchants, poor farmers, and city laborers, among indentured servants and slaves and men and women made into criminals for stealing bread to feed their children, that you will find word of Jesus. That word will come only if they trust you."

She looked at the men in the room, staying a fraction longer on David than the others. "And only to someone who speaks their language."

Holt sent David and Conway back to the rough handling of the movie stuntman while Marie spoke to the three mission controllers.

David was certain that she had changed her mind and was going to come with them. The fact that Marie would be going on the mission with them charged David with conflicting emotions, the most pressing of which was concern for her safety in a pagan world. She was none of his business, but he was drawn to her. And worried about her, as he had been about his wife. What had changed her mind?

Watching Conway fling a spear from a racing chariot, he was again struck by how quickly the man had adapted to ancient weapons. David was a quick learner, but Conway attacked the weaponry with the passion of a man who had waited his entire life for someone to put a sword in his hand. He had a premonition that there would be problems between the two of them. He just hoped the conflicts would be no more than personality clashes.

David knew what his own reaction to the mission would always be: he would carry it out with lethal efficiency. It was the most important assignment in history; no man, at any time, had been handed a greater burden than the one he and Conway were given. The whole world relied upon them. But he had his own agenda—to kill the Zayyads and get back to save his wife.

Conway had so quickly adapted to his role of noble Roman, David wondered if the man indeed was a great actor, or just getting caught up in his role. A couple of times Conway's tone of voice and mannerism to him suggested that David was less than equal. *Maybe I'm just not adapting well to the role of subservient Jew*, David thought.

Footsteps crunched behind him and Marie approached. She had Isaiah, the shepherd boy, with her.

"Hello," David said.

"Hello."

They looked at each other for a moment, each feeling awkward.

"You changed your mind, you're coming with us?" he said.

"Yes. Back to the ancient world. It's going to an amazing adventure. Like nothing anyone has ever done before."

"It's going to be dangerous."

"For all of us," she said. "For Isaiah, too. And he's just an innocent bystander in this world."

"I'm curious, why did you change your mind?"

She looked away for a moment before answering. "I'm tired of this life, I want to try another."

He nodded and looked out to where Conway was driving a chariot.

"What about you?" she asked. "Why did you change your mind?"

He raised his eyebrows and shrugged. "I made an exchange. They're getting something they want and I'm getting something I want."

There was a change in her face, like a cloud had just passed over.

"What's wrong?" he said.

"You make it sound so . . . so mercenary."

"It is. I don't give a damn about the world." He did not intend to sound so harsh, but the words came out that way.

Isaiah picked up on the disturbance between the two and he shifted uneasily and eyed David with suspicion.

Marie put her arm around the boy to reassure him that everything was all right. "This is Isaiah Ben Ebed, better known as Isie."

He stared at David with cautious eyes, keeping a tight grip on the leather sling in his right hand. On impulse, David stuck out his right hand to shake hands with the boy but Isie took a step back, his eyes widening, the sling at the ready.

Marie spoke sharply to him. The boy relaxed and then politely nodded his head at David, bowing just slightly.

"I'm afraid that's the best I can do," she said. "He doesn't know about handshaking, and he's not going to let go of his sling while he's among strangers."

"I don't blame him. What has he been told about the mission?"

"That two evil men are trying to harm his people and we are going to stop them. He doesn't understand anything about having come forward in time. He doesn't comprehend that the future could bring great technological change because it never happened before the age he was born into."

Conway steered his chariot to them. "Welcome aboard the mission," he said to Marie, saluting her with the handle of the horsewhip.

"Thank you."

"C'mon, I'll give you and the boy a ride."

"I don't think—" was as far as she got.

Conway leaped from the chariot and took her arm. "You'll love it. It's a life-sized toy. Tell the boy to hop aboard."

She spoke to Isie in Aramaic as Conway led her aboard the chariot. Isie wavered between terror of the strange contraption and humiliation that a mere woman would take a ride and he wouldn't.

"C'mon, Isie!" Conway yelled, cracking the whip over the head of the horses. The boy jumped aboard as the horses went into a run.

David ate their dust. And the pangs of jealousy. Conway was a real live movie hero.

CHAPTER TWENTY-SEVEN

SEA OF GALILEE

Amir Zayyad's thoughts went back to his father's funeral as he watched fog cloak the dark waters of the lake. The wind had raged across the blistered plains as if angered by another death. He stood by his brother, Jair, while four men in dusty black suits lowered his father into a shallow hole. His grandmother, an old woman whose face spoke of war and misery, knelt and wiped the tears from his eyes with her black veil and then carefully draped the veil across his father's head to cover the bullet hole.

That had been two decades ago and Amir wondered if all the fighting and killing was worth it.

Blood for blood.

He squashed a big black spider with the heel of his boot. He knew they were being watched. His quick, nervous eyes picked up shadowy figures moving among the trees on the slope beside them. Amir had to fight an urge to run and hide, even though he knew he could trust his brother to handle the situation.

They had power that no one could match. Men of destiny is what we are, Jair said. They had the power to shape history, to mold it in their image, *to play God.*

One by one the shadows became men in black cloaks:

Sicarii terrorists, Jewish assassins who lurked in dark places, waiting to put a dagger in the back of a Roman. Jair had impressed the Sicarii with his power, and had spread gold among them, doubling their reasons to accommodate him by arranging a meeting with the queen.

Amir's mouth was dry, his skin electric, as he waited to see whether the gold paid would net them a clandestine meeting or a knife in the back.

Something thumped behind them and Amir whipped around. A rowboat washed ashore like a dead body. Four Sicarii were on board, shrouded wraiths in black cloaks transporting passengers with tickets to hell.

Jair chuckled. "Our honor guard has arrived."

Other rowboats beached and Sicarii swarmed aboard as Amir and Jair took their place in the boat with the wraiths.

The fog bank was a hundred meters offshore and the fleet of rowboats pushed into it, guided by a distant drumbeat that coursed through the misty night like the steady beat of a heart.

Galilee. The lake some called a sea. In Amir's native tongue of Arabic, the lake was called Buhayrat Tabariya. He had been born south of it in the Judean Hills above the Jordan River valley.

Jair's plan to exploit the turmoil between the Jews and Romans with a scheme so bold and incredible awed Amir by its very madness. He intended not only that they kill the man named Jesus but that they wrestle power from the Romans. To do that, they needed someone who could raise an army that could use the weapons he and Amir would build. Salome had that ability.

The ominous beat of the drum grew louder as the ghost fleet moved toward the center of the lake.

Amir's eye caught sight of a dark hulk in the fog and he leaned forward to get a better look, snapping back as fire roared from a dragon's mouth.

"Don't panic, little Mouse," his brother whispered. "It's the royal barge of Salome."

The drum stopped and the dragon slowed, black smoke

gushing from its mouth. The rowboats swarmed to it like gnats flocking to a garbage can.

Amir followed Jair and the Sicarii up a ramp and onto the deck of the ship. He quivered with excitement. The royal barge of Salome, Queen of Jews, the temptress who danced naked for her uncle, King Herod Antipas, and claimed the head of John the Baptist as her reward. Renowned only for her cruelties and lust, Salome was a tarnished page of history.

A centurion of the Royal Guard was waiting with a squad of men at the top of the ramp. Torches defined their path across the broad, deserted deck. Amir took a dozen paces before he realized Royal Guards were lined up in the darkness beyond the flaming path. Salome was taking no chances with either the notorious Sicarii or the mysterious strangers.

They followed the centurion down a passageway to the second deck and along a corridor lit by flames that flickered from the mouth of silver fishes mounted on the wall. At the end of the corridor, Nubian warrior-slaves stood like giant statues on each side of golden doors. The doors swept open as the troops approached.

Salome was on her throne at the far end of the audience chamber. The Queen of Jews was full busted with that Siren's appeal that has sent men to their doom since time immemorial—long, thick golden red hair curled around aqua green eyes. Ambition and spite, cruelty and bad temper, all radiated from her face.

Near the queen's feet was a dog, no pampered royal pet but an ill-gotten cross between a wolf and a jackal. The beast was chewing on a round chunk of black hair and bloody flesh. It looked up from its gruesome meal and caught Amir's stare. The creature had one yellow eye and one gray eye. Amir looked away. He felt as if he had locked eyes with the devil.

A purple curtain had been erected near the right wall of the chamber. The curtain looked out of place, as if it had been hastily arranged to hide something. Amir forced himself not to speculate on what might be behind the curtain.

Naked girls and boys well into puberty, but with all body

hair shaved off, stood by to serve the queen. Some were painted gold, others silver. Standing behind her was a tall, crisp twig of a man who kept his hands chest high, palm to palm, like a praying mantis. Amir suspected he was the royal vizier, the queen's chief advisor. And often coconspirator, the Sicarii had told them.

The vizier had a white beard and crocodile eyes. He stroked the beard as he surveyed the Zayyad brothers. "You spread gold in the marketplace and among men who practice death, enticing a greedy soul to arrange an audience with the queen and the Sicarii. What you have bought for yourselves will no doubt prove more than you can stomach."

"We are Jews." Jair spoke Hebrew in a hoarse whisper. A thin scar ran the width of his throat, mute evidence of the cause of the rasp in his voice. "We have come a long way at great hardship to stand with the other sons of Abraham against the Romans."

Salome scoffed. "Do you take us for fools? If the Romans suspected me of conspiring with the Sicarii, Roman legions would tear down the walls of Bethsaida and we would all end up on the crucifixion posts. You have been sent here as Roman spies, to lure me into plotting against our benefactors. You will soon find out how we treat spies."

The centurion swaggered closer to the throne. "If they be Jews, their tribe must indeed be a poor one if this is the best they can muster to fight the Romans, Your Highness. I detect the foul tongue of a barbarian in this base creature's attempt to speak Hebrew. My Queen, give me your leave to punish these Roman spies. The eyes that have seen Salome and the Sicarii together must be darkened."

The vizier kept his hands chest high as he leaned closer to Salome and spoke loud enough to be heard by the others. "These strangers claim to have a power mightier than Roman legions. Perhaps we should hear their tale before they are punished."

Salome eyed Jair, two coiled snakes squaring off. "Tell us of this power you claim to possess."

Amir realized everything that had been said had been rehearsed. He started to whisper to Jair, but his brother waved him off.

"We have a power that would make your army stronger than all the legions of Rome, a power that could topple the walls of Rome so your soldiers can rape the empire."

The centurion howled with laughter. "A power to destroy Roman legions? From this ugly beggar?! What is that power? His own foul breath?"

Jair stiffened. The movement was so slight only Amir picked up on it. The centurion had doomed himself. Rather than having pity for the man, Amir felt pride for his brother. Jair spoke softly. "I will destroy the Roman empire and build a new empire in its place that will last a thousand thousand years. I shall sit on the throne of that empire and you will be at my side as my queen."

The centurion drew his sword. "Your Highness! The dog must die for this insolence."

Amir's eyes darted to his brother. Jair's expression had not changed, but his right hand had moved into the folds of his robe.

Salome waved her hand at one of the naked servant girls. "Show our guests what is in store for them."

The girl pulled a cord that dropped the purple curtain.

A body was crucified on a cross. Bloody steel spikes pinned the hands and feet. The body was headless.

Amir stared at the bloody hunk the mad dog was gnawing on. The hunk had turned over and Amir made out a nose and ear and an empty eye socket. It was the Sicarii who had carried the message to Salome, requesting a meeting.

Salome's features hardened. "You see your own fate unless you please me. You boast of power that can destroy armies and win my favor. Tell me of this power . . . and pray that I am awed by your tale."

"You're a woman," Jair baited the centurion.

The centurion charged, his sword raised. "Prepare to die—"

A clap of thunder exploded in the room. The folds of Jair's robe on the right side moved as if whipped by wind. The centurion stopped, his face stunned. He touched a neat round hole in his silver breastplate. The sword slipped from his hand and clattered to the floor. He dropped to his knees and fell face down on the floor.

Salome sat stiffly on the throne, her face blank, but her eyes betrayed panic.

Jair's hoarse voice chilled the room. "The Sicarii will be the vanguard of an invincible army that will conquer the world in my name." He stared at the crucifixion. "Before we build that army, we must kill a man who walks the shores of Galilee."

CHAPTER TWENTY-EIGHT

THE SYNCHROTRON AT LOS ALAMOS

Their final briefing was by a physicist who explained the "time event" that had been created by the facility.

"Earlier this morning, each of you got up and dressed for this meeting. What happened to that moment of *time*, in which you were dressing? To that first day of school when you were a child? That moment you first made love? Those events are still there, not just in your mind but in the physical world. In an experiment gone wrong—or terribly right, depending how you think of it—we accidentally accessed one of those past moments in time, in this case an event nearly two thousand years ago.

"The fact that time travel is theoretically possible is not questioned by the scientific community. Einstein opened the door by theorizing that the faster one went, time would slow down. The problem is how to do it *physically*. Science moves infinitely slower than the imagination. Science fiction writers have always been ahead of the scientists, proving ideas that eventually take root in physics. It took more than half a century to get Dick Tracy's radio-watch off a comic strip page and onto our wrists, and H. G. Wells envisioned a time machine over a hundred years ago, before Einstein postulated that time was relative to the observer.

"You cannot separate science from science fiction," the physicist said, with enthusiasm. "From Jules Verne and H. G. Wells right up to the current sci-fi books on the racks, you'll find fictional concepts scientists later turned into fact. You can trace the evolution of science from science fiction. I am, in fact, working on a book in which I demonstrate that the imagination of writers was almost always ahead of scientists in their laboratories, that the sci-fi books stimulated scientific discovery."

"We'll look for an e-book on the subject when it comes out, Professor. But right now we're a little short of *time*." Holt rolled his eyes at Bornstein and whispered in an aside, "Where the hell did you find him? At a Star Trek convention?"

The professor cleared his throat. "Now, within the past few years experiments in superluminal transmissions have sent light faster than what was once thought to be possible, so fast that the light exited a chamber *before* it entered. In other words, the future event—the exit of light from the chamber—occurred *before* the current event—the entrance of the light into the chamber. By analogy, if it had been a human being sent instead of a beam of light, the person would get to their destination *before* they left and could watch themselves make the journey. Speed up the light even further and you push time back further and further. The superluminal transmissions, in conjunction and the all-optical atomic clock that produces a quadrillion 'ticks' per second, demonstrate how 'elastic' time is.

"Now, human beings are not beams of light," the professor said. "To the science community, a human being can't be transported because we lack the power source to send an object that has physical mass. However, in the next few decades, that power may be available through quantum physics.

"Most current theories of time travel see travel as a process called teleportation. Speaking in the most simplistic terms, the theory is that there is a past, a present, and a future. You can think of it as a straight line, say along a length of wire. Information can travel down the wire if it is converted into electronic form, just as we scan information and transmit it by computer or fax.

"Obviously, we can convert a picture of a person into an electronic format and transmit it. It's done millions of times each day. In theory, there is no reason why we couldn't convert an entire physical body into electronic format and transmit it at superluminal speeds, sending the person's body back to a time before the person was even born. In a way, the superluminous method creates a wormhole, those mysterious objects in space that astronomers believe are doors to—"

"Professor, perhaps we could cut this down a bit," Holt interrupted.

"Yes, well, superluminous transmissions, teleporting, wormholes, alternate dimensions"—he frowned at Holt—"each of these theories have in common the fact that humans would have to be converted to an electronic format and transmitted at superluminal speeds. But there is a fundamental flaw with all of them." He shook his finger at them. "*You can't fax a soul*. We can transmit the physical body, but it may arrive as inanimate as a brick, without its thoughts, feelings, and ideas."

"So how do you send us back in time with our thoughts and bodies intact?" Conway asked. Like Holt, he was impatient to get the show on the road. He had the greatest role of his career to play.

"We're not going to send you back in time. *We will bring time to you*. The time event here at the synchrotron revealed that time is not in a straight line, it's not a parallel universe, not a trip through a wormhole—it's not a function of *travel* at all. To understand what happened, we need to consider the nature of the universe.

"The big bang theory is that the universe was created by a massive explosion with everything flung out from a central core. In a simplistic way, although what we call stars and galaxies were formed from gases created by the explosion, we can think of everything in the universe as chips off the same block. It's important to understand that while things may look different, *everything* in the universe has a common source.

"We know that nothing in the universe is actually solid. Everything, from an ant crawling on the window to a piece of steel and a supernova, is composed of minuscule particles we can loosely refer to as atomic and subatomic particles. Subatomic particles are in turn composed of infinitesimally smaller particles we'll call nanoparticles. Thus, the building blocks for everything from our thoughts to empty space and giant stars are composed of the same basic substance. The universe is not empty space with hard objects flying around but a vast cosmic soup made up of nanoparticles, some of which have clumped into bigger pieces until protons, atoms, ants, and planets are formed. These nanoparticles that make up the cosmic soup are held together by an energy force I'll call electromagnetism for want of a better word. And, despite the fact that we can't see the movement, the energy force keeps the particles in constant motion.

"Because information is stored on a computer disk in an analogous way to the cosmic soup, the universe can be thought of as a giant computer in which we—each of us, the ant on the window, the stars overhead—are all bytes of information on the same disk. We could click on the earth with a computer mouse if we had a big enough one and somewhere to stand." He chuckled to himself and wrote a note on his papers. "I'll use that phrase in my book."

"Professor—" Holt started.

Only David got the joke—a play off Archimedes' boast that he could lift the earth if he had somewhere to stand and a long enough lever. No doubt only scientists and computer nerds would appreciate the humor.

"Yes, we must move along expediently." The scientist cleared his throat again. "All the nanoparticles that make up the universe we are experiencing at this moment, the configurations that create us and the stars, are in constant change, continuously being reconfigured. We see this 'reconfiguration' as time passing. I lift my arm, the earth rotates around the sun, the galaxy spins—and the particles change configuration. 'Time passes' only because there is movement creating changes in the configuration—if the soup froze in place, the particles becoming inert, there would be no passage of time because there would no reconfiguration of the particles.

"Now, if time runs *forward* because the nanoparticles stay in motion, we can literally run time *backwards* by reconfiguring the particles into the same configuration they were at a past time. I walked into the building an hour ago. The particles were positioned in a different way than they are now. But they can be reconfigured to what they were an hour ago. It's not unlike accessing an erased file on a computer disk.

"What happened at this facility is being called RE for Reconfiguration Event. In the doughnut hole, a place infinitesimally less than a billionth of a nano part of the universe, reconfiguration of the particles occurred, opening the door to time. But the shepherd boy was not 'transported' from one time period to another. Instead, the physical world around him changed, reconfigured, into what it is today. He personally was not changed because the spot he was standing on, what we're calling a rabbit hole, was not reconfigured. The dirt in the doughnut area was tested and we discovered that an area about a dozen feet square has the same mineral-vegetable composition as the Israeli-Jordanian region where we believe the boy lived."

"Are you saying the entire universe was reconfigured?" David asked.

"No. As Einstein said, time is relative to the observer."

"Briefly explain how the synchrotron created the time event," Holt said.

"Well, the synchrotron is an attempt to discover the power that fuels the universe," he said. "By tapping into the magnetic field of the earth itself, and uniting it with the type of energy created by solar wind, phenomena created by sun flares, the scientists here hoped to duplicate the fierce electronic storms that occurred in outer space and provide a clue to the true source of the power called magnetism.

"The earth is surrounded by a vast magnetic field that is generated by the spinning of its molten core. The planet can be thought of as a giant electric generator, a machine producing unimaginable power. You might say that the synchrotron tapped into the very power source of the earth, a connection to the power that turns the earth and keeps the soup of the whole universe stirred. No one has ever tapped into such a well of power."

"Professor, I hate to hurry you, but let's wrap this up, these people have an appointment with destiny," Bornstein said.

"Yes, of course. I just want to add how much serendipity played a role in the matter. Besides the unexpected connection to a vast energy pool, the involvement of a particular time, place, and the shepherd boy was all purely accidental. The boy's lottery number simply came up."

"Can we see what the future will be?" Conway asked.

"We're not sure there is a future. We may be the future. Who knows, we may be the past. The concepts of 'past' and 'future' assume that there is a beginning and an end. But the universe has expanded from time immemorial. We may be the front end of the time expansion or somewhere in between. But we don't know."

"Can the machine be reprogrammed to do other time periods?" David asked. This was a critical question concerning David's participation.

Holt reacted to it to immediately. "Yes, I explained the dinosaur incident. Sorry, Professor, the lesson is over *now*. These folks are going to need rest before they begin their assignment."

After David, Marie, and Conway left the room, Holt put his hands in his pockets and pursed his lips. He met Bornstein's eye and then spoke directly to General Scott.

"I had a conference call an hour ago with the president. You apparently requested that Ben-Dor and the woman be eliminated from the mission. The answer is no. They stay in."

Scott grinned and saluted Holt with his cigar. "You can't kill a guy for trying, can you?"

Bornstein said, "Our psychological profile people have studied the videotapes we've made of all four. The boy and Marie have bonded. And Ben-Dor definitely has feelings for

Marie. He lost a wife to violence and Marie will be in jeopardy. Conway is keeping his distance from both, although he is courteous and professional."

"Good, since he may have to terminate them at some point," General Scott said.

"Let's hope that won't be necessary," Holt said.

"It wouldn't be if they were left out of the mission."

Holt shook his head. "You're beating a dead horse, General. The only way they would be left out is if they chose not to go. And that doesn't look likely."

Scott left the room, his jaws so tight he bit through his cigar. He had made a mistake in leaving management of the project to civilians. This was a military maneuver. Conway could be trusted because his records reflected that he had been a good soldier. Ben-Dor was a Jew. That made him even more dangerous than the woman.

General Scott was talking to MPs in the corridor near the door to David's room when David returned from training. The general greeted him as if it were a chance meeting, but David suspected the man had been waiting for him. Lying in wait for him was more accurate, he thought.

"Did you want to speak to me?" David was not in a mood to hide his dislike for Scott. The man's blood-and-guts approach reminded him of his own father.

"I wanted to let you know how pleased I am that you're a member of the team. Conway needs a pro backing him up and you couldn't come with a higher recommendation than an Israeli army uniform."

A complete moron, David thought. *He has to know that my tour of active duty with the army was less than meritorious.* He wondered why the man was patronizing him, but he was too tired to care. He started to walk around Scott but stopped as the general's words caught up with him.

"It's too bad that the Gauthier woman accepted. She's going to be a big problem for you and Conway. We picked her up on the streets of Marseilles, you know. She's a prostitute."

He turned back to face Scott. The smug arrogance on the man's face was a tempting target for a right cross, but he kept his fists at his side. He now had something to lose. The chance to save his wife.

"You know what, General? She couldn't be any bigger whore than the politicians who run the world and the military officers who flutter around them, feeding off their droppings."

Scott licked the end of a cigar with his tongue. "I guess we have different tastes in women. You were married to some Arab slut, weren't you?"

David laughed. He had seen the verbal punch coming and was ready for it. "Trying to get me kicked off the mission, General?"

He opened his door and paused before stepping in, and looked back at Scott. "You're not a very bright man. You must have kissed a lot of political ass to get those stars."

CHAPTER TWENTY-NINE

General Robert E. Lee Scott didn't let David's accusation faze him. The product of a military family, he considered anyone not in uniform as someone to be tolerated or eliminated. His father had been career military, a master sergeant who saw action in both World War II and Korea.

He had enlisted early in the Vietnam War as a private and won a Purple Heart, Bronze Star, and an officer's commission. By the time of the Gulf War, he was a bird colonel and on the White House staff. He went to the Gulf as an on-site advisor to the chairman of the House Military Appropriations Committee and was an active advocate of making the Gulf campaign a military hardware trade show in which America demonstrated and tested its weapons on Iraqi targets. He got his first star upon returning from the Gulf. His second star had come only recently. During the intervening years, he had worked up a good rapport on Capitol Hill with congressmen and senators who favored the pork barrel military budget.

He was not considered a particularly bright man, except perhaps by his wife. But he had that pit bull mentality that made him invaluable when going for the jugular was appropriate. Unfortunately, his only plan of action in almost any situation was to rip out someone's throat. While this made him popular at Washington cocktail parties with the guns-and-guts crowd, he was less favored by those who thought diplomacy or something less than a nuclear firestorm might be appropriate in most situations.

For the past few years, he had been degrading mentally. His wife had died several years before. They had no children. She had been his only respite from living a military life twenty-four hours a day. With her gone, he had moved into officer's quarters where he ate, lived, and breathed the army.

His aide, a major, had begun to notice that the general had moments of memory loss and sometimes his thinking was a bit fuzzy. He suspected that the meat, bread, and potatoes diet the general had spent his entire life on had plugged his arteries and that the man just was not getting enough oxygen to his brain to keep him sharp. Three months ago, when he suggested to the general that his arteries might be plugged, General Scott had unholstered his military-issue pistol and threatened to plug his aide's arteries for good.

The subject had not come up again.

Conway was stretched out on the floor in his room and in a yoga position when he heard a knock on his door. He opened the door and let General Scott in. The general was carrying a paper sack.

"Sorry to disturb you," General Scott said. "Blast-off is in a couple hours and I needed to talk to you alone."

"Have a seat."

"No, I'll make this quick so you can rest. I know what a hell of a position you've been put in. You're not just the only pro on the mission, you're the only one that can be trusted. We've teamed you with a Jew and a whore and we're sending you up against a couple professional killers with both hands tied behind you."

Conway smiled politely. He wondered what the hell the general was getting at.

"You heard Bornstein's comments about the effect on the world if the secret of Jesus is revealed," Scott said. "You and I know there's only one answer to that. Jesus is the Son of God. But you're going back with a Jew and a woman who has rejected religion. You can bet your sweet ass that if they come back from this mission, they'll spread lies about him that would rip apart the free world."

"What do you mean by 'if they come back'?"

General Scott took a goatskin waterbag out of the paper sack. The waterbag was a duplicate to the one Conway had been issued to carry back with him to the ancient world. The general handed Conway the waterbag.

"Switch this for the one you have."

Conway squeezed the bag. It was filled with water, but he could feel something hard inside. "What's inside?" he asked, even though he was sure he knew.

"An equalizer."

"Do Holt and Bornstein know about this?"

"It's been authorized at the highest levels," General Scott said. "The highest levels."

CHAPTER THIRTY

They were taken to the center of the synchrotron, to the circular dirt patch where Isie had materialized. The scientists at the synchrotron reasoned that duplicating Isie's exact location would send them back to his time. When Isie and a patch of dirt had come forward, it replaced the dirt and brush that had been in the doughnut hole. The assumption was that the boy and his dirt patch had traded places with the modern spot. Everyone hoped the assumption was correct.

The only clothes they had were the ones of handwoven cloth that they were wearing. In their pockets were a few small gold and silver coins; larger gold coins were sewn into the lining of their clothes. For underclothes, each wore a loincloth. Atop that, they had a tunic, a garment that Conway hated because it made him feel he was wearing a dress. Each had a robe. Conway's was a Roman toga, a heavy white woolen robe that enveloped the whole person. It was cut in a semicircular fashion, and consisted of cloth five meters long by four wide. Of much finer material than the coarse robes of servants and farmers, it was graceful and dignified in appearance. Conway had spent a couple of frustrating hours learning how to fold it around his body. Since only Romans were permitted to wear a toga, the robes worn by David, Marie, and the boy were all the same: coarse woolens resembling blankets. Commoners used their robes as blankets at night and coats during the day.

They were all outfitted with a waterbag, a three-day supply of stone-ground flour, strips of dry salted beef, a pouch of salt, and flint and hard iron to start fires with. Flour, water, and salt would be combined to make a hard unleavened bread that would be laid on fire coals to cook.

David and Conway had each been issued two daggers and a short sword. David's sword had to be kept hidden because Rome forbade Jews to possess weapons. A leather sheath was rigged up so he could carry the sword on his back, inside his clothes, and draw it from behind his neck in an emergency. One dagger was kept in a sheath hung around the waist, the other concealed under their robes. Marie had been offered a small dagger to hide in her clothes but she refused it.

Now came the frightening part: a journey into the unknown.

"We can't guarantee anything," the director of the facility told them. "Try not to move around too much or touch anyone else. You might end up with someone else's nose or a shirt button for an eyeball.

"Just joking," he said, when he saw the expressions on their face. "Obviously the boy put up quite a struggle and had a frightened sheep in his arms, and they both came through intact. But nonetheless, try to stay still. Who knows what will happen? There will be a lot of wind, at this end and the other."

The man had the personality of a funeral director, David thought, as he positioned himself next to Marie, with Isie on the other side of her. She did not appear frightened. Rather, she seemed resolved. Her decision to come had lifted a weight from her shoulders. But what was she resolved to? he wondered.

Conway could not hide his glee. He grinned at David, at the boy, anyone who came within his range. Things could not be more perfect for him as an actor—and he did not even have script control.

David and Marie exchanged smiles. "I'll see you . . . in a couple thousand years," he said.

Isie had taken a position on the other side of Marie, his

sling in hand, ready to defend her even against an enemy he couldn't see. She put her arms around him and hugged him. "Everything will be all right, Isaiah. The journey will last only for a blink of an eye and then you will be home."

The area was cleared of people, all except the four guinea pigs, looking a little awkward, all feeling a little nervous except the grinning Conway—two men, a woman, and a boy in a barren field marred by the ruts of chariot wheels and the blood of terrorists.

No sounds, no shouted warnings told them that the synchrotron had been activated and the process of returning to the past by restructuring the atoms of the present had begun. The clue was a breeze, mild at first, then picking up momentum, blowing faster and harder and kicking up sand until they were choking from the whirlwind.

David fought panic as a dark maelstrom engulfed them. He shot one last glance at Marie and Isaiah, fearful for their safety.

The panic almost instantly melted into a mellow ecstasy, like the hot flash of an orgasm. He felt his body exploding into thousands of tiny stars and the stars exploding into thousands of more pieces, raining through the universe all the way to eternity.

There were millions, billions of pieces, yet each piece was all of him . . .

STAND STILL, YOU EVER MOVING SPHERES
OF HEAVEN,
THAT TIME MAY CEASE AND MIDNIGHT
NEVER COME.
—*Christopher Marlowe,* Doctor Faustus

THE HOLY LAND

CHAPTER THIRTY-ONE

David fell into a smothering funnel, a fall to Doom off the end of the earth, a dark burning wind wrapping around him like the inferno of a black hole. Light shone at the end and the black fires began to melt as all the millions of him flew back together as if attracted by the magnetic glue of his soul. His body was stunned-dead. A gasp of breath sent a hot burst of life shooting through him like a lightning bolt, igniting a billion nerve ends, heart pounding, blood surging through his veins, carrying a tidal wave of consciousness into his brain. He swayed dizzily from the rush of blood and put up his hands to block the eye-aching glare that had melted the black fires.

The glare became the light of a bright day. Trembling fingers touched his numb face, feeling his cheeks, his nose; he stared at his fingers, ten of them, and looked down at his legs, at the toes sticking out of his sandals—he was whole!

It was daytime. He was in a meadow of wild grass surrounded by a stand of cypress trees on a gentle tapering hill.

Marie swayed beside him and he steadied her. "Are you all right?"

"Yes . . . a little dizzy. Where's Isie?"

The boy was a few feet behind them, sitting on the ground, staring about the strange terrain with mouth agape, dazed by the "magic." Conway was nearby, on his feet.

They were no longer at the synchrotron, no longer in the New Mexico desert, but where exactly had they landed? And when? The grass around them lay flat, beaten down by the winds that had heralded their arrival.

Conway flexed his fingers and lifted his feet up and down, getting circulation going. "It worked. We're here, but where the hell is here?"

Through the foliage David could see hills to the west and he hurried to higher ground for a better look. The others came up beside him as he stared, almost in disbelief, at the hills in the distance.

"The Golan Heights," Marie whispered, emotion gripping her voice. "The Holy Land." Her lips trembled.

A wave of excitement hit David. He felt young and foolish, ready to laugh, on the verge of tears. The ancient world! My God, it had really worked. They had stepped through a hole in Time itself. He knew how Columbus must have felt when he sighted land, or the feeling generated by that first step on the moon.

He stared up at the sun, shading his eyes. "Probably ten or eleven in the morning. Now all we have to figure out is what year it is."

Lush green plains fanned between them and the Golan Heights. Too green, David thought. "This area is dry and barren in our own time. I hope we don't cross the hills and find dinosaurs stomping around a swamp where the Sea of Galilee is supposed to be."

"Not likely." Conway pointed east where a brown trail stretched the length of the valley. A long line of donkeys, mules, and camels, loaded with goods, moved along the trail. A caravan, hundreds of people and beasts, stretched back half a mile or more.

"It's big, bigger than any caravan I've seen in the Middle East," David said.

Caravans in the modern Middle East supplied only villages too remote to be reached by truck, and typically were small, a fraction the size of the procession spread out below. He wished he had a pair of binoculars to pick out more details.

"What do you think, Marie?" She was the mission's expert on lifestyles in the first century.

"From what I can tell, there's a variety of clothing, a variety of races. I see clothes that look like those worn by Jews, Egyptians, Persians, Mesopotamians. The robes are more or less the same, but the headgear varies. I'll know more when I can see their jewelry and hear them speak. Look! Toward the rear—those are sedan chairs."

"The ancient limousines of the rich."

"Not so ancient," Marie said. "Sedan chairs were in common use, even in the early part of the twentieth century. The clothing isn't going to tell us anything, either. Clothing changed very little from a thousand years before Christ to a thousand years after."

David met Conway's eye. "The only way we're going to find out is to go down there and ask. Hopefully not too bluntly." Conway had been appointed leader of the mission and David committed himself to following Conway's orders—so long as he believed in them. The last condition was solely his own.

Isie spoke to Marie in Aramaic.

"Isie says there's a water hole a couple hours down the trail. He remembers being there once, with his father. Caravans stop there for the night."

"Good." Conway shifted the goatskin waterbag hanging from a strap over his shoulder. "We'll join the caravan while it's on the move so there'll be less opportunity to ask questions. The water hole and the caravan will give us a chance to practice our act for Bethsaida."

Conway and Isie led the way down the hill. The boy picked up a gnarled branch to use as a staff and kept his leather sling dangling in the other hand.

"Off to slay a giant," Marie said, "as another young David did." She glanced at David, then quickly turned away.

"Look!" Conway pointed at the caravan when they got closer. "The caravan looks as if it rolled off a movie set. Sedan chairs carried by slaves, girls walking alongside fanning fat merchants. It's history and we're witnessing it."

"We're living it," Marie said. "The men with the long, braided beards, they're the ones I said might be Mesopotamians, people once called Babylonians. They have only a few camels, so the merchandise must be very valuable, probably fine jewelry and exotic perfumes. They were the Cartiers of the ancient world. They are taking trading goods across Palestine to be shipped to Rome. They'll make the return trip with new goods. It's like long-haul truckers. They drop off one load and pick up another, but in the ancient world the traders themselves usually went with the merchandise."

"Can you give us a date in history?"

"No, all of these races were around for a long time, not always as an empire but as a distinctive people. The men with the mules loaded with pottery might be Greeks. The Greeks were famous for fine vases and exotic sculpture. The men behind them in purple robes and camels loaded with furs could be Phoenicians. Phoenicia is north of here, so they're probably on their way home after trading. Their most famous export was Tyrian purple, a dye in great demand in the ancient world. The furs may have come from Africa."

Conway pointed at a group of white-robed men leading camels. "They look like modern Bedouins."

Marie spoke in Aramaic to Isie before replying. "They're Nabataeans from the desert kingdom to the south. Before the Romans defeated them, the kingdom was fabulously rich from tribute levied on caravans flowing east and west. Now the Romans collect the toll."

"I see Jews," David said. The tunics and cloaks of the Jews were little different from what most of the other traders wore, but the curly temple locks of the men set them apart. Another distinguishing feature were the big, buckskin-colored donkeys carrying their goods. Other caravaners used camels, mules, and horses. The yellowish donkeys seemed to be reserved for Jews.

Conway glanced back and spoke softly. "We have a problem."

A group of men had split off from the caravan and were

moving to intercept them. Each man carried a javelin, a shield, and had a short sword strapped to their side. They wore metal helmets and leather breastplates.

"Maybe they're caravan guards," David said.

Marie shook her head. "They're Roman soldiers. You can tell by the bronze helmets and the eagle standard."

David mentally compared the group marching toward them with the pictures of Roman soldiers they had been shown during the history lecture at the synchrotron. The soldiers carried two spears, a light one held in hand and a heavier one strapped to their back. The light spear was thrown into the enemy's shield, wedging there, knocking the opposing soldier off balance while the legionnaire came in and finished him off with the short sword. If the light spear didn't work, the heavier spear was used for infighting.

Their shields were oblong, three or four feet high, made of wood and covered with a thin layer of metal, probably bronze since the men were common soldiers. Romans didn't wear pants, considering such dress suitable for barbarians. Each soldier wore a heavy tunic that fell halfway between the hip and the knee, with a "shirt" of light mail, again probably bronze rather than iron, nearly completely covering the tunic. Their sandals were similar to Conway's, leather straps rising from a leather sole and crisscrossing halfway up to the knee, but the leather was thicker and rougher than the Roman patrician variety made for Conway.

The group marching toward them was a rugged, tough-looking lot, not the glittering legionnaires of the army of Cecil B. DeMille. For the first time it came home to David that they were in a cruel and barbaric era, a time of no human rights, when might was right.

Conway took a deep breath and quickened his pace, boldly approaching the file of soldiers. David started to catch up, but slowed when Marie called to him.

"You're out of character. You're a lowly Jew, a household servant. You can't go strutting up to soldiers of the master race as if you were an equal."

"You're right." He gritted his teeth, but forced himself to smile as humbly as he could. "It's hard to be a free man and think like a slave."

She started to say something, but it was lost as the leader of the soldiers cracked a command. The soldiers smartly formed two ranks with their commander in front, javelins at the ready.

David brushed the hilt of the sword hidden under his cloak. Conway had better do some fast talking, he thought. They were outnumbered and outgunned; they wouldn't stand a chance if it came to a fight. "They seem worried about our little band. We couldn't pose much of a threat."

"We might be decoys for a larger force or villagers fleeing a plague and carrying the sickness with them."

Conway raised his arm in a Roman salute and hailed the commander in Latin.

As he watched Conway conversing with the Roman commander, David tried to look appropriately subservient, but his hand kept touching the hidden sword. "How's he doing?" he asked Marie.

"He's telling them we were attacked by bandits. The commander is of low rank, a leader of ten, something like a corporal in a modern army."

This was the first time Isie had seen a Roman in the flesh. They were famed for their battle prowess and cruelty and he had been raised to fear the very name. He took a protective stance next to Marie, his sling loaded with a stone.

The soldiers seemed to relax as Conway talked, and Marie's voice lost its anxious edge. "They're impressed. Conway's Latin is better than theirs. It isn't their native tongue. I think they're mercenaries from northern Greece. They were stationed in Damascus and are being transferred to the household guard of Pontius Pilate in Caesarea." She glanced at David. "We obviously have the right time period."

The commander said something to Conway that caused the soldiers to laugh.

"They're excited about passing through Bethsaida," Marie said. "The city has a reputation of being a den of iniquity.

Conway has the commander intimidated with his Roman patrician act."

David looked sideways at Isie. He and Conway had had some fear that the boy would turn them in as "demons" the first chance he had. The boy's protective attitude toward Marie pretty well settled the issue.

Conway subtly handed the commander something and from the pleased smile that spread across the Roman's face, something more valuable than friendship had passed hands.

They joined the caravan, moving into line behind the legionnaires with Conway walking beside the commander. David got another jolt of adrenaline as he walked in the caravan. He could see Marie shared his excitement. And Isie, too. The boy gawked at the caravaners with their colorful array of clothing and merchandise.

Conway dropped back to David. "We made it over the first hump, but these soldiers are peasants. There's a Roman trader at the rear of the caravan. I'm going to talk to the man, see if I pass muster with a real Roman."

David glanced back to check on Conway's movement down the caravan line and caught the eye of a man leading a donkey, a Jew about David's age, with shoulder-length black hair, beard, and long locks falling over his temple area and down the sides of his face. He wore a coarse brown woolen cloak over a gray linen tunic, a simple piece of camel-hair rope looped in front for a belt, and hobnailed sandals similar to the ones David wore. A half dozen other young Jewish men were to the rear of the man, each leading a donkey loaded high and wide with straw.

David spoke to him in Hebrew. *"Shalom."*

"Shalom."

David slowed his pace to drop back beside the man. "To where do you travel with your straw?"

"To the marketplace in Bethsaida." He spoke cautiously, stiffly.

"This is my first trip to the land of my fathers," David said. "I am a Jew."

The man eyed David's short hair and clean-shaven face

and glanced at the clean-shaven Roman soldiers. "Perhaps you are a Roman Jew," he murmured with great innocence.

"My mother was taken from Jerusalem when I was a baby and made a slave in a household in Gallaecia. My name is David Ben-Dor."

"Yoseph Ben Esau." The name was given begrudgingly. A man behind Yoseph said something in Aramaic and David just caught the gist of it. The man wanted to know what David was saying. David realized he had lucked out that Yoseph spoke Hebrew.

Marie suddenly broke into the conversation, greeting the men in Aramaic and speaking to Yoseph in Hebrew so David could follow the conversation. "We are wandering Jews whose steps have taken us to faraway places." She gave Yoseph a big smile. "Our feet have finally brought us to the Promised Land. Is it true that all the streets in Israel are paved in gold, that milk and honey flows in the Jordan, and that the men are the strongest and bravest in the world?"

Yoseph laughed. "Woman, you have been told only the truth!"

However suspect David was, the expression on Yoseph's face left no doubt that Marie—Mariam—was welcome to the Promised Land.

Isie dropped back and happily rambled away in Aramaic to the men behind Yoseph. David was more than a little concerned when he looked at Marie, but she gave him a reassuring smile. "Isie's only asking where the men have traveled."

When Conway returned, David was about to introduce him to Yoseph but Marie shot him a warning glance. It would be out of character for a member of the master race to socialize with a Jewish peasant.

David and Conway moved ahead of Yoseph's group to talk.

"It's the first of Nisan," David said. "That's close to the first day of April by our calendar. Jesus was crucified on the fourteenth. That means we have thirteen days to work with."

"Considering how slow this world moves, that doesn't give us much time to find the Zayyad brothers. It'll take almost two days just to walk to Bethsaida and Bethsaida's a long ways from Jerusalem." He looked back to where Marie and Yoseph were chatting behind them like old friends. "Who's he?"

"His name's Yoseph. He and his friends are farmers on their way to Bethsaida to market straw. They've agreed to sell us one of their spare donkeys when we get to the water hole. We can barter with other caravaners there for whatever else we need."

"Being accepted by the straw sellers will keep down the suspicion of others. I also made a contact. Quintus, the Roman trader I went back to see, has a villa in Bethsaida. He's invited me to be his guest." Conway chuckled. "He offered stable room for my animals and servants. He's already been a good source of gossip about Bethsaida and Salome."

Conway looked back again. "Your new friends don't strike me as farmers. They walk loose-kneed like fighting men."

Dark riders high on a ridge spied down on the caravan. Only one man had his face uncovered, and he scanned the caravan with darting rodent eyes.

Amir Zayyad had been sent by Jair to watch one area while Jair watched another. He had seen the four people join the caravan. It was too far away to see faces, but one figure seemed familiar to him. And it made sense that they would send David Ben-Dor.

CHAPTER THIRTY-TWO

David and Marie watched a long line of men and beasts pouring into the oasis while Conway went off with the Roman commander to select a campsite. Strings of caravan animals moved into the oasis like diesel rigs pulling into a truck stop: ivory from Africa tied to the sides of one-humped Arabian camels, minty balm from Jericho filling woven baskets strapped to yellow donkeys, fragrant spices from faraway India carried in sacks piled on the backs of Bactrian camels, the shorter, hairier, two-humped cousin to the Arabian beast.

"That's papyrus from the Nile in those bundles." She pointed to bales carried on a train of camels. "The men leading the camels are Egyptians. You can tell by their jewelry."

"They're light complexioned," David said.

"They're pure Egyptian. Modern Egyptians are a product of the successive Arab and Turkish conquests."

Conway came up behind them. "You two are gawking like farmers on their first trip to the city."

"I know how Galileo felt when he looked through his first telescope and saw heaven," David said. They had chosen English to communicate among themselves. Its sound was no stranger than the babel of other languages bouncing around the oasis like radio stations battling for airtime. "Did you find a campsite?"

Conway grinned. "The best. Right next to the water's edge where it'll be coolest. Other people had already staked a claim, but the Roman soldiers cleared out a space for us and Quintus."

"That'll make us popular," David said.

"It'll make us feared. This is a world where only might is right."

"Oh . . . no."

David followed Marie's startled gaze.

A line of men, women, and children chained together like animals were marched into the camp. Slaves. A cargo of human misery. Brutish slave masters with coiled whips flanked the line. At the head of the procession, a fleshy, handsome young man lounged on a litter carried on the shoulders of husky slaves.

"Quintus," Conway said. "I'm dining with him tonight. He offered to let my servants share the sop left over from dinner, but I suspect you'd rather fix your own."

"Where did he get them?" David couldn't keep the chill from his voice.

"They're booty captured in the war the Romans are waging against Parthia, an empire to the east, roughly where Iraq and Iran are. Quintus bought them from field commanders. He's a slave trader. From what I gather, one of the wealthiest Romans living in Bethsaida."

A disturbance broke out in the slave lines as a woman cried out in pain. The woman was pregnant. Other slave women gathered around her as she began giving birth on the ground. The moment the baby's cry was heard, the still-bloody baby was taken from the woman and given to another slave woman, as the slave woman who gave birth lay crying on the ground, wailing for her baby.

"What's going on?" Conway asked.

"They're giving the baby to another woman so the birth mother won't get attached to it," Marie's voice trembled. "The baby will be sold separately from the mother. If it lives."

Quintus approached them, hailing Conway. Preceding him

was a small boy on a leash attached to a collar around his neck. The boy was dressed in animal fur. In the costume, he looked like a monkey with a babyish little human face.

"A pet," Marie whispered, "a pet slave. Rich Romans keep them for amusement. And sometimes as sex toys."

Quintus' eyes stayed on Conway as he approached. He never gave any indication that there were two other human beings, *servants*, standing next to Conway.

"Marcus, my friend, look at that one." Quintus pointed to a young girl of about ten or eleven. "In another year or two, she will be ripe. I love watching them at this age, as their breasts are about to form and they start to get juicy between their legs. Unfortunately, I won't be the first to pick the fruit because she'll be shipped to the slave market at Delos along with the rest, but I'll put a good price on her. Men will pay extra for being able to bed her at that precise moment that she becomes a woman."

Conway followed along with Quintus as the Roman proudly pointed out other slave attributes.

"Look at that one's muscles. Not a big man, but short and powerful, the kind that are hard to fight. He'll go to the arena for training as a gladiator. The one with only one hand—a thief at some time in his life, but amazingly he can write both Latin and the Parthanian language. He was a scribe for a Parthian governor. He'll bring a good price from a merchant. . . ."

David and Marie gathered up their packs as well as Conway's.

"He left his stuff for us to carry. He seems to be adjusting nicely to his role," David said.

"He's a good actor."

"Maybe."

Marie's features were troubled.

"You okay?" he asked.

"I was thinking about that little girl and the baby. This is a brutal age. Romans are no more cruel than other people, in some ways they're much more civilized, but slaves are property, chattels, a work animal no different than an ox or a mule. The owner has absolute power over them, even life and death."

"If they mean money, they will probably make sure they stay reasonably healthy."

"Reasonable people will. But in any society, there are a certain percentage of people who are crazy, perverted, or both. In modern Russia when executions were done by volunteer citizens, people lined up for the opportunity to legally kill someone. Look what happened in Germany during the Nazi era. Serial killers, men preying on women and children in ordinary times, leaving their mutilated bodies along roadsides, suddenly were able to rise to power when the decision was made to kill millions. What worries me, David, when I look at that little girl, is that some crazy pervert may buy her. And she will be completely helpless because he will be able to do anything he wants to her. And the baby? Could it end up in one of the troupes of performers, raised from childhood to perform every imaginable sex act on each other and on the people watching their performance? The children—"

She stopped as David swung around to stare back at the slaves. She grabbed his arm and pulled him back around.

"I shouldn't be saying these things," she said. "We have roles to play and a mission to accomplish. We're here to save the world, not a little girl and a baby. They're expendable." She could not keep the bitterness from her voice.

"Ho! Friends." Yoseph hurried to them carrying a tangle of ropes, poles, and hopsack. He dropped the bundle at David's feet. "I have come to help Mariam bargain for goods. I am the best haggler in all the land."

David nudged the bundle with his toe. "What's this?"

"A tent my companions can spare. I have already haggled a very nice price for you." Yoseph took Marie's arm and grinned at David. "You can put up the tent while I take Mariam around the camp. Later, I will show you the fine donkey I have haggled for you!"

David frowned down at the almost incomprehensible mess of poles, ropes, and cloth. Conway was off hobnobbing with a rich Roman, Marie was waltzing around the camp with a flirtatious young Jewish stud, and Isie was running around satisfying his boyish curiosity. That left him to do the dirty work. What bothered him most was that he was a highly trained engineer and had more technical knowledge than *anyone in the world*, but he didn't have the faintest idea as to how the ropes, cloth, and poles made into a tent.

Dinner was a mixture of rice, leeks, and chunks of lamb that Marie cooked in a bronze pot over a fire built in front of the tent David finally managed to erect a few feet from the water's edge. Yoseph gave them a loaf of unleavened dough, which Marie covered with fire coals to bake into bread.

"The bread's delicious," David told her, after he helped himself to a piece of it. "It has a strange taste, a little gamy like venison."

"The fire ash is dried camel dung."

"Uh, sorry I asked."

He tried to help her prepare dinner but she shooed him off. "This is woman's work, remember. It wouldn't be in character. Tend to the donkey Yoseph sold us."

Donkeys had not changed in two thousand years.

Yoseph and his friends howled with laughter as David nearly lost a finger to the donkey's teeth and barely missed having his head kicked off. Finally, Yoseph came over and gave him a hand.

"Maybe you should stick to women's work and counting the coins of your Roman master," he said, good-naturedly.

"You sold us a wild ass!"

Yoseph shrugged. "Of course."

"And that tent has holes in it big enough to stick your head through!"

"That small! I was misinformed. I must charge you more!"

David left the donkey tied to a palm tree and went looking for more dried camel dung for the supper fire. Everything burnable anywhere near the oasis had long since gone into campfires and he had to walk several minutes back on the caravan trail before he found droppings dry enough to burn. He filled a square of cloth with the stuff and returned to camp.

Marie was not at the tent and he went to Yoseph's campsite to see if the hay farmer had seen her. He was approaching Yoseph's tent when he heard laughter and a second later Marie came out of Yoseph's tent with Yoseph behind her, both of them laughing and flushed. Her features instantly fell to concern at the look on David's face. "I came to borrow onions from Yoseph. We went into his tent to get some and found a gopher raiding the food."

"That's your business." He was angry at himself for the possessive feeling he was having toward Marie. And for his stupid suspicions about her ever since Scott told him that she was a prostitute. He turned on his heel and walked away, foolish at his own stupid reaction to the innocent situation.

She caught up with him before they reached their tent. "What's the matter? What do you think I was doing back there?"

"It's none of my business."

"Don't do that, I want your trust and respect. If you don't want me here, I can return to the meadow and wait to be taken back!"

"No, Marie . . . I'm sorry." He took her arm. "I'm the one who should adjust best to this culture and I find myself stumbling. Let's get dinner going. Everyone's looking. They think I'm a henpecked husband."

Conway came by their camp only briefly before returning to the large tent of Quintus. As night was falling Isie gulped down his dinner and shot off to watch a wrestling match between an Assyrian caravaner and a camel.

"It's a bloodless match," Marie told David as she gave Isie coppers for his admission. "Isie says the camel is the Assyrian's best friend."

David and Marie sat across from each other and sipped wine from clay bowls with the last of the campfire's glowing embers between them. The heavy red wine pressed from the grapes of Galilee had to be diluted with spring water.

"You've adapted well to the living conditions," David said.

She poked the coals with a stick. "Don't forget, I lived for a year in a village among people who hadn't changed their lifestyle since the time of Christ. You were pretty efficient yourself, starting that fire without matches."

He did not feel entirely comfortable with her, through no fault of hers. He was still angry at himself for his reaction when she came out of Yoseph's tent. Something in him stirred that had been long dead. He felt guilty about his feelings toward her, a feeling that he was betraying the memory of his wife. And also perplexed at how someone as caring and full of heart as Marie could be a prostitute. He didn't think Scott would have lied about something that could be disproved with a single question to Marie, but the accusation just didn't fit with the soft innocence she projected. There were several times she had caught him sneaking looks at her. Did she suspect that he knew?

"I learned to use a flint in the desert. Matches are too quirky to rely on. I wish I had learned something about donkeys." He stopped relying on matches when he had gone out into the desert to avoid capture by the police. He wondered what Marie had been told about him. Did Scott tell her he was a loose cannon? That he might turn on them in a murderous rage, as he once turned on the project he had created?

She smiled softly and he felt some of the tightness leave him.

"Yoseph likes you. He says you are a stupid but honest man, despite the fact you count the gold of a Roman."

"That's equivalent to fraternizing with the enemy to Jews. He obviously took a liking to you." David smiled shyly. "I guess I got kind of possessive back there."

She blushed. It surprised him. "It's all right." She looked at him over the rim of her cup. "It's nice to have someone who's concerned about me. Other than Isie, of course."

A whip cracked at the slave camp, followed by the cry of a woman. The whip cracked again and the cry became a whimper. The wine bowl shook in Marie's hand.

David set the bowl aside and took her arm and helped her up. "Come on. Let's take a walk."

They strolled along the water's edge; a warm breeze rustled the palms and drew ripples in the moonlight shining on the dark waters. She leaned against a palm tree and stared up at the night sky while he knelt by the pond and tossed pebbles into the water.

Palm fronds rustled from a gush of wind. The breeze felt good, cleansing. "I love an oasis," he said. "They're tranquil islands in a sea of light and air. Bedouins equate them with heaven. I suppose it's because Bedouins don't have much—a dinner fire and a tent at night, a few animals to graze. We spend our entire lives gathering things, houses and cars and clothing and money to keep the houses and cars and things. The Bedouin can't do that, he's restricted to whatever meager possessions he can load onto the back of his camel. That leaves nothing between him and God."

The minty fragrance of balm drifted on the breeze.

"It's a cruel world," he said. "Seeing those slaves, realizing that the Roman soldiers would have cut us down if it suited their whim this morning, it just drives home Holt's remarks about barbarians with atomic weapons. We have to stop enjoying the scenery and begin our search for the Zayyad brothers."

"There's something else, isn't there, David? I sense something in your voice, something *personal*, when you talk about the Zayyads. I know you're the person who can identify them. But was there something else between you?"

"It's very personal. The Zayyads are a Ben-Dor problem and a Jewish problem. I'm a Ben-Dor and a Jew. I stood beside my father when he shot their father between the eyes."

"My God."

"But you have to understand who we're dealing with. The Zayyads aren't religious fanatics. Other than being born Islamic, I don't know if they even have any serious religious beliefs. They're psychopaths, insane killers, who, had they been born in other cultures, would have thrown babies into ovens in Nazi Germany, chopped up children in Rwanda, blown up abortion clinics in Georgia. They're not driven by pious religious beliefs but single-minded hate. If they didn't hate Jews, they would find something else to hate. What my father did directed the hate. But whatever my father did doesn't justify the Zayyads leaving bloody footsteps around the world."

"Of course not." She quickly changed the subject. "Now that Conway has found one of his, uh, own class, I suppose you and I will end up trying to find a lead to Jesus in the marketplace by ourselves."

"That would suit me." He stared at the dark waters. "They were both there that night."

"Who?"

"The Zayyad brothers. They watched their father die." He had not told anyone, not even his mother, what happened that night, and it came out now. "I was fifteen." Fifteen and if not an executioner, an accessory to one. "They paid us back, picking off the settlers one by one. They got my father a few years ago, a bullet between his eyes, the mark of the vendetta."

"But they never got you."

"Not yet." He grinned without humor. "Maybe because I moved around a lot, to Tel Aviv, Galilee, to—to the Negev. I was always in motion." He needed to talk, to unburden something he had carried around for years. "Did they tell you anything about me back in New Mexico? Did they tell you I froze when a suicide bomber ran into a crowd when I was on guard duty?"

She shook her head.

"It wasn't the bomber that made me freeze. It was the Zayyad brothers. When I heard the commotion, I turned and saw them. They were standing on a street corner across the street, with a group of people waiting to cross. I—I froze. I was petrified, as if I had turned and come face-to-face with ghosts."

"They were there, with the bomber?"

"I suppose so. Probably there as moral support for the poor kid who had explosives strapped around his waist. When the commotion broke out around me, I just stood there, staring at the two ghosts from my past. I didn't even see the kid. I was . . . I don't know what. Mesmerized, I guess."

He poked sand for a moment with the stem of a palm frond.

"I'm glad I was selected for this mission," David said. "But I wish it involved someone other than the Zayyad brothers. I know I should hate them, they're cold-blooded terrorists, killers who would kill those around them if they didn't have someone else to hate, but I can't help but remember what happened to their father. And my own father. I always thought my father was the toughest, bravest person in the world. Now I realize he was a very frightened man, so scared of another Holocaust he would do anything to prevent it. In a strange way he was better able to die for Israel than live for it." He shook his head. "It's ironic. My father always resented the fact that I never fought a war for Israel, and now I'm going to fight one he started."

She looked off into the darkness. "At fifteen, you were just a kid. I was twelve the day my life became a nightmare. They got to us young, didn't they?"

"They?"

"Whoever's pulling the strings. I don't mean to sound bitter, it's just that . . . that some of us seem to take a wrong turn and never get back on the right path again. If my parents had been more understanding about the stigmata instead of getting swept up in the hysteria . . ." Emotion choking her, she stood up and leaned back against a palm tree and stared up at the starry night.

"The stigmata?"

"When I was twelve, my hands bled like the Crucifixion wounds of Christ. After that, I belonged to the Church. I was a nun, before—I—" She didn't finish and abruptly got to her feet and walked back to the tent.

He stood after her, puzzled by his feelings for her, mystified by her revelations. He suddenly felt sad and lonely. The stigmata. He had heard of it happening to people, religious nuts at Passover, but it was unimaginable that it would happen to a lovely young woman like Marie.

Twelve years old. He wondered what it was like to have your life suddenly take an odd and bitter detour at that young an age. Children die at twelve and younger, or get hideous diseases that affect them the rest of their life.

The revelation deepened the mystery of Marie to him. Ever since the day she walked out of the meeting at the scientific facility, announcing she wasn't going on the mission, he had had the feeling that she bore some special knowledge. Was the fact that she had suffered the stigmata merely coincidental on this mission to save Christ? He shook off the thought and tossed another stone in the water.

"When I die," he murmured to the night, "I want my ashes scattered in an oasis."

CHAPTER THIRTY-THREE

Conway and the slave trader, Quintus, lounged on couches and picked food from an assortment of dishes that were placed on a low table between the two couches.

Using his training from the preparation he underwent for his role, Conway had remembered to approach the couch from the rear. He started to stretch out on it when a servant bent to take off his sandals. He paused before putting his feet up, grateful that he had not made a social mistake. Once on the couch, he lay on his left side, facing the table, his left elbow supported by a cushion, imitating Quintus, who faced him on the other side of the table.

He was given a bowl of water to rinse his hands, then wiped them on a warm towel the servant provided, thinking this was at least a custom he found familiar from having eaten in Asian restaurants.

He didn't, however, find the reclining position a comfortable one for eating. What made it manageable to the Romans is that the food was picked bite size off plates or literally put in their mouths by servants. It was no position to be in if one had to cut a steak.

The first course of their meal, *gustus*, was hors d'oeuvres consisting of salad, dried fish, and a sweet wine. Strong wine was not served with the appetizers because it was thought to be too potent on an empty stomach, so a wine-and-honey concoction called *mulsum* was presented.

The meat course, *cena*, followed with lamb, chicken, and dove, all cooked in heavily herbed sauces and also included fresh mountain asparagus, artichokes, beans, a bowl of salt, and wine. Conway had been instructed during their training sessions to drink sparingly at all times, especially at this stage of a meal. It was considered bad form to imbibe wine heavily during the main course.

Permeating the tent was the smell of incense and roses. To reduce intoxication, Conway remembered from his lessons. The Romans believed that sweet smells of perfumes and flowers helped retard the effects of the large quantities of wine that they drank.

The main course was followed by *secundae mensa*, an arrangement of fruit marinated in juices or sweetened with honey—apricots, melons, and pears—along with sweetmeats and pastry. With dessert, wine was served undiluted. This was the point where one was permitted to drink to satisfaction— or satiation, whichever came first. It wasn't a thick wine that had to be watered down but a fine aged wine, pressed from grapes grown at his uncle's villa, Quintus explained.

All the plates and bowls holding the food were silver. Only liquids were poured from earthen jars, and the jars were finely etched and painted. After each serving, a bowl of water and a towel for rinsing the hands were provided, a necessity since the only utensils used were fingers. The food was cut by the servants before being brought to the table. Nor were there individual plates for the diners—food was picked off the platters with fingers or handed to them by the servants.

Conway noticed that one of the servants wore a metal collar around his neck. On his forehead was branded the letter *F*. Words in Latin were etched on the collar: The man was a criminal, a runaway slave. The collar was for identification if he ran again. And was his death warrant if he was found.

"I must apologize, Marcus, for the crude fare, but when one is camped out at an oasis, it is the best that can be done."

"The meal is fit for a king." He was not lying. It was incomprehensible how a multicourse meal of such delicacies could be turned out on what was essentially a camp-out. But this was a society in which a few lived like kings and the many who served them lived from hand to mouth.

Conway carefully watched his host's dinner manners to avoid a faux pas that could bring his Roman ancestry into question. He found Quintus to be an arrogant ass, a bully to the servants, and a braggart. Unlike Conway's simple white wool toga, the one Quintus wore was made of fine Eastern silks. The white silken toga had a purple trim along the bottom, the royal purple that was forbidden to any but kings. The colors and materials were apt to be worn by Roman dandies rather than well-bred gentlemen.

The Roman toga could not be confused with the robes worn by other nationalities. It was the most important and most Roman of all pieces of clothing. As Virgil wrote, 'The Romans, lords of deeds, the race that wears the toga.' Conway would have been more comfortable in blue jeans and a T-shirt. And a pair of Jockey shorts instead of the loincloth he had wrapped around him like a diaper. How did Romans win wars wearing a dress and a diaper?

He had been told that Roman men wore little or no jewelry except a signet ring used to seal and validate letters. Conway had been equipped with a single iron ring that bore his initials, a signet ring. The signet ring that Quintus wore was a fancier one made of gold, and he wore a different ring on each of his fingers. He was of the ilk of Romans who had inherited an empire, not fought for one, and who were so pampered, they considered any activity beyond eating and sex as beneath their dignity.

A blind flute player was wrapped in the shadows of a dark corner of the tent. His whimsical melody floated through Conway's mind on the high created by the potent wine.

Quintus noticed Conway eyeing his purple-trimmed toga, and chuckled. "Not quite the forbidden purple of kings. But close. You know, of course, how the Phoenicians came to learn the secret of royal purple dye?"

Unsure if he was supposed to know, Conway lifted his eyebrows rather than giving an answer.

"The dye is obtained from the murex snail found along beaches. Hercules was taking his dog for a walk along the shore when his dog crushed a snail in his jaws. The juices from the snail ran out of the dog's mouth, staining his muzzle a bright purple."

Conway saluted Quintus with his wine goblet. "It is most fortunate I encountered a fellow Roman in this forsaken outpost."

"It gives me great pleasure to share dinner with one of my own kind," Quintus said, then frowned. "My grandfather, Publius, sent me to this hellish place to learn the trade firsthand. He has no sons, my brother and I are his heirs. Soon I return to Rome to manage the family businesses and estates."

"You will not insist on staying in this land of Jews?"

"I would rather mingle with swine than these dogs that call themselves Jews. What good can be said about a people who have only one insignificant god to protect them and only one large temple in all their land?"

The two servants were scantly dressed twin girls. They were an interesting pair and Conway studied them as he bantered with Quintus. They were dark-skinned, delicate creatures, with long fingers, slender bodies, and small busts. At first Conway thought the girls were young teens, but as the evening wore on he decided they were in their early twenties.

"What's your name?" Conway asked the girl serving him.

"I am called Janus." Her eyes flirted with him each time she brought a dish. He wondered if she was going to be dessert.

"And you," he said to the girl serving Quintus, "what is your name?"

"Janus," the girl replied.

"They are both named Janus?"

Quintus chuckled. "Of course. Janus is a god with two identical faces."

"But when you call their name, how do they know which one is to come?"

"Simply by my tone of voice when I shout the name Janus. At first they failed often and the wrong one would come. They were beaten a good deal. Now they fail not at all."

Conway shook his head. "That's incredible."

"That's privilege," Quintus said smugly. Quintus saluted him with his wine goblet. "The wine these Jews drink is not fit for oxen. This is Caecuban, the wine our most godly Augustus called the noblest of all. My family has it pressed at our own vineyard near Terra Ciana. It does not have to be diluted with water like the swill legionnaires and the Jewish rabble drink."

Conway chuckled. "You don't think much of the Jews."

"There is nothing good in this place called Palestine. We Romans rule the heart of the world. The Mediterranean is our lake. Roman peace makes it profitable for trade from one end of the empire to the other. But the Jews are a festering sore for us. Greeks, Egyptians, Gauls, even barbarians like those half-naked savages called Britons on that cold, miserable island in the north waters, submit to our authority and pay their taxes. These Jews are so enamored with their own dirty, miserable little lives and their tribal god that they resist every effort to maintain peace in the region. It is not enough that we permit them to worship their own god and have a temple in Jerusalem, they battle us when we circulate coins with the emperor's godly image on it because they do not believe in graven images, and war against us when we tax them to pay for the peace and protection our armies provide.

"The problem is that this squalid little province lies across important trade routes. If it were not for the disruption in trade, Marcus, the emperor would send ten legions into the Palestine and wipe it clean. We could populate the place with bands of monkeys and herds of donkeys that would give us less trouble than these Jews."

"How do you find Bethsaida?"

Quintus shrugged. "Like any provincial city, dull and uninspiring. The tetrarch, Philip, is an admirer of our Roman ways. He built the city in the Roman fashion, with marble and statues. There is a good set of baths. My own villa would sit proudly on the Quirinal without shaming me too much."

From the history lesson back in Los Alamos, Conway knew that it would have been more correct for the slave trader to say that the city had been built in a Greek style, not Roman. The Romans had made Greek art and architecture their own. The Quirinal, one of the seven hills of Rome, was a fashionable address.

"What is your opinion of this Philip? As wild as the other Herods?"

"No, to the contrary, Philip is the most prudent of all the Herods. But the same cannot be said about his wife. You have heard of Salome, the wife of Philip?"

"Only gossip."

"Ah, exactly. Salome generates more gossip than the Egyptian gods. I know from personal experience that her sexual appetites are wetter than a Julia."

The reference was to Tiberius' wife. Julia was the daughter of the emperor Augustus. Tiberius was forced to divorce his own wife and marry Julia in order to remain in favor with Augustus and inherit the throne. Her many adulteries were legendary, and no one could carry the tales to Augustus for fear of his wrath. When Augustus did find out that his daughter's licentious life was the talk of Rome, rather than having her killed as the law required, he exiled her for life to the tiny island of Pandateria.

Conway wondered what "personal experience" Quintus had with Salome. He could not imagine the corpulent slave trader satisfying any woman. The man's sexual "conquests" no doubt ran toward helpless slaves and prostitutes.

"But one underestimates Salome if one thinks of her as simply a faithless wife. Philip has taken ill—"

"Poison?"

Quintus grinned. "That is what they say in the marketplace." He shrugged. "Whatever the cause, Philip no longer rules and Salome does. And she does so ably." Quintus gave Conway a sly look. "It is not considered good form for a Roman to become too friendly with these Jews, but I confess that I have Salome's ear. She relies upon me for advice in dealing with many matters. And she has a fondness for money that lends itself to giving special privileges to a merchant such as myself in return for gold."

"On my travels I have often heard this woman mentioned. And the troublesome Jews. There is always talk of revolt."

"We should fear more from our slaves than these Jews. One out of every three people in Rome itself are slaves, and the same holds true for the rest of Italia. Twice in the past slave leaders have formed armies large enough to shake the empire, Spartacus and Eunus before him. Spartacus had an army of ninety thousand, Eunus seventy thousand. It took years and the full might of the empire to put down the insurrections. We lined the Appian Way with twenty thousand crucified slaves as a warning. But if you knew these devils like I do, if you heard their cries for freedom, you would understand why I fear that someday another slave leader will rise and try to topple the empire."

Conway wouldn't be surprised if Quintus, like the mad Herod, would someday run screaming down the corridors of his villa, in terror from the ghosts of the thousands of slaves he helped send into a life of living horror.

The man had been continuously gorging himself with both food and drink as they talked. Quintus waved his hand at the servants, which prompted one of them to hold a bowl for him while two others held a cloth screen to give him privacy. Conway heard the slave trader vomit behind the screen. It was done, according to the Roman history professor, in order to keep eating and enjoying the many courses available to the master race. In fact, wealthy Romans had a special room in their homes, called a "vomitorium," to provide privacy just for those occasions.

After the servants finished with Quintus, they turned to Conway. He shook his head. He had only been picking at his food. Did they expect him to throw up to show his appreciation? Something like belching after a meal with Bedouins to demonstrate that one enjoyed the food? Putting a premium on eating many dishes was the fault of the Romans attempting to ape the Greeks who had refined dining to a state of art. The all-conquering Romans, however, lacked the Greek ease with life and refinement. They tended to become gluttons rather than epicures, measuring their feasts by the variety and amount they could eat, rather than by delicate tastes.

The food was good, although strange tasting. Many of the dishes tended to be sweet and sour. Meat, which he assumed was lamb, was boiled rather than braised, and had a sweet taste. After Quintus finished vomiting, he began eating again.

Another slave come forward and began to play a harp, while reciting poetry that Quintus had written. He was speaking the poetry, mimicking Quintus' voice. Conway glanced at the slave trader and saw the smirk of pleasure on his face.

"Everyone has a slave who can recite poetry, but when I discovered one who could impersonate my voice, I confess I became greedy and refused to market him. It is quite a nice effect, isn't it? To hear my poetry from my own lips, so to speak."

"Quite impressive."

"When we get to Bethsaida," Quintus said, "it shall be my pleasure to have you stay as my guest in my house. I may even be able to introduce you to the queen."

Conway bowed as well as he could from a lying position. "Both acts of benevolence would honor me."

"Are you a member of a club?" Quintus asked.

No one had mentioned clubs. Was he talking about something like a country club? If he said no, he would lose face with Quintus if being a member was a sign of social acceptance; yet if he said yes, he would have to identify the club.

"I realize they are more fashionable in Rome than the provinces," Quintus said, solving Conway's problem. As a traveling merchant, he would not be expected to keep up with the fashions of the great city. "I have been instrumental in forming a mystery club in Bethsaida. There is only a small Roman population, but there was enough interest to establish a club."

Ah, a mystery club, thought Conway, with relief. That was something his classical education would help with. Aristocratic clubs with secret meetings in which food and drink were shared by men were common both among the Romans and Greeks. Sometimes the authorities suppressed the clubs because they hatched political conspiracies. The most famous one was in Athens where several of the aristocratic societies formed a conspiracy to overthrow the Athenian democracy. In order to make sure all members were committed and could not turn on them, common crimes were planned in which all members had to participate to incriminate themselves.

One such incidence happened on a dark night when the members took hammers and broke off the genitals from statues of the god Hermes throughout the city. The act was a crime against religion, punishable by death or exile. But the widespread nature of it signaled that a conspiracy was afoot. The conspirators were tracked down and exiled.

The analogy to the rites of American street gangs was not lost on Conway. Gang membership often required commission of a serious crime to prove the applicant's worth and loyalty.

Quintus went on. "Our club plays tribute to Cybele of Phrygia."

Conway had no idea of who Cybele of Phrygia was, but the lascivious grin on Quintus' face suggested that Cybele did not sew quilts. He toasted the slave trader. "Again, noble Quintus, I consider it a great honor to partake in any hospitality a man of your stature provides."

Something was in the wine besides nectar of the grape. The pleasant buzz that crept from his head down to his toes was not a light drunk but a narcotic flush. Janus, his Janus, had gotten closer and closer until finally she snuggled in his arms. She was dessert. Her hand moved up his robe and she began to gently massage him between the legs. Things haven't changed much in two thousand years, he thought, his mind swaying softly from the drug, the touch, the flute. *Drugs, sex, and rock and roll.* The blind flute player even began to look a little like Ray Charles.

The head of the other Janus disappeared between Quintus' legs. The Roman was sprawled on his back with his eyes closed, smug anticipation lighting his face.

Then Conway's Janus was between his legs with her warm mouth and wicked tongue. He brought her head back up and slipped her robe down to expose her breasts. They were small and delicate, just a mouthful. He tasted each breast, wrapping his tongue around the nipple as he ran his hand under her robe.

His hand closed around an erect penis.

She laughed softly, brushed her lips across the side of his cheek and nibbled on his ear. He pushed her back again and took a good look.

Janus was a boy.

The boy's soft lips warmly caressed him while Conway explored farther with his hand. No sack of testicles hanging under the penis. The boy's balls had been cut off. Janus was an eunuch, but one that was still able to get an erection. That explained the soft flesh and breasts. He didn't know what to do. To act surprised or offended might break his cover. Janus was cradled in his arms, feeling warm and soft.

The boy lifted a cup to Conway's lips and Conway saw the design on it, an older man lying back while sodomizing a youth. He recognized the design from his study of the classics. Erates, an older lover, and Eromenos, a younger one, were common partners in ancient Athens and populated much art of the era. The relationship was not homosexual in the modern sense because it lacked the element of love, and on the youth's side, lust. It was more of a social relationship where the older man became a father substitute for the younger one, teaching him a great deal about life . . . but also using the youth as a lover until the young man started growing a beard.

The Romans, of course, ever aping the Greeks, knew of the custom, but it had not become as dominant in Rome as it had been in Athens and Sparta, but was acceptable, especially, Conway thought, among Romans like Quintus who would consider themselves young and daring.

Conway had never desired sexually another man, but in his mind, Janus was not a man. He didn't look like one or feel like one. Besides, he did not want to offend or make a faux pas in front of Quintus.

What was the expression? When in Rome?

Through eyes glazed by drugs and wine, Conway saw servants peeking in through the folds of the tent.

Quintus' voice came to him as a haze. "They like to masturbate as they watch us."

CHAPTER THIRTY-FOUR

Quintus woke an hour before dawn as was his custom. A slave lit a candle for him and brought him fruit juice to drink. He had never been a good sleeper and his talent for sleeping had diminished since he came to the Palestine. He had told his guest, Marcus Claudius, that he planned to return home, back to Rome, soon, but that was not the truth. He was not just on a business assignment. He had been exiled.

A dispatch had arrived the day before from his family in Rome. He received a long list of instructions from his grandfather, who was head of the family, and a letter from his brother. The letters were written in code, in case they fell into a business adversary's hands. The code his grandfather chose was the simple but effective one used by Julius Caesar whereby each letter of the alphabet in the writing was substituted for another letter two places apart. A slave scribe had stayed up all night deciphering the coded messages.

He set aside his grandfather's letter after reading only part of it. He would give it to the slave who was responsible for most business matters. Business matters bored him. He could not force himself to read through the dry, impersonal details of how his grandfather wanted their business run in the Palestine.

There was one item out of the ordinary in what he had read

though that caught his attention: a list of the type of slaves needed to perform duties in a large household in a district north of the city. The master of that house, a rich landowner, had been killed by one of his slaves. Because the slave who did the slaying could not be identified, all the slaves in the household, four hundred in total, were put to death. Had the killer been identified, only he and his family, including any children, would have been put to death. But to act as a further deterrent, the law required that all the slaves in the household die if the killer could not be identified.

Other than the list of slaves he had to fill, the death of a fellow Roman and his slaves meant nothing to Quintus. He cared only for himself. His heart bled for forgiveness that deep down he knew would never come and for the word that he could end his exile and return. He might as well have been banished to the place of the dead as be banished to this land of coarse, uncultured Jews. Some Romans were transplanted to places like Alexandria or Iberia, but Quintus hated foreign places and foreign peoples. He had been raised with the concept that foreigners were inferior to Romans and that his place in life was lord over them.

His preparation in life had been to live as a Roman, not a barbarian. He received the education provided to upper-class Roman boys. It started in the home with instructions from parents, emphasizing reverence for the gods, respect for the law, unquestioned and instant obedience to authority, truthfulness, and self-reliance, with the concept that being a Roman brought both privileges and responsibilities. His mother taught him and his brother and sisters reading, writing, and basic counting until the age of seven. At seven, Quintus began attending classes given by a hired schoolmaster, learning to perfect his reading and writing in Latin and Greek, writing on wax tablets while working out counting problems with pebbles and an abacus counting board. He went to school accompanied by a slave who carried his tablets and counting board.

His two sisters remained in the home as a companion for their mother while he went to school. Marriage would come early for the girls, sometimes as early as twelve, but no later than seventeen, and there was much for them to learn about managing a household with its staff of slaves. Even though their duties were restricted to the home, inside the home they were absolute mistress, and a woman would often be called upon not only to entertain business and social guests but to give her husband advice in business affairs.

He read his brother's long letter as he sipped the juice. It took nearly two months to get a letter from Rome and he received only about three letters a year. His brother knew how he hungered for the gay life of Rome and always related current events and gossip to keep him informed. He enjoyed the gossip. Reading it made him feel as if he were still part of the social life of the greatest city in the world.

There were juicy tidbits in the letter. The wife of a senator was being sued by her lover for return of expensive gifts the lover had given her over the years after she refused to keep up the relationship. The woman's husband at the same time was suing his son's father-in-law for failing to pay over the balance owed on the dowry for the son's bride. What made the story so reportable was not only the status of the people involved but that the lover was the father-in-law who refused to pay the dowry. He had to shake sleep out of his head to envision the relationships between the parties.

Quintus clicked his tongue in disapproval. To have a senator and his wife make public fools of themselves was a disgrace. Roman women demanded payment from their lovers not for sex but to show appreciation. And they were as eager to get it as a man was to collect a dowry, but not for the same reasons. The women loved the status of being the highest paid.

Had he any word of the most unlucky wedding in history? his brother asked. The bride and groom were of the senatorial class, people far above the wealthy merchant class that Quintus' family belonged to. The chain of misfortunes began when the betrothal ring had to be cut off the bride's finger because her hand swelled up. Betrothal rings were worn on the third finger of the left hand because it was believed a nerve that went directly to the heart was located there. To cut the ring was to invite gossip and superstition that the marriage would not be full of heart.

The next catastrophe occurred at the threshold of the home the bride and groom were to occupy. It was customary when entering the house for the first time for the groom to lift the bride over the threshold in order to avoid the chance of any bad omens. The groom stumbled and both went down, right before all of the assembled guests who followed them to the house in a parade.

Once inside the house, the bride was to light the hearth for the first time, symbolizing her presence and command of the household. She uses the wedding torch that is carried before the newlyweds in the parade to the house to fire the hearth. After lighting the fire, the bride turns and throws the torch to the guests, who scramble for it as a good-luck token. But alas, she caught her dress on fire!

With such ill omens for the marriage, his brother wrote, the groom immediately announced divorce and returned the dowry.

The letter continued with gossip about the emperor, Tiberius Claudius Nero. His life as a youth and into middle age had been so mundane that he was making up for it in his barbarous old age. At seventy-four years old he was homicidal, demented, and perverted. What was it about emperors that drove them to such excesses and madness late in life? thought Quintus.

Elevated to the throne at the age of fifty-six, more or less due to his longevity, the other candidates—most of them better suited and more popular—had either died in war, from disease, or were murdered. Quintus wondered how much of Tiberius's family history had to do with the ultimate madness and bizarre behavior the emperor suffered now.

His mother, Livia, had married a high-ranking Roman at the age of thirteen and gave birth to Tiberius; at the age of seventeen she was pregnant again when she caught the eye of the emperor Augustus, who had ordered her divorced so he could marry Livia, after divorcing his own wife. As was the custom upon divorce in Rome, Tiberius and his newborn brother were sent to live with their father,

It was proclaimed there were only two people that Tiberius truly loved in his life: his wife, Vipsania, and his brother, Drusus. When Drusus was injured while warring in Germany, Tiberius journeyed four hundred miles, riding day and night to see his brother, but arrived at his brother's deathbed.

The second devastation occurred when the husband of the Augustus's daughter, Julia, died. The husband had been a contender for the throne. Julia married another man, Tiberius' father-in-law, but he died as well. With other contenders for the throne dead, the selection fell on Tiberius. To strengthen his ties to the imperial family, upon the death of Julia's second husband, the emperor ordered Tiberius to divorce his beloved wife, Vipsania, and marry Julia.

Quintus had already heard the scandal about Julia. She was licentious, and committed not just adultery but participated in orgies. The stories of her sexual excesses were repeated over and over not only by Quintus' classmates when he was a schoolboy but by all of the adults around him. There were also tales of Tiberius' misery over the loss of his true love. While in Rome on his leave from battle, Tiberius had spotted Vipsania on the street. She had been forced to marry again by the emperor, this time to a Roman senator. He followed her through the streets, weeping, and the emperor, hearing of this, forbade him from ever seeing Vipsania again.

It was not too many years after taking the throne, that Tiberius left Rome and became a recluse on the Isle of Capri. If the emperor had gone to the small island in the belief that his outrages and perversions would be less publicized, he certainly was wrong. Quintus and every other Roman were kept well-informed by the gossipmongers as to the emperor's every nefarious move.

Not that anyone publicly dared to say anything negative about the emperor. Sejanus, the commander of the Praetorian Guard he left behind in Rome, and the Praetorian cohorts that were the supreme military power of the emperors, kept the Roman senate in a state of fear. Sejanus seduced Livilla, the wife of Tiberius' son, and convinced her to conspire with him in murdering her husband. Once he was out of the way, Sejanus married the widow, sealing the connection to the imperial family and his command of the Praetorian Guard, paving the way for the title of emperor.

Sejanus was now dead, his brother wrote. Tiberius had learned that Sejanus and Livilla had plotted the death of his son and ordered his execution. And that the outraged citizens who had suffered at his hands ripped the body to pieces and dragged it through the streets.

On the Isle of Capri, something snapped inside Tiberius. He became a monster. Perhaps the loss of everyone he had ever loved was part of it. His skin erupted with painful sores that smelled. He turned the beautiful isle into a place of torture and perversion. Twelve magnificent villas were built on the small isle and filled with treasures of the greatest empire on earth . . . along with dungeons and torture chambers. He and his courtiers roamed from one lavish villa to another, entertained each night by troupes of actors and dancers who had been trained since childhood to perform every possible sex act imaginable; some of the entertainers were children, especially boys. These little "minnows" were trained to swim with Tiberius in the luxurious baths that were maintained at every villa.

He took a different sex partner every night. When the professional perverts were not enough to satisfy his lust, he sent for the highborn wives of senators in Rome. One woman, the wife of one of the most powerful men in the empire, committed suicide rather than be the victim of his continual lust. He surrounded himself with cruelty and perversion. He killed ferociously and often at random. Since Capri was surrounded by a cliff, to amuse himself he sometimes had a person who fell into his disfavor thrown from the cliffs.

Tiberius also ordered Sejanus' two children to be killed, his brother wrote, out of fear that they might grow up and try to avenge their father's death. The boy was ten, the girl only eight. The little girl was almost saved by ancient Roman law, which held that no virgin could be put to death. Her innocent begging for forgiveness did not stop Tiberius' executioner from raping her so she would no longer be a virgin.

His brother's letter continued with some news about family matters and then closed with the information Quintus received in each of the letters he got from his brother: Quintus was still forbidden to return to Rome. As a matter of family honor, it was best that he stayed exiled, his brother wrote. "I had approached our grandfather with the idea that you return from the Palestine, but his reply to me was that his only emotion toward you was a regret that he had not exposed you when you were born."

"Exposed" was a euphemism for a special way of death.

His grandfather's command that he not return to Rome was not just a matter of his having a financial stranglehold over Quintus but a legal one of life and death. The grandfather had the right and power of pater familias. The word *family* in Rome did not mean only a husband, wife, and children. Rather, it was composed of all those people who were under the authority of the head of the house which usually included husbands and wives, children, grandchildren, the spouses of children and grandchildren, and even more remote descendants on the male side. The legal status of a family member was theoretically little better than a slave; they were a chattel possessed by the head of the house. Until the head of the family emancipated his sons or grandsons, if he did short of his own death, he had complete control of their lives— their money, homes, choice of marriage partners, and even life itself. Although rarely used, he had the right to put to death anyone in the family.

The right to live was granted from the moment of their birth.

When a child was born, it was laid upon the ground at the feet of the head of the family. If he raised it in his arms, he acknowledged it as being part of the family. If he refused to do so, the child became an outcast, without parents or family, forsaken by all. The act of refusal was not done maliciously but to enhance the family. Too many children competing for the same fortune and estates would not only diminish the importance of the family but cause internal disruption.

The rejected child was not immediately put to death. Rather, it was "exposed." It was taken from the house by a slave and left along the roadside to die. Others were dropped at a trash dump. Most babies who were exposed died; though anyone who found the child could keep it. In fact, there were slave traders who kept agents at the dump to watch for exposed children in order to sell them to persons who would raise them for their own purposes. As bad as slave traders were, there were others who hunted for exposed children with even more evil aims—beggar kings who had the children's arms and legs broken and awkwardly bound to twist the limbs to make them pathetic beggars.

Although he was too old to be exposed, if Quintus returned to Rome, his grandfather, as head of the house, still held the power of life and death over him. And he knew the tough old man would use it. His grandfather was no ordinary Roman merchant. Slave trading was not considered a particularly noble profession by upper-class Romans. Only the immense amounts of money the trade generated made the practitioners socially acceptable.

If he set foot in Rome, he knew his grandfather would have him put to death. The only way he could return would be if the badge of dishonor were taken from him by some feat that won him laurels. He was always on the lookout for ways to enhance his prestige. Besides being sycophantic by nature, he flattered and gave outrageous gifts to Salome in the hopes that she might report to the emperor some deed that assisted Rome and its Jewish governors.

With his own expediencies in mind, he had concerns about his dinner guest. Something about Marcus disturbed him, but he could not put his finger on it, a feeling that seemed to want to materialize in his brain but did not condense into a clear thought. His instincts told him that something was amiss with the man. It was not his accent when speaking Latin—many

Romans were born in the outer provinces and had never been in Rome itself. Or even his table manners, which Quintus had learned provincials were often graceless about.

As he was falling back asleep to doze before the dawn, he realized what it was that bothered him about the man. It was the treatment he gave his slaves. Romans carried themselves with the arrogance of a race that had conquered the Western world. Slaves were dray animals, not even noticed unless some task was being assigned to them. When he approached the Roman and his slaves earlier, he had gotten the impression that the man was having a private conversation with them. While it was not impossible for a master to have a trusted slave he spoke to confidentially, no Roman acted informally in public with both his male and female slave.

He must have had very poor training, Quintus thought. But what could one expect from a provincial? Even though he attributed the man's lack of patrician bearing to his provincial raising, it did not answer all of the questions that had formed in Quintus' mind about the newcomer.

He decided to keep a close eye on Marcus.

Perhaps there would be something in the situation that would win him the praise that he needed to end his exile.

CHAPTER THIRTY-FIVE

Staring up at the night sky visible through one of the gaping holes in the tent Yoseph had sold them, Marie listened to Isie snoring beside her and tried to hear David's softer breathing on the other side of the boy.

She knew David had become attracted to her and she worried about her own feelings. Fears. Since he had not been told about her stigmata, she doubted he knew that much about her. Did he think she was a freak now that he knew that her hands bled? What else had he been told about her? What would he think of her if he knew what happened to her in Syria near the Golan Heights?

Her mind rebelled against the memories but they flashed through her head like the fast forward on a VCR.

She had been sent to a small village in a remote area of Syria to learn Aramaic. The area between the village and the Israeli entrenchment in the Golan Heights was a no-man's-land in which Arab irregulars carried on a shadow war of attacks and counterattacks with Israeli army units.

She lived in a small compound with other nuns studying the language. For a young woman barely twenty years old who had become a nun because of strange circumstance rather than zeal, the life of a nun was stifling. A mission to an isolated village that lacked running water, electricity, or even a grocery store, where people lived much as they had since ancient times, was interesting only until night fell, and one went to bed early because trying to do anything under candlelight was more trouble than it was worth.

After being in the village nearly a year, she left one day in search of medicine for a small boy who was running a high fever. The medical supplies of the nuns were inadequate for anything beyond stomach pain and headaches, at best, and supplies of all nature to the village had been cut off by the eruption of fighting from the sporadic warfare that plagued the area.

The only place to find medicine was on the Israeli side. Disobeying the supervising nun's orders, she made her way to the distant hills where Israeli army units were dug in.

As she climbed up a hillside, the cliff she was crawling up turned too steep near the top for her to make it over and she slipped down a few feet, clawing at the dirt with her fingers to keep herself from going into a slide that would send her tumbling down the mountain.

She heard footsteps above. Hanging on, she stopped to catch her breath. And looked up into the face of an Israeli officer. The barrel of a 9mm peered down at her.

He stared at her nun's habit and slowly shook his head. "I've heard of many terrorists disguises, but you're the first nun I've run across."

"I'm slipping," she said, replying in the Hebrew he spoke.

He reached down and grabbed her wrist and helped her up and over the ledge. She lay on her stomach for a moment but when she started to get up, he put the gun to the back of her neck.

"Don't move."

She twisted her neck to meet his eyes.

"I'm going to search you.'

Her eyes lit up with panic.

"I'm not going to rape you," he said gravely. "Is that what they teach you in the convent—that Jews rape nuns?"

"Please, I'll return—"

He put one knee on her back and patted her down from head to foot. His searching hand made no pretense at respecting her femininity. He was looking for weapons or a bomb and his hand felt everywhere.

"Roll over."

"Please—"

"Now!"

She obeyed and his hand felt around her neck. Then the mounds of her breasts. She leaned up and slapped him. Surprised as he, she froze in mortal fear.

He felt his stinging cheek. "A twelve-year-old boy walked into our camp last week to sell goat's milk. There were enough explosives in the milk pail to kill a dozen of my men. You have enough room under your layers of clothes to hide an antitank weapon."

He continued his search, his hand exploring down her abdomen, between her legs and down her thighs, all the way to her shoes. When he stopped searching she met his brown eyes with her own lighter ones. He was young, probably no more than his midtwenties, she thought. He wore captain's insignia on his uniform.

He grinned as she got to her feet. "I've felt better," he said.

She brushed dirt from her habit. "Always at gunpoint?"

He laughed. "Any way I can."

"Thank you for rescuing me," she said. Hebrew, the decreed official language of Israel, was reconstructed in modern times from the ancient one. She had spent several months in Israel retracing the footsteps of Christ before proceeding to the Syrian village, and her pronunciation was perfect, the way the language is employed by professional news broadcasters on the radio and TV.

"Who are you?" His tone was tough.

"I am with the Sisters of Holy Mercy—"

"What are you doing here?"

"I'm with a mission at a nearby village—"

"An Arab village?"

"A village of people who speak Aramaic."

"Aramaic?"

"The people speak the ancient language of the Jews, the language of Christ and the Disciples."

"The people in your Aramaic village, are they Christians?"

"No, they're Muslims."

"They send you here to kill Israelis?" He smiled a little when he said it. She did not answer. "All right, try this one. What are you doing here?"

She rubbed her hands. They were cut and scratched from her adventure on the cliff. "I came for medical supplies. The village is very isolated and the language differences keep them apart from other Syrians. Your warfare has kept supplies from coming. There's a little boy who needs an antibiotic."

His expression went from gravity to astonishment. "You came to the Israeli side to get medicine for Arabs?"

Her chin came up. "The people are poor, there are no doctors."

"Why don't you ask the Syrians? They have an army. Or the PLO and the Hezbollah with all that oil money pouring in?"

"We rarely see a Syrian army patrol. Anyway, they don't carry anything stronger than iodine. We're afraid of the irregulars. The people in the village aren't soldiers, this isn't their war."

"It wasn't our war, either, until the Arabs pushed it on us." He shook his head. "I don't know if I should believe you. Or shoot you."

She brushed aside strands of hair that had slipped out from under her head scarf and fell across her forehead. "If you're going to shoot me, would it be all right if I took the medicine back to the village first and returned to be shot later?"

He tried to keep a straight face but his lips cracked into a smile.

"You don't look like a nun."

"What do nuns look like?"

"I don't know, but you look—and feel—like you belong more in a bikini at the beach than those layers of musty wool."

Her cheeks reddened. "I'll return to the village."

"I can't let you do that. You're a prisoner now. I have to get instructions from headquarters."

"No, please, a little boy is sick."

"You have to come with me, back to my camp."

"Are you arresting me?"

He shrugged. "Maybe."

"If you're going to—"

"I know, give you the medicine and you'll return later to be shot."

Camp was bivouacked on a ridge overlooking the valley, twenty men, a dozen tents, and several large trucks. Her appearance in the camp caused more sensation than if he had walked in with Yasir Arafat.

"Close your mouth," the officer told his gaping sergeant, "you'll catch flies. And get me a first-aid kit."

He gave her water to drink, then she washed her hands and face. "I'm getting your towel dirty."

"That's all right, I have more. I was wondering what you looked like under all that dirt." He led her to a rock overlooking the valley and handed her the first-aid kit. "Sit down and take care of those scratches. I'll be back in the moment."

"Aren't you afraid I'll run?"

"Are you going to run?"

"Would you shoot me if I did?"

"What do you think?'

She studied his face. "I don't think you would shoot me."

"Don't bet on it."

He came back a couple minutes later with bread and cheese and a tin cup of goat's milk to share between them. "My name is Moshe."

"I am Sister Marie."

She glanced back at the camp where the men were trying to pretend they didn't notice her. "Will your sergeant turn me in? He seemed upset that you brought me to your camp."

"He was surprised, not upset. And, no, he won't turn you in, not unless I tell him to. He doesn't understand how a beautiful woman can be a nun. He says Jews have too much respect for a woman's flower to let it dry up and wither because a man isn't watering it."

Her cheeks turned pink, but she didn't look away. "Are those your sergeant's thoughts or yours?"

"Mine."

"I suspected so. Your sergeant looks like a decent person."

"And I don't?"

"What did you do when you searched me?"

He shrugged. "Perform my duty. And maybe a little more. I'm human."

"There's more to life than sex."

"Sister Marie, despite what they may have taught you, there is no life without sex!"

She looked around at the camp. "You must get Arabs through here. There are hapless families and businesses divided by the lines of war. People cross back and forth all the time."

"We tolerate them until we catch them spying. Then we shoot them."

"Have you shot many?"

He smiled at her serious tone and grave eyes. "Not yet. Where is the Aramaic village located?"

"About two hours walk from here."

"What are you doing in that village?"

"Learning Aramaic. It's an almost dead tongue now. The Church is working to keep the language alive."

"Your Hebrew is so good I can't tell your own nationality."

"I'm French. About that medicine. Are there any antibiotics in that medicine kit?"

"Yes, but I can't give it to the enemy."

"Little boys aren't enemies."

"Arabs kill little boys, too."

"I just need a little medicine."

"I could be shot for giving Arabs medicine."

"You could turn the other way and let me take it."

His eyes swept her, the full skirted habit that was still dirty from her crawl up the cliff, her black, high-laced shoes scuffed on the toes. "The life of a nun must be strange. Wearing baggy clothes to hide the body God gave you, living in musty convents among withered old women, dried up priests, and other relics."

Her jaw lifted. "No stranger than wearing a uniform, carrying a gun, and killing your God-given brothers."

"I'm in this uniform because it's my duty."

"So am I! If you won't give me the medicine, I'll be leaving. You can shoot me in the back if you wish."

"You keep tempting fate by asking to be shot." He chuckled. "But I like you. You can have your medicine. I'll probably be shot for giving it to you."

"I'll say a prayer for you."

He groaned. "Not that. If God finds out where I'm at, he'll probably send down a bolt of lightning for what I did to one of his wives. Why did you become a nun?"

"To serve God."

"That's what it says in a textbook. A Christian one. But why did you really become a nun?"

"Why do you say that? As if I should not be one."

"I say that because you look at me like a woman looks at a man."

She stared down at the ground, her face burning. Then lifted her chin in defiance. "I have to go."

"Wait, I'll get some medicines for you."

He escorted her back down the hill, carrying a laundry bag with field medical supplies inside and glanced at her occasionally as they made their way. She tried not to look at him. His comment buzzed in her mind.

When he had accompanied her as far as he dared, he offered his hand to shake. "Take care, Sister Marie. Remember me in your prayers." He grinned. "And your dreams."

She took his hand in a strong, firm shake. "Thank you, Captain."

"Moshe."

"Moshe. The deliverer of his people from slavery and receiver of the Ten Commandments." The Hebrew name for Moses.

Her hand stayed in his grip and pink touched her cheeks as they stared into each other's eyes. He slowly pulled her closer, and she let herself be slowly drawn to him, her eyes wide open in awe and wonderment as his face drew near and his lips gently brushed hers. She closed her eyes but then opened them and swayed as she looked into his eyes. He was still holding her close.

"Marie . . ."

Scarlet cheeked, she jerked away, grabbing the bag from him. She ran down the hill.

"Sister Marie!"

He started after her and stopped. She hurried down a dry gully made by rain water. When she looked up, he was standing on a rock, his hands on his hips. He waved to her.

She hurried away. When she turned to wave back, he was already gone.

CHAPTER THIRTY-SIX

She trembled as she walked, not from fear but from guilt, as she experienced a warm, wet throbbing between her legs, her nipples hard under the layers of holy cloth. It was a sin for her body to react sexually to a man, a sin to kiss a man. And the young Israeli captain wasn't just a man. He was a Jew! Why had he affected her like this? It was just a kiss.

But she had never been kissed. Or touched. Not in that way.

She went back across the dry foothills, back to the three dozen awkward baked mud-and-straw huts gathered around a water well that made up the village where a hundred or so of the last people on earth who spoke Aramaic raised thin sheep and grew scrawny vegetables.

The people in the village lived little different than their ancestors had for over two thousand years. They had no electricity, plumbing, cars, or phones. The only books other than the Koran were stories in the minds of the elders who passed them from generation to generation over supper fires. The only schools were fields where boys tended sheep and the family hut where young girls learned the ancient art of weaving.

The village had avoided the heavy foot of conquerors for a large part of recorded history because of its poverty and remoteness, but was now caught in the no-man's-land between warring entities.

Sister Hortense was the eldest of the three nuns sent to the village. A weathered woman of fifty, she had spent most of her life in the Holy Land and was in charge of the project. Sister Joan, close to Marie's age, was short, plump, talkative, and excitable. Naive, immature, her head full of the ghosts and miracle makers of religion, she was alternately awed and jealous of Marie's receipt of the stigmata.

Marie arrived back at the village an hour before dawn, haggard and exhausted. A patrol of irregulars moving in the night caused her to take shelter in a space between large boulders. She had sat for much of the night, alone under the moonless night sky, reliving what had passed between her and the Israeli officer, her fingers tracing her lips as if searching for a telltale mark that his lips had placed on hers.

The two nuns were waiting as Marie came in the door. Sister Hortense was furious, the wrath of a vengeful God, Sister Joan could hardly hide her un-Christian glee.

"Where have you been?" Sister Hortense demanded.

"At a camp of the Israelis." Marie's cheeks reddened and she avoided their eyes. "I brought back medicine for Raffi."

"A camp of soldiers? You spent the night with men, with *Jews*?"

"I . . . I spent the night in the desert, alone. I spotted an Arab patrol on the way back and I hid. They camped nearby and I had to wait until they were asleep."

Sister Hortense looked close to a coronary. "You have been with men."

"No. I just spoke to one, an Israeli officer, the one who gave me the medicine."

Marie turned away and Sister Hortense grabbed her arm and jerked her back around. "What did you do with this man? Did he touch you? Did he violate you?"

"He kissed me!" She glared at the older nun, her hands balled into fists. "And he touched me!"

"Mary, Mother of God." Sister Hortense made the sign of the cross. Sister Joan made an unintelligible gurgling sound of ecstasy and horror and quickly closed her gaping mouth, making the sign of the cross as Sister Hortense scowled at her.

Marie's knees went weak and guilt overwhelmed her. She stared down at the dusty rug that covered the dirt floor of the hut as Sister Hortense glared at her in cold fury.

"You are not to leave the village again. I will report this matter to Mother Superior in Beirut. Go to your room and pray to God for forgiveness."

"I have to take the medicine to Raffi."

"Go to your room and pray!"

Marie lifted her face, frightened, guilty, but defiant. "A little boy needs this medicine. I will not abandon him." She started for the door and paused, but didn't turn around, as Sister Hortense made a sharp retort to her back.

"It's too bad your devotion to God is not as strong as your animal desires. A man has whispered in your ear and you are ready to forget your vows."

She fled the house and went to the edge of the village where the little boy lived with his father.

Raffi was a small, scrawny nine-year-old whose only possession was also a small, scrawny mongrel about the same age. His mother had died at his birth and his father, the village hunter, disappeared for long periods into the desert in search of game, making the boy the village orphan. Raffi and the dog had adopted Marie and had become her shadow. And the first true friends she ever had.

The boy was asleep on a mattress of animal hides stuffed with straw when she came into the tent. His mutt was stretched out, snoring, beside him. She woke the boy and forced him to take the antibiotics. She cradled him in her arms until he went back to sleep and laid him gently back down on the bed, covering him to ward off dawn's chill. She rested beside the boy, unwilling to return to the fury of Sister Hortense. Reliving the moment of Moshe's lips on hers created a fire in her blood. What would it be like to be a *whole woman*, a wife, lover, mother, to love a man, and share her life with him? She knew her thoughts were supposed to be sinful, but they didn't seem sinful to her, not even when she imagined what Moshe looked like naked.

She had seen naked little boys, running around with their inch-long penises flapping, their little sack of testicles bouncing underneath, had even seen a grown man, though not intentionally. The men of the village were not ashamed of their bodies and one of them casually pulled out his male part and urinated as she was nearby. The practice was stopped after Sister Hortense told the village leader she would whack off the next penis that came out in public.

She imagined Moshe's strong, muscular body on top of her naked body, the muscles of his chest pressing against her breasts, his hands exploring her body eagerly, her legs parting . . . she put her hand between her legs, the throbbing sensation escalating until suddenly a fiery sensation shot through her and she convulsed as if she'd been hit with an electric shock. After the hot flash was over, she lay breathless, surprised at the passion that she had unleashed in herself. Tears flowed down her face, ashamed of having experienced forbidden feelings, and frightened by the realization of what she was missing in life.

A week of cold silence passed between the nuns. Marie tried to keep herself busy and her mind occupied, but thoughts of the young Israeli officer whose lips caressed hers invaded her sleep and every waking minute. Sister Joan had tried to talk to her once, asking gleefully where the Jew had touched her, but Marie ignored her.

Unable to take the tension any longer, Marie walked into the kitchen where the nuns were preparing dinner and told them that she was returning to the camp of the Israeli.

"I need more medicine for Raffi."

"Nonsense! The boy is better!" Sister Hortense snapped. "I forbid you to leave the village. I have reported the matter to the mother superior. You must stay here and pray for forgiveness until we receive her reply."

Marie left the room and walked away from the village.

It was dark by the time a corporal in charge of a patrol brought her to the camp. The corporal saluted as Moshe came out of his tent.

"She says she knows you, sir."

She cowered as Moshe stared at her wide-eyed. "What are you doing here?"

"I—I need more medicine."

"I'll take care of this, Corporal. Thank you."

After the corporal left, Moshe shook his head. "This time I may have you to shoot you as a spy."

She avoided his eyes. She was weary, not from the climb but from tension. Every step had involved a struggle with her conscience.

"You can have more medicine. Have you eaten? My men have gone over to Command for a briefing and I've tapped into my secret hoard for dinner. There's more than enough for two."

Disappearing into his tent, he came back out with a bulging laundry sack similar to the one he had packed the medicine in. "When you've been in the army long enough to call yourself a veteran, you learn to survive in spite of army rations."

He led her to the huge rock overlooking the southern end of the valley. Unpacking the bag, he set out wine and cheese, canned biscuits, dried fish, olives, and marinated artichoke hearts. Returning to his tent for cups and utensils, he came back to find she had spread out the laundry bag for a tablecloth. He handed her a fresh handkerchief. "Cloth napkins. This is a five-star restaurant."

The summer night was warm, balmy, with a taste of moisture in the air. Mediterranean clouds were floating in from the west, carrying a warm storm. A bolt of lightning flashed in the clouds, white fire, a majestic display of nature's power, spiritual in its power and beauty.

"You didn't tell God I was here, did you?" he joked.

"Maybe he knows I'm here," she murmured.

"Are you happy as a nun?" he asked, groaning aloud after

he said that. "Sorry, I have an American friend who calls those kind of remarks foot-in-mouth disease."

"I haven't been happy since I was fourteen years old. I'm . . . I'm confused. I love God, I want to serve Him, but I'm not sure this is the way, that—a life like this . . ."

"Being a nun?"

She pushed hair away from her face. "It's hard to explain."

"I understand. I really do. I couldn't imagine myself as a rabbi or priest or an Islamic holy man. Even when they're allowed to marry. It means giving up part of yourself. I have too much passion for life to save it for the life beyond."

Tears welled in her eyes and down her face. "I'm sorry." She blew her nose on his five-star handkerchief. "It's been inside of me so long."

"You shouldn't feel guilty about your feelings. They're natural."

"I just want to be like everyone else."

They sat quietly for a long time, watching the sun go down, the moon rise from beyond the mountains. They drank wine and nibbled on the food. No conversation was needed. She felt comfortable in his presence.

Warm drops of rain began to fall.

"Oh, no," she said, "I'll be drenched before I get back to the village."

"You can't go back to the village tonight. It's too dangerous."

She seemed startled at the idea of staying. "I should return to the village."

"No. And this time I mean it. One of our patrols would shoot you if you went stumbling out into the dark—if you were lucky enough not to get shot by the Arabs. You can stay in my tent." He smiled. "Don't worry, my sergeant has an extra bunk in his. I'll bed down there."

The drops became a downpour as they gathered up the remains of their picnic and ran for his tent. They stumbled inside, drenched and laughing. Rain beat the tent canvas.

The tent was spartan—an army cot of canvas stretched between a wood frame, a battered footlocker, two folding chairs, and a portable drafting table. They sat on the cot and shared another glass of wine.

"Wine is one pleasure the Church does not forbid," she said.

He held out his mug. "A toast to . . . to you, to the future. To being like everyone else."

"I've never thought much about the future. The present has always been enough of a struggle." A drip from a tear in the tent canvas was becoming a steady stream and they silently watched it as they sipped wine.

"My men are due back tonight, but I suspect they'll stay the night at Command. The patrol roads we've cut into the mountain turn to mud in these storms."

"I shouldn't take your sleeping quarters. Give me a blanket and I'll sleep in another tent."

"That's not a good idea. My men might be a little surprised to come back and find a beautiful woman in their tent."

They looked at each other for a long moment. He took both her hands and placed them in his. The warmth of his skin radiated his desires to her and excited her. He kissed her, very gently brushing her lips. She didn't turn away and he kissed her again, his lips staying against hers.

She traced the curve of his lips. "I like your lips, they're like the lips you see in medieval murals, well formed and deeply colored."

He kissed under her ear and nibbled on it and slipped down the side of her neck, around her throat and up to the other ear. Her body heat radiated against his face. Thunder pounded somewhere in the night.

He slowly undid the buttons of her habit. She helped him undo the fastenings on the garment underneath. He spread the cloth, exposing her naked breasts. Her breasts were not confined in a brassiere. It was her own private secret, her single defiance against the prison of the cloth she wore. They were small but firm and not quite round, a little narrower than round, with large pink nipples.

Taking her hand, he placed it on the hardness straining against the zipper of his pant. She unbuttoned the top of his pants and opened the zipper and felt the bulge in his shorts, cupping her hand over it, slipping his penis through the opening. She put her hand around it, caressing it, feeling the excitement there. It felt natural to her.

He kissed her lips again, and spread her habit open, his lips following the curve of her throat down to the lush white of her breasts, under her breasts and down her abdomen. It tickled and she laughed softly, delighted, and ran her hands through his thick hair.

She lay back on the couch. "I've waited so long for this moment."

Stripping the layers of holy cloth from her until she was naked, he ran his hands from the base of her throat over her breasts and down her sides, following the curve of her slender figure, pausing at the mound of dark hair guarding her most private place, slipping farther down, along her smooth thighs. Her body was firm from exercise, soft from oils; the body of a woman who cared about her own flesh.

The passion inside her was building, ready to ignite, as lightning and thunder exploded outside. He covered her nakedness with his own, feeling her warmth and softness, touching, experiencing all of her with his whole body.

Thunder shook the earth beneath them.

"This is my dream," she whispered.

Rain beat against the canvas, a great torrent of cleansing water, washing away her sins.

Two hours before dawn, he woke her with kisses as he got out of bed.

"Don't go," she whispered. She could hear activity outside the tent, as if the whole camp had come awake.

He dressed and sat on the edge of the bed. He ran his fingers through her soft hair. "My men are back. There are Arab units on the move in this sector. We're pulling back and a commando unit is coming through."

"I have to get back to the village."

"Not now, not with the Arabs on the move. This area is going to get hot. There's a Syrian tank unit north of here that backs up the irregulars every time they hit us. The word from command is that we're going to clean up this sector."

"Those tanks are not far from the village. We see them once in a while."

"All the more reason not to go back."

"But I should warn the people in the village."

"You'd never make it. The whole area is going to be one big firefight in a couple hours."

"But I have to warn them. The village could be destroyed. Raffi, the little boy, is there."

He pulled away from her and stood up. "Look. I can't let you return. You could jeopardize the whole operation." He jerked open the tent flap. "Don't try to leave the tent. I'm putting a watch on it."

As soon as he was gone, she cut a hole with a field knife and slipped under the back of the tent.

A bloody dawn streaked the horizon by the time Marie reached the hill overlooking the village. A sailor's old adage came to mind as she looked down at the village when she paused to catch her breath.

Red sky in the morning, sailor take warning.

Fighter planes shrieked overhead. She didn't know if they were Israeli, Syrian, or both. Artillery pounded somewhere in the distance.

As she approached the village, Raffi and the mongrel ran to her, both shouting in joy. Loud rumbling came from the north. A solid wall of dust was moving toward the hills, a storm kicked up by Syrian tanks. A rocket flare launched from the heights exploded overhead and she could see the lead tanks moving toward the village.

"We have to get your people out of the village!"

They ran down the hill to where the group of nuns and a hundred excited villagers had gathered at the edge of the village.

Sister Joan rushed to met her, gripped by hysterics. "We don't know what to do! Some of the villagers want to stay in their houses, others say we should flee into the mountains. Show us the way, Sister Marie! *Show us the way!*" The young nun fell to her knees at Marie's feet and hid her face in the skirt of Marie's habit. The people grew silent and stared at Marie. They had been told many times that Marie was a chosen one of God. They were simple people and the medicine and other magic of the nuns was awesome to them.

"Show us the way," Sister Hortense pleaded. The elder nun was also frightened half out of her wits.

Marie's mind swirled in panic. She thought of the tanks coming at the village and imagined the mud huts crumbling under their heavy steel treads. There was no protection in the mountains. The Israelis would be pouring out of them with a vengeance while the Arabs fought their way up. There was only the wadi, a dry riverbed a couple hundred meters from the village.

"The wadi," she shouted, "get everybody to the wadi!"

They huddled in the wash as Syrian tanks rumbled into the village. Marie crawled up to the top of the embankment to check the direction of the tanks. Raffi and the mongrel soon came up beside her. The dog suddenly darted out, barking at the intruders. Marie grabbed the boy as he rushed out and pulled him back. But he screamed for his dog and Marie shoved him into the arms of the two nuns. "Hold him!"

She scrambled out of the wadi and ran after the excited dog.

The overhead jets roared in a dogfight as the Syrians tried to protect their tank battalion. Rockets flashed across the sky and a plane exploded overhead. Marie caught the mongrel by his neck and was thrown to the ground with the dog in her arms from the concussion of an explosion.

A stray rocket had made a direct hit on the riverbed.

She heard the moans and screams of the dying down to her soul.

CHAPTER THIRTY-SEVEN

They left the oasis at dawn, hoping to reach Bethsaida before dusk. David had hoped to tag along with Yoseph's group to avoid entering Bethsaida alone, but they were still loading the stubborn donkey with the tent and supplies when the straw sellers left.

Quintus offered "Marcus" and his servants the privilege of accompanying him to Bethsaida, but David and Marie balked at being part of the cargo of human misery. Conway had not forced the issue because the chained slaves moved slowly and were not due to arrive in Bethsaida until long after dark. It would be difficult enough for the group to safely assimilate into the infamous city without adding nighttime as a handicap.

Before their departure, however, Quintus' overseer arrived with a gift for Conway, a saddled horse to be returned in Bethsaida.

The master race doesn't walk, David thought.

The tack for the horse looked familiar to him, but something was different. The saddle was leather stretched over a wood frame; its horn was a chunk of carved silver that looked suspiciously like a phallic symbol; the harness—bit, straps and reins—all looked conventional. Then it struck him. There were no stirrups. The mounting device had not been invented.

"Your slave will help you mount," the overseer said.

Across the oasis, a servant got down on his hands and knees next to a horse to be mounted by a merchant.

"Go," Marie whispered.

David got down on his hand and knees and Conway stepped on his back to mount. He saluted his fellow Roman as the expedition set out with Conway at the head on horseback, followed by David leading the donkey, and Marie and Isie bringing up the rear.

"That bastard could have leaped aboard," David told Marie as he led the donkey.

"It would have been out of character."

"We're going to be walking in the droppings of Conway's horse. Appropriate, I suppose, since Jews are vassals of Rome."

"You're building up animosity toward Conway in his role as a Roman," Marie said. "He's only doing his job."

"I'm not building up anything," he snapped, then grinned ruefully. She was right. The Romans were second only to Hitler in terms of atrocities committed against the Jews and he instinctively resented Romans—including the one Conway was portraying. Not to mention a bit of envy of the handsome bastard.

"You're right." He stepped to the side of the trail and picked a yellow wildflower. "This is a peace offering."

She contemplated the flower. "It's not a Greek horse, is it?"

"No, I've never been clever enough in my relationship with women to be deceptive."

Their eyes spoke to each other for a moment before Isie ran up, jabbering to her in Aramaic.

"Our Roman master is waving for us to catch up," she said. "If we don't hurry, he might have us whipped."

They had been traveling two hours when Conway turned in his saddle and yelled back to David, "There's a bundle ahead. I'm going to check it out." He galloped ahead and returned moments later with a white bundle about three feet long and a foot wide, tied with camel-hair rope. Conway opened the cloth on one end to expose the contents.

"Swords," he told David, raising his eyebrows. "There's straw residue on the bundle and more on the ground where I found it."

"Yoseph's group."

"There are four swords in this bundle and I'd wager more bundles are under their loads of hay. Jews are prohibited from bearing arms. That means your friends are—"

"Zealots," David said. "Rebels."

"Or Sicarii assassins." Conway eyed the trail ahead. The road ran straight for another couple miles before meandering in the hills that protected the Sea of Galilee. "They might come back looking for the bundle. And they're not going to believe we didn't look inside if we have it. I'm going to dump it."

Conway rode off the trail and dropped the bundle into a ravine.

Isie broke into an excited dialogue with Marie. She told David, "Isie thinks it's madness to throw away the swords. Four swords are worth more than a large flock of sheep."

"We can't have him talking to anyone about them. You better say something to scare him. Tell him they're taboo or something."

After Marie spoke to him, the boy shot a furtive glance at the ravine and hurried down the road. They followed him with the donkey clopping behind on a short rein.

"I told him the swords had a curse on them and warned him not to tell anyone or a demon would come back looking for him." She shook her head. "I hated to pollute his mind with more nonsense about devils, but I couldn't think of anything else."

"He still believes we're demons?"

"He doesn't think I'm a demon." She pointed off to the right. "Look. Isie's chasing supper."

The boy was chasing a rabbit, his sling swirling as he ran.

Marie left the trail and followed him. "Don't go too far," she shouted to the boy.

The region teemed with wildlife. Near where the roadway started into the hills, a herd of antelope raced across the grassland. A lion trotted behind the antelope in no obvious hurry. It reminded David of scenes in safari movies and he marveled at how rich the earth had been before machines and overpopulation sucked the land dry.

A fresher, cleaner world than the one he was born into, not poisoned by chemicals and toxic wastes, a quieter world, not hammered by the noise of cars and trains and planes, but it was a world without a sense of humanity. What would the effect be on history if beneficial modern knowledge was introduced into this world where might was right and people believed human events were determined by gods that sat on clouds and toyed like spoiled children with the fate of mankind?

Atomic bombs were madness in the hands of pagans, he thought, but atomic power in the hands of the ancients could mean reaching the stars long before Columbus sailed the ocean blue. What if he used his knowledge and training to educate the ancient world? He was an intelligent, caring human being who could communicate the sense of humanity the ancient world needed so desperately. It took the Judeo-Christian ethic centuries—a couple thousand years—to instill even a modest sense of brotherly love in parts of the world, but he could spread it at—

Gunpoint! A man's head snapping back as a bullet split his forehead. He shuddered at the memory. His father had played God. Playing God was exactly what he would be doing if he changed the world to fit his own image, but his role in the mission still bothered him.

In New Mexico, General Scott's barbed remark about the consequences to the Jewish people if the mission succeeded had been easy to rebut, no more than an intellectual exercise on David's part, but the reality of the mission had come home to him and he confronted the dilemma the second time that morning: He had taken a covenant to seal the fate of his own people for the next two thousand years by ensuring that a young Jew from Galilee died on the cross.

His father would have been proud of young Zealots like Yoseph, Jewish warriors fighting a foreign enemy. Or would he? If his father had been a first-century Jew under Roman hegemony, he probably would have been a Sicarii, a terrorist, not just an underground fighter for freedom.

As he reached the first bend in the hills, David saw someone dodge behind a boulder to his left. He tensed. Conway had galloped off to get a better look at the lion stalking the antelope herd and Marie was off chasing rabbits with Isie.

Four men in black cloaks suddenly charged out of the rocks.

David jerked the donkey's reins and yelled, stampeding the donkey between him and the men. He drew his sword and quickly slashed out at the closest man, spinning around and slashing the others in a frenzy, his powerful blows and superior sword breaking one sword and backing off all of the attackers.

One man was still off balance from the charge of the donkey and David's violent attack, and he stumbled backward. David's sword cut the man across the chest, opening the flesh. The man screamed, dropped his weapon, and ran. Another attacker came at him from the left and David whipped around, swinging the sword wildly as Conway charged into the melee on his horse.

The fight became a blur of clashing swords and frantic movements as four more attackers swarmed them. Conway's horse screamed and he jumped clear as the beast went down. Two of the attackers immediately tried to rush Conway while he was off balance.

Marie came running up, confused, not knowing what to do, Isie behind her. One of the attackers saw her and split off from the group and ran for her. She bent down to pick up a rock to defend herself when Isie suddenly appeared beside her, his leather sling singing as it swirled, letting fly a stone that caught the man in the chest. The man turned tail and ran back into the rocks as Isie let another stone fly.

A heavyset man charged in front of David and drove his

swordpoint at David's throat but David parried the stroke and for one frozen moment stared into a pair of nervous, feverish eyes.

Amir Zayyad!

An instant later, he was gone, the attackers had suddenly broken and fled back to the rocks. David's guard was still up, his ears buzzing. He didn't understand why the attackers had fled.

Yoseph ran up, grinning broadly. The straw sellers had returned to find their bundle.

David relaxed his stance, relieved, as other straw sellers ran by him, pursuing the attackers into the rocks.

"Come back, friends," Yoseph yelled. "Let the snakes crawl back into their holes."

Conway saluted Yoseph with his sword. "Many thanks, you saved us from those bandits."

Yoseph picked up a dagger one of the attackers dropped. The good humor left his features as he stared at it. "Those were not bandits," he said to Conway. "They were Sicarii assassins. They mark for death Romans involved in the enslavement of Israel." His eyes went to David. "And their Jewish collaborators."

He walked away stiffly, rejoining his friends who had gone back up the trail to their donkeys.

David exchanged looks with Conway as Marie and Isie hurried up to them.

"Are you all right?" she asked.

David nodded. "I saw what Isie did. Tell him we're proud of him."

It wasn't necessary. The boy was grinning ear to ear. He ran off to join the straw sellers, eager to swap tales of the battle.

"Stay close to the boy," Conway said to Marie. "Make sure he doesn't tell the straw sellers about the bundle of swords we found."

Marie went after Isie and David left the trail to retrieve the donkey. The beast had not gone far—its reins had snagged between boulders fifty feet off the trail. He calmed the animal and led it back, joining Conway where he was examining a cut on his horse's side.

"It's not bad," Conway said, "but I'll walk it anyway."

They kept a wary eye on the rocks as they led the animals up the trail.

"That attack established several things," Conway said. "They know we're here, and we know they haven't found Jesus. Nor have they had time to make modern weapons. If they had, they would have attacked openly. It may be that they're not going to make modern weapons until they've completed their object. Once they spread guns around to other people, they will lose the mystery and fear that these people will have for them and their edge of killing power."

"Jair wasn't with them," David said. "I'm sure of that. He's not the type to hide behind a rock and let his younger brother do the fighting. He might be in Galilee—perhaps even Bethsaida—searching for Jesus. Probably sent his brother to watch the roads because he knew a rescue team would show up. Amir didn't have any trouble spotting us. Not with me along."

"Now they know what we all look like," Conway said. He glanced sideways at David. "Watch your back. I didn't get a look at Amir. You're still the only one who can identify both the Zayyad brothers." They walked in silence for a moment before Conway said, "I wasn't impressed with the swords or the swordsmanship of the Sicarii. Their weapons are inferior and they handle them like farmers with hoes rather than soldiers."

"That's because they *are* farmers. And tradesmen. They probably forge their swords in their own blacksmith's shops. And learn how to fight in back of the barn, hitting each other with sticks."

Conway shook his head. "And these people think they can take on Roman legions?"

"We have one question answered."

Conway raised his eyebrows.

"Yoseph and the straw sellers are not Sicarii, they're Zealots. Zealots don't get along with the Sicarii. But Romans are the common enemy. I suggest you watch your back, my *Roman* friend."

CHAPTER THIRTY-EIGHT

Bethsaida.

David shaded his eyes from the sun and gazed at the distant city. Walls of granite rose near the banks where the holy Jordan was swallowed by the Sea of Galilee. Gilded rooftops of palaces and public buildings protruded above the walls and glowed in the late afternoon sun.

Conway caught David's eye. "Excited about seeing your first Jewish city?"

"I'm excited about seeing an *ancient* city. Bethsaida isn't Jewish even if many of the people living there are. The city's a pagan place with marble palaces for the rich and mud-walled tenements for the common people. It's built in Greek style, not the architecture of Israel." Its builder, Philip, had been more "Greek" than Jew, David thought. The city had been a sleepy fishing village until Philip rebuilt it in Greco-Roman fashion.

"The New Testament characterizes the city as a place made wicked from Salome's lust and intrigues," Marie said. She emphasized what they had been taught about the city. "After creating his first miracle here, Jesus warned people from coming here, although several of his Disciples were from here."

"Has Isie ever been to Bethsaida?" David asked Marie.

This was Isie's first time to the city, but he had heard many things about it, he told Marie. It was a place where a man could find pleasure with a woman or meet death for the contents of his purse.

On a hillock just before the city they came upon a grisly sight. Crucifixion crosses. Three men, their bodies bloodied and broken, their faces death masks of horror.

They walked silently by three crosses reeking of pain and death, flies feasting on the blood of Jewish rebels.

The straw sellers stared grimly at the crosses as they passed. Yosef glanced back at David, who read the unspoken message: Look what your Roman masters have done to the Sons of Israel, O Roman Jew!

David took Marie's arm. Her face was pale and drawn. "It's—it's all my nightmares come true."

"Don't think about it," he said. "Look! A pagan city! We're entering a living museum, walking across a page of history," his voice cracked.

Conway hurried back to them. "Are you two okay?"

"Fine. Let's keep moving," David said, taking a deep breath. He reminded himself that this was the pagan world.

"It's the most brutal form of torture ever devised," Marie said, "the ultimate form of humiliation and pain. They crucify people naked to increase the humiliation. Even more horrendous is when they crucify them upside down. Peter asked to be crucified upside down because he said he was not worthy of being crucified in the same manner as Jesus."

David didn't try to stop her. She needed to talk it out. She had spent most of her life dealing with crucifixion wounds. Now she needed to verbalize her anguish.

"What makes it so horrible is that the victims don't die right away. They are nailed to the cross and left there for their bodies to slowly shut down. They literally die of suffocation as their lungs and internal organs slow down from the pain and exposure. To increase the torture and speed death, the victim is whipped, scourged, till they are bloody and their flesh hangs in strips. They are hung up to die slowly. An act of mercy is taking a sledgehammer and breaking the person's legs so he bleeds to death or taking a spear and puncturing the abdomen."

She became breathless as she spoke.

David didn't need the history professors to tell him about crucifixion. He knew it had never been a Jewish form of punishment. Ordinary capital offenses, like murder and adultery, were punishable by stoning, with the accusers throwing the first stones. The Romans used crucifixion for what they considered heinous crimes, things like treason and rebellions and slave insurrections. So many Jews were crucified by the Romans, tens of thousands, that the cross became a symbol of brutal oppression.

She stared back at the crosses. Her voice became coldly calm, so devoid of life and emotion that it caused the hair to raise on the back of David's neck. "Iron spikes were driven through the palms of my hand. Nobody saw them but me. I screamed when they ripped through my bones and flesh." Her face was pale and drawn as she looked at David. "They made me experience His pain so I would know that I had been chosen."

The marketplace spread out before the main gate of the city was an ancient version of a shopping mall, part mercantile, part theatrical; a place where one stall sold chickens with their feet tied together and at the next stall humans were on sale with chains around their necks; where fortune-tellers told your fate and pickpockets sealed it.

City guards at the edge of the marketplace inspected new arrivals and their packs.

Yosef and his friends split off, taking a side road that led to the camp of the caravaners who were bypassing the city. Yosef looked back, but did not wave.

"They must be wondering whether we're going to turn them in," David said to Conway.

"They obviously don't want their hay searched. I imagine they have their own way into the city."

The Roman legionnaires from the caravan reached the

guard station and rudely shoved their way past the city guards, who were not legionnaires.

Conway grinned. "Seems the master race doesn't have any respect for the local rules. Well, when in Rome . . ." He arrogantly pushed a barrier aside and as a guard stepped up to him, Conway shouted at him in Latin loud enough for the legionnaires to hear.

The Roman commander turned around and yelled to the guards, who quickly backed off, letting the group through without a search. Conway waved his thanks to the Roman commander and the man grinned and waved back.

It had been an unnecessary display of daring, David thought, but it worked and he kept his mouth shut. He didn't breathe easy until they were well beyond the barriers and swallowed by the crowd. He still had a tight grip on Marie's arm and she pulled away to stay beside Isie as they meandered between the stalls and piles of goods.

"I'm all right now," she said.

Starting at the city gates, merchandise was sold from wood stalls, canvaslike canopies, tables in the open, blankets laid on the ground, and sometimes, just in the hands of people who wandered around, accosting shoppers and offering their goods.

"Look at the lost arts," David said. Most of the merchandise displayed in the marketplace was made in the same shop that sold it. Walking by rows of wooden stalls leaning against each other like pilings of driftwood, he paused to watch a merchant and his two sons casting molten brass and shaping the metal into bottles, bowls, and vases at the rear of a shop while the man's wife and daughter sat in front of the shop and etched designs on the merchandise. They passed shops where clothing was woven, bronze worked into pots and pans, jewelry carved from copper and cut from stone, glass blown, rope, saddles, pottery, and lamps made, decorated and sold, merchants taking orders on wax tablets, weighing grains and fowl on scales balanced with stone blocks of varying size.

The "manufacturing" process alone was amazing. The baker didn't simply knead bread and shove it into an oven. The process began in the rear of the shop in an hourglass-shaped stone vessel sitting on a round stone with a channel in it. Grain was poured into the top vessel, the vessel was turned by a donkey strapped to it, grinding the grain, flour flowing out of the channel in the bottom stone to a wide-mouth jar. Flour from the jar was spread onto tables where it was moistened with water, kneaded, mixed with grapes or other fillings, and baked in hard clay ovens before being placed for sale on tables in front.

The noise level was beyond rap music. It was like being in an electronics superstore in which all the speakers for sale were turned on—full blast. The sounds of hawking, arguing, and negotiations in a babel of tongues, each merchant yelling as if decibels increased the value of the goods, each buyer shouting back to beat down the seller's decibels. Peddlers of bronze utensils and melon farmers from the other side of the Sea of Galilee fought for airtime. Shopkeepers of cloth and lamps argued with lower-class women who did their own shopping, as well as the slaves who shopped for rich households.

Added to the bedlam of voices was the tapping of shoemakers, hammering of blacksmiths, chopping of wood sellers, sawing of furniture makers, chiseling of stonecutters, and a dozen other sounds of the manufacturing processes.

The voices and manufacturing mixed with the creaking axles of carts—axles greased only with animal fat or olive oil, turning wheels that were big, thick wooden disks—the belligerent baying of donkeys, the thump of oxen hooves, and the baa of lambs being herded to the butcher's stall. A flurry of curses rose as the sheep, on their way to slaughter, got too close to a pottery maker's jars and bowls.

"The talent and hard work in this place is incredible," David said. "Each shop literally starts from scratch and creates a finished product. We're from a world where things are made by machine and thrown away when they break. Almost every person in this marketplace has a talent for making something useful. We would call these people artisans and craftsmen, but here they are just the norm."

Marie nodded toward a fuller's shop where clothing was woven, bleached, combed, shrunk, softened, sewn, and sold. Alkaline clay was used for soap and the cloth was bleached by hanging it on wooden frames with burning sulfur beneath. The fuller's shop gave off a variety of stenches.

"Yes, the human talent is incredible, but there was also ignorance," she added. "Part of that smell from the fuller's is urine collected from the public lavatories. They use urine as a chemical to thicken and mat the cloth. When men and women stomped the cloth, they often got skin diseases that were untreatable. They knew nothing about lead poisoning and produced pottery that killed millions."

"We have factories costing millions and employing thousands to produce what these small families are producing in small shops."

"And those skills are being passed from father to son, mother to daughter," she said.

"Skills we've built machines to perform," David said. "A few people in our time learn how to engineer the machines, but most don't get beyond simply pressing the on and off button." The engineer in him was dazzled by the manufacturing processes. "I can't get over what we've lost to machines."

Several women wearing elaborate hairdos and silken togas were being waited on at what appeared to be a cosmetics counter, a place where oils and creams mixed with spices and aromatic gums were sold, along with a black substance to darken eyebrows, brass and silver combs, and bronze tools to cut and trim nails. Another shop attracting a similar group of women had a counter full of jewelry, bracelets of copper and bronze, anklets, long strands of beads made from colorful glass and stones, rings of all sizes and shapes, the larger and gaudier pieces being the most numerous. Bronze, copper, and iron seemed to be the most popular metals for the rings and bracelets, but wealthy women dripped with gold and silver chains around their neck and in their hair.

"Gold and silver and precious stones are sold in shops safely tucked within the city walls," Marie said.

From their fancy clothes and elaborate jewelry, David assumed the wealthy women frequenting the cosmetic and jewelry counters to be Roman, but Marie didn't agree.

"I heard several of them speaking a mixture of Hebrew and Greek. I imagine they're wealthy Jews. Look at the contrast between them and the lower classes. The Jewish women working in the shops and the ones that look like farmers' wives have modest dresses similar to the tunics men wear." The women's dresses were decorated with embroidery, as were the shawls they wore around their shoul-ders and the scarf on their head. "You notice how much jewelry the rich women wear? Some even have gold rings in their noses."

"It was an age of class differences," David said, "and the women dressed to show their superiority, just as Romans wore togas to distinguish them from others. While wealthy Jews aped their Roman masters, commoners like Yosef carried on a secret war for freedom." The same had been true during the struggle to birth the nation of Israel. While Jewish patriots fought for freedom, there were still Jews who thought living under the British Mandate was acceptable.

Most Jewish males wore the same type of clothing he was wearing, though his was more coarsely woven, befitting his station in life as a slave. Many of the men and women David took to be farmers or laborers wore a square cloth affixed around the head by a cord. It was similar to the Bedouin kaffiyeh headgear that David had worn during his sojourns in the desert.

There was magic in the marketplace. They passed a small crowd huddled around a snake charmer who was lying on his back on the ground with a coiled cobra on his stomach. The man used a stick with a small ball dangling from a piece of twine like a fishing line to keep the snake's attention while a woman beseeched coins for the performance. An old woman, looking much like a Gypsy, approached David and jabbered something in Aramaic.

"She's offering to tell your fortune," Marie said.

He laughed and walked on. "Tell her it would ruin her day."

They were assaulted by an army of beggars and avaricious tradesmen as they moved around piles of fruits and vegetables grown locally and dried goods from the desert nations.

David caught a little Hebrew here and there, plus a language Marie said was ancient Greek, but the most common tongue of the marketplace was Aramaic. As they neared the gate of the city a pitiful creature in rags came toward them shouting something and Conway steered them away from the man.

"He was shouting, 'unclean!'" Marie said. "He's a leper and by law must warn others of his presence. Poor soul. This really was an age of ignorance. They believed the disease was God's curse."

Conway eyed the crowd. "Half the men in this crowd look like the assassins who attacked us. I've changed my mind about staying at an inn. We'll be better off at the villa of Quintus where we'll have a little protection by being the guests of a Roman." He grinned. "I hope you like the stable."

Conway strutted arrogantly by the guards posted at the city gate. The guards let them pass, already forewarned by the legionnaires.

David experienced another thrill of discovery as the main thoroughfare of the city was before them. Porticoes with tall columns and triangular roofs lined each side of the street, stately entrances to the buildings that created the impression of a long colonnade on both sides of the street. Statues of the twelve divinities of Olympus, idolatry no orthodox Jew would tolerate and that would have caused riots in Jerusalem, but that the descendants of Herod displayed to toady to the Romans, lined the way. The thoroughfare passed under an arch of triumph and beyond that they could see the walls to the palace of Salome and the bedridden Philip.

Passing Roman baths, a naked Apollo at the one side of the entrance, a naked Venus on the other, the smell of mineral waters permeated the air.

Marie said, "The baths are like modern health spas with hot mineral waters to relax the muscles, icy pools to stimulate the blood, and steam to cleanse body and soul. Men frequented them more than women. Sometimes they were like social clubs, others were little more than brothels."

David saw the look Conway gave Marie. An angry rush of blood went to his head.

CHAPTER THIRTY-NINE

Quintus had sent a messenger ahead to announce the arrival of his Roman guest and servants to ensure that all was in order to provide hospitality for the guest.

Observed from the street, the house looked severely plain, with white stucco, windowless walls, and a slightly slanted roof of red Mediterranean tile. The house fronted the street. David noted that the walls were not the hardened mud-and-straw bricks of a poor person. The material was an amalgam of ground stone and volcanic ash.

The front entrance was through an open courtyard, the *vestibulum*, lined with shrubs, flowers, and statuary, and floored with gold-veined marble. As they came into the entrance, they were startled by two dogs, big mastiffs with hanging lips, drooping ears, and short, thick, tan coats. The dogs, chained in the courtyard, were as noisy as jackals and mean enough to take on a lion.

"Burglar alarm," Conway said of the dogs as the animals snarled and dripped saliva through sharp teeth.

The dogs strained their short chain, trying to get at them. Everyone stayed well away from them except Isie, who got within biting range of one of them. His own snarl and swing of his sling caused the dog to close its mouth and shut up.

The threshold to the doorway had an elaborate mosaic of

Roman soldiers battling barbarians. Set into the tiny bits of glassy ceramic was the word *salve*.

"It's a wish for good health to any who enter the house," Conway said.

The entrance to the house, a doorway called the *ostium*, was next. Above the broad, bronze door engraved in stone was the phrase, *Nihil intret mal*.

Conway again liberally translated the Latin. "Nothing bad or evil is to pass through the door."

As was their custom, they talked freely in English, certain that no one could understand what they said; an alien language was not suspicious in an empire that encompassed dozens of languages.

"Marcus the Roman" and his three servants presented themselves at the front door where the head slave greeted Conway with lavish praises for him and his illustrious family, which of course the slave knew nothing about, not even the fictional Roman one created for the mission. He looked at Conway's servants with distaste. "Servants enter the stable at the rear."

"They will accompany me first to better acquaint themselves in serving me," Conway said. "Show me to my quarters."

Conway had guessed that his servants would be barred from the main house, but he wanted David and Marie to see the layout in case of an emergency.

Passing through the doorway, they entered the *atrium*, the core of the house. The rectangular room, long and wide, two stories high, was a vast cavern with a large hole in the center of the roof. Below the hole was a fountain that collected rainwater that came through the opening. To the others, it was just a beautiful room. To David, who had designed a large building incorporating the features of an atrium, it stirred emotions.

"It was a very effective design," he said, mainly speaking to Marie, who stood beside him, "in the days when the outer walls of houses didn't have windows for safety reasons. Light came through this hole in the roof that was used for escape of smoke for the cooking fire in the days when even Roman houses were mud huts. As Roman homes became palaces, the atrium became the main room that one entered from the street."

The rooms leading off the atrium included a library with papyrus, leather scrolls, and clay tablets, a drawing room, and dining room. A second story included baths and bedrooms. The upstairs rooms had windows on the interior side of the house to provide more light and air.

The atrium room itself, resplendent in its statuary and furnishings, was much like the modern living room: for display purposes only. The pillars holding up the ceiling-roof were made of polished variegated marble, as were the walls and floor. Adorning the walls were figures in relief, scenes from Roman history and the machinations of the gods. In the space between each doorway leading off the atrium were statues of distinguished ancestors, emperors, gods, and famous warriors sculptured in marble.

The ceiling was a dark, rich hardwood encrusted with silver and ivory designs.

The fountain in the center of room was a marble basin. Encircling the foot-high wall of the basin were gold reliefs of nine muses: Calliope, holding a writing tablet of epic poetry; Urania, the muse of astronomy holding a globe; Euterpe playing a flute; Clio with a scroll of history; Melpomene with her tragic mask; Erato with her love poetry; Polyhymnia singing; Terpsichore dancing; and Thalia with her comic mask.

"The bedrooms, reception area, dinning room, and baths are heated," the head slave told Conway, with ostentatious pride.

David could feel heat rising from the floor. His engineering and architectural training clued him on the heat source as he explained it to Marie.

"There is a furnace or two under the house, maybe one upstairs. Water is heated and carried through the house in tile pipes to hollow areas in the floors and maybe even some of the walls."

There were also portable heating units, metal boxes called *foculi,* that were filled with hot coals and carried into a room that needed to be heated.

"Space heaters," Marie called them.

Conway was delighted to discover that the bathrooms had toilets with running water. The water was collected and stored in cisterns on the roof of the house and flowed gravitationally down to the bathrooms.

"We're so thrilled for you," David said, without hiding his sarcasm. Marie gave him a warning look. Even if the head slave could not understand the words, vocal tone and body language were universal.

While the marble and statuary were palatial, what one would expect if touring an ancient palace, the furnishings were spartan, David noted.

"It was said that there was not a comfortable bed in all of Rome," Marie said, reading his and Conway's mind as they stared at the sparse furnishings throughout the house. "And the same can be said of couches and chairs, which comprised most of the furnishings. You notice that there is none of the jumble of furnishings that modern houses contain. No mirrors on the walls, no desks or writing tables, no bookcases, dressers, not even a hat rack."

The couches were most often a seating place by day, a bed by night, she told them. While the wood was ornate, the coverings of costly fabrics worked with gold and silver thread, they were not places to flop into and be a couch potato. Chairs were basically four-legged stools without a back. Quintus' chairs tended toward the fancy curule chairs that had four legs of curved ivory topped by a fancy cushion.

Tables were small and ornate except for the large dining table that was covered by cloth to protect the precious wood from hot and wet bowls.

At the far end of the atrium, enormous bronze doors, twenty feet high, unclosed in warm weather, opened to two broad marble steps that led down to the *peristyle,* an area larger than the atrium.

The peristyle was similar to the atrium in that doorways led off to rooms that lined both sides, but it was more open to the elements. It was essentially an almost open courtyard, with the roof opening encompassing almost half of the ceiling area. The fountain-pond in the center was correspondingly larger to accommodate the large opening to the sky. Like the atrium, the courtyard was adorned with marble, relief on walls, statuary, shrubs, flowers, and trees, but not as richly scaled. Likewise, the walls left and right were lined with doorways to rooms—kitchen, scullery, storerooms, slave quarters, and all the other facilities that a great house required.

"It's almost two houses," David said. "The atrium is elegant and quiet, the place where the master eats, sleeps, and entertains. The peristyle is a pleasant courtyard and contains all the support facilities that kept the main house operating." David paused to look at two clocks during the walk-through.

In the courtyard of the peristyle, a sundial measured the hours of the day by the shadow cast by a bronze finger. More interesting was a water clock in the atrium that measured the hours of the day and night. An idea borrowed from the Greeks, the water glass worked similarly to an hourglass, but was more useful. It consisted of a vessel filled each day at the same time. As the water dripped from it, the passage of hours could be told by a scale.

"A water clock, even made with precision, would never be very accurate because of the ways hours were counted," he told Marie. "The Romans simply divided up daylight into twelve 'hours' and nighttime into twelve more. The problem is that an hour in a winter month would be much shorter than an hour in a summer month."

"But they didn't need accurate time," Marie pointed out. "Journeys and other events were measured by days, weeks, and months, not minutes or hours in a car or plane."

There was a third area in the complex, to the rear of the house: a stable for the horses. Above it was a hayloft that also served as accommodations for the servants of guests who stayed overnight.

The loft above the stable smelled of hay and manure and horses.

Their "bathroom" was the stable floor.

"Just pick a spot and squat," David said. "You know, I already hate Romans and I've only met one so far."

"You are impossible," Marie said. "You fit nicely into this era where stiff-necked Jews fight the Romans to death. Literally."

He shrugged and grinned with as much innocence as he could muster. "I'm guilty, but I'm trying to change. Trust me."

Marie sighed and sat down on hay baled with twine. "Impossible. Besides, I don't have the energy."

He sat down beside her. "It's one thing to read in history books about what arrogant, ruthless bastards the Romans were, and another to see Quintus treating slaves worse than we treat cattle. I guess I'm having the same sort of reaction that I would have if I was transported back to a pogrom in Nazi Germany and had to stand about helplessly as I saw injustices all around me."

"We promised not to change this world," she said. "We are here to do just one thing, and that's to prevent the terrorists from changing it."

"I know that, but I have a couple thousand years of persecution running in my veins. I was numbed by how my father reacted toward the Arabs. Because I saw what he did to the Zayyads, the bloodshed, I froze inside. Coming back here, seeing how the Jews were treated, my blood is defrosting."

"Mine is just tired," Marie said. "And so is Isie's."

The boy had curled up on a pile of hay with his robe wrapped around him.

After they spread blankets on fresh hay, Marie fell into an exhausted sleep almost immediately. A beam of moonlight sneaking through a crack in the roof touched her like a spotlight from heaven.

David lay awake and watched the gentle rise and fall of her breathing. He was on a mission to save the world from the very tentacles of an ancient evil in a city from the Arabian Nights. At his side was a beautiful woman.

What more was there in store for him?

———

Late that night, Quintus arrived home. His head servant reported the preparations he had made for Marcus the Roman.

"Is my guest pleased?" Quintus asked.

"Very pleased with the magnificence of your hospitality."

"Good." He did not ask his servant what he thought of his guest. One did not ask a slave for an opinion about a fellow Roman.

After he had snacked on sweetmeats and drunk a goblet of wine, he sat down in his chambers and wrote on a sheet of papyrus.

"A stranger has arrived in the city," he wrote. "A Roman. The man has raised my curiosity because he is accompanied by a Jewish servant who does not appear to be a Jew and who is not treated in all respects as a servant. This and the man's sudden appearance from a direction in which there was no caravan trail with a story of having been waylaid by bandits has aroused my suspicions . . ."

When he was finished, he folded the letter and used his signet and warm wax to seal the letter. Quintus stared at the letter in his hand, weighing the consequences of his act. He made up his mind and handed it to his overseer.

"Take this to Rahm, the captain of the Royal Guard. Tell him it concerns strangers who have entered the city. It is for Salome's eyes alone."

CHAPTER FORTY

Yoseph left the house of a cousin where he was staying in Bethsaida. The straw sellers had stabled their donkeys and straw with a hostler outside the city and entered a secret passageway under the man's storage shed. The passage led to natural underground catacombs that had been leached out by water eons before the city and its walls went up. They carried with them bundles of swords.

Inside of the city walls, they resurfaced in the shop of a goldsmith. From there, they divided up, each taking a bundle of swords to be hidden where they resided during their stay in the city.

Yoseph knew well that it was both the pride and the misfortune of Jews that their small land of Israel occupied a strategic location on the trade routes. By the time the Romans became the dominant power in Israel, the Jews had suffered and survived slavery in Egypt, exile to Babylon, domination by the Persians, Macedonians, and Syrians, plus endless warfare with neighboring countries. It was claimed that in Babylonian times, Nebuchadnezzar blinded and sodomized the captive chieftains of Judah, to humiliate them and make it easier to keep their people in captivity.

But the Jews' worst enemy was always themselves.

After all of their struggles to throw off the yoke of foreign empires, Roman hegemony came not from conquest by the mighty Roman legions but because they were invited in to settle a dispute between two Jewish princes of the Hasmonean dynasty. Divide and conquer.

Now the Jews chafed under the Roman heel. The Romans claimed they offered peace and prosperity to the world under their control, but it came at a frightful price. They took away the dignity and pride of the dominated people. They taxed them with a zeal that made one wonder whether gold was their god. And they trampled on religion when it got in the way of their aspirations.

Things were not well in Israel for persons of Yoseph's ilk. He was a farmer. Not a poor man. Far from being a rich one. And it was others like him, the farmers and tradesmen who formed a small middle-class, who suffered under the Roman heel.

The most aggravating effect of Roman dominance was taxes and the brutal way they were collected. The Romans taxed everything. There was a poll tax—a personal tax on each person merely for being alive—a tax on meat, salt, roads, houses. The Romans would tax the air if they could.

The right to collect taxes was sold by the emperor to men who paid him the full value of the estimated taxes. They then collected as much money from the people taxed as they could, pocketing the excess. To squeeze every cent possible, gangs of thugs went to farmers and merchants to collect, beating those who resisted, imprisoning their families and applying torture when mere violence was not persuasive enough.

The Herod toadies, kept on golden thrones by Roman legions, added their taxes atop the pile of resentment.

The taxes were just the most obvious point of contention. The Jews were a religious people, emboldened by faith in their God. To have Romans issue coins, statues, and banners with graven images was an offense to Jews. An offense to their pride, God, and their dignity. Yoseph and his Zealot brothers believed that Israel would never be great, her people never prosperous, nor the land be healthy and bountiful, as long as they had to kneel to the Romans as slaves do to their masters.

Unlike most of the other provinces of the empire, they had the courage to take up arms against the overwhelming Roman military forces. The source of their courage was an unyielding faith in God. They had a powerful god, the *one* God in a world in which other nations had a confusing pantheon of deities.

The Jews were the Chosen People. They believed that when they rose and took sword in hand, their God would not let them fail.

Yoseph was keenly aware that others had tried. And failed. After Herod the Great's death, Archelaus, his son, put down a rebellion by massacring three thousand Jews. Roman troops arrived and took control of Jerusalem. The Roman commander stole the temple treasure and part of the temple was burned when Jews in the city rose against the thief.

In Galilee, a Jewish patriot known as Judas of Galilee, the son of Hezekiah, another Jewish patriot murdered by Herod, raised an army and fought the Romans. The Romans brought in legions from the empire and brutally put down the rebellion, destroying the rebel city and crucifying thousands of rebels and those who supported them. But out of that defeat and chaos rose an underground Jewish resistance determined to drive the Romans from Israel—the Zealots.

One such Zealot was Simon, a former slave of Herod, who gathered an army and a following in Perea and fought the Romans until he was defeated. Another, Athronges, a shepherd, was said to have the strength of Hercules. Supported by his four militant brothers, he proclaimed himself the heir to King David, and fought to gain the kingdom itself.

Each was defeated and thousands of Jews were crucified. But that did not deter Yoseph and the Zealots who were preparing for another great battle against the Romans. The ones who revolted before did not have the support of the Lord. This time they would wait for a sign. And when they received it, they would rise.

Yoseph stepped into a doorway and stood still as a squad of soldiers went by. They were not legionnaires but Salome's personal guard. When he was younger, he would have spat as they passed, but he was a Zealot leader now and his duty was to prepare for a war, not end up in a dungeon because of a moment of bravado.

After the soldiers passed, he moved quickly. It was nearly curfew time and anyone caught on the streets after the second hour of darkness was stopped, questioned, and arrested if they did not have a good excuse—and a bribe for the soldiers.

The meeting of Zealots was held in the house of a wool merchant. They never met twice in a row in the same house.

Yoseph, whose farm was outside a village ten leagues from the city, did not know all the Zealots of Bethsaida, but he had met and befriended Ezra Ben Ephraim, the leader of the city's rebels.

When he entered, he was greeted as a brother and friend by all present. The Bethsaida leader, Ezra, steered Yoseph to a seat on a bench and the group gathered around them. Ezra's snowy beard, barrel chest, and massive arms and legs gave him the powerful profile of a blacksmith rather than the leather merchant that he was.

"Any word of my brother?" Yoseph asked.

No man at the table met his eye for a moment. Ezra stood beside him to pour him a cup of wine and then sat down, heavily, the world on his shoulders.

"Your brother is still alive. Sadly." Ezra spread his hands. "We tried to slip poison in with the prisoners' food but Salome's dungeon guards snatched it when one of their own men became ill. The swine died but your brother is still in the hands of the queen. She has received permission from Rome to proceed with his crucifixion and has set the day after tomorrow for the act."

"I appreciate your efforts," Yoseph said. His brother had been captured in a Zealot raid on a Roman tax collector's caravan. The others had escaped into the wilderness but his brother's mule had gone down, taking him down with it.

"The tax collector's money your brother's raid gained will buy twenty swords," Ezra said. "Each one of those swords will take five Roman lives." He reached across the table and squeezed Yoseph's arm. "Your brother's life will cost the enemies of Israel a hundredfold."

"I know that. More importantly, he knows that. But I cannot let the blood of my family be spilled as a public spectacle by the Jezebel." Yoseph's hands shook as anger gripped him. "Dogs ate the flesh off of Jezebel's naked body after she was brought down. Salome will get no better treatment after we drive her Roman masters from Israel."

"What are your plans?" Ezra asked.

"To kill my brother."

Each of the men at the table understood. Salome did not plan to simply execute Yoseph's brother. To put terror into the hearts of her subjects, she planned to turn the death into a circus of horror, crucifying him in such a way that he died agonizingly slowly, in great pain, making him beg for death as a crowd of her bootlickers and courtiers, mostly non-Jews, looked on with glee.

"I have a plan," Yoseph said. "One that involves myself and three of my cousins who accompanied me here. We will not put our Jewish supporters in the city at risk for my brother. This is a family matter and we shall take care of it."

"You cannot save your brother," Ezra said. "The dungeon is too well guarded."

"Yes, I know."

Ezra looked down at his strong hands, clenching them open and shut, as if he had Salome's neck in his powerful grip. "There is other news we must deal with," Ezra said. "A spy we have in the Sicarii informs us that those murderers have allied themselves with strangers possessing a power."

"A power?" Yoseph asked.

"We have no knowledge of what it is. The Sicarii leaders are not speaking of it even to their own kind. But rumors leak through their ranks and our friend in their midst says that two men from outside Israel are in league with the Sicarii. What their intent is, we are not sure. But if they have a weapon that would be effective against the Romans, we need to know."

Ezra's voice was filled with contempt for the Jewish terrorists. They were patriots, too, but men who would murder others in cold blood were not to be trusted. They were too dominated by their own insane passions. The look on Yoseph's face drew his attention. "You know something of this, Yoseph?"

"Not for certain." He shook his head. He related how David and the others joined the caravan with a tale of having been robbed, and the subsequent fight with the Sicarii.

"Two men, a Roman and a supposed Jew, a woman, and a boy. A strange Jew." Erza pursed his lips. "Do you think they are Roman spies?" he asked Yoseph.

"At first I did, but now I am unsure. The Romans are not fools. They have paid spies in every city and village in Israel. Why would they send us a Jew whose hair and lack of beard would bring his religion into question? And Marcus, his master. They would not send a Roman to spy upon us."

"Perhaps they are the two men the Sicarii are in league with," Ezra said.

"They were attacked by the Sicarii."

"A false attack to eliminate suspicion?"

"It was not a fake attack. I am sure of it. The emotions were too strong. The battle too violent. We came upon it only moments after it started. I don't know how it would have ended, the two men were outnumbered, but they would have taken many Sicarii lives with them had we not frightened away the attackers."

"Then who are these strangers?" Ezra shrugged. "Perhaps no more than ordinary travelers?"

"No, of that I am certain. They are here for a purpose. Not to trade. Their Roman master, Marcus, is not a man of coins. His trade is that of a soldier. And David Ben-Dor does not count coins for a master. He is also a fighter and more than that. He was armed with a sword, a weapon forbidden even for a servant of a Roman. And not a poor-quality sword like those we make but one of hardened iron that only Roman officers carry."

He hesitated, trying to find the right words. "The woman, Mariam, is of Israel. I know by the way she speaks Hebrew and Aramaic. David speaks only Hebrew. I am not a priest, but his Hebrew has a strange sound to my ear. I befriended the boy who accompanied them. He is bright and he avoided my probing questions about the others, but I learned that he barely knew them. The way he avoided my questions told me that the journey the three were on was one cloaked in secrecy. We know from him that they found the swords we dropped. He said nothing, but his face revealed what his tongue refused to say."

"And the attack by the Sicarii? A coincidence?" Ezra asked.

"No, I think not. True, it was a small party led by a Roman, perfect bait for a Sicarii attack. But I spotted one among them who was not Jewish."

"Not Jewish? Attacking with the Sicarii?" Ezra looked at the others with astonishment. The Sicarii were the most fanatical of Jews.

"If he was Jewish, he was one of the tribe of David Ben-Dor. He lacked the beard and locks."

"What do you make of all this?" Ezra asked.

"A puzzle for sure. They could have turned us in at the city gate. I was certain they would. We had saved their lives, but a Roman would not have cared that he owed us his life. They had to know we were rebels when they found the swords. Yet they seemed to have no interest. They must be here for another purpose. They are spies of Rome, for sure. But I do not believe they hunt for Zealots. Not at this time, anyway."

"The men who are in league with the Sicarii. That may be their purpose. Their mission may be to hunt down these strangers. It would fit with the attack on them by the Sicarii and their lack of interest in having rebels captured."

"There is one other thing I must tell you," Yoseph said. "Something else unusual about the man and the woman,

David and Mariam. I liked them." Ezra lifted his eyebrows and Yoseph smiled. "I do not find deception in them. They may not be who they claim to be, but I find no malice in them. And I agree with you. They may have some conflict with the men the Sicarii are scheming with."

"I want to meet these strange Jews, this man named David and the woman, Mariam," Ezra said. "We need to know what nature of spies they are. They did not turn you in today, but who knows what the morrow brings? They may have confederates who followed you and are planning to seize all the rebels in the city in one swoop. We need to know their intention. We have an army gathering in the Ghor. We must keep them supplied with food and weapons as they train for war against the legions of Rome.

"If God wills it, the people of Jerusalem will rise against the Romans at Passover. When they do, our army must be ready to come out of the wilderness to drive the Romans from Israel. If this beardless Jew and the woman stand in our way, they must be disposed of."

Ezra looked around the table, meeting the eye of each man. "Many strange things are happening. More than have ever happened in my lifetime. We must be ready when the fire ignites at Passover and we must pick up our swords and do the Lord's bidding."

CHAPTER FORTY-ONE

David awoke to find Isie sitting on a stack of grain sacks near Marie's bedroll. Marie was not in sight. He sprang to his feet. "Marie!"

"I'm over here." Her voice came from behind a tall stack of grain sacks where she was dressing.

He sat back down, taking a deep breath. "Sorry. I had a bad dream. I dreamed I was being transported back to the future holding a dog. When I got there, I had the head of a dog."

She stepped out from behind the sacks, brushing her hair. "I've sure Freud would have said it has something to do with lusting after your mother. I'm afraid that's all I know about dreams."

The boy said something to Marie in Aramaic.

"Isie says he's going with Conway today. The two have apparently bridged the language gap with gestures and faces."

David combed back his hair with his fingers. He had a fine-tooth wooden comb in his pack, but his fingers did the job just as well. "Conway told me last night he's going to make the rounds with Quintus today. He probably needs a servant around to wipe his feet."

Marie came out from behind the sacks. "I'm going down to the stable to wash up. We can get something to eat in the marketplace."

She left, taking her twelve-year-old shadow with her.

David kicked off his blankets and got up to dress. He had slept hard, but awoke tense. He had had another dream that he did not mention to Marie. In his dream, he had been a Nazi war camp officer who exterminated Jews. He didn't need Freud to tell him that he was burdened with guilt about a mission in which his job was to make sure two thousand years of persecution of the Jews occurred.

Shake it off, he silently told himself.

He got dressed to go downstairs and clean up in the stable.

"I'm going to wash in the horse trough," he said aloud, "and that Roman bastard is probably being scrubbed by naked virgins."

Conway accompanied Quintus to the public baths. They went aboard two litters, each carried by four husky slaves through the crowded streets. He tried to portray features reflecting a bored Roman master-race countenance, but it was difficult for a person raised in the modern world to keep a straight face when he was being treated like a king in an ancient world.

The baths had two entries: one for men, the other for women. Shops lined the street on both sides of the entry ways.

As they walked into the baths, Quintus expressed his contempt for the provincial facility.

"I must apologize for the poor quality of these miserable baths. But they are the best that can be provided this far from Rome."

Before they stepped through the front door, they were bowed to by the doorkeeper but no attempt was made to collect the entrance fee. Quintus confided in Conway with fake modesty, "I have a small financial interest in the baths. They were built with gold from my slave transactions. The income is shared with the queen."

The marble used in the public structure lacked the fine detail and precious gold and silver used in Quintus' palatial house. The statuary too, of the pantheon of Roman gods, was impressive but did not have the exquisite expression and form of the works of art found in Quintus' home.

They entered a warm anteroom where they removed their clothes and put them in a locker overseen by a slave. The purpose of the warm room was to acclimate their bodies for a hot bath. Conway was surprised that Quintus was the only man in the place who did not walk around naked. The slave trader kept a loincloth on.

"A skin problem," he told him. "Embarrassing but not painful."

They soaked in the hot bath. Like the heating system at Quintus' house, the public baths were heated by underground furnaces fed by slaves.

Quintus introduced him to some of the other men, all Romans businessmen who lived in or were visiting Bethsaida.

"Are the baths available to Jews?" Conway asked.

"To rich ones. But they have their own entrance and baths around the side. They object to the statues of the gods in the main entrance. I could have omitted the statues, but I confess, I lack charity in my heart for these troublesome provincials. There is another entrance, in the back, where common tradespeople enter. Their facilities, of course, are the most basic. You can sometimes hear the noise of these vulgar bathers and the cry of vendors offering grilled meats and honey cakes. I would not have bothered providing facilities to the common people but Salome believes the baths and the games in the arena make the people love her."

One Roman bather was a tax collector, Quintus revealed to Conway, his words dripping with envy. "I have asked my grandfather to place a bid on tax collecting in the area. With my knowledge of the locals, and a good gang of slaves taken from war prisoners, I would be able to double our money."

They were served a cool honey-and-wine mixture while they lounged in the hot water. After the bath, they went to a room where they were massaged and rubbed with soothing oils. One slave picked unwanted hair from their bodies and another shaved them.

"We will have lunch in my private bath," Quintus told him.

The slave trader's private bath was a small, warm pool with a smaller, cold plunge bath beside it. After a light lunch served by slaves, Conway slipped into the bath to soak his muscles again while Quintus took a short nap.

When Quintus awoke, he clapped his hands and two women entered the room. "Celestial virgins," Quintus said, smirking.

One of the women came to the edge of the pool where Conway was sitting in the warm water. She had a Eurasian cast to her complexion, a golden honey tone that Conway had always found sensuous. She let her robe drop. Her sculptured body, melon breasts with nipples tilted up, flat stomach, shaved V, and firm thighs, were all original equipment. Her lips were full and red. Someone once told him that red lips were sexually arousing because they imitated the labium lips in a woman's genital area that swell with blood when aroused. He enjoyed both sets of women's lips and really did not care what the sexological significance was.

She slipped into the water with him and took a sponge and leisurely rubbed his chest. Meeting her eye, he realized one thing about her: She was virginal in name only.

Snuggling against him with her wet naked breasts caressing his chest, she licked his ear with her tongue as her hand went between his legs. As she slipped his erection inside her, he wondered when in hell the Romans found time to make war. . . .

CHAPTER FORTY-TWO

David and Marie wandered through the marketplace, making an occasional purchase. Breakfast was hard, dry barley bread, grapes, and warm goat's milk. The bread had to be dipped in the milk to keep them from breaking their teeth on it.

"Don't complain," Marie said. "Most servants and common people only have a little watered-down wine and a chunk of hard bread for breakfast. It's not a big meal like we're used to. What we call lunch is substantial and dinner somewhat less."

They passed shops with loaves of leavened wheat bread lying beside tubs of honey and butter, sweet rolls and cakes smothered with fresh fruits, and a dozen other delicacies. The process for making cane sugar was not known so the delicacies were sweetened with honey and thick jellies made from grapes, figs, and dates.

"We can't have any," Marie told David, as he stared at freshly baked wheat bread and honey. "We're servants, poor people. We eat coarse barley bread sprinkled with a little olive oil. We can't afford honey."

"Dogs and Indians," David said.

"What?"

"Dogs and Indians. When the British ruled India only two types weren't allowed into the plush country clubs and restaurants—dogs and Indians. Hell, Conway's part British *and* Roman."

The round loaf of barley bread had a strong taste of millet, a cereal grass used in the raising process. Marie's campsite camel dung bread tasted better.

They passed another baker, this one specializing in cakes that fired David's taste buds. He saw women pay a copper for a cake and he veered over, grabbed a cake, dropped a copper on the counter, and hurried back to Marie. He broke off a piece for her and stuffed his own mouth.

"Hmmm, good. Tastes a little like almonds," he said.

"Locust."

"Locust? You mean as in . . . grasshopper?"

"They bake them, grind them, and mix them with flour. I've eaten them in the village where I learned Aramaic."

"Bugs or not, they're good."

"You've got to learn to be more humble. Servants don't act like you do. They don't assert themselves."

"I'm working on it. How would it be if I leaned over like a hunchbacked dwarf and dragged one leg?"

"Better than you strutting around like you have a chip on your shoulder."

He stopped and faced her. They stared at each other intently. David looked deep into her eyes, trying to find the real person hidden beneath.

"You're right," he said. "As usual. Regardless of what my own feelings are, I shouldn't put you in danger. I'll try to act more humble."

She brushed cake crumbs from his tunic. "You'll try . . . again . . . but I'm not sure you're trainable." She smiled as they walked along. "It's funny. I want you to act humble because I'm concerned about your safety. I don't care what happens to me. You want to act humble to protect me. You don't care about what happens to you. It's too bad that each of us can't care about ourselves as much as we do other people."

———

As they examined the goods around them, Marie inquired about healers. "My sister is blind," Marie told a lamp merchant.

The man sat on a short wooden stool and worked pedals that turned a mound of clay. He shaped the clay as he listened.

"I seek a healer. I have heard of a rabbi named Jesus Ben Joseph whose touch gave sight to a man in Bethsaida."

"I know of no healers," the merchant said abruptly. He stopped his work and went into the back of his shop.

"That's the second time someone has panicked at the mention of Jesus," David said, as they moved along. "And two others clammed up."

"The woman at the leather stall has a friendly face. I'm going to try her."

David pretended to examine a saddle while Marie asked about healers as the woman stitched a belt.

The woman cautioned Marie to be silent. "It's the Baptist," she said. "The queen fears the Baptist has returned and seeks his revenge. The queen's men are hunting for healers, taking them to the dungeon to be examined."

The woman's husband, working leather at the rear of the shop, threw down his tools and rushed to them. He pulled his wife into the interior of the stall. "Leave my shop," he told David and Marie.

They walked away slowly, trying to appear casual. Other shopkeepers gave them wary looks.

"What did she mean about the Baptist?" David asked.

"King Herod Antipas had nightmares about John the Baptist. He thought John had come back in the person of Jesus for revenge on him and Salome. It's one of the reasons Jesus had to conduct an underground ministry."

David thought for a moment. "If Salome is intriguing with the Zayyad brothers, she would want to attract Jesus to Bethsaida, not drive him away. Maybe she's making things so bad in Bethsaida that Jesus will be compelled to come to the city to help."

"Or maybe the hunt for healers began before the Zayyads arrived," she suggested.

An old beggar approached and gestured with his begging bowl. The man was a leper.

Marie smiled and dropped two coppers into the bowl.

"The Lord be with you," the beggar said.

A city guard shot by and lashed out with a short whip. The old man screamed and fell to the ground as the whip split the cloth on his back and cut into his flesh. As the guard reared back with the whip to swing again, Marie cried out and stepped in front of the leper. The guard was about to lash Marie when David grabbed the whip and jerked it from the guard's hand, sending the man staggering backward. On Conway's orders, he had left his sword at the stable in case he was stopped and searched. The guard drew his sword and David cocked the whip back to defend himself. When Marie yelled at the guard in Aramaic, the man hesitated, looking confused.

"I told him you were the servant of a Roman. Say something in Hebrew. He may not understand, but it'll impress him because it's the language of the upper classes."

The old beggar got to his feet and ran.

"I'm going to have your head for drawing that sword. Queen Salome is my personal friend," David said in Hebrew.

The guard picked up on the queen's name and his confusion increased. Marie exchanged words with him in Aramaic and then with David in English. "Give him back the whip. Let's get out of here while we still have our heads."

David threw the whip at the man's feet. A crowd had gathered and David pushed through with Marie behind him. He swung around when he heard a familiar voice.

"Hurry! Come with me." It was Yoseph. They followed him through the crowd and down a narrow, twisting street. They put several blocks behind them before stopping.

Yoseph shook his head. "You take your life in your hands when you fight with city guards. The queen will have you joining Zealots on the crucifixion crosses if you interfere with her bloody sense of justice."

"Where we come from people aren't treated like animals," David snapped.

Yoseph raised his eyebrows. "Where do you come from? Heaven?"

David started to reply, but stopped.

"Why did the guard beat the old man for begging?" Marie asked.

"You are strange people. Did you not see that he is a leper? He has to keep announcing that he is unclean so people can avoid him."

David nodded at Marie and grinned. "Actually, Yoseph, I was just trying to finish a fight that Marie started. Sometimes she forgets that she is a lowly servant and causes trouble."

"We should talk," Yoseph said. He looked behind them. "Before you are murdered in the streets or dragged off to the queen's dungeon. There is a wedding this afternoon at the house of a friend, Ezra Ben Ephraim. Come to the celebration. There will be good food and much joy. You will see the ways of your brothers of Israel when they are not beset by fear."

Conway was waiting for them when they got back to the villa.

"Lunch with Quintus and the Roman clan proved interesting. A crisis is brewing. Salome has gone out of her way to provoke the Zealots. She's going to crucify one tomorrow. And she's turning it into a Roman circus, if you'll pardon the expression."

"She's harassing the poor and the sick," said Marie.

"I think Salome's trying to attract Jesus to the city," David said. "Beating on the poor and sick and crucifying people will draw him here."

Conway nodded. "Sounds like something Salome would do."

"Jesus was linked with the Zealots," David said.

"The evidence is strong that he was one," Marie said.

"Then let's say he was," David said. "Salome has two reasons to hunt down Jesus. We learned in the marketplace that she and her uncle, Herod Antipas, are both superstitious about healers because of what they did to John the Baptist. And by now she's probably been contacted by the Zayyads and has double reason to track down Jesus. I think we should spread talk around the marketplace, let people know we are looking for Jesus and will pay for the information."

"It'll attract instant attention to us," Marie said.

"Exactly. The clock's running. We need to get aggressive about looking for Jesus. We've been invited to a wedding this afternoon," he said to Conway. "A friend of Yoseph's. Maybe a nest of Zealots. We may get a lead there. And if we don't, I think we should create one."

"Watch yourselves," Conway said. "The scuttlebutt among the Roman crew is that the Zealots have had it with Salome. They never cared for her morals and now she's spilling their blood. The local Romans think there'll be an insurrection and have secretly petitioned Pontius Pilate to send a legion to Bethsaida. Quintus told me there's little hope of getting troops until after Passover since every spare man has been committed to Jerusalem because it's almost inevitable that there'll be trouble in the holy city during the festivities."

Conway had traded in his simple merchant's garb for an expensive Roman toga and finely crafted sandals. He looked well fed, manicured, cleanly shaved, his haircut and nails trimmed, the residue of oils from the rubdown on the baths giving his bronze good looks a young, dynamic aura.

He grinned at David and Marie.

"Quintus has graciously told his servants to throw whatever's left from their dinner, which is the leftover from our dinner, into a bucket for you two."

He touched his clean-shaven face. "We Romans like to spoil ourselves."

CHAPTER FORTY-THREE

The house where the wedding took place was surrounded by a tall earthen wall. Behind the wall was a green, cool Tyrian courtyard with date palms, fig trees, and pomegranate bushes gathered around a well in the center. The house fronted three sides of the courtyard. Like Quintus' house, there were no street-side windows. Unlike the slave trader's palatial house, this one was constructed of mud-and-straw bricks with a roof of large timbers. It was not the house of a rich man but of a tradesman of modest means.

David felt a warm aura as he entered. It was a home for people, not statues. House of the Zealots, is how he thought of it.

"The wedding will last seven days because the bride is a virgin," Yoseph told them. His cheeks were flushed with wine and good cheer. He met them as they came through the front gate and handed them goblets overflowing with wine. David suspected they had been watched and their progress reported as they approached the house.

"Israel is a civilized country," Yoseph said. "We celebrate our weddings with virgin brides for seven days and that of widows for only three. It makes great sense, does it not?"

"Great sense," David said. "My people have the bride and groom wed on Wednesday because that way if the blood does not come, the groom can go to court on Thursday and demand that the marriage be set aside."

Yoseph threw up his hands. "Exactly! We have the same custom. You are not such a foreign Jew!" He took them by the arm. "Come, you will have wine to quench your thirst and food to still the cries of your hunger. Later I will introduce you to our host, Ezra, the father of the bride and the owner of this fine house. My own father is a member of the same *shusbinut* as Ezra. My father is ill and I have come as his representative."

Yoseph led them to seats near tables heaped with food and drink. He was pulled away by a young woman who wanted him to dance while she played a tambourine, leaving David and Marie alone for a moment.

"What did he mean when he said his father was a member of the same *shusbinut?*" Marie asked.

"A *shusbinut* is a group of men who each contribute money when a member's son gets married. The individual contributions are not large, but in total ensures a larger wedding and more prosperous start than relying on a single family's resources. It was not, uh, uncommon for a member of the *shusbinut* to sleep in the house of the bride and groom on the wedding night to act as a witness in case virgin blood doesn't come."

"Charming," Marie said.

"It wasn't a very enlightened attitude," David admitted. He smiled. "You're the history expert, you're supposed to be telling me this stuff."

"I'm afraid I missed *shusbinut* in my studies. They seem to serve a good purpose, all but the part about virgin blood. Besides the double standard, some women who have never been touched by a man don't bleed when they make love for the first time."

The talk about sex caused Marie to blush and look away. The blush melted the hard reserve that she hid behind and suddenly she seemed younger, more innocent, more vulnerable. He wondered for a moment how a woman who apparently had been a prostitute could blush when sex was mentioned. He put his hand on hers and softly squeezed it.

"Hello," he said. "I don't know if you remember me, but I'm someone you met about two thousand years ago."

"Two thousand years ahead," she corrected.

"I guess we were ahead of our time."

"I'm going to ignore that terrible pun, Captain Ben-Dor." He groaned. "I hate being called captain."

"I know, Captain. But I'm just getting back at you for letting me make an error and getting between that leper and the guard. I almost created a disaster for both of us."

David laughed. "Is blaming me for your mistake after you gave me a lecture some sort of twisted feminine logic?"

"Exactly." She squeezed his hand. "Thanks for saving me from that guard. Although getting whip marks across my face would have probably improved my looks."

"There's nothing wrong with your looks that an occasional smile wouldn't cure."

She blushed again and tried to pull her hand from his but he held on tight.

"Why are you always drawing away from me?"

"Did you know that the business about virgin blood was only one aspect of this society in which woman were treated as little more than chattels?"

"Are you changing the subject?"

She ignored his question and went on. "But even though there are double standards in regard to the rights of men and women, woman of this time period were treated better in Israel than most of the ancient world. They could travel freely and they didn't have to wear veils, but the laws treated them unequally."

Marie nodded at the bride. "Legally, she can't inherit her husband's money, can't even inherit anything but her dowry from her own father. Only the males of the family can possess property. Her husband can even void contracts she enters into because she is considered incompetent as a matter of law, as if she were a child. A woman can't even testify in court because she's considered incompetent in legal matters.

"Sometimes women are treated as no more than slaves. If a man goes broke, after he sells his house and lands, he can 'sell' his daughter into a type of betrothal in which the daughter is promised in marriage for a price paid to the father."

She met his eyes with an innocent look. "Do you want to know what the worst double standard was?"

"I'm dying to hear."

"It's the double standards concerning sex. A woman's adultery is punishable by death if she's caught in the act. Usually, she's strangled. If she's merely suspected of the crime, she's 'tested' by being forced her to drink a terrible concoction which includes dust from the Temple floor. If she vomits or becomes sick from the mixture, she's dragged into the streets and stoned. Do you know what they do with men who commit adultery?"

"Not a thing," David guessed.

"Very clever of you to deduce that."

They both laughed and she squeezed his hand. It felt good to David.

"Marie—"

"Let's get something to eat before we insult our host by ignoring his table."

The food tables were piled with fruits and desserts, honey and pomegranate cakes, dates, grapes, figs, and almonds and an abundance of that strong Israeli red wine that had to be diluted with water. Other tables had more substantial food: a stew of mutton and lentils, plates of fresh cucumbers, beans, leeks, olives, and dried fish.

"The chickens are really small," David said.

"They're pigeons. Chicken was expensive and hard to find. Earthenware dishes were considered unclean," she told David as they put food on shallow bowls of bronze.

He paused by a stack of flat, saucer-shaped bread chunks and hesitated. The bread looked too hard to eat.

"That bread isn't for eating," she said. "There may not be enough metal bowls to go around and some guests will use the bread to put food on."

"An early form of paper plates?"

"That's probably the idea."

"They need to improve the design of wineglasses."

The "wineglasses" were cone-shaped metal containers with pointed bottoms similar to the paper cups used in 1950s soda fountains. They could not be set upright on the table, but were placed in holders.

They had finished eating by the time Yoseph returned, sweating and flushed from kicking up his heels on the dance floor. "Come, I will introduce you to the master of the house."

Yoseph led them to a bear of a man with a great beard, barrel chest, and massive arms and legs.

"Ezra, my friend, these are the two foreign Jews I told you about."

"My house is your house," Ezra said. To David's relief, the man spoke in Hebrew. He had the vocal tone of a muffled cannon.

Yoseph grabbed Marie's hand. "Dance with me so I can prove to my friends that my boasting that a beautiful woman looks upon me with favor is not untrue." He pulled Marie away, leaving David alone with Ezra. David had the feeling the move was planned.

Ezra examined him with large, grave brown eyes. "Yoseph tells me you are from Tarraco in Hispania. I have heard that Seneca, the governor, is a wise and fair man."

"Seneca?" David raised his eyebrows. "The governor is Lucius Calpurnius." He held his breath while he waited for the bear's reply. The governor's name had been scholarly guesswork by the two history professors at the synchrotron.

Ezra smiled slightly. "It must have been another province I was told about. Tell me, what brings you to Galilee?"

"My Roman master is a merchant of fine daggers. He has come to Galilee to buy sicas."

The answer surprised both of them. Sicas were the short daggers used by the Sicarii. David had blurted it out deliberately. He plunged recklessly ahead. "I understand the biggest supply of the daggers is found in the backs of Romans and their Jewish collaborators."

Ezra stroked his beard and eyed David thoughtfully. "Your master is a strange Roman. He lets his servants roam far from the leash to ask many questions in the marketplace." Ezra suddenly smiled, a bear grinning. "Word has it that the emperor himself sends spies to Galilee." He saluted David with his wine goblet. "Galilee has an undeserved reputation as a center of dissent against Roman rule. The true Jew is a patriot of Rome. Pax Romana!"

"Roman peace has given you tyrants like Salome and the crucifixion cross."

Ezra frowned. "We do not talk insurrection in this household."

"You do more than talk it. You are Zealots. Yoseph was smuggling swords into the city to be used against Salome." David stepped closer and lowered his voice. "I need your help. I am no friend of Rome or its despots."

The expression on Ezra's face was a mixture of amazement and consternation. David wondered if he went too far.

"We cannot talk here," Ezra said. "Come with me."

Ezra led him to the back of the house where he opened a cellar door and gestured for David to enter ahead of him. "The wine cellar is the most private place in my house."

David stepped by Ezra and started down a flight of stairs lighted by wall candles. He had gone down half a dozen stairs when it suddenly occurred to him that it might be dangerous to be alone with Ezra in the "most private" part of the house. He stopped and turned around to face a dagger in Ezra's hand. The dagger was less frightening than the expression on Ezra's face and the sheer size of the man.

"Keep going," Ezra growled.

When he reached the bottom of the stairs, Marie, Yoseph, and three men armed with daggers, were already there. David took a protective stance next to Marie and faced the men.

"They've been questioning me," Marie said in English.

"Speak Hebrew!" Ezra snapped.

"Is this how you make your guests welcome? Daggers and dark places?" David asked.

"This is how we welcome Roman spies."

"If we were spies, Yoseph would have been arrested at the city gate with his cache of swords. And we would have brought city guards with us today. They could have gathered up half the Zealots in the city."

Yoseph shrugged. "Perhaps you are waiting to snare an even greater catch."

"There will be no more of this foolishness," Ezra said. "You ask questions in the marketplace for your Roman master about healers who are Jews and friends of our cause."

"We are seeking a healer for my blind sister," Marie said.

"A lie," Ezra growled. "You would not seek a healer in Galilee for someone who lives on the other side of the empire."

David hesitated. This was the critical test and they had to pass it or they'd never leave the cellar alive. "We are seeking a healer. Men from our land have come here to kill this person. This healer has great significance for the people of my land and if he dies at the hands of these assassins, great harm will come to my people."

"You have explained nothing. Who is this healer? Who seeks him?"

David could not tell them the name. If word got back to Jesus, he could alter his pattern of behavior and change history. "I don't know his name, but it is written that a man who has performed miracles on the shores of Galilee will free the people of my land from the paganism of Rome. The men who seek to kill him call themselves Jews, but they're not Jews. They're Roman spies who have fooled the Sicarii into thinking they oppose Rome."

David almost laughed at the irony of it. How could he explain to Ezra that he had come to Galilee to ensure that a Jew dies on a crucifixion cross, thus guaranteeing two thousand years of persecution of Jews?

Ezra eyed David intently. "I do not believe you."

David returned his scrutiny. "The assassins from my land have linked up with the Sicarii and will bring harm to my people and your people."

"The Sicarii are not great friends of our cause, but they are the enemy of our enemy. They fight the Romans as well as we do."

"You fight the Romans as patriots with a vision of a free Israel. The Sicarii are fanatics who would drive the Romans from Israel only to replace them as tyrants. They are intriguing with Salome and she is the handmaiden of the Romans. Salome has never been a friend of the Zealots, but isn't it obvious something has changed? She now openly seeks to destroy you. She fills her dungeon with your comrades."

"And why does she do this?" Ezra stroked his beard and spoke almost in a whisper.

"Because she believes these evil men from my land have the power to make her master of Israel. Salome, the Sicarii, and these men have joined together to destroy the Zealots. If Zealot blood is not already flowing from their intrigues, it soon will be."

David could see from their expressions that he had made a major point.

"The man to be crucified is my brother!" Yoseph burst out.

"What do you seek from us?" Ezra asked.

"Help us locate this healer."

"That will never happen. We would violate all of our duties to our God and our brothers if we turned over a brother to strangers." Ezra stroked his beard and frowned at David. "If you are a Jew, you are a strange Jew. Tell me, strange Jew, where do you carry the symbol of your devotion to God?"

"In the tassel in the bottom of my cloak. Like each of you, there is a blue thread."

Ezra gestured for Yoseph to follow him upstairs. "Watch them," he told the other three men in the cellar.

David gave Marie's hand a soft squeeze. The jury was out. The cellar was built like a dungeon. Whatever the verdict was, they were not going to be able to appeal it by escaping.

Ezra and Yoseph returned a few minutes later. Their faces were stone.

Yoseph suddenly grinned and raised his hands in exasperation. "What are we doing in this dark cellar when there's good food and dancing upstairs?"

Since Yoseph loved to dance and flirt, he spent the rest of the evening heaping attention on Marie. David frowned as he watched the action. *I'm jealous*, he told himself. Admitting that he was jealous didn't help the pangs.

A break in the music occurred and he stole Marie away from Yoseph.

"I'm jealous," he admitted.

She looked up at him in surprise and her cheeks colored with blush again. "It doesn't hurt for me to be friendly with Yoseph. He can help us."

"It wouldn't hurt for you to smile at me occasionally, either."

Her reply was lost as the music started again and Yoseph grabbed her for another dance. He felt like kicking himself. Jealousy was juvenile, but damnit . . .

David discovered too late that the local wine had a mule's kick. As he and Marie made their way along dark streets toward the villa of Quintus, he felt more inclined to dance with Marie over the cobblestones than keep an eye out for danger.

The fact that two of Ezra's sons, chips off the same mountain, followed them to ensure their safety home, gave David the luxury of relaxing his guard.

"You're drunk," Marie said.

"I'm drunk from the moonlight in your eyes."

When they reached the villa's rear gate they waved goodbye to Ezra's sons. The gatekeeper had to be woken up to let them in. David flipped him a silver coin to ease the resentment.

"You're out of character again," Marie said. "One servant doesn't tip another and certainly doesn't have silver coins to toss about."

They stepped inside the stable and were greeted by the warmth and smell of horses and manure. David grabbed her as she started up the stairs to the loft and pulled her to him.

"I'm tired of role-playing."

"You're not very good at it," she said, pushing away. "I keep telling you, you're not humble enough."

His balance wasn't good, but he held on to her.

"Make love to me and I'll be humble."

"What?"

"I said—"

"You're drunk."

"My body is drunk. My mind is clear as . . . as . . ."

"Mud."

She started up the stairs and he pulled her back into his arms and held her close, their lips a kiss apart. "You're like poison," he said. "You infected me from the moment I saw you and I haven't been able to get you out of my system."

"Telling a woman she's poison is not a compliment."

"You're as lovely as a rose, as—"

"And you smell like a winery."

He tried to kiss her but she buckled her knees and slipped out from his grasp. She ran up the stairs with him stumbling behind her. Before she reached the top, he grabbed that back of her robe and she went down to her hands and knees.

The liquor was overpowering him. He crawled up beside her, his face flushed, eyes glazed. "What's the matter," he slurred, "you hung around with Yoseph all night. I'm not as good as him?" He leaned toward her. His breath was eighty proof. "I'm not as good as the men you've whored with?"

She struggled away from him and ran up the rest of the stairs.

Wine and emotions curdled in his gut. There were so many things he wanted to say to her, but his body wasn't willing. He made it to the bedroll spread out on the hay, sank to his knees, and fell facedown. He was out before his face hit the blankets.

Marie's body trembled. David's words swirled around her like snakes as the brooding darkness pressed down on her. She wanted to deny his accusation, to tell him that he was wrong, but there was no easy way, no magic words, that would untwist what he had been told about her.

She was so confused, so terribly mixed up, she wasn't sure she could even discern fact from fiction in her life. There was much she wanted to tell David, so many things she needed to share with him, but she didn't know how to break through the wall she had put up between them. She was attracted to him, even wanted to make love with him. But then his words slashed at her.

Nothing had ever come easy for her. Not even love.

She had to get out into the cool night.

The gate to the street was cocked open. The guard's back was to the wall and his head hung down. As she walked toward the gate she thought at first the guard was asleep. His awkward pose did not sink in until she saw the blood on his chest. His throat had been cut.

The shadows around her took the shape of dark cloaked figures. Before she could cry out, a hand went over her mouth and a dagger was pressed against her throat. A man with nervous rodent eyes stepped in front of her.

"It's the woman. We'll take her back and can use her for bait."

The assassins hurried Marie down dark streets, neither speaking to her nor among themselves. They kept the blade against her back.

Fear choked her. She stumbled on the cobblestones street and they jerked her upright so viciously she cried out. The dagger went back to her throat and unclean breath blew in her face as one of the assassins whispered, "Fall again, woman, and I will cut your throat."

The assassins led her through the gate and into the marketplace while the city guards looked the other way. The kidnappers turned into an alley and stumbled, cursing as an old beggar scrambled out from around their legs.

Marie exchanged a frantic look with the beggar as he scurried off. She recognized him. It was the leper she saved from a beating.

They stopped at the side door of a blacksmith's shop and tapped lightly on the door. The door slid silently open and they hurried her into the shop, shutting the door behind them.

They steered her into a room with shelves crowded with bits

and pieces of iron and tools of the smithy's trade lining the walls. In the open area in the middle of the room, a huge stone pit glowed ashy red. A stairway to the right led up to a loft and a hole in the roof where the charcoal pit smoke escaped.

Two men tied her wrists with a coarse rope and slipped the loose end through an iron ring high on a post near the stone pit, wrenching the rope until her hands were above her head and she had to stand on tiptoes to relieve the strain. The Sicarii huddled in a corner of the room to confer, while the blacksmith, grimy from baked-on sweat and charcoal, sat on a bench next to the door and ate apples from a barrel.

The blacksmith was more than dirty, a lifetime of charcoal dust and a dearth of soap had left him and his clothes permanently gritty and smelly. He had been honing the blades of sica daggers when Marie was brought in, work that could only be done in the secrecy of night.

The huddle broke up and four Sicarii left, including the man with the nervous eyes. She had already guessed that the man with the nervous eyes was Amir Zayyad; his body language fit the description David gave of the man. One man was left behind to guard her. She had heard only a few scattered words from the huddled conference of the assassins, but it was enough.

They were going back to finish their deadly work at the villa.

David jerked awake. Someone hovered over him.

"Shhh . . . ," Isie whispered.

The boy pointed to the stairway down to the stable. A footstep creaked on the stairs. Every nerve in David's body snapped to attention. Isie held up two fingers. Two men.

Isie smelled of wine. He had been at the camp of the caravaners beyond the marketplace when he returned to find the gatekeeper dead and two men sneaking into the stable. While the assassins crept up the stable stairs, Isie had raced up a wooden ladder mounted on the side of the building.

Another creak sounded. The men were nearly to the top of

the stairway. David rolled quietly to his feet. Marie's bedroll was empty. He gestured at the bedding and Isie shook his head; he had not seen Marie.

The boy pointed to the window, but David waved him away. They would have knives in their back before they made it out the window.

David slung a heavy sack of grain onto his shoulder. The noise alerted the men on the stairway and their footsteps pounded as they dropped any pretense of surprise. David made it to the stairwell as the first man shot up. He drove the grain sack into the man with his shoulder, letting go of the sack as the man fell backward. The two assassins tumbled down the stairs like bowling balls.

He grabbed his sword and leaped through the rear window after Isie, hitting the ground and rolling to break the fall. Isie was already on his feet. David caught up with him near the back entrance to the main house.

The boy jabbered in Aramaic and pointed at the bushes near the door. A pair of feet poked out of the bushes. The doorman was dead. Assassins had gone in after Conway as well.

The door was cracked open and David burst through, nearly tripping over a body. The doorman had taken an assassin with him. He ran through the villa with the boy behind him, hitting the double doors to Conway's quarters dead center with his shoulder and crashing into the room.

A whirl of activity centered on the bed, Conway on his knees wielding a dagger against an attacker trying for a kill with a sword. The assassin broke for the window and Conway's dagger flashed across the room, catching the attacker between the shoulder blades. The man ran into the wall, bounced back, and fell to the floor.

Conway's naked body was spattered with blood. He shook his head grimly. "Not mine," he told David.

A bloody body was tangled in the bedcovers. It could have been a young boy or girl, David couldn't tell for sure.

"Janus," Conway said, "a servant."

The Sicarii guarding Marie in the blacksmith shop went into an adjoining room. He left the door open so he could watch her as he sat at a table to break bread and drink wine. Marie's blouse had been ripped and one of her breasts threatened to fall out. The blacksmith sat by the door with a half-eaten apple in his hand and stared at her breast, openmouthed. He lifted his gaze from her breast and she met his eye. He was the animal side of human nature.

Wiggling until the rest of the breast popped out of her blouse, she looked to the blacksmith and tried to smile, her lips trembling. His eyes were wide and his mouth gaped open. She gestured with her head at the door to the room where the Sicarii was.

The blacksmith got the idea. Dropping his apple onto the floor, he got up and shut the door, sliding an iron bar across, ignoring the yelling from the man on the other side.

He shuffled to Marie and reached for her bare breast. She twisted around, using the post to block him. "Free me," she said in Aramaic. "Free me and I'll pay you."

He clawed at her, tearing more of her blouse. She wrapped her legs around the pole and pressed against it. "Stop! I have gold, gold! Let me go and I'll give it to you."

Something akin to animal cunning ignited in his eyes.

"Gold," she whispered breathlessly, "you can be rich."

He undid the cord holding his tunic and spread the tunic open. His flesh was matted with thick black hair and painted with charcoal dust. He palmed his penis and masturbated. She buried her face in her arms for a moment to hide her disgust. "Yes, that too. Cut me loose and I'll give you pleasure and gold."

He grabbed her again and she hugged the pole. He ripped her blouse down to her waist. "No! You have to cut me loose so I can use my hands to give you pleasure."

Grunting, he grabbed a broken sword from a pile near the burning pit and sawed the rope from her hands. His sour odor was choking her. She tried to run, but he jerked her to him, shoving his penis at her as if he believed it would go through her robe. She jabbed a thumbnail in his eye and twisted out of his grip, getting a step away before he caught her across the side of the head with his hand. She fell to her knees beside the smoldering charcoal pit.

He grabbed her hair and forced her back to her knees as she tried to get up, shoving his erect penis at her face. Struggling to get out of his grip, her hand landed on the wooden handles of a pair of metal tongs lying on the rim of the burning pit. She grabbed the tongs and clamped the white-hot tips onto his penis.

He screamed and went berserk, staggering around the room, crashing into shelves.

She ran up the stairs to the loft. He got the hot clamp off and came after her like a crazed animal, the stairway shuddering under the pounding of his feet. As she reached the top of the stairs, she ran for the smoke hole in the ceiling. The ceiling tapered down until she had to bend to keep from bumping her head as she got closer to the hole. The opening was slightly higher than her waist.

Leaping up to the opening, she had almost scrambled all the way onto the roof when the blacksmith got a hold of her foot and pulled her back inside, knocking against the loft railing as he stepped back. She kicked blindly with her free foot and he let go as he grabbed for support. The railing buckled under his weight and he broke through, waving his arms wildly as he lost his balance and fell. Pushing herself the rest of the way through the opening, she slid on the slanted roof, unable to stop herself, and went over the edge, crying out as she dropped into the darkness. She crashed onto the roof of a merchant's stall and rolled off, landing in a pile of trash next to the stall.

The wind knocked from her, she lay stunned on the cold cobblestones, hovering on the edge of consciousness, dimly aware of the excited voices of men coming from the blacksmith's shop.

She passed out as someone took her arm and dragged her over the cobblestones.

CHAPTER FORTY-FOUR

David sat on the edge of a fountain in the courtyard of the Roman villa. Conway stood in front of him, with Isie a few feet away poking with a stick at fish in the pond.

"We have to leave immediately for Jerusalem," Conway said. "There's trouble brewing in the city. Salome's crucifying a Zealot this afternoon. I recognized the name when Quintus told me. It's Yoseph's brother."

"I'm not going anywhere."

David kept his face blank. Conway gave no clue to the servants with his body language that he and David were at loggerheads. A Jew who disobeyed his Roman master would have been flogged—not argued with.

"I can't leave without Marie. I'm going to find her and the crucifixion today is a good place to start. Her whole life has been dominated by visions of a crucifixion. If she's still alive, she'll be there." He spoke the last words with difficulty and struggled to maintain his composure.

"I'm not concerned about your problems with Marie. She was an asset—now she's a liability. It's as simple as that. We have a job to do. Bethsaida is getting too hot for us. Jesus is probably already on his way to Jerusalem for Passover. We have to intercept him before the Zayyads do."

"I didn't ask for this mission and neither did Marie. We

were dragged into this mess. You can head for Jerusalem or hell for all I care. I have to find her."

Conway maintained his composure, but his eyes revealed his feelings. He was analyzing data like a computer, not reacting emotionally to David's remarks but analyzing the situation in terms of what the loss of David and Marie—and Isie, because the boy would opt to search for Marie—meant for his chances of success.

David could have mouthed the pros and cons for him. It meant Conway would lose his Aramaic interpreter, David's knowledge of the Zayyad brothers, and would have to travel alone. Romans did not travel without servants. That fact alone would subject him to suspicion. He could hire servants . . . but none that he could trust.

"You have twenty-four hours," he told David. "If you won't continue with the mission by that time, I'll kill you."

David smiled. He wanted to leap up and grab Conway by the throat and it took all of his willpower to keep himself down. He spotted Quintus watching them from a second-story landing.

"You arrogant bastard," David spoke through clenched teeth, "it's all a game to you. Just another role for you to play. If you cause any harm to Marie, your next role will be that of a corpse."

Shocked and disgusted at the mob mentality he saw around him, David shoved through the crowd gathered to watch the crucifixion of Yoseph's brother. A Jewish patriot was to suffer a horrible death, and the atmosphere was not outrage but that of a circus. Vendors hawked food and drink, jugglers performed, thieves picked pockets, and women offered favors for a price.

The expectant faces of the people in the crowd were a study in human nature. Some had come to be thrilled, some to be horrified, but all were there to be entertained by the grim drama. It reminded David of the crowd scenes in movies about the French Revolution, jeering human beings watching other human beings go to the guillotine, the gleeful horror of an executioner quickly grabbing a head out of the basket and holding it up for the crowd.

What quirk in human nature permitted people to enjoy, or at least be fascinated, by the pain and suffering of their fellow man? He remembered a story his father had told him about a guard at the Auschwitz concentration camp. The guard's job was to throw Jewish children into ovens, yet the guard broke down and cried when he came home one evening and discovered his own little girl had fallen and hurt her leg.

David reached the high ground where the crucifixion posts were mounted. Except for a narrow roadway kept clear by Royal Guards, the area between the posts and the city gate was a press of people. Conway had taken a position on the roof of a building near the city gate to have a bird's-eye view of the crowd, paying a fee to the building owner who sold prime seats for the entertainment.

David spotted Yoseph in the crowd near the edge of the roadway. Yoseph looked grim and David wondered if the Zealots would try to rescue Yoseph's brother, one more loose end he had to think about as he searched for Marie in the crowd and worried about a Sicarii dagger in his back.

Not trusting the Roman Quintus, he took Isie to the house of Ezra. If something happened to David, he didn't want the boy to end up on the slave trader's auction block.

David had spoken to Ezra only briefly.

"It is a day of mourning in this household," Ezra said, in reference to the crucifixion. Ezra claimed he had heard nothing about Marie. David believed him.

A wave of electrified anticipation swept the crowd.

The condemned man was coming. The poor devil dragged the crossbar of the crucifixion cross through the city gate. David trembled with anger and pity. The man had been drugged and beaten to make him docile when he walked through the streets. His tunic was shredded and bloody from whips laid across his back by Salome's guards.

The man dragged only the crossbar because the post was

already in the ground. When he reached the crucifixion post, his hands would be nailed to the crossbar, the crossbar hoisted up, and his ankles nailed to the post. Ezra told him that the young man would not have the mercy of a spear jab in the abdomen or his legs broken which allowed for bleeding to hasten death. He would take a couple of days to die at the least.

A torture invented by the devil.

David tore his eyes away from the poor bastard and looked to Conway, who pointed behind David, raised two fingers, and then made a cutting motion across his throat. Two men were making their way toward David. He couldn't see them; he needed to make it to higher ground, and started pushing his way though the crowd to get closer to the crucifixion posts, the highest ground in the area—and the "best seats" in the house.

Four men carrying a rich man's litter put the veiled litter down halfway into the crowd. Reaching into the curtained area as if to pull back the curtain for whoever was supposed to be sitting inside, one of the bearers pulled down a trap door and fled as huge rats charged out, squealing.

The people around the litter exploded in panic, blind fear spreading like wildfire through the crowd. Terrified people who didn't even know what they were supposed to be fearful of trampled each other trying to flee. The line of guards holding the roadway to the crucifixion post wavered and broke.

Yoseph darted past the guards and embraced his brother.

"I love you," he whispered before he plunged a dagger into his brother's heart.

He gently lowered his brother to the ground. Footsteps pounded behind him and Yoseph swung around, dagger in hand. A Royal Guard blocked Yoseph's dagger with his shield and another came up behind him and bashed the young Zealot on the head with a club.

Thundering chariots, as well as Royal Guards on foot, poured through the city gate to quell the disturbance. As the last chariot rumbled by the building, Conway leaped from the roof and onto the back of the chariot. He threw the startled driver off and grabbed the reins.

David struggled his way to a clearing around the crucifixion posts and let the crowd surge by. Two men were fighting their way through the panic to get to him.

The man closest to David broke into the clearing and came at him with a dagger. There was no time for David to grab the short sword hidden under his cloak. He sidestepped a thrust at his stomach and grabbed the man's wrist, using the assassin's own momentum to throw the man off balance. Slamming a kick behind the man's knee, he pulled the man to the ground with a hold on his cloak. The man twisted his dagger hand out of David's grip and lashed out, cutting the front of David's clothes. David seized his wrist again and twisted the blade back toward the man, suddenly throwing his whole weight onto his hands, shoving the dagger into the man's chest. He jumped back as the goggled-eyed assassin thrashed on the ground in death throes.

Another man broke out of the crowd and rushed at him.

Amir Zayyad.

For a moment the two men froze in place and stared at each other. An instant flash of a youth paralyzed with fear as Simon Ben-Dor executed their father appeared in David's mind. Emotion convulsed Amir's features.

For one crazy moment David considered shouting out to him, telling him he was sorry for what his father had done that night, asking him to turn around and walk away from the blood feud, but it was too late. He had always known the past would catch up with him and that time was now.

Amir charged him with a short sword drawn from out of his cloak. David parried with his own blade. Amir swung his sword wildly, using it more like an ax than a precision blade. In some ways Amir was more dangerous than a good swordsman like Conway, who made precise, if not predictable, moves. David dodged back, fending off the wild lunging and hacking

Sidestepping to the left to avoid a wild slash, David

tripped on a rock. He tried to keep his balance but Amir was maniacal, hacking and chopping at him with the sword. David fell back, hitting the crucifixion post with his right shoulder, still keeping up his guard as he went down, rolling to his left away from the terrorist's frantic swordplay.

The sound of a chariot rumbled behind Amir. He spun around, stumbling back against the crucifixion post as the chariot that Conway commandeered bore down on him. Conway leaned out over the right side and drove the charioteer's spear through Amir's stomach, pinning him to the crucifixion post.

Amir grasped the end of the spear with both hands. His eyes bulged as he gaped at David, who froze in place. David was as paralyzed as Amir had been the day Amir had seen his father shot.

Amir shuddered and slumped lifeless, still pinned to the crucifixion post.

The Royal Guards and chariots had already swarmed in as Conway wheeled the chariot to return to David. The lead charioteer charged Conway and threw his spear but Conway ducked the spear and lashed out with his sword as the chariot came by, nicking the man's face. He tried to wheel the chariot again, but was dragged off the back of the chariot as Royal Guards swarmed it.

Surrounded by a dozen guards with drawn swords, David had no choice but to throw down his sword and let them take him. He was thrown to the ground, his arms and legs spread-eagle. A moment later Conway was slammed onto the ground beside him.

The charioteer that Conway had dueled with touched the cut on his cheek and glared down at them from his chariot. He wore the silver breastplate and plumed helmet of the captain of the Royal Guard.

"I will have you two drawn and quartered," he spat. "Prepare the slave first. I want this bastard to see exactly what is going to happen to him."

Four charioteers positioned their vehicle while foot soldiers tied ropes from the back of the chariots to David's arms and legs. David struggled and a guard kicked him in the head, hard, but not enough to knock him out. They wanted him awake when the horses shot off in four different directions, ripping his arms and legs from his body.

"Rahm!" Quintus hurried to the scene aboard a sedan chair carried by slaves breathing hard. He pointed an accusatory hand at Rahm. "Stop your men!"

Rahm glared at Conway. "Why do you interfere?"

"That man is a citizen of Rome. You have no authority to punish him."

"I am captain of the Royal Guard. The wretch drew my blood!"

"Kill a Roman and the queen will have your head because the emperor will demand hers. Not even the queen can order the death of a Roman citizen."

Rahm trembled with rage. He pointed at David. "Take that dog to the dungeon. I have something special in mind for him. The Roman is to be kept in chains until he appears before the queen."

He drew his chariot closer to Quintus. Angry words were exchanged between the two, but the words were spoken too low for David or Conway to hear.

CHAPTER FORTY-FIVE

At the direction of Rahm, David's hands and feet were bound and a pole slipped under the bindings. "Take the pig through the crowd so the people can thank him for spoiling their entertainment."

He was paraded through the streets of Bethsaida, carried by Royal Guards at each end of the pole, like a pig on its way to market. He was jeered at by an angry crowd. One of the angry citizens kicked him. "Bastard!" the man spat.

"You let Romans rape your wife and daughters!" David retorted.

The man kicked him again. "I am a Roman!" Others in the crowd soon joined him. The unsympathetic guards slowed down so everyone could get their turn, even Jews. David cursed them for being Roman lackeys.

Salome's praetorian guards got in their kicks and taunts as he was carried through the palace gates and across the palace courtyard. Inside a building off the courtyard, the guards dumped him on the floor and cut him loose from the pole. He was jerked to his feet, his hands still tied. Behind him was more commotion as Yosef and three Zealots who helped him were brought into the courtyard.

David stood at the foot of a grim stairwell, a dark, dank, dreary place. He didn't have to be told that Salome's infamous dungeon was somewhere below. He was dizzy and in

pain from the blows he had taken. Rough hands pushed him
forward and he twisted his body to take the fall on his side
and brought his legs in, hitting the stone steps with a bone-
crunching jar and tumbling down more steps.

He was jerked up by his tied arms and dragged down to a
guard station at the bottom of the steps, through a doorway
and into the dungeon. He was only half-conscious. A cell
door opened and he was shoved inside, the door clanging
shut behind him, as he hit the floor. He lay still, pain racking
his body, blood pounding in his head, his ears ringing. He
pushed himself up from the cold, slimy floor and crawled
into a sitting position with his back to the door. The cell was
a ten-by-ten cubicle with a tall ceiling that had only a flicker
of light, which came though a tiny Judas window in the door
and along the crack at the threshold. The rest of the cell was
lost in darkness.

Yellow eyes of *God-only-knew-what* stared at him from
the dark recesses of the cell. Something touched him and
David almost jumped out of his skin. A long brown snake
slithered over his legs. He jerked his feet back, which the
coiled snake interpreted as a threat, a king cobra, raising its
head and fanning in anger. David was afraid to breathe. He
would have melted into the door if he could.

A rat scurried between him and the serpent. The rat sensed
danger and froze in place, then lifted its head and sniffed.
The rat darted as the snake struck in a blur, disappearing into
a dark corner with the rat in its mouth.

He hoped to hell there were more rats than snakes in the
cell. David stood with his back against the door, his knees
weak.

Conway was brought in chains to the queen's audience chamber, a long narrow room with a vaulted ceiling and arched
windows. Fifty feet below the windows on the left side of the
room was a duck pond; on the right side, a cobblestone courtyard. More than one person who displeased Salome exited

right. Both sides of the room were flanked with guards; royal advisors, seers, servants, and toadies crowded before the stairs leading up to the throne.

Rahm commanded Conway to kneel, but Conway ignored him and spoke directly to the queen. "A Roman kneels for no one but the emperor."

Salome stared at him coldly, reminding Conway of a pouting child. Though this vicious-tempered woman was not a little kid who pulled wings off of flies but a despot who could have his arms and legs ripped off.

"You have not been brought before me as an honored citizen of Rome but as a criminal who killed men in the marketplace, attacked my guards, and conspired with Jewish traitors." A dog sitting at her feet growled, a wild, mad-looking creature with foam at the corners of its mouth. The creature was so strange and unexpected that Conway did a double-take before looking back at the queen.

"You have been misinformed," Conway said. "My servant was attacked by thieves and I went to his aid." He carefully avoided mentioning the Sicarii. Labeling the attack as political would create too many other questions.

"You lie! Your servant created a distraction for a rebel to break through the guards and kill the prisoner who was to be crucified. You tried to help your servant escape."

"You have been advised falsely, Your Highness. I went to the marketplace with my man to find a runaway slave, a young woman who took care of my household. The diversion was caused by rebels who released rats in the crowd."

The queen's vizier leaned beside her and whispered, her features emotionless while he spoke.

As soon as the man straightened up, Conway took another shot at intimidation. "If I am not released, a message will be sent to Pontius Pilate in Caesarea and to the governor in Syria to inform them that a citizen of Rome is being held. I would regret having to advise my fellow Romans that the streets of Bethsaida are so poorly governed they are unsafe for a Roman."

The court parasites exchanged furtive looks and whispered among themselves. The mad dog at Salome's feet growled and foam dripped from its lips.

The queen addressed Rahm. "Admit Quintus."

Quintus entered and bowed to the queen. "As a citizen of Rome, I have come before you to vouch for my fellow Roman and friend, Marcus Claudius Verro."

"You are welcome before this court, Quintus," the queen said, "but word of this man's activities disturbs us. Speak to your friend. We hope he will heed your counsel and save his life by telling us what we must know."

Quintus moved closer to Conway and lowered his voice. "Word has come to the palace that you seek the men from a foreign place who have been scheming with the Sicarii. You have killed one of them and the other does not confront you openly despite great power the man possesses. The queen suspects you have an even greater power."

Zayyad's gun was obviously the great power. "I don't know what you're talking about. I'm a simple trader."

Quintus waved aside the lie. "You must tell the queen about this power. It will save your life."

"I am a citizen of Rome and I have been unjustly attacked. Romans cannot be treated this way by provincials."

Quintus turned to the queen. "Your Highness, I witnessed the events in the marketplace. It was not Marcus but his Jewish servant who killed the two men and conspired to kill the condemned man."

He was throwing her a bone, Conway thought. By placing all of the blame on David, the queen could save face. She could not kill a Roman, but she could report the matter to Rome and ask for instructions. And hold him for months until she received word. He didn't correct Quintus—he needed to get out of the mess if he was going to continue the mission.

The vizier bent down and whispered to her again.

Rahm suddenly spoke up. "My Queen, this rabble attacked me. If it is not within the queen's power to punish him because he is a Roman"—the captain shot an angry glance at Quintus—"I demand personal satisfaction."

"I accept!" Conway said.

"Silence!" the queen snapped. "Another word from either of you and you shall both be cast into the dungeon." She stared hard at Conway. "You are free to go, but you are not to leave this city until we have heard from Rome about your claim of citizenship and the punishment that will be decreed by the emperor."

She suddenly smiled, an unfriendly smile. A raptor grin just before it rips apart helpless prey. "Quintus, bring your friend to the arena tomorrow. He will get a preview of what it is like to be ripped to pieces by wild beasts and desperate men."

Conway's chains were removed by a begrudging command from Rahm. He and Quintus made it to the great doors leading out of the audience chamber before the queen got in her last jab.

"Of course, your Jewish servant will be put to death."

He swung around to object but was pushed through the doorway by her guards, her laugh echoing through the great doors that clanged shut.

Marie awakened on a bed of straw in a cave dimly lit by a candle. She struggled into a sitting position, cold air and a chill gripping her. A shadowy passageway led out of the mouth of the cave and into what appeared to be a maze of tunnels and caverns as quiet as a crypt. She heard the shuffle of feet and tensed as the dark figure of a man stepped in front of the opening to the cave.

He spoke to her, but her mind was spinning and she didn't catch the words. More feet shuffled into the cave. She collapsed back onto the straw.

An old hag with one eye and half her face wiped away by burn scars knelt beside her and adjusted the tattered blankets to bring them higher on Marie's body. "We mean you no harm. This one," she gestured at one of the others, "saved you."

The man came closer and Marie recognized the old leper she and David had helped. The others assembled around here were all outcasts.

"Where am I?"

"You are under the city. This is our home. The queen's men have driven us underground to live like moles."

Burning with fever and shaking with cold chills, she felt herself fading, slipping back into the void of unconsciousness. She asked, "Have you heard of a man named Yeshua Ben Yoseph?"

Jesus, son of Joseph.

"Yes," the old hag cackled, "yes, he is one of us."

The sound of his cell door being unbolted jarred David awake. Four guards entered and grabbed him, slamming him facedown onto the stone floor. They shackled his ankles. With rough hands, kicks, and curses, they dragged and pushed him out of the dungeon and put him into a cart with two other prisoners. The prisoners spoke a language unknown to him, but he had heard it spoken in the marketplace, some Middle Eastern tongue other than Hebrew or Aramaic. They talked to each other in fearful tones. One of them tried to communicate with him, and when the language barrier came up, the man made a slicing motion across his throat.

He was telling David that they were going to die.

The cart left the palace courtyard and rumbled along cobblestone streets. David recognized the route. They were heading for the city gate. The same route they had taken the first day they entered the city. It led out of the city, through the marketplace, and up the hill to the place of crucifixion.

"They're going to crucify us," he told his two companions.

But when the cart came out of the city gate and passed through the marketplace, it turned from that road and instead went onto a bumpy road. He wondered if they were taking them to another prison . . . or a quiet place to kill them.

The cart bounced for several minutes along the road and then a structure loomed in the distance. It was the largest structure he had seen in or around the city. Its rounded shape reminded him of a sports arena.

His companions started jabbering and one of them pointed at the structure and again made the slicing motion with his hand across his throat again.

He shook his head, a little confused. Why take him out of the dungeon to kill him? Salome and her storm troopers would not be squeamish about killing him on the main street of Bethsaida. It didn't make any sense to him.

The cart bumped along the road and then into an open gate at the structure. It rumbled in darkness under the structure and through another gate, his eyes momentarily blinded from the sudden infusion of bright sunlight. The cart came to a halt in a wide dirt area surrounded by the rows of seating of an amphitheater.

Two dozen men were engaged in mock combat with wooden weapons—swords, daggers, spears, nets, pitchforks. Their "armor" was leather rather than iron or bronze.

The men fought one another, following the commands of an instructor who stood on a raised platform. Burly guards with real weapons stood around the group to make sure none of the amateurs escaped.

"You must give a good account of yourselves," he shouted. "Any man who fails to act bravely and go to his death fighting will find death in a slow, painful way that will cause you to pray to the gods that you be taken."

David met the eyes of his shackled companions and they grinned knowingly. They were going to be killed. But rather than having their throats cut, they would die in the arena. Fighting history's most deadly warriors.

They were amateurs to be pitted against professional killers—gladiators—to the roar of the crowd. Or would they be sentenced to fight lions or other savage beasts that had been tormented and kept starved up to the moment they were turned loose against hapless victims?

David was led off the cart and into a holding cell. A youth of about seventeen or eighteen was already in the cell barely big enough for the two of them to sit down in side by side with their legs folded up to their chests.

The boy was terrified and tearful. "I want to kill myself," he told David. "But they won't let me. They want to see me die in the arena."

He told David he was a slave who had been caught with his master's wife. He was a tutor who taught the master's children to read and write.

"The woman forced me. I tried to refuse her, but after my resisting for months she told me that she would tell her husband that I had raped her. He found us lying together. He killed his wife and bedded with me as a woman before he sold me."

David was not surprised the man did not kill the boy on the spot—why destroy a valuable piece of property? The man sodomized the boy to humiliate him and then sold him to the gladiator school. He got rid of a problem wife, regained his "honor," and made a profit on the deal by selling the boy. This boy knew nothing about fighting. He would not last more than a couple of minutes in the arena against a professional killer. But that was the idea.

David was in the cell about an hour when he, the boy, and other newcomers were taken to the arena where the master of the gladiator school awaited them.

A human fighting machine, David thought. A mass of fight scars and bulging muscles.

"Despite your crimes and the miserable punishments you deserve, you have been chosen to die a quick and honorable death in the arena." He paused and let the information sink in. "There may even be one among you who will live to fight another day. I was a gladiator in the arena. Seven times I fought. Seven times I won.

"You will fight, just as I once had to fight and thousands of others have had to. You will be given training today in the weapons you will use in the ring. When you appear before the queen and the crowd, you will not cower but will fight for your life. If you do that, you show that you are worthy of a honorable death, you will die quickly. If you can best your opponent . . . he will die and you will live."

He walked around the group, sizing each man up. They were a pathetic bunch, David thought. Slaves who had disobeyed their masters, petty thieves, prisoners taken in the war against Parthia who were too hacked up from battle to fetch a good price at the island of Delos where ten thousand slaves a day were marketed. Not one of them had the strength and speed to go up against a professional killer. The gladiator master knew it.

He paused in front of David and looked him over from head to toe.

"You have been chosen for a special fight," he said. He ordered the guards, "Take them all inside to be introduced to the Ram."

The Ram was a huge bronze statue of a horned ram. It was big enough to put a man inside its belly. Once the man was inside, the hatch he entered was locked.

"A fire is built underneath," the gladiator master said. "And the person inside slowly bakes. His screams come out of the Ram's mouth and it appears the Ram is bellowing." The gladiator master pointed to a body off to the side that looked like an ancient mummy. "He is taken from the Ram while still alive and rolled in a mixture of sulfur and salt. His death is the most agonizing one imaginable."

He pointed an index finger that had been chopped off at the first joint, jabbing the air before each man to get across his point.

"Any man who fails to die honorably in the arena will be slowly baked in the Ram. You will be begging for death after a few minutes of baking." He grinned. "Make sure you handle yourself well. If you turn and run, you will go into the Ram."

The group was taken outside and given wooden swords and other weapons for practice. David was not given a practice weapon. The men would be given real weapons for the actual combat, but it would not alter the results. They were not being trained to defend themselves, David thought. They couldn't learn that in a few hours playing with a wooden sword. They were being shown how to present themselves professionally so they would look good when they were struck down. If it was too easy, the crowd would be displeased. And so would the queen.

Gladiators were expensive; criminals, rebels, runaway slaves, were much cheaper to replace. The gladiators performed at another part of the field. They practiced with real weapons. Like pampered professional athletes in modern times, the gladiators were being treated to special food and rubdowns. They even had iron weights resembling barbells to pump their muscles.

While the others were training, David was taken back to his cell and chained in front of it. When an hour had passed, two gladiators came with the gladiator master. One of the gladiators was a huge man with long black hair, a beard, and massive arms and legs. The other was a foot shorter and built like a bullet.

"This is the one." The master pointed at David.

The big man looked at David and grunted. "He is nothing."

When the two gladiators left, the schoolmaster whipped out a dagger and cut David's right shoulder. "The queen doesn't like her favorite to lose."

CHAPTER FORTY-SIX

Conway arrived at the arena on a litter carried by slaves provided by Quintus. Lounging on pillows elevated above the crowd was not a clever way to protect oneself against an assassin's blade, but it gave him an exhilarating sense of superiority. From the size of the crowd pouring out of the city gate, it looked as though everyone in the city were going to the arena.

No word had come concerning Marie or David. Before leaving for the arena, Quintus had promised to use his influence at the palace to get David released. "We must move slowly, let the anger over the incident at the marketplace die."

He and Quintus took seats in the Roman section at the bottom row of the arena, an amphitheater with a wall at least twelve feet high to protect the spectators from the participants. The small Roman community in Bethsaida stuck together and had the best seats in the place, literally the fifty-yard line. "Of course, it's not as large as the arena in Rome, but you will find that the crowd is just as noisy and bloodthirsty," Quintus said.

The queen, carried aboard a golden throne by her slaves and surrounded by the Royal Guard, entered in the style accustomed for royalty. She deliberately paused for a moment, nodding to the Romans, and meeting Conway's eyes.

As Conway listened to the acclaim for her—and saw her agents in the crowd rewarding those who shouted the loudest—he could not suppress some admiration for her. It was a brutal world for all, but especially for women who lacked the physical strength to stand up against men with swords. Although the women of Rome were known for their influence in the affairs of state, in most places women were treated as work animals or sex objects. For a woman to rise to power required twice the intelligence—and twice the cunning and cleverness—of a man.

She was pagan, part barbaric queen, part patron of Greco-Roman culture. He had perceived aspects about her that were incompatible for a woman who ruled a country with an iron fist and was universally hated—fear and innocence.

Despite her outward appearance of ruthless expediency, he sensed she was frightened of her own ignorance. The source of the fear was obvious: she was a product of a family where murder and madness were the order of the day, where any sign of weakness meant being devoured by her own ambitious relatives if the people on the street did not rip her to pieces, and where there was always a Roman administrator or spy looking over her shoulder, waiting for her to stumble and ready to have her head chopped off when she did. Among the Herods, suspicion and reprisal took the place of brains.

Her innocence came from the sheltered life she had led. It was not an innocence of sex or the bestial nature of man but ignorance. She knew no other existence than the cauldron of insane emotions and ambitions she was raised in. She understood how to deal with Roman administrators and avaricious relatives. Herod had had fifteen wives and left a huge brood, not all of whom he murdered but all of whom aspired to a throne. No doubt she must be totally mystified in dealing with strangers with a power outside her experiences, Conway thought. In some ways she acted like a spoiled child who was not getting her way.

The blare of trumpets announced the start of the games.

———

Chained to an iron bar in a holding area, David watched as the professional gladiators and amateurs marched onto the sandy arena. The games took place midday under a bright sun, and the combatants were resplendent in their bright, colorful uniforms.

They marched completely around the ring, spectators yelling the names of their favorite gladiators. The entire group lined up in a square formation with the gladiator master out in front and saluted Salome:

Morituri te salutant!

We who are about to die, salute you!

The formation marched back and disappeared into the rabbit's warren of rooms under the stadium. Trumpets blared again. The games had begun.

A cart with a covered cage was dragged out into the middle of the arena. The cage shook and the sound of a primeval beast roared from the cage.

A female gladiator, a tall, ebony woman, taller than David's almost six feet, with well-developed muscles, came into the arena. She was dressed in black leather and bronze armor and carried a spear and round shield. The crowd knew her and cheered.

She gestured at an attendant by the cage to release the wild beast inside. He opened one end of the covered cart, putting down a ramp. Three "creatures" rushed out: dwarfs. Each was dressed as a gladiator and carried a small sword.

They rushed the women warrior and a mock battle began. The dwarfs tumbled and rolled, poked her with their swords, then scrambled from her spear. Soon the audience was laughing at their antics.

The warm-up entertainment had begun.

Conway, watching the battle of the Amazon and the Lilliputian gladiators, decided it was analogous to the rodeo clowns that warmed up audiences before a show. Get the spectators loosened up and relaxed before what they really came for—blood—flowed. He had seen gladiator battles in movies, had played roles himself, but he had never realized how close the entertainment was to modern contact sports like football, boxing, and wrestling, how caught up the audience would be, shouting for their favorites, demanding blood.

Two men on horseback engaged each other, each with a curved sword. What made the match unusual was that they fought with visors that had no opening for their eyes. Quintus called them *andabataes* and despite his aversion to the senseless violence, Conway found himself fascinated by the contest between two men who tried to scope out his opponent with just hearing.

When they came into range of each other, one man swung wildly. The other blocked his blows and hit him in the back of the neck with a curved sword.

Quintus laughed gleefully. "The champion is actually blind, of course."

Gates into the arena suddenly burst open and two chariots rumbled out. One of them had a professional driver and an *essedarii*, a gladiator who fought from the back of the chariot. "A Britany from our Britania providence," Quintus said, of the *essedarii*, "a real savage and a favorite of the queen."

The two men on the other chariot appeared confused and bewildered. The one holding the chariot reins definitely looked like he would be more comfortable guiding a cow on a rope than the two horses pulling the chariot.

The professionals rode in circles around the ring several times, waiting for the crowd to get worked up before the chariot was turned toward the amateurs. The panicked driver of the amateurs whipped the horses. His companion, trying to hold a sword with one hand and hold on to the chariot with the other, fell off the back. The oncoming chariot ran over him, stomping him under the hooves of the horses and crushing him under the wheels. They went after the amateur driver, pulling up beside him. The gladiator reached out with a pole with a sharp hook on the end and pulled the driver off the back.

Conway turned his head and looked at the crowd as the charioteers played cat and mouse around the arena, slowing tormenting the man who had been pulled off. When he was finally flat on the ground, the gladiator stood over him and looked to the queen. Shouts of *"Habet!"* came from the crowd, signifying that the man was wounded and it was time for another drama to play out, one the crowd played a role in.

The wounded man on the ground held up a trembling hand, lifting his forefinger to implore mercy from the crowd. People throughout the crowd, Quintus among them, pointed their thumbs to their chest, indicating that they wanted the man stabbed.

"He does not deserve to live," Quintus said, annoyed at Conway for not joining in, "he failed to amuse us."

Conway took out a handkerchief and waved it, joining the small minority in the crowd signaling their desire that they wished the man to live.

Salome raised her hand to signal the audience to tell her their decision. Thumbs down greatly outnumbered handkerchiefs. Salome gave the audience their wish: the gladiator cut the man's throat.

Conway kept his eyes averted. It struck him again how similar the rowdy crowd was to those at the mock wrestling matches in his time. How would a modern crowd react if they had a choice of seeing a defeated wrestler put to death? He wondered how many ordinary people would turn thumbs down. His cynicism about people made him conclude that they would be just as bloodthirsty as the arena crowd. A crowd mentality, a bully mentality, like a pack of dogs chasing a rabbit and then ripping it to pieces when they caught it, put blood in the mouth of ordinary people who go to church on Sunday.

As soon as the chariot battle ended, a group of slaves dressed as demons from Greek mythology, ran into the arena to remove the bodies. They first poked each man with a red-hot iron to see if they moved. One of them, the one that got trampled, flinched. Conway glanced away as a slave dressed as Charon, the boatman who ferried the souls of the dead across the river Styx to Hades, smashed the man over the head with a heavy wooden mallet to finish him off. Two of the demons snagged the bodies with hooked poles and pulled them from the arena, leaving bloody furrows in the sand.

"You don't enjoy the sport, Marcus?" Quintus asked.

"Sport? You mean slaughter. War is for men who enjoy action. The arena is for men who get their thrills watching others."

After the wreckage of men, horses, and chariots were cleared, a small stage for a play was created in the middle of the arena.

"They're putting on a play?" Conway asked.

Quintus grinned with glee. "A performance I designed myself. My brother writes me that it is all the rage in Rome."

Actors took to the stage. At a signal from the queen, the audience grew quiet so that the actors' voices could be heard.

"They're not real actors," Conway said as he listened to them shouting their lines clumsily in Greek.

"Of course not."

Despite the awkward performances, Conway recognized the play. It was Euripides' *Medea*. Medea was an enchantress in Greek mythology, a goddess with the gift of prophecy, who helped Jason and the Argonauts steal the Golden Fleece from her father, King Aeëtes of Colchis. She later married Jason, who deserted her for the daughter of the King Creon of Corinth. In her revenge, Medea murdered Creon, Creon's daughter, and her own two sons by Jason, and took refuge with King Aegeus of Athens.

Conway knew the story but had no idea why the crowd at the stadium listened so quietly and intently as the actors shouted their lines in a mixture of Greek, Hebrew, and Aramaic, using whatever language the actors knew.

The crowd certainly could not be caught up in the play's dramatic value, not the way it was being presented.

Quintus and the Romans around him seemed to take particular interest in one of the actors, a man dressed as a woman. Each time he spoke they leaned forward, to catch his every word.

Quintus slapped his knee. "Did you hear that?"

"What?"

"The quiver in his voice. He's scared. He's thinking about what will be happening and it frightens him. Now he'll lose the sympathy of the queen and the audience."

Action on the stage stopped and the actors looked up to the queen. She nodded.

The actors grabbed buckets of a liquid and doused the nervous man with it. Another man ran up with a burning torch and set him on fire. He screamed and tried to beat out the flames, but the liquid he was soaked with was inflammable. Probably something like naphtha, Conway thought, one of the ingredients of Greek fire, the mysterious fiery compound that later helped Constantinople hold off the Islamic onslaught for hundreds of years.

He recognized the scene. Medea was supposed to have used her powers to cause her rival to burst into flames. Conway felt nauseous as he turned his eyes from the screaming man trying to beat out the flames as he ran. The fire did not kill him. He was finished with a mallet and dragged from the arena.

"Artose, the queen's favorite gladiator, will be fighting today," Quintus said. "He's a vicious brute, a veteran of the arena in Rome itself. I guarantee you will enjoy his performance. He's quite a crowd pleaser. He never kills his victims outright, but works slowly, crippling one arm and leg at a time. Only after the victim is helpless on the ground does he deliver the final blow."

"I can hardly wait," Conway said, keeping a straight face.

Quintus nodded up toward where the queen sat. "Artose will fight extra hard today. The queen has been offended and has told him she expects him to restore her honor."

Her entourage occupied a dozen of the top rows. Quintus and Conway were seated closer to the action, but Conway realized Salome had chosen the upper level for security reasons. The queen's old vizier stood beside her in his praying mantis posture. He leaned down and spoke to her, then looked down to Conway. She favored Conway with a deceptive smile. The captain of the guard followed her gaze and stiffened when he saw Conway.

Conway grinned back at him. He also flipped him the bird, realizing the gesture would not be understood. "I see the queen has brought golden boy to the games. Is Rahm her lover?"

"The captain of the guard is not just a military position but a social one." Quintus grimaced. "It's the honorary title held by the queen's current lover."

The crowd suddenly broke into a cheer. A man armed only with a club and a shield was pushed into a large cage containing a bear that had been beaten and whipped until it was in a killer rage. The man cowered from the beast.

"He's making a mistake," Quintus said gleefully. "His only chance is to dominate the animal."

There was no way any human being could dominate the tortured animal.

Conway turned sideways and wished he could plug his ears. Once in a gladiator movie he and a stuntman had gotten carried away in a fight scene and fought each other until Conway had drawn blood. He loved the surge of excitement that the moment of sword combat had given him. He'd love to be in the arena himself. But not to slaughter some poor fool who couldn't defend himself.

The bear reared and came down on the man, its great claws ripping as the crowd roared. The bear and its bloody plaything were separated as the bear was pulled back by men grabbing the long chain that was left dangling from its neck. They tricked the bear back into its cage and removed the body. Another bloody furrow in the sand.

Two old men armed with short swords were pitted against a gladiator aboard a chariot. The gladiator wore an armor vest, had a large shield, spears, net, and sword.

"A couple of farmers caught poaching the queen's game," Quintus said. "By the gods, is it not exciting! I often thought about taking a turn in the arena myself, but naturally my grandfather wouldn't permit it."

Conway kept himself from laughing. It was true that the intoxicating roar of the arena crowd had even lured some young Romans of noble birth into the arena, winning fame or fortune or a glorious death to the thunder of thousands, but it was hard to imagine pudgy Quintus as one of them. He had read about Commodus, a mad emperor of the next century, so caught up in the games that he imagined he was the god Hercules and fought in the arena. Naturally, he won all of his matches until the Romans could not tolerate his insanity any longer and had him strangled by a wrestler during a match.

Even when Conway looked away, he was inexorably drawn back to witness the slaughter. The amateurs had little chance against the pros and savage beasts. A skinny young boy caught stealing in the marketplace was pitted against a condemned killer who was bigger and stronger.

Quintus gestured at the killer. "The man is a robber captured raiding a caravan. He should be fighting a gladiator, but his clan met the queen's price and they pitted him against a boy."

Conway avoided looking as the robber battered the boy to the ground and killed him with clumsy blows to the head. The savagery was almost unreal to Conway. He was actually watching human beings kill each other to amuse an audience. What bothered him most was the pounding of his own blood, the fiery urge to jump out of his seat and face a challenger in the arena to the roar of the crowd. It was intoxicating, the blood and danger and cheers more seductive than a woman. He had always known he was more than an actor; he was a man who had to live his parts. What a curtain call it would be, to stand before cheering thousands with the taste of blood in his mouth.

Quintus nudged him. "That's Artose, the queen's champion."

The crowd cheered as a man with arms and legs swollen with cords of muscle strutted into the ring.

"You're going to enjoy this. Artose is a crowd pleaser."

Conway stared in disbelief as the gladiator's victim came into the ring. He swung around to Quintus and the Roman shrugged.

He patted Conway's leg. "Things will work out nicely this way. The queen will have her revenge and you can find another servant."

David was equipped with a wooden shield that looked like a toy and a short sword. His "armor" was leather padding. He raised the sword up and down and flinched from pain as he tried to exercise his shoulder.

Conway's surprise turned to icy anger. "They've wounded him. He's working the muscles in his shoulder." He had been set up, lured to the arena by Salome. Quintus was conspiring with her. *They want to see if I'll use the power they think I have,* Conway thought.

Quintus shrugged and ate a honey cake, dropping crumbs down the front of his toga. "Gladiators are expensive."

Unlike David, Artose, the gladiator, wore a metal breastplate, had a long sword strapped to his side, carried a three-pronged spear in one hand and a net in the other. The idea was to tangle the victim's feet in the net, jerk him off his feet, and spear him like a frog.

"It won't be a fair fight," Conway said.

"Of course not, but the crowd will love it. And so will you. Artose is quite a master. He will pin your overseer to the ground with his spear and chop off the man's hands and feet with his sword before dispatching him with a stroke to the neck. He takes his time, letting the audience see each amputation bleed before he does the next."

Quintus was taking obvious pleasure in the situation, pretending to be Conway's friend while he played the queen's game.

"I will give your servant credit." Quintus raised his eyebrows as he watched the action. "He faces death like a man and not a cowering dog like most of these Jews. The queen is punishing your servant because she suspects you have a power you are withholding from her. I do not know how long my influence will keep *you* out of the arena." He blinked with mock innocence.

Conway ignored him and kept his eye on the action. David had squared off against the gladiator, showing more confidence than he felt with the odds stacked against him. He actually envied David and wanted to be in the arena himself, battling for life and death, the roar of the crowd drowning out all sounds but the whisper of death.

The gladiator charged, hurling the spear. David ducked and scrambled out of the way as the gladiator swung the net. Artose ignored David's en garde position and casually walked over and picked up his spear.

"He could batter your servant to the ground with his sword, but that would be too quick. He prefers to play for a while."

Using short spear thrusts and sweeps of the net, the gladiator closed in. David dodged and kept moving back because his shield had little effect in warding off the spear.

A wave of approval surged through the crowd.

"Oh, lovely, he's going to back your servant up against the arena wall and pin him. It's quite a sight."

David tripped and stumbled back against the wall. The crowd went up on its feet, Conway with them, as the gladiator charged with the spear to pin him. The spear bit deep into the wall, but David wasn't there. He sidestepped and lashed out with the sword at the exposed tendons at the back of the gladiator's leg. Artose screamed as the sword cut deep into the flesh above his heel. The audience reacted with a gasp of surprise.

He tricked him! Conway smiled. *He's hamstrung the bastard!*

His adrenaline was pumping, ready to blow like a new oil well. He could barely keep himself seated. A life-and-death drama was taking place before his eyes and being a spectator was not a role he played well.

The gladiator struggled to his feet, using his spear for support, and pulled his sword. Even though David had cut the tendons in the back of the man's leg, the man had an animal instinct that kept him charging, using the spear as a crutch and dragging one leg.

Lashing out at David with his sword, Artose went off balance and fell to the ground. David jumped past him as the gladiator was getting to his feet and sliced the muscles behind the knee of the man's good leg. The gladiator was completely helpless, unable to get to his feet. He sat up and stared down in disbelief at the blood flowing onto the sand from behind his legs.

Rahm had left the queen's entourage and went down the arena two steps at a time. He leaped onto the railing overlooking the combat pit and paused dramatically to let the crowd catch sight of him. Turning to the queen, he saluted her with his sword and jumped into the arena.

"He's going to save the queen's honor!" Quintus exclaimed.

Another man rushed into the arena as Rahm jumped down. He also went for David.

"That's Zakor, Artose's lover."

Conway had seen the small, husky, bullet-shaped man earlier acting as an animal handler, working the animals into a killer rage by beating and torturing them. His adrenaline on fire, Conway jumped to his feet, drew his sword and stepped up onto the railing.

"Are you mad!" Quintus screeched.

Conway paused to salute the queen and the Romans. He leaped, grinning, into the arena.

Rahm commandeered a chariot from a guard post and whipped the two horses into a run, steering them for Conway while Zakor attacked David like an angry bee, darting in and out with quick sword strokes. David frantically parried the thrusts and kept moving because Artose, the wounded gladiator, had joined the attack, pursuing David on his hands and knees, a mindless beast trying to back David against the arena wall again.

Rahm hurled a spear from the chariot as he charged Conway who swiftly dodged his spear. He wheeled the horses around and tried to run him down but Conway threw himself to the side. As the chariot rolled by, Rahm snagged Conway's clothes with a four-pronged grapnel tied to a rope, the hooks gouging the flesh on his left side. The slack in the rope disappeared and Conway was dragged on the ground behind the chariot. He grabbed the rope and hung on to keep the hooks from burying deeper in his flesh.

The crowd surged to its feet, roaring.

Rahm turned sharply with the chariot, creating a slack in the rope. It allowed Conway to gain his footing and grab the rope a couple of feet ahead of the hooks so he could unwedge them from his flesh. He ran for the chariot as Rahm whipped the horses. The horses shot forward and almost took Conway off his feet, but he kept his balance and ran up to the back of the chariot. He tossed the hooks at Rahm, snagged the man's clothing, and holding on to the rope, threw himself to the ground, using his own weight to drag Rahm off the back of the chariot.

Conway pulled his dagger and grabbed a shield that had fallen off the chariot. He turned to defend himself as Rahm charged with a sword. He was no match with his dagger and shield against Rahm's sword. He backed up. The driverless chariot came around again and Conway jumped for it, leaping aboard and steered the horses to where his sword was on the ground. He jumped off the chariot and picked up the sword at a run.

The roar of the crowd fed the fire in his blood. It wasn't just an audience—he felt as if the whole world were watching him. What a heroic role! The side of his face was cut when Rahm pulled him behind the chariot and the taste of blood was in his mouth. It was a sweet taste and he spat some of it onto the dirt as he closed in on Rahm, his thoughts blind with the excitement of the moment. It was the only part of his own blood that he planned to spill in the arena.

When he had played Julius Caesar on stage he had died nobly on the steps of the Roman Senate. But there was no honor in bleeding to death in the dirt of the arena.

To achieve glory, Rahm must die.

Across the arena, the wounded Artose and his lover were trying to pin David to the wall. Zakor was built like an artillery shell and had the speed and nimbleness of an acrobat. He backed David toward the arena wall with short, quick jabs of

Artose's three-pronged spear, keeping a little distance to David's left, as Artose, crawling like a crippled tiger, sword in paw, flanked David on the right.

Sweat poured down David's face and into his eyes. He tore the leather helmet from his head and wiped sweat from his face with his sleeve. The helmet made his head feel like it was in a vice and it wouldn't have stopped a blade. His adrenaline rush had taken him beyond pain and he could no longer feel his shoulder. He was not even aware of the crowd. The roars that vibrated the stadium were blocked out of his mind by the immediate danger of the two men trying to kill him. He was facing death for the third time in days—his life or theirs. He was exhausted but his mind and body were on fire with the desperate urge to live. And kill.

His left foot brushed the net Artose had used earlier and he picked it up with his free hand. Zakor charged at him, bouncing first to his left and then to his right, jabbing with the spear. He threw the net, entangling the spear, and lunged at Zakor, grabbing the spear with his free hand and striking out at Zakor's head with his sword. Zakor moved under the blow and David's fist smacked into the man's steel helmet.

David tried to break away but the man held on to him. He saw Artose crawl frantically toward them and David shoved the little man backward over Artose. He didn't move away fast enough as Artose got a grip on his ankle. Rearing on his knees, Artose accidentally knocked his lover aside as the little man tried to get back into the fight. David blocked Artose's sword and lashed out, cutting deep into the thick cord of muscles on the side of the gladiator's neck. The spray of blood hit David and he backed away, too breathless to gag but horrified at the sight of the body writhing in the dust.

Seeing his lover's bloody body engaged Zakor. He came screaming at David like a cannonball. The little man grabbed a spear off the ground ready to kill, but David sidestepped and buried the point of his sword in Zakor's throat.

Conway taunted Rahm as he expertly countered the man's swordplay. "It's not so easy when you have to fight fair, is it?"

The roar of the crowd was deafening as Conway attacked him, dazzling the crowd with his swordplay. He could have killed Rahm, but the crowd was going crazy over the way he was humiliating the man.

Rahm's confidence broke. He turned and ran.

Salome screamed a command at the archers posed along the railing. They let their arrows fly, dropping on Rahm in a rain of death. She screamed more commands and her soldiers poured into the arena from every entrance.

David and Conway came together near the wall to the Roman section, David en garde, ready to take on Salome's whole army, while Conway ignored the soldiers and saluted the crowd with his sword as he reveled in the deafening roar. Without turning and taking his eyes off the soldiers coming at them, David said, "Thanks."

"Take as many as you can when they charge," Conway said. "I want people to write songs about this day."

The crowd grew silent as the soldiers formed a giant circle around the two victors. Everyone in the arena knew what was happening. The queen's champions were dead, the victors were supposed to be rewarded, but the queen had been affronted.

Throughout the arena people stood, silent, expectant, thousands with thumbs up or waving handkerchiefs, signaling the queen that they wanted the victors spared.

Salome was on her feet, her face dark with anger. She suddenly laughed shrilly, loud enough to be heard across the arena.

"There cannot be two heroes of the day," she announced. She pointed down at David and Conway. "They must fight to the death!"

The crowd rocked the arena with its roar of approval. Conway waited for the noise to die down before he shouted his reply. "Is the queen commanding a citizen of Rome to fight to the death with a Jew? A slave?"

The group of Romans in the audience stood up, one by one, and challenged the queen with their glares. Only Quintus slumped despondent in his seat. He looked as if he had lost his best friend.

Conway knew that the Romans didn't care about him, but they thought he was one of them. A fat salt trader Conway had met at the baths with Quintus bellowed up at Salome, "Your captain violated the rules of the arena by interfering when the servant of a citizen of Rome gained advantage during the fighting. Marcus defended his servant against unlawful attack."

The vizier whispered frantically to Salome. The expression on her face changed from anger to cunning as she listened. She pointed down at the two victors.

"The Jew is free. As for the Roman, he shall be my guest at a feast befitting a hero of the arena."

CHAPTER FORTY-SEVEN

David returned to the villa of the slave trader Quintus, his tunic torn and bloodied. His shoulder ached and throbbed, but he had more important things on his mind than pain.

The rear gate guard hurried inside when David approached.

A moment later Quintus came out of the villa flanked by his overseer and the guard. Quintus was drunk, distraught, and arrogant. "You are not welcome here."

David stepped by the men without saying a word and went to the stable to get his things. Everything of value was gone and he left the stable, tight jawed.

Quintus staggered behind him. "Run, Jew, run. The dogs have been loosed!" He threw his wine goblet. "There is no place for you to hide, Jew!"

David never looked back. Quintus was too cowardly to put a knife in his back. He would have enjoyed teaching the Roman some manners, but it would have meant another visit to Salome's dungeon.

He went to the house of Ezra the Zealot. He had nowhere else to go and received a hero's welcome, the great bear hugging him like a long-lost cub. Isie was there, shyly happy to see him.

David scrubbed down and put on fresh clothes that Ezra's wife had rummaged from somewhere. It felt good to be clean, to have the filth of the dungeon and the arena washed off his body. Afterward he and Ezra sat in the cool courtyard and broke a fresh loaf of bread, drank wine, and picked at dates and figs.

"Good Jews do not go to the arena, but word of your victory is sung in every household. The games are rigged in favor of the Romans and you are the first to avoid their treachery. A Jewish hero of the arena will not sit well with Salome or the Romans. You must be on guard against more treachery."

"Has there been any news of Marie?"

"It seems the woman was swallowed by the earth. Our ears are everywhere and hear nothing of her. Perhaps she has fallen into the hands of friends."

"We are strangers in the city. She would not seek aid with anyone besides you or Yoseph. Before we left the arena Con—uh, Marcus told me he hadn't seen her. He also said Quintus had only been pretending to be his friend."

"You have not been around Bethsaida long enough to know the local gossip. Quintus is not only a great friend of Salome and no doubt spied on you for her but Rahm was his lover. And hers."

David shook his head. The place had more plots than a soap opera. "I'm amazed by the scandal of Salome's court."

"The madness and debauchery run in the blood. The descendants of Herod have freely indulged in murder, lust, and incest to increase their fortunes and power. Herod, who called himself Great, murdered his beloved wife, their two sons, brother, grandfather, and mother, not to mention his own firstborn and other sons. Is it any wonder that we fight to rid Israel not only of the Romans but corrupt and immoral tyrants like Salome?"

"You have a good and just cause. What news do you have of Yoseph?"

Ezra's features went dark. "He is in the queen's dungeon. The queen has sent a messenger with a petition to the governor in Syria and Pilate in Judea to have Yoseph and three others crucified without waiting for word from Rome. She claims rebellion is being plotted and the punishment will dissuade rebels." His nostrils flared. "No more blood of our brothers must flow. This Roman Jezebel who calls herself the Queen of Jews must be stopped. Our people in Caesarea say Pilate plans to grant the petition, but is waiting until after Passover because he wants to reinforce Salome's army with a Roman cohort before the crucifixions."

"So your people want to strike now."

"Exactly. Word has spread and our followers from throughout Galilee gather in the wilderness. Soon our army will be strong enough."

"It will cost many lives to free the men in the dungeon."

"Thousands of Zealots have been crucified. To strike a blow against the Romans and their puppet despots and show that we will fight back may save many lives in the future even though the cost today is great."

David clasped Ezra's arm. "I have little to offer, but I'm willing to help all I can."

"We need every sword we can muster. But your own plans, this mysterious quest about a prophecy, does it not take you to Jerusalem?"

Ezra's question was a dilemma David had been struggling with almost from the moment he had walked out of the arena. Time was running out.

"Yes, I must be in Jerusalem during Passover. But I can't leave Bethsaida without word of Mariam and my friend."

Ezra raised his eyebrows. "You call your Roman master friend? No, do not answer. You are a strange Jew from a strange land. Indeed, the way the Roman fought side by side with you in the arena, if he is not your friend, he must be a madman."

Fever and chills racked Marie's body, her days and nights were one, filled with delirium, her mind wandering to dark places, remembering terrible things.

The outcasts were always there, nursing her, keeping her warm in the dank, chilly cavern. To Marie they were dark shadows hovering around her bed of straw, the old hag nursing her while others brought dry blankets to replace the ones soaked from her sweat or torn in the fury of her dreams.

On the third day the leper who had brought Marie into the caverns told the old hag, "She is going to die."

The old hag nodded in agreement. "Demons attack her and she cries out in a strange tongue. There is only one that can save her."

In a brief moment of lucidity she realized that her body was in a life-and-death struggle and that she wanted to die, wanted her body to surrender to the infection spreading through her system. Her dreams were a surrealistic reliving of the past, a replay of pain and ghosts, a church in a French village where frenzied people greedily tried to gain salvation by touching her; the sorrowful face of a little Arab boy whose flesh melts from his bones as he asks her over and over why she led him to his death.

The specter faded before a glow of light that began at the end of the tunnel and slowly moved toward her. It was not the flickering yellow of a candle flame but a soft white glow, growing larger and brighter as it neared.

Through vision blurred by fever and pain she saw a man in a pure white cloak. Kneeling beside her, the man reached out to touch her moist brow.

When Marie woke the old hag was sitting beside her grinning. She felt Marie's forehead. "Your fever has gone. The demons have left you. You slept peacefully for many hours."

Marie struggled into a sitting position. Other outcasts gathered around her, a circle of friendly, ugly faces. The illness had broken, but she was still weak.

"I had many dreams, but I only remember one. A man came into this room and spoke to me, a man in white."

"Death was upon you and we sent for a healer. After he touched you, the demons ran from your body."

"Where is he now?"

"Yeshua Ben Yoseph is gone."

Her strength slowly came back. She rested on the bed of straw and was mothered by the old hag and the crew of outcasts who brought her broth and bread and fruit and treated her like a queen.

She had inherited a family, a strange clan of cripples and freaks, more grotesque than Snow White's seven dwarfs and more loving than anything she imagined. That most appeared to suffer from leprosy did not frighten her. Despite its biblical reputation, she knew the disease was not highly contagious and many skin afflictions were mistakenly believed to be leprosy.

The outcasts gathered around her bed for hours at a time and told her about Bethsaida, of the golden days before King Philip took ill and Salome used the reins of power to drive them underground to live like worms. Poorest of the poor, the dregs of society, they still had hopes and dreams for the future.

"A place warm and dry where the sun shines all day," the old leper who helped her said, "that's where we will go when King Philip is well and drives that wanton whore from his throne."

On the day they guided her out of the caverns they brought her flowers, fresh fruit and a delicious apricot cake from the marketplace. She realized that they had sacrificed to give her the treats and her eyes filled with tears. The old hag told her not to cry. "It's all right. We stole all of it."

They trooped through the caverns like an honor guard for a queen as they escorted her out.

"The caverns are long forgotten by the authorities," said the leper. "They were under the old city that was here before King Philip built Bethsaida. Our people used them to store food during times of war. No one uses them now but us."

Water flowed down the middle of some of the tunnels.

"The aqueduct is above us and leaks in many places," said the leper.

The old hag gestured for silence. "We've come to the place of the cries," she whispered.

Marie heard an eerie whine, hardly audible. The old hag pointed to a crack in the ancient stone wall.

"Beyond that wall is the dungeon of Salome. You hear the cries of the tortured souls that have died under the rack in that hellish place."

They took her to Ezra the Zealot, from whose house had come word that she was sought by friends.

David was sitting on the wall of the well in Ezra's courtyard sharpening a sword with a wet stone when Marie walked into the courtyard.

She met his eye only briefly and looked away, as if she was unsure of her welcome.

He set aside his work and ran to her, taking her into his arms. She held on to him, urgently, burying her head against his shoulder.

"I'm sorry about that night," he said. "I was stupid and drunk." He gently lifted her chin so he could look into her eyes. "I've been so terribly afraid for you."

"It was my fault," she said. "I was insane to leave the stable that night."

"Where have you been? Ezra and Yoseph have been turning the city upside down for you."

"Only a mole would have found me. I was under the city in a place were the poor and downtrodden are hiding from Salome's whip."

Ezra came out of the house, grinning and stroking his beard. "I think this house will soon see another wedding," he said.

Ezra's wife served them dinner in David's room to give them privacy. They spread the food on the floor in front of a roaring fire.

"I ran because the poison was choking me," she said. "I realized what they must have told you about me, what you must think."

"We don't have to talk about it."

"No, we have to face it. Sometimes I feel as if I've been

nothing more than a spectator of my own life, watching as the rest of me moved helplessly in and out of shadows."

She told him what happened in the Aramaic village, of wandering into the desert numb with shock, of being found by bandits. And gang raped.

"When I was in the hospital in Marseilles, recuperating from—from what happened, I saw street girls brought in battered, brutalized, by men, drugs, life itself. I can't explain why, but seeing those girls, knowing that they needed someone to help them, saved my own life. I honestly think I would have killed myself if I hadn't suddenly found some meaning in life among the magdalenes."

"Magdalenes?"

"Magdalenes is a name for prostitutes, after Mary Magdalene, the prostitute Jesus saved from a reprobate life. Afterwards, she followed Jesus on his ministry and witnessed the Crucifixion and Resurrection." She buried her hands in her lap. The palms burned.

He took her hands in his own and kissed each palm. "It doesn't matter, whatever it is, it doesn't matter."

"I feel guilty when I'm with a man after what happened—"

"We're together, that's all that matters." He cupped her face with his hands and drew her lips close to his, and kissed her tenderly. "You don't have to feel guilty about love anymore. It's not something we planned, not a crime we premeditated. We fell in love. We don't have to make excuses for it."

She threw her arms around him and squeezed with all her might. "David, you could never imagine how many times I dreamed of this moment, how many times I cried because I had never experienced real love. I loved you from that first moment in the corridor at the science facility, from the moment you made a hole in a bathroom wall with a knife to talk to me."

"We never have to be apart again."

They came together that night as lovers long apart.

They slept on blankets piled on the floor in front of the fire and he woke her as he got up to stir the ashes in the fireplace.

She nestled contentedly in his arms after he crawled back into the blankets. They lay quietly for a while, but neither could fall back asleep.

"It's not over yet, is it," she said. "We can't go away and just be with each other."

He was bothered by another thought. He had fallen in love with Marie. But he had a duty to his dead wife, whom he also loved. A duty to bring her back to life. He did not know how to tell Marie about his plan for his wife.

He sighed warily and stretched his arms. "No, it's not over yet. We still have the mission. Do you think Jesus is still in the caverns?"

She shook her head. "No, the old woman said he had come just for me and was leaving Bethsaida afterwards."

"What did he look like?"

She shook her head. "I never saw his face. Everything was a blur. I was only half-conscious, if that. If I had been well, I would have said something to him, perhaps arranged it so we could join him in his travel and protect him from the Zayyad brothers."

She felt his body tense at the mention of the two terrorists. "It's haunted you, hasn't it, the Zayyad brothers, knowing they would come for you someday."

"More than I've been able to admit myself. I knew they would come someday, for me, my wife, children, whoever they could get to. That's one of the reasons I kept moving around, why I went into the desert. They couldn't surprise me in the desert, put a bomb under my car or wait as I passed an alleyway. And . . . there was the violence in me, the way I reacted to the death of my wife. It was an accident, a tragic one. She drove between the fools as they were firing at each other.

"I'm too much like my father. It's ironic, he literally disowned me because he thought I was too much like my mother. I just can't seem to win, I guess." He squeezed her hand. "Amir Zayyad is dead. I wish I could have taken the devil out of him instead, but . . ."

"Don't think about it."

"I have to. Jair is still out there. And we have a mission to complete. We have to get back into contact with Conway. Time is running out."

"David . . . let's run away! From Bethsaida, from Israel. Let's go together to the other side of the world. Somewhere we can be alone, just you and I."

"We can't abandon the mission."

"I've spent my whole life worrying about other people, on one mission or another. There's so little time left for us."

"Would you abandon the world to Jair Zayyad? Let him twist history into his own rotten image?"

"No, no, I wouldn't. But—damn, damn, damn—nothing in my life has ever been simple. There's always something else that I have to take care of before I can take care of myself. David, promise me you'll be careful, promise me nothing will happen to you. I don't want to lose you. You're the only decent thing that has ever happened to me."

He kissed her tears. "When I came on this mission, I was only half trying. I wasn't sure that the world was worth saving." He shook his head. "Marie, we have a lot of problems in our own time, but there is a savageness that we are usually able to control. It gets out once in a while, with a Hilter or a Stalin, genocide in Africa or chaos in the Balkans, but it's sporadic. I know now that I can't leave the world to the Jair Zayyads. Whatever humanity we've created in two thousand years we need."

She searched his face with haunted eyes. "I'm afraid, David, I'm afraid that we can give the world a future only at the price of our own." She put her head against his chest, listening to the beat of his heart.

"We've got to try and contact those people who helped you in the caverns. They may know where Jesus went."

"I want to help those poor people. They're desperate. Is there anything we can do for them?"

"We have gold coins sewn into our clothing. A few of those could buy them a new life. I wish we could repay Yoseph that easily. The Zealots are planning an attack on the dungeon. Getting Yoseph and the rest of their people out will mean the death of many others. Ezra doesn't want to admit it, but there's a good chance the dungeon guards will kill the prisoners the moment an attack begins."

She shuddered. "There's a terrible place in the caverns where a draft seeps through a crack in a common wall with the dungeon and makes a sound like the cries of tortured men."

He stared at her. "Are you saying the dungeon is at the same level as the caverns?"

"Yes, I think so."

"And there's a crack in the wall between the caverns and the dungeons?"

"That's what the outcasts told me."

"We have to tell Ezra. This may be the miracle he needs to ward off a massacre."

The Zealot leader came out of his bedroom grumbling like a bear disturbed in midwinter, but quickly became alert as David explained about the crack in the cavern wall.

"Can you find your way back to this place?" Ezra asked Marie.

"No, but I'm sure the beggars will show me."

Ezra was excited and David decided to press his luck. "Now I need a favor. I have to find a healer from Nazareth named Yeshua Ben Yoseph."

Ezra frowned. "We do not reveal information about our comrades."

"We mean him no harm."

"Why do you seek this man?"

"I can't tell you that. I have to ask you to trust me."

Ezra studied David's face. "I must trust you. If you were untrustworthy, I would not be in this room with you at this moment but in Salome's dungeon with my comrades. The man you seek, this man who is known to us as a healer and teacher from Nazareth, has been in Bethsaida recently. He is a sympathizer of just causes and helps us. He is gone now, not to Nazareth, but is taking food to our army that has gathered in the wilderness."

Marie and David exchanged looks. The New Testament said Jesus fed five thousand men in a desolate place.

"Ezra, I need to find this army."

Ezra shook his head. "That I could not tell you, not for friendship, not for the lives of myself and my own family. But I will tell you this. It is too late to seek him there. By the time you reached the army, the healer and his comrades will have delivered the food and left. Their plans are the same as all good Jews at this time. They go to Jerusalem for Passover."

"We have to be in Jerusalem for Passover, too," David said.

CHAPTER FORTY-EIGHT

The feast Salome threw for Conway was an orgy that would have made Harold Robbins blush.

He approached the great doors of the banquet hall accompanied by an honor guard stepping to the beat of military drums. Palace guards lined both sides of the corridor and saluted him with raised swords, the great doors drew open, trumpets heralded and the banquet guests rose as a body, roared their welcome, and gave him a clenched-fist salute.

The banquet hall was a long, rectangular room with two tiers of couches lining a sunken entertainment area in the center.

The queen's couch was on top of a pyramid at the far end of the room. Leading up two sides of the pyramid were steps that the servants used to bring her food and drink. A servant girl in a black spider's costume dangled in midair next to Salome. The other end of the weblike rope disappeared in the darkness above. The spider girl picked delicacies from a golden tray and handed them to Salome.

Conway thought a colorful butterfly would have been more in tune with a woman's taste, but the spidery creature was more in character for Salome. His couch was in a position of honor at the queen's right, slightly elevated above the couches of the other guests, but nowhere near as high as the queen's lofty enthronement.

Salome stared arrogantly down at her guests, not hiding her scorn for those beneath her. All the guests were men despite the fact that the person hosting the party was a woman. Apparently women were deemed worthy only of serving food, providing sexual pleasure, and ruling a country.

The entertainment began with acrobats jumping and bouncing to incredible heights; jugglers and clowns took a turn at amusing the crowd, followed by a man who first ate fire, then a sword, and finally swallowed a snake whole. Only the fire and sword came out again. Conway decided it was either an extremely clever trick or the man had one hell of a digestive system. Watching the guests was as entertaining as watching the performers in the center of the room; fondling the servants took preference over eating.

He soon realized after the first few sips that the dinner wine was drugged, more potent than the one he drank during orgies with Marcus, but the flush spreading from his head to his toes indicated it was already too late to worry about it, so he might as well enjoy the high, the music, and the action. Drugs, sex, and rock and roll.

A magician appeared center stage and the crowd quieted and gave him their attention. He wore black robes that fell to the floor and a steel helmet with an iron spike erupting up from it. He had wisdom's white beard and reptilian black eyes.

He walked around the entertainment floor holding up a white dove to the audience. Off to the side, four assistants stood by with a large, black sheet. The magician paused dramatically with the dove in one hand and a dagger in the other. He flicked his wrist and cut off the bird's head, spraying the floor with blood and threw the white body onto the bloody floor, the bird flip-flopping for a moment before becoming still.

His assistants held the black sheet over the bloody area. The magician walked around the sheet waving his dagger in the air, drawing a secret incantation with its magic point and throwing handfuls of an ashy substance from a pouch carried around his waist. The ash sizzled when it hit the sheet, like water sprayed onto a hot frying pan.

After making an incantation at all four sides of the sheet, he threw a big handful of the gray material that exploded with a huge puff of smoke, clouding the sheet. The assistants snatched the sheet away to reveal a naked young girl on the floor where the dove had been.

The girl lay still, her lips spread in a narcotic smile.

The magician held up a small, bright green snake. He cut off the snake's head and sprayed blood near the girl on the floor, and threw the writhing green body on the bloodied area. Again, the assistants hovered over the spot with their black sheet and more incantations and magic smoke spewed before they whipped away the sheet. The audience gasped. A monstrous green snake, a full-grown python, a dozen feet long and as thick as a man's leg, was coiled on the floor. The girl was only a foot from the snake.

She's obviously drugged, thought Conway. *Probably a prostitute*. Her face was young but hard, and her drug-dazed smile was a little cocky, a little lewd.

The magician knelt beside the girl and whispered in her ear. She squirmed with sexual desire, spreading her legs and using her fingers to spread herself open.

Conway's mind wasn't too finely tuned after a few glasses of the potent wine and he found himself hot and aroused along with the rest of the men.

One of the assistants held a line tied to the snake's neck. He tugged on the rope and guided the uncoiling snake onto the prone girl. She welcomed the serpent into her arms as a lover, wrapping her legs around the creature and moaning aloud as its round, firm body coursed between her thighs.

The magician jumped back as the powerful snake suddenly began coiling around the girl. The snake flopped her over and twisted around her. Once again the assistants fluttered their black sheet over her and a handful of magic ash clouded the scene. When they snapped away the sheet, a live white dove and a little green snake were on the floor.

All at once the room grew darker. The guests and servants quietly left, leaving Conway sprawled on his couch. He stared wide-eyed at the top of the pyramid.

Salome was slowly descending the pyramid in the arms of the spider. The spider was real to him, a great black creature with grasping arms. He tried to resist the illusion, but drugs had taken over his brain.

The spider unfolded its legs and Salome stepped out of its embrace and began dancing, her body coursing with an eerie melody that filled the room. Her golden robe slowly unraveled as she swayed to the strange music, revealing round, firm breasts, nipples hard and erect. The V between her legs had been shaven bare.

Lust radiated from her. Instead of sensual desire came the sexual rage of a jungle beast in heat.

The pounding in his head moved to his groin and he unconsciously slipped off the couch to go to her. She faded into the darkness as he approached her and he stood, confused, wrapped in shadows and erotic music. The darkness began to fade and he found himself in a cool garden with tropical birds, broad-leafed plants, and slender palms.

He was naked, yet it seemed natural.

A serpent in a tree stared at him and flicked its tongue as he approached. He knew he should be frightened of the snake, but his feet kept taking him closer and closer until he was standing beneath the snake. The snake slowly slid from the limb and wrapped around his naked body, sliding around his neck and down across his chest, around his waist and between his legs, coursing against his groin. The creature was warm and smooth and he thought that strange because serpents were cold-blooded. He trembled and squirmed as the silky creature rubbed against his testicles and penis.

He closed his eyes and floated to the ground and lay on his back with the warm body of the creature wrapped around him. The creature flicked its tongue in his face. He opened his eyes and stared into the face of Salome. She sat up with her hands across his chest and spread herself over his groin.

As she swayed back and forth on top of him, he thought

about how exciting it was to make love to a woman with a shaven cunt.

The next morning, they lay naked on a bed of soft feathered pillows floating on a pond in the middle of the palace garden, soaking in the morning sun, Salome on her back with her eyes closed, Conway gently teasing the erect nipples of her breasts with the stem of a flower.

Watching them from the shore was the mad dog that stood guard by her throne. The dog had the look of evil incarnate. If the devil decided to pay a visit, the dog would be a perfect guise for the dark lord to assume, Conway thought. "Why do you have a creature like that as a pet?" he asked.

"He's the only one I completely trust. He hates everyone except me and only tolerates me because I feed him. He desires neither gold nor power, fears neither man nor beast, and is too mad to appreciate danger or love." She opened her eyes and turned on her side to face him. "Two men come to Bethsaida in search of a third man, a teacher from Nazareth. Then you come seeking this teacher and kill one of the men."

Conway drew a circle on her stomach with the flower stem. "The man we seek has importance in terms of a prophecy, but he does not have power or gold to fill your treasury."

She stared at him with half-closed eyes, a lizard eyeing a fly. "The brother of the man you killed has a power that roars like thunder and can kill a man without the use of an arrow or sword. You, too, must have this power."

It made sense, Conway thought. The terrorists also had to believe the rescue mission came armed to the teeth. That's why Jair had not risked an open confrontation. He probably thought he was outgunned.

"You have been trying to make my life miserable with Quintus," he said. "Must he be part of our arrangements?"

"Quintus the Eunuch? No, I only use him. He means nothing to me except the gold he pays to be accepted at the palace."

"Why do you call him a eunuch?"

"Because he is one."

"He was castrated?"

"He castrated himself. He is a follower of Cybele of Phrygia, the cult whose members go into a sexual frenzy and castrate themselves during their orgies."

Conway shuddered at the thought of Quintus inviting him to a Cybele of Phrygia festival. Unbelievable. Even though it was not that bizarre. Cult members in modern times practiced mass suicide and mass murder. A little castration paled in comparison to drinking poisoned lemonade.

"That's why he cannot go back to Rome. He has dishonored his family." She ran her fingers through the hair on his chest. "This power could give my army the might of a dozen Roman legions—"

"A thousand legions."

"Power that could give me the throne in Rome itself. The man who helps me win an empire will sit beside me on a golden throne."

"Why don't you make a deal with the man in league with the Sicarii?"

"He cannot be trusted. He is like the dog, madness festers within him, but it takes more than a bone to keep him from devouring those around him. He only wants to use me. When he has control of my army, he will cast me away."

Conway grinned. Smart girl. "If you keep my stomach full and step on my tail once in a while, will I be trained to sit at your feet and foam at the mouth?"

"You will be a king of kings."

"Before we can make any plans, we have to get rid of this man. Where is he?"

Salome shrugged. "How do I know I can trust you? How do I know for certain that you have the power?"

"You can trust me as much as I trust you." He kept a straight face. "Tell me where this man is and I'll demonstrate my power by destroying him."

"We shall see, we shall see" she murmured, running her

hand through the hair on his chest. "This man has powerful friends. I must know I can trust you before I challenge them. We shall see how you perform your duties."

He raised his eyebrows. "Duties?"

"You killed Rahm, the captain of my guard."

She clapped her hands. Servants came to the edge of the pond carrying a silver breastplate, a helmet with a long golden plume and the uniform of the palace guard.

She laughed at the startled look on his face. "You are the new captain of my guard. Your first assignment will be to rid the city of a festering sore of Zealot traitors."

CHAPTER FORTY-NINE

Marie spotted the leper in the marketplace. The old man hurried away as David and Ezra closed in on him, but Ezra's sons intercepted him before he could get away, herding him to the back of a weaver's shop.

The weaver exchanged knowing looks with Ezra and went on working at the front of the shop as if nothing had happened.

Another Zealot, David thought.

Ezra's sons stepped back from the leper as soon as they got him into the back room. Leprosy was a sign of damnation, not to mention a walking plague.

The beggar protested his treatment in Aramaic and Marie switched him to Hebrew so David could follow the conversation. David almost laughed. Leave it to a beggar to be a polyglot.

"These men are friends," Marie told the leper, "patriots of Israel. You must take them to the place in the caverns where the cries of tortured men are heard. You will be rewarded if you help," she added.

"You'll be hamstrung if you don't," Ezra said, darkly. Like his sons, he did not relish rubbing shoulders with the damned.

It was dark when the old leper led them down the back

streets of the marketplace to the cellar of a building abandoned to rats and roaches after its owner had been murdered by tax collectors. The building's neighbor was the blacksmith's shop.

"It doesn't surprise me that the blacksmith is host to a nest of vipers," Ezra said to Marie. "He has less sense than a camel." Ezra grinned. "Word has come that he broke both his arms in a terrible accident. Much time will pass before he forges another Sicarii dagger."

Marie and the leper led the way in the cavern, with David a step behind and Ezra following, their path lit by candles. They carried torches for extra light. The outcasts in the caverns melted back from the intruders, hiding in the darkness, watching with wary eyes as invaders trampled their domain. They passed under water gushing from the city aqueduct and over rocky debris from a crumbling stone pillar supporting the waterway.

Ezra shook his head. "It will not be long before that old pillar collapses and the city will be without water." He grinned. "I, good Jew that I am, will supply the queen with water from my own well. In exchange for her nose."

David examined the stone pillar. "It wouldn't take much for this thing to come tumbling down and turn the caverns into an underground river."

The old leper led them to the wall that 'moaned' because of a tyrant's cruelties.

David enlarged the hole with an iron rod, working slowly in case the digging could be heard on the other side. He stopped when he could see light from the other side.

He peeked through and moved aside for Ezra. "I think it's the dungeon," David said, in a whisper, "but I'm not sure. I didn't get a look at much of it during my stay."

Ezra leaned against the wall and peered into the hole. He stuffed the hole with a piece of cloth before he stepped back.

"It's the queen's dungeon, for sure. I was once a guest in that miserable hell. It cost my family a year's income to win my freedom for the heinous crime of turning my back rather than throwing myself on the ground and groveling as the Roman whore paraded through the streets. It is a sign of God's blessing that I am here today to talk about it," he said darkly.

"What part of the dungeon is beyond the wall?" David asked.

"The racks and the guard station." Ezra took a stick and scratched the layout on the ground. "The dungeon is two levels below the palace. The barracks of the palace guard are at ground level and the kitchen for the barracks below that. You enter the barracks to get to the stairs that lead down to the dungeon."

"I went down those steps. Headfirst."

"And I. It is a little joke of the guards. They bet on the number of broken bones the falls inflicts. A massive door leads from the passageway into the dungeon. I could see the door through the crack. It's directly across from us. The area between this wall and the door contains the racks the jailers use to torture prisoners. Off to the right is a corridor leading to the cells. Three or four steps lead up to the jailer's station in front of the door. That's why you cannot see the racks in between. The rack area is lower than the guard station."

"I saw four or five guards during my short visit, but I didn't see the whole dungeon."

Ezra shrugged. "There are not more than six or eight guards on duty at a time, but they can pull a rope that rings an alarm bell in the barracks above."

"The dungeon door blocking the passageway to the barracks is thick, even thicker than that big neck of yours," David said.

"It could hold off a small army."

"Then it could hold off the palace guard."

Ezra didn't understand and David drove the point home. "The door is built to hold off attackers from above. We can use it to lock out the palace guard. That way we would only have to fight the dungeon guards on duty at the time."

"It would take too long to breach this wall," Ezra said, pointing at the wall with the crack. "The guards will hear the pounding and half the palace guard will be waiting for us when we break through."

David shook his head. "I can design something that will breach the wall instantly."

Marie gave him a troubled look. He knew what she was thinking. He could whip together enough gunpowder to blow Salome and her whole palace to hell. But it wasn't gunpowder he was thinking of; he wasn't going to break his covenant not to introduce modern weaponry into the ancient world.

He ran his fingers along seams between the blocks of stone on the wall. Each stone was about a foot square.

"There's no mortar between the stones. They're held by their own weight on top of each other."

"It's a very old and very strong wall," Ezra said. "The stones have been here so long they have grown together. It would take a dozen men with a battering ram an hour to breach it."

"We can breach the wall with one blow and create a hole big enough for our men to rush through, overwhelm the jailers and lock off the door."

"No battering ram could breach the wall with one blow. Not one small enough to be brought into the caverns."

David walked around and examined the cavern as he spoke. "I can build a large enough battering ram here in the dungeon."

"You have knowledge of the machines of war?"

"Yes."

Marie followed him as he paced the distance up the cavern from the wall. "What are you planning?"

David knelt and looked back down the passageway to the wall. "He's right. A conventional wood battering ram wouldn't do it, at least not something that uses muscle power. What I have in mind is a freight train."

He laughed at the look she gave him. "We'll build a battering ram of stone on wheels. Take a couple sets of chariot wheels, put a track of timber under each wheel, and tie down a load of big stone blocks on it. The ground between here and the wall is slightly sloped. The slope can be increased with shovels. If we get enough weight on the cart, enough men behind it and enough grade down to the wall, it'll breach that wall with one mighty blow." At least that's what he hoped.

Ezra joined them and David explained his "machine of war." The Zealot leader was awed, incredulous, and worried.

"If you push away the wall, the ceiling will come down."

David pointed at timbers studding out from above the block wall. "We'll brace those timbers."

Ezra stroked his beard and eyed David. "You have built such a machine of war before?"

David grinned. "Never. But I've studied the works of Greeks and Egyptians who have built such machines."

"Greeks and Egyptians build machines of the devil."

David started to point out that both countries had managed to enslave Israel, but decided not to risk having his own head used to breach the wall.

"I'm sure my plan will work. The most critical part will be getting good sets of chariot wheels. They have to be strong enough to carry a big load of stone."

"I have to trust you, foreign Jew. If your plan works, the lives of many of my people will be saved. And if it does not, I will see that you are spared crucifixion by killing you myself." Ezra suddenly grinned. "The best wheels in the city are on the chariots of the officers of the Royal Guard. I am sure they will not mind 'loaning' us a few."

"We'll need skilled carpenters who can build the ram, men to dig the slope and brace the ceilings, more to carry stone, not to mention a couple dozen of your best fighters to rush in and free their comrades after we knock down the wall."

"You will get all the help you need. We have skilled carpenters and many hands to help. And fight."

"We also need an escape plan." David asked the leper, "How far do the caverns extend beyond the city walls?"

The leper hesitated and looked to Marie. She nodded and he answered. "One goes to the camp of the caravaners beyond the marketplace. The tunnel was dug so the king's soldiers could get behind attackers at the city walls. The opening is hidden in a clump of trees near the camp."

"Can you show us the way?"

The leper grinned. "I have used it many times to visit the caravaners at night and borrow goods."

Ezra grunted. "You mean to steal."

"It would be better to exit by way of that tunnel and flee into the wilderness than to try and hide the escaped prisoners in the city," David said.

"True, and we can have horses ready to make the escape. But it is a long way from here to the camp of the caravaners, and I remember something else. Once there was a rebellion among the prisoners in the dungeon and they overpowered the jailers and barricaded the dungeon door. The palace guards made short work of battering down the door because there is a secret known only to the officers of the guard of removing the hinges to the door."

"We'll have to block the door as best we can. I've been mulling over our escape and I have an idea. The aqueduct's ready to burst. We could give it a hand, breach it on our way out and flood the caverns to hinder pursuit."

Ezra's jaw dropped. He started to say something about "mad foreign Jews" and choked on it.

David couldn't help but grin at the look on the big bear's face. "We can seal behind us the passageway that leads to the cavern camp," he told Ezra, "so we don't drown."

"Aren't you forgetting something?" Marie asked. "The caverns are the only home these people have."

David turned to the leper. "I am told that you and your friends are tired of living like moles, that you want to go somewhere dry and sunny."

"There is no place my kind are welcome."

"Ezra, we have gold these people can use to buy land to farm. Where can they move to?"

"They can live in Hades for all I care. But there is a place near the waters of Meron where people of his kind can go and are not driven away. At this place are followers of this healer from Nazareth you seek."

"The waters of Meron are a wild and terrible place!" said the leper.

Ezra shrugged. "Wild, but not so terrible. It has been to the advantage of our movement to spread tales of the dangers there."

If the Zealots spread tales about the region, it must be one of the places where their armies form before striking, David thought.

Marie asked Ezra, "Would they be safe there?"

"They would have a far better life than the streets of Bethsaida with Salome's soldiers whipping them like cattle. They would have a far better life thanks to a strange Jew who knows not only how to build machines of war but the alchemist's trick of weaving gold."

Conway lounged on a couch near the pond's edge in the palace garden. One servant girl fed him sweets and a cool drink, a second fanned him with a gilded palm leaf, while a third girl gently stroked a harp.

It was an idyllic moment. He felt . . . kingly.

He had been born into the wrong era, he thought. He was a pagan at heart. The ancient world was the place for him. It was so much more *dramatic*. Perhaps it was just his ability to adapt to any role. He had always amazed directors and other actors by his ability, no, his fanatic assumption of any role he took. But there had never been anything like his present role. The combat and victory in the arena had excited him more than anything had before. Killing held no thrill for him, but the danger, the life-and-death struggle to the roar of the pagan crowd, had been more exciting than sex or money. He had been serious in the arena when he told David to take down enough guards with him to make the event legendary. He was willing to give his life for a moment of glory.

He had made love to a queen and she wanted him to help

run the world. Why not? he wondered. He could mold the world into a decent place for eons to come.

His thoughts were interrupted by an officer of the Royal Guard. The guards were a mixture of competent fighting men and royal lackeys—mostly the latter. Conway had already pegged the centurion as a lackey. The man swaggered, walking or talking, and was arrogant to the men.

"The queen commands your presence in the dungeon, Your Excellency. The jailers are in need of your good services to make the tongues of the rebels wag."

Conway followed the arrogant officer down the shadowy passageway to the dungeon, resisting the urge to give the man a kick in the ass that would send him tumbling down the steps. *If I were king . . .*

The thought jarred him. It was becoming a recurring theme in his thoughts.

Two guards were playing a dice game at the bottom of the stairway. Their uniforms were dirty and their hair unkempt. One of them got lazily to his feet and pulled on a rope that rang a bell inside the dungeon, signaling the guard station inside to open the door.

The officer sniffed. "These jailers spend so much time in this foul place, they become brother to the roaches and rats infesting it. I would never permit swine like this in my unit."

The door swung open and they passed through to the guard station in the dungeon. The stench of human excrement and putrefied flesh fouled the air.

"Take us to the prisoners being interrogated," the officer snapped to a dull-eyed, slovenly jailer.

They followed the jailer to a set of racks two men were stretched across. Conway had to draw on all of his training as an actor to keep from gasping. One man was hardly recognizable as human. So many bones had been cracked and so much flesh peeled from his body, he looked like a red jellyfish.

The man on the second rack was Yoseph. They had just begun their torture on him, but it was an ugly beginning. He was being peeled alive, starting with the skin on his chest. The creature performing the torture was also hardly human.

His scarred, pockmarked face spoke of cruelty, his black eyes had the aimless gaze of the blind.

The officer picked up on Conway's discomfort and smirked. "Not like being entertained in the queen's bed, is it."

Conway elbowed him in the face. The blow was aggravated by the metal arm protectors Conway wore. The man's nose splattered; he flew back and fell over a rack.

"He made a remark about the queen's chastity," Conway told the torturer. "Throw him in a cell until I discuss his punishment with the queen."

The torturer stared wide-eyed at Conway. "Yes, Excellency." He yelled at two jailers who rushed to seize the bleeding officer.

"This one," Conway pointed at the hapless jellyfish, "what have you learned from him?"

"Nothing, Excellency. The man has endured more punishment than any I have dealt with in years."

"Kill him."

"Kill him?!"

"Kill him. Quickly, now." And God rest the poor bastard's soul, Conway thought. "You have failed your task miserably. The man is a living example of the ability to resist your torture. The other rebels take heart by his defiance of your best efforts."

"But, Excellency—"

"Silence! Or you'll take his place on the rack. This other rebel," Conway indicated Yoseph, "what have you learned from him?"

"Nothing, Excellency, but I have just begun."

"Did you starve and beat him before beginning the torture?"

"Of course—"

"Fool! No wonder you can't pry information from prisoners. You make them too weak to withstand the interrogation. Give this man food and water and return him to his cell. He is not to be tortured until I personally inspect him and can declare he is strong enough to suffer and confess instead of dying under your hand."

Conway clenched his teeth on the way back up the stairs.

He was not a man who flinched at death. Battle was glorious, but torture was a dark side to violence.

He had repaid Yoseph for his help when they were attacked by the Sicarii. The score was even. He was a man who repaid his debts, tit for tat. But he was not a sentimentalist.

David spent the next three days directing the men and equipment that Ezra poured into the caverns. He felt the pressure of time. Passover was less than a week away and he and Marie, with or without Conway, had to be in Jerusalem by the fateful day.

He worked day and night, taking only an occasional catnap, driving himself and those around him with such frenzy that Ezra proclaimed to anyone who would listen that they had a madman on their hands.

Obtaining a supply of stone blocks for the battering ram proved easier than expected. They braced the cracked aqueduct with timbers that could be jerked away at the critical moment and then disassembled the stone pillar that had supported the waterway.

Ezra was impressed with the wood device that David had designed to trigger the collapse of the aqueduct. Because of the great force exerted from the weight above, he had to strain his engineering skills to rig a support that could be readily collapsed.

"Pull the rope, the support under the timbers slip, the timbers come down and . . . boom! All the water in the city will rush into the caverns."

He gave David a hardy slap on the back that nearly sent David staggering across the cavern. "Very good my friend." He gave him his bear's grin. "And if we do not get to the door to escape the cavern quick enough, we will drown like rats."

David had a door built at the entrance to the passageway that led to the caravan camp. The men who triggered the flood would be the last ones through the door. The length of the rope was limited because the longer it was, the less strength the rope would have and the more likely it would break before the support structure gave. It would take two men to pull the rope hard enough and he had already decided he would be one of them. Ezra had claimed the "privilege" of being the second man. If they didn't make it to the door before the water got there, or if the door did not hold, they would end up as Ezra's drowned rats.

"You are the best carpenter I have ever seen," Ezra told him. "And the first who works with his mind and not his hands. After we drive the Romans from Israel, come back and you can build real Jewish cities for us."

"I gather you dislike the cities designed by the Greeks."

"Bah! The Greeks know only how to carve naked idols. Even their pillars look naked. Their buildings are pretty to pagan eyes but lack the strong heart that comes when the dirt of Israel is molded into building materials by the hands of the chosen people." Ezra glared at him. "You have not heard a word I said. You stare at the door to the passageway like it is a man stealing your wife."

David used his sleeve to wipe dirt and sweat from his face. "I'm so tired I'm forgetting things. We have to build a brace behind that door if we plan to make it to the caravan camp without drowning."

"Why? Salome's soldiers will be too busy swimming to batter down the door. And the water will not strike it directly because it is around a sharp bend in the cavern."

"I'm worried about the wind."

"Wind? There is no wind in the caverns!"

"There will be after the aqueduct breaks. When the water comes roaring down the cavern, air pushed in front of it is going to blow that door off its hinges if it's not heavily braced."

Ezra stroked his beard and stared at David with the indulgence of a father for a mad son. "Wind in the caverns? Good friend, it is time you went to my house and rested before the battle."

David walked quickly, his cloak over his head, his face turned from the people he passed. As weary as he was, if he was challenged he would roll over and play dead, he told himself.

Marie and Isie were in the garden sitting next to the well when he came through the gate of Ezra's house. The boy had been despondent since word of Conway's infatuation with Salome had spread in the streets. At first David had tried to excuse the stories on the grounds that Conway might be intriguing with an intriguer, but as the days rolled by and the word coming from the palace was not a message to them from Conway but stories of the queen bestowing wealth and honors upon him, David began to wonder whether the man had succumbed to the temptation of power.

The boy had taken the matter to heart.

"Isie comes from a shepherd's culture with very simple mores," Marie told him. "A friend should never betray a friend, and if he does, the betrayal is answered in blood."

Isie got up as David neared the well and spoke to David in Aramaic, looking to Marie for the expected translation.

"He says he has found a group of pilgrims we can travel with to Jerusalem tomorrow after the release of Yoseph. They're herding sheep to sell during the Passover celebration. Isie thinks the sheep will be a good cover to get us past Roman patrols."

David ruffled the boy's hair in a fatherly fashion. "Good work."

Isie spoke again and Marie hesitated a moment before translating. "He wants to be in the caverns tomorrow when the attack begins. He wants to help, to be part of it. So do I."

"That's impossible. We can't have a woman and a boy getting in the way during the fighting."

"This woman and boy weren't told they would be 'getting in the way' when we were made part of the mission and accepted the danger. We want to help."

"You have helped. We wouldn't know about the caverns if it wasn't for you. Now you can help by staying clear of the fighting. You and Isie can leave the city with that flock of sheep before we attack the dungeon. Ezra has a plan that will take us to Jerusalem along back roads. I haven't had a chance to go over it with him. I'll talk to him and send a messenger with instructions as to where you and Isie are to meet me."

David knew the flock of sheep would move slowly. He intended to race to Jerusalem as soon as Yoseph was freed.

He was literally staggering from exhaustion by the time he reached his room. He stripped down and stretched out on the bed. He was too tired, too full of nervous energy, to sleep. It was the worst state for him; he needed sleep, but his mind roamed and his body ached.

Marie slipped quietly into the room. He held out his arms and she came to him, covering his body with hers.

She kissed his nose. "You're tired."

"And grumpy. And worried. We have only a few more days. We should be on our way to Jerusalem, not taking sides in a civil war."

"Do you still believe Conway has abandoned the mission?"

David shook his head. "I don't know what to believe. He hasn't contacted us. Yet . . . I don't know. I'm not even sure Conway knows."

"What do you mean?"

"I'm beginning to think he gets so caught up in his roles that he becomes the person until he's diverted by events into another role." He shook his head again. "Forget it. I'm too tired to think straight. Maybe he's just being seduced by the power and glory of being king. Or playing God."

"What about you?" She brushed the hair off his forehead. "Don't you have the urge to change the world? To restructure it in your image?"

"I've thought of it, about the good I could do, thought about the revolt that's coming, the terrible things that are going to happen to my people at the hands of Roman legions.

The Zealots and the Sicarii will rise and fight Roman legions. But the empire will rape Israel, crush it under their heel, destroy the Temple, the symbol of my people, and leave them homeless for two thousand years. In the end, the cities will be destroyed, the people scattered. There will not be another Israel until six million Jews die in the Holocaust and the survivors reclaim their ancient land because they have no other place to go.

"I've truly come to terms with my father, with my own past, with my childhood that saw so much conflict between Arab and Jew. There is no right or wrong with what's happening in the Middle East during our time. It's just people on both sides trying to survive, shoving each other back and forth to get room to live. Hopefully someday they'll see that there's room for everyone. It's their minds that are keeping them apart, not the lack of space."

He took her hand and rubbed his bare chest with it. "A story I read years ago has been haunting me. It was written by the American writer, Ray Bradbury. I don't remember exactly how it went, but it had something to do with tours of the past being sold by some future travel agency that had conquered time travel. One of the time-traveling tourists stepped off the electronic path in prehistoric times and accidentally squashed a bug. The loss of that single insect caused a gap in the food chain and altered history, changing the world the hero returned to."

"The kingdom was lost for want of a horseshoe nail."

"Something like that. I thought about the story last night when I was digging in the caverns and cut a worm in half with my shovel. I wondered if a fish would die because of the loss of that worm, and a person would starve to death because of the loss of that fish, and if the dominoes would just keep falling until a man was never born. I began to imagine that man was me."

Neither spoke for a long time.

"If there was one thing in this world that I could change," she said, "I would make sure that every man and every woman experienced the miracle of love, that each had the chance to love and be loved by someone."

He pulled her to him and held her tight, his heart beating against hers. "You're my miracle," he said.

David pushed aside the blanket and she came to his nakedness.

CHAPTER FIFTY

There were twenty-three of them: David, Ezra, and twenty of the best fighting men the Zealots could muster. Isie completed the contingent. David tried to get the boy to stay with the men tending the getaway horses staked out near the opening to the caravan camp, but Isie pretended he didn't understand David or the interpreter. The boy, who only spoke Aramaic, suddenly could not understand a word of it.

Ezra had sent his son, Hezekiah, back to his house with a message for Marie. She was to go with Hezekiah to the south end of the lake where David would rendezvous with her after the attack on the dungeon. If David failed to show, Hezekiah would take her on to Jerusalem.

David knew it was a relief for Ezra to find an excuse to get his son out of the attack on the dungeon. His other son helped tend the getaway horses.

"No house should have more than one man in the fighting," Ezra told David. "That way no family can suffer the loss of more than one."

Ezra chose midnight as the time to begin the attack. "We can't attack any sooner. We have to be certain the palace guards in the barracks above the dungeon are in bed. The time it takes them to get out of bed and put on their clothes and boots can be the difference between us being guests at a victory feast or at a crucifixion afterwards.

"We can't attack any later because we will need the hours of darkness to cover our retreat. Thanks to your madness we are attacking like moles underground with a handful of men instead of storming the city walls like Jewish warriors. The Royal Guards outnumber us a hundred to one. If we are still around the city when the sun wakes up, they will take us back into the dungeons to patch the wall before they skin us alive."

David groaned. "If just one of the disasters you've conjured up strikes us we'll be lucky to get out of this with just losing our skins. It's three hours until midnight."

"We must rest and pray."

Ezra's son, Hezekiah, came out of the passageway through the trapdoor that the leper used on his visits to the camp of the caravaners. His brother and two other men were watching the horses. Hezekiah took his brother aside and whispered a personal message from their father and then set out by himself through the marketplace.

He was near the city gate when men in dark cloaks stepped out of an alley and blocked his way. He reached for the sword hidden in the bundle he carried, but daggers were against his flesh before he could unleash it.

They took him to the blacksmith's shop and stood him against a wall. Six Sicarii formed a half circle in front of him. They moved apart to let a captain of assassins and Jair Za-yyad through.

"He is the son of Ezra Ben Ephraim, the Zealot who has befriended your enemies," the captain of assassins said. "He would not be out alone in this part of the city unless he was on a mission for his father."

"Or he's carrying a message to the woman from her friends," Jair said. He stepped closer to Hezekiah. "What message do you carry?"

Hezekiah spat in his face.

The assassin captain lunged forward with his dagger and Jair's hand shot out and caught the man's wrist.

"No!" Jair wiped the spit from his face with the back of his hand. "We have to make him talk." He looked at the wooden wall behind Hezekiah and smiled. "Nail him to the wall," he whispered hoarsely. "Crucify him."

Rebekah, the wife of Ezra, stood at the courtyard gate and nervously wiped her hands with her apron as she watched Marie disappear down the dark street with the two men who had come for her.

The men said they carried a message from David for Marie: she was to accompany them to a rendezvous point.

Rebekah knew she shouldn't worry, but she could not shake a sense of dread. She had expected her husband to send one of their sons back. Instead, two strangers came.

She wondered if she should have told Marie that she did not recognize the men.

The two men led Marie through the city gate and across a bridge spanning the Jordan. A group of horsemen were waiting at the foot of the bridge.

She wasn't suspicious until they brought her face-to-face with a man with cruel eyes and jagged features. She tried to run but a pair of strong hands grabbed her and propelled her to Jair.

"Your friends killed my brother," Jair whispered hoarsely. His hand snaked out and grabbed her throat. "Before I'm finished, you'll beg me to kill you."

David made a last-minute nervous check of the battering ram.

With two sets of wheels spread apart by timbers and large stone blocks strapped on top, the battering ram looked like an incredible Stone Age weapon. He didn't think it would bounce off the dungeon wall. More likely, it would get stuck halfway through, or worse, bring the ceiling down. But Ezra and his Zealot friends were awed by the "machine of war."

Ezra positioned the men behind the battering ram, a defiant Isie among them clutching his rock sling.

"Are you ready?" Ezra asked David.

David looked up the cavern to where the men were gathered behind the battering ram and down the narrow wooden track constructed to keep the wheels in line. The absurdity of the situation struck him. He was a highly trained engineer, a man with more technical knowledge than any other person in the ancient world. He could make explosives capable of destroying cities and weapons that could wipe out armies; he could turn Rome into a city of skyscrapers; and he had used his knowledge and training to build a crude stone club mounted on wooden wheels.

"If Archimedes could see me now."

"Archimedes?"

"The father of carpenters."

Ezra spat. "A Greek."

At David's command the blocks were removed from in front of the wheels and the battering ram started down the track with the men pushing.

In seconds the heavily greased wheels picked up enough speed to leave the men behind. It hit the wall like a runaway freight train; the concussion knocked the men in the cavern off their feet.

A shudder ran through the dungeon that was felt in the palace above.

When the dust cleared, David gawked at a gaping hole in the dungeon wall big enough for two men abreast to run through.

David got to his feet and cried, "Follow me!"

He charged through the opening with sword in hand, Ezra one step behind and the rest of the Zealots at their back.

The queen was already in the audience chamber when Conway rushed in. He had been napping in her chambers when he felt the palace shake. A moment later a panicked guard yelled that the queen needed him.

She was surrounded by a group of nervous parasites wringing their hands and guards brandishing their weapons.

"The dungeon has been attacked," she told Conway. "The whole palace may be under siege."

She was wide-eyed. It was the first time he had seen her totally rattled.

"Who's attacking?"

"Rebels! Stop them!"

She came off her throne and pointed her finger at him.

"Use your power. Stop them or I'll have your head!"

"They breached the wall between the dungeon and some caverns under the city," a guard officer told him as they hurried from the audience chamber.

The man was one of the few officers of the guard Conway respected.

"A jailer got out before the rebels barred the dungeon door. He said they broke through the wall with a giant battering ram."

"Is the palace itself under attack?"

The officer hesitated. "I don't believe so. If the attackers were trying to take the palace they would not have blocked their own path by sealing the door. Our men are already working at disengaging the hinges on the door."

"That means they're trying to rescue the prisoners," Conway said.

They took the dungeon steps two at a time with the centurion shouting, "Make way! Make way!" at the swordsmen and archers lining the dim stairway.

Eight men were slamming a handheld battering ram against the door. "We've disengaged the hinges. They've reinforced it, but we'll bring it down any moment," an officer told Conway.

"The guard station platform is just beyond the door," Conway said. "We'll clear the platform with swordsmen so the archers can shoot at the insurgents from an elevated position."

He never thought about whether he would be fighting

friend or foe. He was the captain of the Royal Guards, sworn to defend the queen with all his might.

It was just another role for a good actor.

David had a dozen men positioned near the dungeon door while Ezra and the rest of the Zealots were helping the last of the prisoners through the gap. Every prisoner had been tortured, beaten, and starved.

Yoseph was one of the last of the prisoners to be released and he refused to be led out with the others, grabbing a sword and joining David at the dungeon door.

"Thank you, brother," Yoseph said.

David grinned. "I had a debt to repay."

They had stunned the dungeon guards with their explosive entrance. Only one guard had gotten away. The few who had resisted were quickly cut down and the rest herded into a cell.

David had hoped the only "rear guard" necessary would be the flood from the aqueduct, but things had gone slower than planned because the prisoners had been in such poor condition. Now they faced the grim prospect of fighting a rear-guard action.

The dungeon door trembled more each time it was hit with the battering ram.

"The door isn't going to hold," David shouted. "Fall back, clear the landing."

The door shook from another blow, teetered for a second and fell, hitting the floor with a clap of thunder.

Royal Guards rushed in with Conway in the lead.

David was the last to retreat as the group defending the door fell back for the escape hole. For one startling moment he faced Conway, the two men staring at each other, swords en garde, but forced apart by a rush of men as Ezra roared back into the fighting. More Zealots poured back through the gap, only to retreat as the guards pushed back.

The fighting was toe to toe and the archers Conway posted on the platform could not loose their arrows for fear of hitting their own men.

Suddenly Ezra was beside David. "Retreat. There are too many of them. I have archers waiting in the caverns."

There was no orderly retreat into the caverns; the Zealots simply moved back as they were driven back, until only Ezra, Yoseph, and David were left with their backs to the exit hole.

Conway tried to break through his own men to get to them. David grimly watched his progress out of the corner of his eye. Conway was the deadliest sword in the room. If anyone faced the man's blade, David wanted it to be himself.

"Fall back," he told his two Zealot friends.

David was the last man out of the dungeon, holding two guards at bay with his sword as he backed through the opening. Isie was suddenly beside him whirling his leather sling. He let a rock fly and it struck a guard between the eyes. The other guard slipped by David's thrust and caught the boy in the abdomen with his blade.

David cut down the man with a vicious slash to the throat as Isie fell to the ground.

"Isie!"

"Down!" Ezra yelled. He pulled David down as arrows flew at Conway and the Royal Guards trying to enter the caverns.

Conway fell back into the dungeon and yelled to an officer, "Bring up the archers and shields!" A moment later Conway led swordsmen and archers through the hole and into the cavern.

The Zealots had already fled.

An explosive collapse of stone sounded and echoed throughout the caverns.

Conway froze and strained to listen. The men around him stared wildly about. Wind whistled by and the caverns trembled underfoot.

Conway wondered, 'What the hell . . ."

Then he saw it coming, a wall of raging water roaring around a turn in the passageway.

"Back!" Conway yelled, but his men had already thrown down their weapons and were crowding back into the dungeon.

Conway was the last man back through the gap. As he ran

up the dungeon stairway, he had to admit to himself that that
damn engineer had some clever tricks up his sleeve.

David ran down the cavern with the boy in his arms. Ezra had
pulled the pin on the aqueduct! The Zealot leader was coming down the cavern with a wall of water behind him. Wind
pushing ahead of the raging water almost knocked David off
his feet.

He set Isie down inside the tunnel to the escape hatch. As
soon as Ezra came through the doorway, David put his
shoulder to the door. He couldn't budge it against the force
of the wind!

Ezra came up beside him, breathing hard. The big man put
his shoulder to the door and the two of them pushed.

The door closed and they frantically threw wooden braces
against it. Wind and water smacked the door like a bomb,
pieces of wood blowing off the door and flying at them as
shrapnel. The door creaked and bulged and water sprayed
through the cracks, but it held.

Suddenly it was quiet.

David realized he wasn't breathing. He took a deep breath
as Ezra leaned back against the wall of the tunnel and closed
his eyes. The bear was breathing heavily.

"A hurricane in a tunnel," Ezra said. "You are an alchemist
of war."

As they came out of the tunnel, Yoseph and Ezra's son
were waiting with mounts. David quickly checked Isie's
wound and decided the cut wasn't deep. Yoseph helped the
boy mount behind David, and the Zealots left the camp on
the run.

Salome was waiting on the balcony overlooking the palace
courtyard when Conway came out of the dungeon.

The courtyard was lit by flaming torches. Conway looked
up to the queen on the balcony and waited.

Salome trembled from rage.

"I should have your head! Cowardly dog, you let my enemies escape."

The officer who had fought beside Conway stepped forward. "My Queen, I swear that this Roman fought the boldest
of all. I have never battled beside a commander braver than
this man. If the aqueduct had not collapsed and flooded the
cavern, we would have won the battle."

Salome pointed an accusatory finger at Conway. "Why
was your power not used?"

It was a good question and Conway didn't flinch. He had
been thinking about it all the way up the dungeon steps. "Because I knew you would not want your palace destroyed to
prevent the escape of a few dogs."

She didn't know whether to believe him or not, wavering
between murderous rage for his head on a platter and fear of
the power he claimed to possess.

Fear won the battle and she turned and fled into the palace.

Later that night Conway heard someone sneaking into his
room. He slipped his dagger out from under his pillow and
waited.

A ghostly white figure came across the room and leaped
onto the foot of his bed.

He kicked off the covers and was coming up with the dagger when he realized it was Salome. Her milky flesh glistened with oil.

She attacked him savagely, clawing, beating, biting,
gouging.

He took hold of her wrists and she spread over him, slipping back and forth, rubbing her naked body on his, trapping
his penis between her naked thighs and squeezing.

"Bastard."

Conway awoke hours later with a dagger at his neck.

"Lie still so you don't get your throat cut."

He froze. Salome sat on the edge of the bed, a servant girl
with a bowl of hot soapy water beside her. Salome took the
knife from his throat and applied a hot cloth to his face. An-

other girl stepped up with a long towel and put it full length down Conway's body. A girl removed the towel from Conway's face and applied a scented oil. After the oil was on, Salome began shaving his face.

"Are you going to slice me up or shave me?"

"That question is still undecided." She worked slowly and carefully. When she was at his throat again with the blade, he felt the tension down to his toes.

"A man with the power to defeat Roman legions would not be afraid of a woman with a single dagger," she said.

"You're no ordinary woman," he murmured.

The flattery appeared to please her. At least she did not cut his throat.

The towel was removed and a servant girl oiled him. All over.

Salome began shaving his chest. "I hate hair on men. When I am empress of the Roman Empire, I shall decree that every man in the empire shave his entire body everyday."

"You wouldn't get much work done, if you did that."

"True, but think of all the babies that would be future warriors and farmers that would be born because women found it more pleasant to love their man."

The blade worked its way down to his stomach. When it started below that, he got nervous and started to sit up. "Perhaps we should discuss this—"

Two giggling servant girls pulled him back down.

As Salome shaved his pubic hair, she said, "I find eunuchs interesting, don't you?"

"Only at a distance."

She pulled his member up and shaved at the base of it. "Did you know there was more than one kind of eunuch? Some have their sack cut open and the two balls thrown away, others actually have their male stem cut off." She took his testicles in her hand and began to shave around the sack.

"Interesting." His leg trembled involuntarily.

"Have you ever thought of what it would be like to be a eunuch?" The blade paused and pressed against his sack. "If that happened, you would grow plump like a hen and have breasts like Quintus."

"Uh-huh."

The blade pressed harder against his sack.

"Tell me about the power."

"Why don't I show you? The best demonstration is to kill you."

She flinched and he felt the blade cut in. "I can destroy your manhood."

He leaned up and looked her in the eyes. "And I will take your life."

She got up and tossed the bloodied knife into the bowl.

"We leave immediately for Jerusalem. Trouble is expected in the city. The way you handle it will be your last chance to convince me of your power."

CHAPTER FIFTY-ONE

David kept Isie beside him during the long ride from the city to the other end of the Sea of Galilee. A large Zealot force was waiting for them on the south side of the lake. When they reached it, Ezra pointed at flaming torches passing signals from hilltop to hilltop.

"One Roman torchbearer signals another. By dawn news of the attack on the dungeon will have reached Pontius Pilate. By sunset there'll be a couple Roman cohorts kicking up dust on the road to Galilee."

A cohort was usually about five or six hundred men, David thought. Two would not be much considering the size of Galilee, but the fear they inspired exceeded their size in terms of numbers.

"We haven't been followed," David said. He and Yoseph had brought up the rear, riding more slowly than the others because of Isie's wound.

"Good," Ezra said. "Our people must disperse immediately. They must be peaceful workers and farmers by morning or they will be guests in Salome's dungeon before the day is gone."

As soon as his feet touched ground, Isie was off, telling tales of the Romans he'd slayed and showing off his wound to anyone who would listen.

The raiding party and dungeon prisoners happily greeted

each other, joyous over the victory. David was pointed out as the hero of the day, and a man, no older than David but wasted and aged by torture in the dungeon, hugged David and cried, trying to say thanks, but unable to speak. The man's friends led him away, taking him back to the family and farm he had not seen in months.

Ezra clamped a big hand on David's shoulder. "You are truly a master of war machines and a master of swords. Thanks to you we have won a battle not just for the Jews of Bethsaida but of all Israel. If I knew your father, I would send word to him of the victory you won for our people."

David mumbled an embarrassed thanks and went looking for Isie. He found the boy telling another group of men of the many Romans he had slayed and interrupted the boasting long enough to examine the boy's wound. It was a flesh wound to his abdomen, probably painful though the boy wouldn't admit it, but not serious.

Yoseph found David examining Isie's wound and gave him disturbing news about Marie and Hezekiah. Ezra's wife had become fearful and sent a message to her son tending the getaway horses. Hezekiah never made it home. Marie had left with strangers. "Ezra must leave immediately for Bethsaida."

Ezra gave David a great bear hug before leaving for Bethsaida. "May God's wrath fire your sword, for your enemies are my enemies."

As soon as Ezra rode away, David told Yoseph, "I have to go to Jerusalem. If Jair Zayyad has Mariam, he'll take her there."

"You will also seek out the healer in Jerusalem?"

"Yes."

"And I will go with you to cleanse myself at the Temple. And to be a sword beside you when you need it."

David clasped Yoseph's arm. "Thank you."

Yoseph scratched his beard. "I do not understand your Roman master. When I was on the rack he risked his own life to spare mine. But during the fighting he could have joined us at any time and he chose not to."

"Our swords almost crossed in the fighting. It would have been a fight to the death."

"But the man fought at your side in the arena!"

"He fought for the glory and the roar of the crowd."

"And what do you fight for?"

"Israel," David said. He had finally said it and he felt a sense of relief.

Yoseph grinned. "And I, too. And for my God." He scratched his beard again. He had picked up vermin in the dungeon. "I do not know what manner of king you have in the strange land from where you come, but your Roman master will find to his sorrow that the family of Herod is a nest of vipers and that the bite of Salome is the deadliest of the lot."

A more pressing problem than his "Roman master" was Isie. His wound was not serious, but David had to travel fast and the boy would slow him down. As David watched the boy talking to a Zealot from the same region as Isie's family, he could see the boy was homesick.

It was time Isie returned home to sit around the evening fire and entertain his family with tales of the battles he fought, side by side with strangers from a strange land. He used Yoseph to interpret as he told the boy he could return to his home.

The boy was both happy and sad. "What of Mariam?" he asked.

"She's fine. We'll stop at the house of your father before returning to our own land," he lied.

David pulled Isie close, giving him a big hug. He was going to miss the boy. And his lethal slingshot. He wanted to reward the boy, but hesitated about giving him money. The boy's pockets were already stuffed with coppers and silver, more money than his sheepherder father had ever possessed. To give Isie more money would subject him to suspicion and thieves. Instead, David gave him the fine dagger he had been issued at the synchrotron.

"We must ride now," Yoseph said, "and may luck ride with us for we not only must survive the wild beasts of the Ghor but the ghost men of the Dead Waters and the haunted palace of Herod."

David struggled with the horse's cinch. He assumed the Dead Waters Yoseph referred to was the Dead Sea and that the "ghost men" must be the Essenes, the strange Dead Sea sect that wore white robes and might have spawned both John the Baptist and Jesus of Nazareth, but the haunted palace was a new one.

"What tales do you weave now, Yoseph? What haunted palace?"

"It is not a tale but a truth. We must pass the precious balm trees of Jericho that the Roman warrior Mark Anthony gave to his Egyptian whore, Cleopatra. At Jericho is the summer palace of Herod, who lied and called himself both King of Jews and Great. He murdered most of his family in the palace. Their ghosts wandered the corridors and called for him at night, finally pulling him down to hell itself."

Jericho, a sweet oasis with fine, tall palms, was prized not for its water or scenic beauty but for its balm, a resin worth its weight in gold because of its use as a fragrant ointment for healing and anointing. David didn't need Yoseph or the history professors back at the synchrotron to tell him about Jericho. It was the stuff of Israeli schoolboys.

It was to ancient Jericho that Herod retreated to relax—and to commit some of his worse atrocities, including the murder of the sad and lovely Mariamne, said to have been the most beautiful woman in Israel. He built a magnificent palace at Jericho, a heavenly retreat in the Greco-Roman style with colonnaded courts, marble columns, and roof galleries called loggias projecting over second-story corridors. Herod spent his last and maddest days there, his guts eaten by cancer and infested with maggots, in unbearable pain, terrifying those around him with murderous rage while he cowered from the ghost of Mariamne.

The palace was no more than an archaeological ruin in the modern world, but David had studied its design in books. With its serene terraced gardens, water fountains and stately palms, it was the archetype of David's own Oasis Project.

Yoseph took the horse's cinch from David and tightened it.

"You should stick to woman's work," he scolded. And grinned. "And fighting."

"How long will it take us to get to Jerusalem?" David asked.

"If we ride like the desert wind and get fresh mounts from our friends, we can reach the city in two days."

Two days. It was the eleventh day of the Jewish month of Nisan. Jesus was crucified at the time the Passover lamb was slaughtered on the fourteenth day of Nisan.

Marie was there. He was sure of it. And he had to find her.

"JESUS WAS PREACHING POLITICAL AND RELIGIOUS HERESY. SOMEONE WAS BOUND TO KILL HIM."

JERUSALEM

CHAPTER FIFTY-TWO

O JERUSALEM!

They saw Jerusalem from Jericho Road atop the Mount of Olives.

Dismounting, they stood beside their tired, sweating horses and stared down at the city. They had ridden like the "desert wind" and reached the city in two days, as tired and dusty as their fourth set of horses.

About thirty-six hours left, David thought. To find Marie. To stop Jair. To save the world. He was bone weary, but nothing short of death would stop him from pushing on.

"Tell me the truth, brother," Yoseph said, "is there no sight short of heaven as beautiful as the one you are beholding?"

Separated from Mount of Olives by the Kidron Ravine, the city sat like an emperor's golden crown on two hills, great buildings glittering like precious jewels, surrounded by mighty walls of tawny golden brown the color of a lion's mane.

Pictures in history books took life before his eyes—the Temple of the One God, its roof fiery yellow from golden spikes, the mighty Citadel of Antonio, the powerful fortress Herod named for Mark Anthony before the Battle of Actium, and another wondrous Palace of Herod with the Towers of Hippicus, Phasael, and Mariamne, the same Mariamne whose spilled blood had haunted him in Jericho. Hippicus had been Herod's friend and Phasael his brother.

Center of the Jewish world, the birthplace of Christianity, holy also to the Muslims, in the first century the city was first and foremost a fortress garrisoned by Roman troops headquartered in the Citadel.

Galilee was the heart of the Jewish resistance against Roman rule, but it was in Jerusalem when the city was packed with pilgrims that the smoldering hate was fanned into defiance. Self-proclaimed messiahs, false prophets, and revolutionaries beseeched the crowds at festival times to throw off the Roman yoke and storm the Citadel. The upper classes and priests of the Temple, beneficiaries of Roman rule, resisted the freedom cries of their own people and helped the Romans nail Jewish patriots to crucifixion crosses.

Glittering jewel, tempest, fortress, it was all that and more, David thought. "I've never seen a sight more wondrous," he told Yoseph.

Jericho Road wound down Mount of Olives and branched off to city gates protected by tall towers. An endless throng of people poured in and out of the Golden Gate, the east entrance to the Temple. A gray river of sheep, thousands of head, flowed into the city through the Sheep Gate, sacrificial lambs to be sold for slaughter during Passover.

"How many people come to Jerusalem for Passover?" David asked.

"It is said there are two pilgrims for every man, woman, and child who live in the city."

Probably over a hundred thousand people, David thought. Out of which he had to find a man capable of hiding in his own shadow.

Mount of Olives had been turned into a vast camping area with thousands of tents erected in the olive groves.

"The city is surrounded by tents of the pilgrims," Yoseph said. "The law says that Jews who live in Jerusalem must open their homes to pilgrims without charge during holy days, but the city could not hold all the pilgrims even if everyone obeyed."

Across the Kidron Ravine, David could see beggars and cripples hobbling toward the Pool of Bethesda, the "miracle" waters. The pool was outside the city walls, near the gate to the lower end of the city. A natural phenomenon caused the pool to periodically empty and refill itself, as if God Himself were directing the waters. The sick, the old and the dying, beggars and rich men, rushed into the waters to be cured by its holy touch as the pool refilled itself, crying "Hallelujah! Hallelujah!" The Lord be praised.

To the north was the Roman-style amphitheater that Herod the Great had built to "entertain" the populace with bloody spectacles. Below the city was Herod's theater, rows of stone seats carved into the hillside.

Yoseph pointed across the ravine. "We'll enter by the Golden Gate. It is the most heavily used and the guards are not stopping anyone. Today we merely cross the Temple courtyard, but tomorrow after we have cleansed ourselves we will go to the Temple together and I will show you the greatest wonder of our people." Yoseph's features tightened. "When you have finished your tasks, return to Israel and help us drive the Roman swine from our streets." He shook his fist. "The time is coming, good brother, when the people of Israel will rise against the Romans and drive them into the sea."

Yoseph would strike him dead if David tried to explain to him that when the Zealots rose, Roman legions under Titus would take Jerusalem during the revolt, and that the victorious legionnaires would be turned loose on the city, slaughtering twelve thousand people outright, raping and pillaging and murdering, cutting the stomachs of thousands to find gold and jewels they could have swallowed.

The Romans believed in setting examples and the roads from one end of Israel to the other would be lined with the crucifixion crosses and stained with young blood. It would take eighty thousand Roman soldiers to conquer thirty thousand Jewish farmers and craftsmen who would take up arms. The last battle would not be at Jerusalem but towering Masada, where the Jewish warriors turned their swords on their wives and children to spare them from the atrocities they would suffer if they fell into the hands of the Romans. Their families dead, the men would turn the swords on themselves, with ten men chosen to kill the others, and finally one of the ten, chosen by lot, killing the other nine before taking his own life.

The Temple would be destroyed, never to be rebuilt, and the Jews would be an exiled people passed from hand to hand of successive conquerors for two thousand years. Would Yoseph, no longer a young man, die in that revolt? Would he be at Masada, committing suicide when the last pocket of Jewish resistance was betrayed and crushed?

He, David Ben-Dor, the reluctant Israeli warrior, was there to make sure the people of Israel kept their tragic rendezvous with history. It was a fatal destiny that he had the power to change. Jewish patriots armed with the weapons he was capable of forging could conquer the world. But he could save the past only at the expense of the future.

"Come," he told Yoseph, gruffly, "time is running short. I have an appointment with destiny."

A few minutes later two young Jews late of Salome's dungeon passed by Roman guards posted at the Golden Gate and entered the great courtyard of the Temple of the One God. David stared at the glorious Temple in awe. He was witnessing more than history—the Temple was an act of God!

It took forty-six years and ten thousand men to build the great Temple that soared a hundred fifty feet high with walls of virgin white marble, its roof laced with golden spears to keep birds from landing and fouling it. The massive, walled esplanade surrounding the Temple was a quarter of a mile long and almost as wide, with the corner stones set precisely on the foundations of the temple Solomon built and Nebuchadnezzar destroyed.

The only remains of the Temple in the Israel that David was born into was the Wailing Wall, a small piece of the western wall of the Temple that had somehow survived two thousand years of successive conquerors.

Near the Temple was a slab of stone carrying a warning: the penalty for a gentile to enter the Temple was death. Beyond the railing were great bronze doors leading into the Court of Women. All Jews were permitted to go that far, but except during special occasions, only men went beyond to the Court of the Israelites. After the Court of the Israelites was the Court of Priests where the great sacrificial altar burned perpetually; beyond the altar was the Holy of Holies where the high priest recitied himself once a year to commune with God.

Every inch of space along the courtyard wall was taken up by the tables of the money changers and the sellers of sacrificial animals.

Each male Jew over twenty years old was required to give a silver coin to the Temple each year and only ritually cleansed money could be donated. The money changers did a brisk business changing street money to acceptable coins.

Every Jew also had to make a sacrifice at Passover, an offering to God for passing over the Israelites when He struck down the Egyptians. Families and friends too poor to offer a whole lamb joined together to make an offering. Doves, goats, sheep, even oxen, were sold for the thousands of other sacrifices made at Passover and throughout the year. The cages of the sellers of sacrificial animals were near the tables of the money changers.

Because the courtyard would not hold the thousands of lambs offered for sacrifice, they were brought in from the other side of the Temple, through the Gate of Sheep. Pilgrims purchasing a lamb for sacrifice first exchanged their money for ritually "clean" money at the money-changing tables and then used the clean money to purchase a lamb from the sellers of sacrificial animals, not claiming the actual animal at that time but a slip of parchment that gave them the right to an animal.

The pilgrim then went to the other side of the Temple and got in line, exchanging his parchment receipt for a live animal when his turn came. With the lamb by the ear, the pilgrim got into another line, this one leading into the Court of the Israelites where only male Jews were allowed. Once inside, he lined up with a couple dozen others making a sacrifice at the same time. As silver horns blared, those offering the sacrifice placed a hand on the head of the lamb, transferring their sins to the lamb.

Again the trumpets would blare and each man threw his lamb to the floor and with a sharp knife, cut the throat of the animal while Temple priests scurried to catch the blood in silver bowls. The bowls of blood were passed down a line of priests to the Court of Priests where a priest dashed the blood on the golden altar and roaring flames.

The dead lambs were then hung on a nail and dressed, the fat removed and burned by the priests in the raging inferno at the Altar of Sacrifice while trumpets blared and a chorus of Levites, members of the tribe of Levi chosen to assist the priests, sang the Hallel, repeating the text until the sacrifice was completed.

At the end of the religious ceremony, each pilgrim gathered up the carcass of the lamb in a cloth he brought for that purpose and took it back to where his family and friends were camped outside the city. That night they would dig a hole in the ground for a fire and roast the lamb on a spit made from an olive branch.

The Temple courtyard was bedlam. David and Yoseph entered a sea of pilgrims shouldering each other, the smell of the burning flesh and entrails of the thousands of animals sacrificed each day in the temple fire fouling the air, undisguised by the tons of incense burned at the same time. Rituals, prayers, and slaughter were conducted with fervor and joy punctuated by the blast of trumpets, sages shouting the laws of the Torah and the bleating cry of sheep and goats.

David took an instant aversion to the chaos and stench of burning fat. The ancient Israel he admired was not that of the Temple's ritual and blood sacrifice but the courage and innocent idealism of the men and women of Galilee who reminded him of the Israelis who built the Israel of his day, men and women who faced the tanks of five Arab nations with homemade bombs and raw courage.

For the first time David heard Hebrew spoken as commonly as Aramaic and he was able to pick up on conversations around him.

"Am I hearing right?" he asked Yoseph. "A man, a young Jew from Galilee, overturned tables of money changers this morning?"

"Shhh, Roman spies are everywhere. So are those of the High Priest. Do not rejoice too much, brother. The poor fool who flouts the authority of the Romans ends up on the crucifixion cross."

"I must find this Galilean—"

"Tomorrow, brother." Yoseph grinned and slapped David on the back. "We must eat and rest so we have the strength to vanquish your enemies."

An aristocrat dressed in a white silken robe trimmed with costly fur and followed by slaves strode by them. David was surprised to see from the man's golden jewelry that he was a Jew and not a Roman.

Yoseph frowned as the man and his retinue passed, and whispered to David, "Sadducee." He spat the word and David glanced back at the man with interest. The Sadducees were competitors of the Pharisees for what little political and religious rule of Israel was left over after the Romans and their kingly puppets nearly picked the bones clean. Rich and privileged, speaking Hebrew and Greek, and living in grand houses staffed by slaves, they looked to the Romans to maintain the status quo and were contemptuous of the "rabble" from Galilee, ignorant peasants who spoke Aramaic, the crude language of the marketplace, and who were foolish enough to try to upset the applecart created for the Sadducees by Pax Romana.

"They will be swept away with the Roman dogs," Yoseph whispered to David. "Fools listen to the Sadducees, presuming that their wealth is a sign of God's favor. Those same fools wait for a messiah to come and drive the Romans from our land. We will drive the Romans away with the sword, not miracles."

David and Yoseph left the courtyard and followed a narrow street packed with pilgrims entering and leaving the Temple area.

"The Temple stays open every hour of the day and night during Passover week," Yoseph told him. "It is the only way all who want to pray and make their sacrifice can do so."

Ezra had sent a messenger along the shorter high road between Galilee and Jerusalem so they would be expected at the home of a wine merchant.

"Is Ezra's friend the Zealot leader in Jerusalem?" David asked.

"He's one of us, but not even Ezra knows the names of all the leaders. That way not all will fall from words squeezed out on the rack."

The city was a maze with three and four-story houses crowding narrow streets. Every few blocks the streets opened into city squares lined with merchant shops.

"These are the homes of merchants and shopkeepers. To our left is the lower city and the Pool of Siloam. That is where the common people live"—Yoseph grinned—"the best people, the ones who do work with their hands besides counting gold. Those streets are very narrow and a house that is home for one family here provides for six families there."

"Do the wealthy live on this street?"

Yoseph shook his head. "The rich are in the shadow of Herod's palace and that of the Hasmonaeans. These are the houses of merchants. More homes of merchants are near the Pool of Amydalon and it is there that Ezra's friend resides."

The beat of military drums sounded and the crowd on the street cleared the way in panic as a Roman legion goose-stepped down the middle of the cobblestone street. The legion standard, bearing the bronze image of the Emperor Tiberius, was covered with cloth to keep from affronting the Jews whose religion forbade "graven images" of man or beast. The Jewish prescription against graven images arose from the biblical commandment forbidding such images because they gave rise to worshiping false idols.

This respect for Jewish customs was only observed during religious festivals when tens of thousands of people converged on the city and the potential for riot and revolution was great. Surprisingly, it was Herod the Great, Arab not Jew, who caused one of the greatest conflicts over graven images when he mounted the golden eagle of Rome at the Temple entrance. He burned at the stake the leaders of the riot that followed, but removed the eagles after a complaint was made to Rome.

The faces of the Roman soldiers were a surprise to David despite the fact that he had served in an army. There were few youths among the marching troops—the average legionnaire appeared to be a tough professional, with more the look of a hired mercenary than a citizen-soldier. The days of the citizen armies of Rome were over.

Behind the legionnaires came men in cages on carts pulled by slaves.

Yoseph's features hardened. "Condemned men for the arena. The Roman swine like to entertain during holy days with festivities of their own. Curse the Jews that attend the bloodlettings."

David grabbed his arm. "Look!"

Heading a company of Salome's Royal Guards down the street was Conway, in a chariot made of finely carved ebony and ivory. He was ablaze in silver breastplate and silver helmet.

Gasps and murmurs swept the crowd as Salome came into view. She was lounging on pillows piled high on a platform carried by her husky slaves. The queen's full-length gown was composed entirely of tiny black pearls from the Persian Gulf. She wore a single piece of jewelry, an incredible golden snake that began as a tiara on her head, the serpent's gaping jaws exposing fangs of uncut diamonds, and then extended around her neck and stretched down the middle of her body to her toes.

David deliberately kept his face exposed. He wanted Conway to know he was there regardless of the risk.

Conway did not look his way as the chariot carried him by.

Yoseph spat. "Bitch."

———

The house of Ezra's friend had two stories and a Tyrian courtyard similar to that of Ezra's house in Bethsaida.

They ate dinner with the family in the courtyard, and afterward, tired from the journey, they begged off from joining their host for wine and talk. They used an outside stairway to climb to the flat roof of the house where they spread their bedrolls. The sun was setting behind the western hills, tinting the sky red in its passing.

"The sun bleeds because it leaves our beautiful Israel for the hot sands of Egypt," Yoseph said as they watched the gathering dusk. Moments later he was snoring.

David lay awake, too tense to sleep. It was the eve of one of the most significant events in all of history. By the next evening, a young Jew from Galilee had to be arrested by the Temple guards, setting off a series of events that would profoundly change the world.

He had to make sure it happened, but his thoughts kept turning to Marie. He finally slipped into a troubled sleep, worrying about her.

Marie heard voices in the other room and inched like a snail across the dirt floor to the crack at the bottom of the door. Her hands and feet were bound.

She was being held prisoner in a warehouse where oil was pressed from olives and stored in wooden barrels and huge clay jars, a building in a grove of olive trees just off Jericho Road on the Mount of Olives. To the west was the city wall and the Golden Gate to the Temple.

She had been to the spot many times when she was a nun traveling in the Holy Land. In modern times it was the location of the Basilica of the Agony, with its serene Garden of Gethsemane. The Church of St. Mary Magdalene was nearby.

Gethsemane was the Hebrew word for oil press. It became a Christian word for betrayal. Jesus had come to visit friends camped near the Gethsemane the night Judas Iscariot betrayed him to Temple guards.

Marie had gotten only a brief look at the place when they brought her in and locked her in a small storage area no bigger than a walk-in closet. The rest of the building was a large, open warehouse area with a huge oil press in the center and a storage loft above filled with hay. Barrels and jars of oil were stacked on the ground floor along the west side. The other side contained a corral for the donkeys used to turn the oil press.

The building hummed with activity during harvesttime, but it was off season and the only visitor was the caretaker who came each day to feed the donkeys.

She had been tied up and left without food or water, but there were worse things than being ignored by Jair Zayyad. She was thankful that the man was too busy with his schemes to have paid any more attention to her than an occasional angry taunt and kick.

The Sicarii leadership in Jerusalem had not quickly fallen into line with their Bethsaida brothers in support of Jair. Another player had entered the game, a Roman championed by Salome who was now her captain of the guard. The Sicarii wanted a showdown between the two before they committed themselves.

Straining to listen, she heard male voices and laughter, but couldn't make out all the words. She heard Jair speak the name Judas.

Judas Iscariot. Judas the Sicarii was the translation. Daggerman. The Sicarii would know the location of one of their own and it would not have been hard for Jair to get them to direct Judas to him.

There was another explosion of laughter and the crunch of footsteps moved toward the storeroom. She struggled to move away from the door as it flew open. Jair stepped in, his face a mixture of triumph and poison.

"So you heard. I have decided only to tamper with history a bit, a small change, you might say. Instead of waiting for the Temple priests to bribe Judas, I gave him thirty pieces of silver tonight to betray his friend." Jair laughed. "I thought thirty was a nice touch. In a little while Judas is bringing Jesus here to meet a man in need of a healer."

Jair drew his gun and aimed it point-blank between Marie's eyes. He pulled the trigger and she flinched as it clicked on an empty chamber.

"Not yet, my friend, but soon. I'm waiting so your lover can watch you die." Jair kicked her. "When I'm finished with your miracle man from Galilee, I'm going to have my revenge."

CHAPTER FIFTY-THREE

Yoseph shook David awake at midnight.

"First you cannot sleep and then you sleep like the dead. Here, an old beggar brought this a few minutes ago." He handed David a small piece of papyrus rolled into a tube and fastened by cord.

David pulled off the cord and unfolded the paper. Three words were printed in crude Hebrew letters: *The woman. Gethsemane.*

Gethsemane, a warehouse where olives were pressed for oil. David had seen the building as they followed Jericho Road down Mount of Olives.

"What is it?" Yoseph asked. "Your hands shake like wheat in the wind."

"A message about Marie—Mariam. It says she's being held at the oil press building on Mount of Olives."

"Who sent it?"

"I'm not sure." He took a deep breath to calm his nerves. "It could be Jair, the man I seek, or perhaps my former master, Marcus. It doesn't refer to her by name. But if it was sent by Marcus, I am sure he would use her name. Unless he wants me to believe Jair sent it."

"It must be from this man you call Jair. Your Roman master just arrived in Jerusalem. There has been no time for him to find Mariam. I think the note is meant to lead you into a trap. The Roman is too busy groveling at Salome's feet to care about you or your enemy."

"He has to care. Salome is intriguing with Jair and the Sicarii. She has to pit Conway against Jair and go with the better man. And Salome would know where Jair is."

Yoseph stroked his beard. "You believe Salome has told the Roman where Jair is to provoke a fight between them, and the Roman is pitting you against Jair?"

David fingered the message. "Jair's an animal. He would have sent a stronger-worded message. But I'm not sure."

"Tomorrow we will find out. I will gather a dozen good men and we shall see if Mariam is held at the oil press warehouse."

"I can't wait until tomorrow. I have to go there now."

"Now? In the middle of the night? That's exactly what your enemy wants. He sets a trap for you."

"I don't have a choice. We can't go storming the place in broad daylight in full view of the Roman soldiers on the city walls. Besides, if we attacked openly Jair would kill her." David pulled on his tunic. "This is my fight, good friend. Stay here and sleep. You deserve it."

"And let you get all the praise for rescuing Mariam!"

Yoseph picked up his own tunic and looked askance to the heavens.

"He is not mad, Lord. It is I who has been robbed of my senses for am I not venturing into the jaws of death when I could be sleeping like a babe?"

Mount of Olives was aglow with moonlight and campfires.

Despite the lateness of the hour, a thin but steady line of pilgrims moved down the hill to the Temple while others were returning to the hillside.

The two men making their way to the oil press station went unnoticed except by an old beggar following them. Campfires were scattered around the oil press station, but the building itself was dark. David and Yoseph circled the building, pretending to be two pilgrims looking for their campsite.

Yoseph spotted a nest of Sicarii camped on the north side of the building.

"How do you know they're Sicarii?" David asked, after they had made a second run by. A man was sitting by a campfire burning between the two tents.

Yoseph estimated there were seven or eight men asleep in the tents.

Yoseph spat. "How do I know that one snake bites and another has no fangs?"

"There might be more inside the oil press warehouse."

As David spoke, it occurred to him that if Jair was in the building, there would not be many Sicarii inside. Jair trusted no one.

"I will gather good men today and when it is night again we will return and drive the Sicarii away. There will be no pitched battle that will attract the Romans. The Sicarii are even less anxious to come to the attention of the Romans than my comrades."

"I don't have time to wait."

Yoseph touched David's arm and spoke softly. "I know you fear for Mariam, but we have no choice. The two of us cannot manage this deed alone."

David did fear for her, but even if she weren't in the building, he knew he couldn't wait for the next evening. By that time Jesus had to be arrested near the oil press building by Temple priests.

David stared at the campfire of the Sicarii. Yoseph suddenly broke into his thoughts.

"You are smiling. Have you devised another machine of war?"

"Maybe. You said a minute ago that the Sicarii would run away rather than risk attracting the attention of the Romans."

"They will not run from the two of us. They will cut our throats and leave our heads on stakes for the crows to pick our eyes."

"They might not run from us, but how about from their own fame? Can you get a big jug of the oil used in lamps?"

Yoseph looked at him the same way Ezra did when he talked about knocking down dungeon walls with one mighty blow.

"You plan to drive off assassins with lamp oil? Are you mad? No, no, it is already decided. It is I who am mad."

"If my trick works, the Sicarii will go away without a fight. I want your promise that you will also leave. Jair Zayyad is an old enemy. The fight with him is personal."

The merchants at the makeshift marketplace thrown up for holy week outside the Golden Gate were sleeping by their goods. David sent Yoseph down to wake up a merchant who sold lamp oil.

While Yoseph was gone, David made a trip around the building again. Wide, barn-type doors were at the front and back. Yoseph told him that not only barrels of olive oil were stored inside but the donkeys used to turn the giant press were also stabled within.

David guessed the donkeys would be housed at the back side of the building because the rear doors opened into a corral. The doors were two-piece, Dutch type. The two-piece construction might make them easier to pry open than the front door, he thought.

He crouched in bushes near the corral and waited for Yoseph to do his work with the lamp oil.

Yoseph carried a jug of oil to the side of the hill just below the Sicarri camp. Only fear of getting his throat cut kept him from laughing out loud. David was a clever devil, he thought. After David finished his own business, he must help his brothers drive the Romans from Israel.

He spread oil in the pattern David told him, then fired it and ran.

The burning oil spelled out a flaming message: SICARII

He couldn't help it; he stopped and turned back and laughed. He didn't see the shadowy figure in a black cloak step out from the trees behind him, a Sicarii lookout posted beyond the perimeter of the camp.

Yoseph felt a single sharp jab of pain as the assassin stuck a dagger in his back.

CHAPTER FIFTY-FOUR

The Sicarii abandoned their camp, fleeing in such haste that they left their tents and equipment behind. Two men came out the back door of the warehouse and fled into the darkness. The top half of one door was left ajar as they hurried away.

David slipped through the corral fencing. Keeping low, he ran to the building and crouched by the doors. He could hear donkeys fidgeting inside, their keen senses awakened.

He tried to pull open the lower door, but it wouldn't budge. It was locked from within. The upper half was cracked open, probably to give the animals some air. He jerked open the upper door and dove through headfirst, landing in smelly straw on the floor of the stable area. He crept in a low stance using the donkeys for cover, moving among the nervous animals to the corral posts.

The big olive oil press was in the center of the warehouse, with its long wooden spokes extending from the circular basin where the olives were pressed. When the press was in operation a donkey was tied to the end of each spoke and walked in a circle to turn the press and squeeze the oil from the fruit.

Marie was on the ground, her hand tied to a spoke of the oil press, hay piled around.

She was staked out as bait.

"It's been a long time, Ben-Dor."

The voice came from the loft to David's right. The only light in the warehouse was a single oil lamp on a stack of barrels behind Marie and it left the loft cast in darkness.

"Run, David!" Marie struggled with her bonds. "It's too late. Get out before he kills you."

Jair's words floated down to him. "I'm glad it's you. Blood for blood, that's how it should be. I've waited a long time."

"It's too late, David, save yourself!"

"She's right," Jair said. "It's too late. You failed. I beat you Jews to it." Jair's voice reeked with sarcasm. "He looked a little like you, Ben-Dor, just another young Jew from Galilee. That gave me extra pleasure when I killed him."

"Still hiding in the dark, Jair? You always were a cowardly bastard." David changed position as he spoke. He brushed against something as he moved, a pitchfork. "I'd ask you to come out and fight, but that's not your style. A bomb in a trash can is how cowards like you operate."

Jair's hoarse voice came out of the darkness like a chill from the grave. "My style is winning."

A flame flew out of the loft and into the pile of hay around Marie. She screamed and fought at her bonds as the hay burst into flames.

David froze in utter horror. *The son of a bitch was burning Marie alive to drive him into the opening!* He went wild, grabbed the pitchfork, slammed open the gate, and drove the donkeys out of the corral. Panicked by the fire and commotion, the donkeys stampeded around the oil press.

He crouched low among the animals, trying to keep from being trampled as he made his way toward Marie. Jair came to the edge of the loft, gun in hand, trying to spot him.

David sprang up, throwing the pitchfork like a javelin. Jair saw it coming and dodged, tripping sideways over a barrel of oil and falling off the edge of the loft, crashing into the barrels stacked against the wall. The barrels broke loose, the stack collapsed like a house of cards, taking Jair down with them.

Frantically David kicked the flaming straw away from Marie and slashed desperately with his knife at the ropes binding her. Oil from barrels that burst when the stack fell exploded into an inferno. The ropes around Marie's wrists suddenly gave and David jerked her to her feet.

She screamed and David whipped around, getting a flash of Jair on his feet, taking aim with his gun. David pulled Marie down with him as the shot exploded. A donkey dashed in front of Jair as the assassin pulled the trigger and the bullet hit the donkey. The beast went down and another donkey suddenly swerved and knocked against Jair as it avoided the fallen animal.

David charged as Jair rolled over and was getting to his knees, gun still in hand. He leaped over the fallen animal and dove at him. David's shoulder connected with Jair's chest and sent him and the gun flying. Jair regained his feet a split second before David and flew at him, hands and feet chopping like ax blades. David threw himself at the assassin in a logroll. Jair stumbled over him, hit the ground, and bounced back to his feet like a rubber ball. When he came erect he had the gun in hand. He pointed it at David and smiled.

"Blood for blood," Jair said.

Something flew out of the darkness to the rear of David and hit Jair in the chest. The impact caused Jair to stumble backward a couple of steps, dropping the gun, gaping in horror at the dagger stuck in his chest.

The old beggar who had followed David rushed by and kicked Jair, sending the man backward into the raging flames. He stooped and picked up Jair's gun and turned to face David and Marie, removing his false beard.

Conway grinned. "You're lucky I'm good with a knife," he told David. "I risked him shooting you rather than break my promise that I wouldn't use a gun."

He saluted them with the gun General Scott had concealed in his waterbag.

CHAPTER FIFTY-FIVE

A crowd of sleepy-eyed pilgrims gathered to gawk at the warehouse inferno as David, Marie, and Conway fled the burning building.

They went along on Jericho Road, trying to be inconspicuous among the pilgrims milling about as the flames from the warehouse roared. Guards on the city walls spread the alarm and the city gates slammed shut as legionnaires scrambled to the walls in anticipation of an attack.

They left the road and followed a path that veered up the side of Mount of Olives to a cluster of rocks. David led the way, drawn to the area because it looked deserted, a dark spot in a sea of campfires. Something about the strange rock formation struck a familiar cord with David, but he didn't immediately place it. He made out three tall objects in a clearing a short distance away, monuments of some sort. It occurred to him that people deliberately avoided the place. The whole mountainside was swarming with pilgrims, but none had chosen this spot to camp.

David's thoughts went to his father as he stood on the rocky outcrop and watched the warehouse burn. It had all come full circle—a shot fired in righteousness, a man's head snapping back, a youth named Jair with death in his eyes.

Marie told them what happened at the warehouse in the hours before David rescued her.

Jair had won.

Years ago he had left David's father facedown in the dirt to avenge his own father's death. To avenge something more subtle, perhaps life itself, Jair left a man named Jesus Ben Joseph and his betrayer, Judas Iscariot, facedown in an oil press warehouse. He had lured Jesus to the warehouse by bribing Judas and had waited patiently in the shadows, repaying Judas with a knife in the back rather than the promised fistful of silver.

David held Marie close and she wept against his chest.

"What's the matter?" Conway asked.

"We lost," Marie said, "the world was at stake and we failed."

"Don't count on it." His voice was hard. He was not a man who liked to lose. "This is a strange spot. I wonder why no one's camping here."

"Look behind you," Marie said. The tall forms behind Conway had become visible in the light cast by the raging warehouse fire below.

Crucifixion crosses.

"This is Golgotha, the Skull. Pontius Pilate had Jesus crucified here."

Conway stared at the crosses. "The Skull. I should have known. The rock formation is supposed to resemble a human skull when you look at it from the city." He walked around the crucifixion posts, staring up at them. "Do you realize the most dramatic moment in history occurred right here on this spot? More books have been written about the Crucifixion than any other event in history."

"The books will never be written," Marie said, "because now it will never happen."

Conway gave no indication that he had heard her as he continued to walk among the crosses, staring almost reverently up at them as if he were enthralled by their very existence. "Jesus had to die, of course. He was preaching political and religious heresy. Someone was bound to kill him. They always do. Gandhi, Martin Luther King; people who are afraid of the truth can't let them live."

David had never perceived Conway as particularly devout or even having any sort of religious leanings, and as he watched Conway he realized the man was more caught up by its dramatic effect than the religious significance of the event. All the world was a stage to an actor and Conway was standing center stage where the most passionate religious moment in history had taken place.

"All we need for the greatest drama in history to take place is a man to be crucified," Conway said.

"What are you talking about?" Even as he asked the question, David understood the other man's train of thought and it sent electrified chills through him. "It can't be done," David said. "People know what Jesus looks like."

"No, they don't. Remember what Marie said? Judas had to point out Jesus to the Temple guards because they didn't know what he looked like. It was a kiss, wasn't it?" he asked Marie. "Judas used a kiss of death to finger Jesus. Right here on the Mount of Olives."

"Close friends kissed each other on the cheek when they met," Marie said. "Judas pointed out Jesus for the Temple guards by kissing Jesus on the cheek."

"The kiss of death," Conway mused, "a knife in the heart from one friend to another. Judas was a fascinating character, weak, greedy, probably jealous of the attention and respect his friend received. A meaty role, but of course Jesus got top billing."

Marie finally understood. "It can't be done. Jesus is Jesus, not a role to be played."

Conway shook his head. "I don't know who Jesus was, but what we all know is that a young carpenter from Galilee died the death of a man, in pain and agony, on the cross. His name was better known than his face except among his friends. And doesn't the Bible say that his friends denied knowing him? No doubt most of them fled the city the minute he was arrested."

"But someone might know—"

"What difference does it make as long as the masses believe the man is Jesus of Nazareth? The New Testament wasn't even written by people who actually saw the Crucifixion. Besides, who can say that this isn't God's plan? What do people say—the Lord acts in mysterious ways?"

"He's right," David whispered. He felt cold, and shivered.

Conway was flushed from excitement. He didn't look at them as he talked, but walked among the crosses, staring up at them dreamily.

"Imagine the agony and the ecstasy. My God, what a meaty role." His voice dropped to a whisper. "Facing Pilate and the Temple priests, humiliated by the guards, the crown of thorns, bearing the cross on my back through the streets while the multitude cried—no, jeered—but I turn those jeers into tears as I gaze at them with my face shining in spiritual bliss—"

Tears rolled down Conway's cheeks as he "experienced" the emotional impact his performance would have on his audience.

"They'll write books about this moment, sing of the power and the glory forever." He suddenly whipped around to them and glared at David. "The kiss of death. You'll have to carry off the part of Judas and give me the kiss of death. Start thinking about your role, the man's shifty eyes, his false pride, his shallow arrogance, petty greed. You can blow the whole thing with a wrong look, the wrong body language. You must become the sort of scum who could sell out a friend for thirty pieces of silver. You must not think you're acting—you must think you're Judas Iscariot, Judas the Sicarii!"

He jabbed a finger at Marie. "You'll have to brief us. You know the story of Jesus and Judas, you know the history. Wait! There's a role for a woman, a prostitute. How fitting! Marie is the French name for Mary. Mary of Magdalene was at the Crucifixion."

"She witnessed the Crucifixion and the Resurrection," Marie said. "She was the messenger of God, carrying word of the Resurrection, the miracle she witnessed."

"Yes, I remember. Damn, I wish I had spent as much time reading the Bible as I did the classics, but thank God for Cecil B. DeMille and Martin Scorsese. At least I've seen the movies. She gave him something when he was on the cross, a drink of water, wasn't it?"

"A bitter vinegar used to kill pain. She soaked a sponge in the vinegar and lifted it to his lips on a long stick."

"Yes, that's right, I remember the scene."

"There's a problem, isn't there?" David said. "You can't pass for Jesus. You're not a Jew, you don't look like one, you don't speak the language. The moment Salome sees you, she'll expose you. You might get away with playing Judas if you wore a kaffiyeh, but you'd have to avoid speaking."

"We have to find another way," Marie said, "it won't work."

"You know it will," David said. "All we need is a young Jew from Galilee."

David stared at the breaking dawn seeping up from the hills to the east, firing the golden roof of the Temple. Now he knew why he was born, why he hid from life in the desert, why he ran, haunted by the specter of violence and slaughter all around him.

He smiled and wiped a tear from Marie's cheek. "You always knew, didn't you."

She buried her head in his shoulder and cried.

He felt a jabbing pain in the palms of his hands, terrible pain, as if a knife were plunged into each palm and twisted.

"I was born in Galilee," he said.

CHAPTER FIFTY-SIX

NEW MEXICO

CIA Director Holt, Martin Bornstein, the president's national security advisor, and a squad of marines were the last people airlifted away from the synchrotron.

Holt checked his watch and spoke to Bornstein, raising his voice over the roar of the jet copter. "Thirty-six minutes."

They both looked out portholes, getting their last look at the synchrotron. In thirty-six minutes the facility would be ground zero for U.S. bombers with international observers aboard. Bornstein muttered something.

"What'd you say?"

"Nothing, I just thought of an old Chinese proverb—an inch of time cannot be bought for an inch of gold. I always wonder at these moments what would have happened if we had a little more time."

"If General Scott had had a little more time, he probably would have erased both of us from history."

Too bad about Scott, Bornstein thought. He didn't like the man but he had been with them all the way—right up until he cracked when the president gave the order to destroy the facility.

The general had tried having himself sent back in time to 1968 so he could rearrange a little Vietnam War history. Scott

had been "detained" at Holt's orders and the ⌐
abruptly accepted his resignation, a little ahead of Sco⌐
ing it.

Holt sat back in his seat and lit up, ignoring the No Smok-
ing sign. He touched his briefcase again, the reassuring feel
of the guns.

"Two guns," he said to Bornstein, "we send three people
back in time and we get back two guns, no people. One gun is
the Korth automatic Jair Zayyad had. The one Scott hid in
Conway's waterbag was never fired. The guns are obviously
a message telling us that the mission was a success.

"If they decided to stay in the ancient world, and the Mission Evaluations computer had given an eighty-one percent
probability that that is exactly what would happen, I can see
them sending back the Zayyad gun to let us know the mission
was a success. But when we found out about Scott's gun and
queried the computer on that, it gave a ninety-two percent
probability that anyone who stayed in the ancient world
would keep the gun for protection—"

"As a model for a thousand more," Bornstein interjected.
"What it means is that we were dealing with people with too
much integrity for a computer to understand."

"What do you think happened?" Holt asked. "I know it's
pure speculation, but what do you think came down?"

"We know they got the Zayyad brothers, the gun proves
that. I presume the mission was a success, everything seems
normal, no tidal waves in Time. At least nothing we're cog-
nizant of."

"I think Conway pulled it off, he was the pro," Holt said.

"True, but I wouldn't write off David Ben-Dor. There was
something about Ben-Dor. And don't discount the woman. I
had a feeling about her. She—"

"Christ, what an incredible time Conway must be having.
That bastard, he must really be enjoying it. The Roman Empire, the Greeks, the ancient Holy Land, the living Bible with
the living classics. He would sure soak it all up. Hell, I
wouldn't be surprised if he plays a Roman emperor for real."

Holt coughed and spat nicotine out the window. "I have a

confession to make. The reason I was so sure Scott would make a move to alter history wasn't just because of his personality profile but because I had thought of it myself. Can you imagine—not only experiencing another period in history . . . but playing God?"

"Which time period had you planned to go back to?" Bornstein asked, a little amused.

"The same damn one Conway's living right now. The Roman world. And you—no bullshit, now—you must have thought of it."

"I rather fancy the Renaissance—Columbus discovering America, da Vinci's painting *Mona Lisa* and creating engineering marvels, Michelangelo hanging from the ceiling of the Sistine Chapel while petty princes warred to be pope. It was the rebirth of art and science and culture, the most glorious—and chaotic—time in history."

"Hell, it was a time of war and anarchy."

"True," Bornstein said, "and maybe that's why there was so much creativity. It's like what Orson Welles said in that movie, *The Third Man*, directed by Britain's Carol Reed. Trying to explain to Joseph Cotten why he was such a bastard, Welles ad-libbed one of the great lines of cinema. He pointed out that in thirty years under the Borgias, a time of war, murder, and lust, Italy had produced some of the greatest art and science of all time. And with four hundred years of peace and prosperity, the Swiss had produced the cuckoo clock. Maybe that's why New York and L.A. produce—" He stopped in midsentence. Holt hadn't listened to a word he had said.

"Climbing the walls of castles in the air?" Bornstein asked him.

"I don't know." He snicked ash from his cigarette onto the copter floor and then took a deep drag as he stared out the porthole. "In another few minutes the greatest scientific discovery in history will be turned to dust."

They were both silent for several moments.

"I wonder what happened to her," Bornstein said.

"Her?"

"The Gauthier woman."

Holt shrugged. "Who knows? What do you think she was . . . a saint or a whore?"

"I think she was more complicated than even that." Bornstein sighed and leaned back against the seat. He was tired, bone weary from sleepless nights and nervous exhaustion, but without the stimuli provided by Holt's endless cigarettes and muddy coffee.

"Know what I think happened?" he said. "Pure and simple—*a miracle*."